MW00782260

THE WOLF TREE

THE WOLF TREE

BY LAURA McCLUSKEY

G. P. PUTNAM'S SONS
NEW YORK

PUTNAM
— EST. 1838 —

G. P. PUTNAM'S SONS
Publishers Since 1838
An imprint of Penguin Random House LLC
1745 Broadway, New York, NY 10019
penguinrandomhouse.com

Map by Clare Ainsworth

LIBRARY OF CONGRESS CATALOGING-IN-PUBLICATION DATA

Names: McCluskey, Laura, author.
Title: The wolf tree / by Laura McCluskey.
Description: New York : G. P. Putnam's Sons, 2025.
Identifiers: LCCN 2024027794 (print) | LCCN 2024027795 (ebook) |
ISBN 9780593852545 (hardcover) | ISBN 9780593852552 (epub)
Subjects: LCGFT: Detective and mystery fiction. | Novels.
Classification: LCC PR9619.4.M3795 W65 2025 (print) |
LCC PR9619.4.M3795 (ebook) | DDC 823/.92—dc23/eng/20240708
LC record available at https://lccn.loc.gov/2024027794
LC ebook record available at https://lccn.loc.gov/2024027795

Printed in the United States of America
1 3 5 7 9 10 8 6 4 2

Book design by Shannon Nicole Plunkett

The authorized representative in the EU for product safety and compliance is
Penguin Random House Ireland, Morrison Chambers, 32 Nassau Street,
Dublin D02 YH68, Ireland, https://eu-contact.penguin.ie.

For Liv, of course

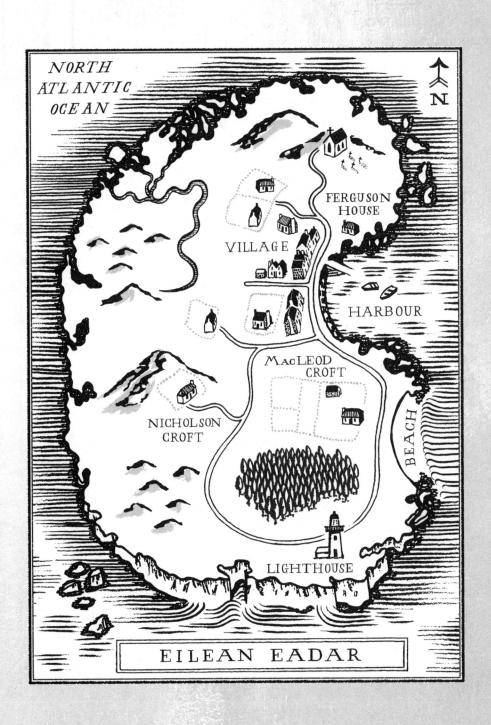

NORTH ATLANTIC OCEAN

N

FERGUSON HOUSE

VILLAGE

HARBOUR

MacLEOD CROFT

NICHOLSON CROFT

BEACH

LIGHTHOUSE

EILEAN EADAR

CHAPTER 1

PEOPLE THINK THAT DEATH BY DROWNING WOULD BE PEACEFUL. BUT IF THERE is any truth to that, it's a peace that comes after the worst thirty seconds of your life. And it's a fate that, until today, George Lennox had never considered might befall her.

With her jaw clenched against both the biting cold and sudden dips, George stands on the heaving deck of the police launch; constricted by the bulk of an orange life vest, a duffel bag over her shoulder. She clutches a leather briefcase in one hand, the slick railing with the other. The weather has changed dramatically in the last few hours. The soft white clouds that farewelled her on Skye have turned black and heavy, and the waves that claw at her feet are splintered iron, threatening to drag her down all twelve thousand feet to the sunless floor of the North Atlantic Ocean.

"It really had to be today?" A burly marine police officer shuffles up behind her. "We couldn't wait for the fucking wind to die down?" He pauses and eyes her chest speculatively. "You know how to use those?"

She follows his gaze, then looks up coolly. "Life vests?"

He blinks, hearing his words over again. "I just meant there's a whistle under that flap, and a wee light over there . . ."

"I'm sure I'll figure it out should the need arise, Constable."

Though he must be at least ten years her senior, the officer ducks his head.

"Righto, *Inspector*," he mutters before moving away.

George just grits her teeth, sucking in a quick breath as the boat angles sharply downward. The condescension is something she's used to, even when they learn her rank. These waves, however . . . She swallows hard, temporarily grateful for the wind that dries her perspiration as soon as it forms on her forehead.

"You might want to step inside, Inspector," a voice calls over the thrum of the engine. Despite his narrow frame, the captain barely sways as he leans out of the cabin behind her. "It's only going to get rough from here." The soft, rolling lilt of his Western Isles intonation is a pleasant contrast to the harsher Glaswegian accent she's become used to.

"This isn't rough?" George asks, incredulity creeping into her voice.

His bushy eyebrows pull together. "The Atlantic gives you hell on a good day," he rumbles, with knowledge born of a long career spent rescuing drunken tourists from dangerous cliffsides or fishing people from the sea—alive or dead. "We're certainly going to test her patience by trying to dock."

George narrows her eyes as a light rain starts to fall. "How far are we pushing our luck?"

He shrugs. "The harbor is to the northeast of Eilean Eadar, and we're coming in on a strong westerly. In this swell it's sheltered once you're in, but it's a fine narrow entrance over the bar." At her nonplussed expression, he adds, "We'll be taking our time coming in, that's for sure."

He takes a moment to shout instructions back into the cabin and receives a muffled response. George clutches her briefcase tighter as a wave crests the edge of the boat and her boots, sending a new chill through her socks and soaking the hem of her trousers.

"Who out here can receive a distress signal?" she asks. "The coastguard should be within range." She peers through the thickening rain at a distant coastline. "Or one of the little islands . . . that's Hirta, isn't it?"

"You'll not find much help there. They're isolated enough as it is. Where you're going . . ." He blows out a long breath. "Even I've only set foot on Eadar once, dropping off some lads when one of their trawlers lost a rudder. That was near twelve years ago. I don't think any police have been there since."

"So if we need a quick exit . . . ?"

He barks a laugh. "I hope you can speak dolphin." But his laughter dies as he squints into the distance, as if his seasoned eyes can see further across the water than hers. "If you're in a pinch, your best chance would be Stornoway; there's the airport there, and the Search and Rescue helicopter team, too. And a good hospital," he adds, as an afterthought.

She rubs a spot behind her ear, the only outward indication of her inner disquiet.

The captain eyes her contemplatively. "The locals don't like strangers coming in unannounced, but you say they're expecting you?"

"They should be."

"Then you'll be fine." Her relief is short-lived, though, as the captain adds, "I just hope someone sees us coming. Docking in this weather without help . . . I don't fancy the prospect."

A shout from the cabin draws the captain away. "Like I said, Inspector, you'd be best off coming in. The radar says we're about to get a soaking."

She nods once, sharply enough that he takes the hint and leaves her alone. Her eyes seek out the horizon, the line becoming increasingly blurred by rain and the pitch of the boat. She readjusts her grip on the railing, looking for somewhere more secure to wedge herself until they reach the island, as a deep voice booms out behind her, "How are your sea legs, Lennox?"

The boat tilts forward suddenly, stealing George's retort as she focuses on keeping her feet. She turns in time to see the upheaval not only wipe the smile off Richard Stewart's lightly lined face but also take his legs out from under him.

She makes her way down the deck and hauls him to his feet, not hiding the effort it takes to bring his stocky body vertical. "You were saying?"

He swipes rain droplets out of his silvering hair, scowling. "Don't test me—not when my socks are wet."

George looks out at the ocean churning around them. "This trip was never going to be cheerful, Richie," she says tersely. She fishes her phone out from an interior pocket of her coat and tries to shield the screen from the rain and spray. "Have you got any bars?"

Richie doesn't even bother checking. "I think we said goodbye to service as soon as we left Skye."

A low growl rolls across the sky like a boulder.

"Do you think the islanders are going to talk to us?"

He shrugs. "*They're* used to not having service. Silence might come more naturally to them."

———

By the time the lonely island of Eilean Eadar comes into view just before midday, the rain has become so heavy that George has acquiesced to stand just inside the cabin door, her hood pulled tight around her eyes. Strands of dark hair whip in the wind, stinging her forehead and cheeks. The sun is shuttered behind the murderous clouds, so George's first impression of the tiny island thrown far off the west coast of Scotland is a sheer, dark cliff. Huge waves smash against the craggy rock face, yet Eadar stands resolute against their rage.

As they skirt around the southeast side of the cliff, George catches sight of a lighthouse silhouetted against the dark sky.

She nudges Richie, who has squeezed himself into the doorway beside her. "Look," she says into his ear, pointing.

His pale blue eyes emerge from under a knitted beanie to peer up at the cliff, face scrunched against the pelting rain. His lips thin when he spots the lighthouse.

It looms larger as their passage takes them closer to the cliffs, and George feels a sudden swirl of dizziness unrelated to the rocking boat. She drops her gaze to the deck and steadies her breathing, sensing Richie's eyes on her. Slipping her phone from her pocket again, she squints at the screen intently until he looks away.

As the captain warned, it's no simple task to dock in Eadar's small harbor. The relentless swell pushes them uncomfortably close to the cliff, so he takes the boat out in a wide arc with the bow pointed at the island. Soon the narrow opening into the harbor appears, a gap between the encircling arms of dark rock. From the silence in the cabin, George can tell the captain and the two officers are concentrating hard, their years on the sea evident in the way they focus on the water rather than the instrument panel. She feels a flicker of regret at her insistence they travel today, but quells it quickly. A tragic death requires investigation. A grieving mother deserves closure.

They make their approach slowly, the engine reduced to a hum beneath their feet, letting the swell push them closer to the harbor entrance. She doesn't realize she is holding her breath until the captain, timing his run perfectly down the front of a large wave, throws the motor to full power and they shoot through the jutting rocks that border the entrance. She exhales slowly; Richie's shoulders relax.

The water is calmer in the harbor, but as the captain predicted, there's no one on watch. He flicks the lights on, the red and blue flashes barely penetrating the sheeting rain. The officers are engaged in a low but urgent conversation about if and how they can safely approach the stone quay without assistance when movement in the gloom ahead catches George's eye. Soon she can make out six figures screwing up their faces against the rain to wave them into a gap between two weather-beaten trawlers, and less than ten minutes later George and Richie alight onto the quay with all the dignity of two wet socks.

"You should thank God that you weren't blown in on a nor'-easter," a squat woman roars at the captain as she loops a rope over her shoulder. "You would have been smashed to bits!"

Another man calls to the woman, and though George can barely hear him over the rain, she recognizes the lyrical patterns of Gaelic.

As the captain is drawn into the bellowed conversation, George and Richie are ushered up a set of uneven stone stairs cut into the seawall. The combination of the rain and cloud coverage means George's first look at the main street of Eadar is of a narrow road that currently resembles a river, and unremarkable buildings. They're urged into a narrow two-story house with warm light glowing in the windows, which is how George ends up stripped to her skin in the small but cozy home of Cecily Campbell with nothing but a scratchy blanket between her and the eyes of Cecily's three curious children.

"Away, away," Cecily chides them as she enters the bedroom that is clearly her own, carrying a steaming pot. The kids scatter into the hallway as she closes the door with her hip. George hears a giggle slip under the door.

"Don't mind them," Cecily says, raising her voice above the sound of the rain lashing the roof. "We get so few visitors out here, especially coming out of a squall the way you did. I've put your partner in the boys' room next door, so they'll be bothering him next." Cecily places the pot on the floor and pushes a chair closer to the low stone fireplace. "Pop your feet in here."

George hides a wince as her frozen toes touch the hot water, but soon the heat is working into her bones and up her body. Despite the welcome relief she sits stiffly in the chair, eyes flicking around the room as Cecily towels away the puddles from George's entrance.

The Campbell home has a surprising warmth despite its rough stone exterior. There's hand-painted wallpaper that is faded in places, a handsome wardrobe with a large scratch running down one door, crocheted throws, and a woven rug beneath her feet. A wide bed dominates the room, the squashy mattress sinking in the middle. George only caught a glimpse of the lower level as she was pushed through the door and up the stairs, but there was a similarly cozy living area and a kitchen beyond.

"You'll be defrosted in no time," Cecily says. "I've spent years thawing out Donald—my husband—when he comes home off a day of fishing. He's still got all ten toes. Only nine and a half fingers, but beer and a very sharp knife are to blame there."

"Was he in a fight?"

Cecily's dark eyes go wide before she laughs again. "Oh, no. He's just all thumbs on land. Get him out on the boat, though, and it's like *Swan Lake*." She crosses to the plump double bed and smooths a crease from the creamy coverlet, then stoops to gather George's wet clothes.

George starts to rise. "Please, let me . . ."

"Don't be silly. Just warm yourself up. Give a chill the chance to set in and you'll be shivering for weeks."

Relenting, George unwraps the towel from around her head, combing her fingers through the tangled curls that fall around her shoulders while Cecily lays out her clothes on the floor in front of the fire. High cheekbones dominate her face; the firelight makes her expression shift between soft and severe with every flicker. Studying her like this makes George realize that the woman can't be much older than herself.

"How long have you been married?"

"Nine years," Cecily says briskly, "though some days it feels like fifty."

"You must have married young."

"And had our first less than a year later." She nods toward a small framed picture of the Virgin Mary taking pride of place among a collection of photos and stacked books on one of the squat bedside tables. "We were quite eager to make things official."

"I see. Did you grow up here?"

"No, actually. I'm a mainlander like you." She moves to the bed and sinks down comically deep into the mattress. "Donald seduced me and lured me across the sea. Been on Eadar ever since, bar the annual trip with the kids to see my parents." The Gaelic word rolls effortlessly off Cecily's tongue—*Eht-ter.* "He and a few of the lads took their boat out this morning. Idiots. If they haven't been capsized, the storm will have scattered the haddock. The other crews saw the forecast and didn't even bother setting out, but Donald . . ." She sighs. "He does what he likes."

Now that she's not facing an immediate risk of drowning, George's bones are becoming heavy, and the crackle of the fire is making her thoughts soft and fuzzy. She tightens her stomach muscles and hauls herself straight again. "Fish are the island's main export, is that right?"

Cecily nods glumly. "If there was a demand for rotting seaweed or mud, we'd be minted. The boys are out there in their wee boats dropping nets against commercial trawlers that can pull up twenty times what we do in a day. It's not easy. Some weeks we're barely keeping the wolf from the door." She lapses into a contemplative silence, picking at a loose thread on a pillow.

George looks out the window, trying to see to the harbor beyond. "When do you expect them back?"

"Depends where they were when the storm hit. Most days they're all back in the late afternoon, but it's not unusual for them to spend a night on one of the bigger islands. Or the mainland, if they had enough of a catch to drop off." Cecily cocks her head. "You're staying out in the Nicholson croft, aren't you?"

"Your guess is as good as mine. We're meant to find someone named Kathy MacKinnon, at the post office. I think she has the keys."

"Ah, that'd be right."

"Is the croft hers?"

Cecily shakes her head. "It belonged to Auld Samuel Nicholson, and when he passed Kathy volunteered to keep an eye on things as nobody wanted to live so far up that hill. She's good like that, always offering to help out. I wouldn't be surprised if she has the spare keys to this place."

George raises her eyebrows. "Is everyone here so trusting?"

"She wouldn't even need keys," she says with a laugh. "The only reason anyone around here locks their doors is to keep the wee ones in at night." Her smile slips, and her slim fingers play with a tiny silver cross around her neck. "We wondered if people would come to ask questions about Alan. But the funeral was two weeks ago. We all assumed the mainland had forgotten about us again."

George tilts her head. "And yet you knew I was a police officer without me saying so."

A flush rises on the other woman's neck, and she draws her knees up to hug them. "Like I said, we don't get many visitors. There's only two reasons mainlanders come here—deliveries or marriage. And nobody's arrived with a ring on their finger since me, which should tell you a few things." Her brief attempt at lightness dissolves into a heavy pause that George allows to stretch.

"To be honest," Cecily continues finally, her eyes boring into the floor at George's feet, "we're all a little surprised that you and your partner are here. What happened to Alan is tragic, but not exactly a mystery."

George, recalling the documents she was poring over last night, counters, "Alan Ferguson climbed to the top of that lighthouse for a reason. Don't you want to know why?"

A conspicuous absence of sound triggers an instinct in Cecily that's absent in George; in two long strides she's thrown open the bedroom door and stares down at her children, three ears at the approximate height of the keyhole. They blink up at her with identical expressions of guilt. She banishes them to the living room with a curt dismissal, swatting the rump of the girl who stares over her shoulder at George with unabashed curiosity. Cecily closes the door again and turns to face George with a strained expression. "They don't need to hear that," she says, her hand rising to fidget with her necklace again.

"You didn't tell them about Alan?"

"They know he died, but . . . do you have children?"

George shakes her head.

Cecily closes her eyes. "It's terrible," she says. "Incredible, of course, and the most joy I've ever felt in my life. But truly awful sometimes, the worry and stress. Especially out here."

"What do you mean?"

"We're surrounded by water on all sides, half the buildings are boarded up, and there aren't enough children for a proper school. All we really have is our families." Already pale, Cecily's color drains further, and she crosses herself vigorously. "His poor mother," she says in a shaky voice. "Catriona has already suffered so much. I pray for her every night, and our priest leads us in prayer every morning."

George glances at the briefcase, picturing her notebook inside. "Do you have much to do with the Ferguson family?"

"In a community this small, everyone knows everyone. Catriona works at the bakery, so add in church and I see her almost every day. But Alan was much younger than Donald and me. I heard he was planning to go to university on the mainland, but that was months ago. I suppose he changed his mind."

"Maybe," George says lightly, then rises, bunching the blanket so the ends don't dangle in the water at her feet. "We need to get going."

"But your clothes aren't dry yet. I can send my eldest to get the key for you."

"I have a change of clothes here."

Cecily departs, and George hears her check in on Richie in the next room. His deep, cheery voice vibrates through the walls.

"Dry socks make all the difference," George mutters, then stifles a yawn. After a restless night, she was up before dawn reviewing the case notes, and the tumultuous boat ride drained what little energy she had left. As if summoned by the memory, a familiar pain pulses behind her right eye and she firmly presses her thumb into the brow bone. It deepens the ache for a moment but she grits her teeth and holds it, counting to ten before exhaling and lifting her thumb. The technique only brings temporary relief; she knows she'll need to rest soon. But rest comes after resolution, and Alan Ferguson needs her focus now.

She takes another deep breath and slaps her cheeks, willing herself to look alert. Based on her limited knowledge of Eilean Eadar, the residents are known to be wary of strangers. She wonders if that attitude is a result of their isolation; as the crow flies, where she's standing right now in Cecily Campbell's squashy bedroom is approximately 220 miles across wild land and sea from her own sparse flat on a bustling Glasgow street.

Her eyes flick to the door, ear cocked for Cecily's return, and then she crosses to the window and looks out, but she can't see far enough to the right to catch sight of the lighthouse. When researching Eadar over the past three days, she found an online forum devoted to what happened there a century or so ago. It's the kind of spooky story that is told at high school sleepovers—a tale that has morphed from fact into folklore over the last century. She suspects it's another reason the islanders might be mistrustful of visitors; they don't want their home to become a ghost tour for gawking tourists.

The rain has eased—through the pattering drops, she's able to see down to the street below. The passing of the storm seems to have coaxed residents outside. A handful of people dart between buildings, some hurry down the steps to the harbor—to check that the fenders kept their boats from being smashed against the stone, she assumes.

She half turns to pull her duffel bag toward her when a prickle runs across the now-warm skin of her neck. Keeping her movements slow, unhurried, she casually glances back at the street below.

And spots someone in a hooded coat looking up at her.

George resists the instinct to jerk back, even as the hairs on her arms rise beneath the blanket; instead, she leans closer, trying to make out the watcher's face between the raindrops on the glass. But her vision is further marred when her breath fogs the pane, and by the time she's wiped it away with a corner of the blanket, the watcher has disappeared into the swelling stream of residents. She scans their faces, but she didn't get a clear look at the watcher.

By the time her host enters with an armful of blankets George is lacing up her boots, her duffel bag open on the bed beside the briefcase.

"It's still raining a little, but you can take the red umbrella by the door," Cecily says. "And I don't know if Kathy has made the beds up, but I'll send these with you. It gets bitterly cold up on the hill during the night."

George takes the blankets from Cecily. "You've been very kind, Mrs. Campbell. Thank you for everything."

"I'll send one of my boys to show you to the post office. I'm sure you want to be getting on with your investigation." Her tone shifts, becoming pointed. "We all look forward to his mother finally getting the peace she deserves."

As she hears Cecily collect Richie and lead him downstairs, George hesitates, then flicks open the latches of the briefcase. From an inner pocket, wrapped in a pair of thick socks, she withdraws a pill bottle. Pausing to listen to Richie's muffled voice rise up from the ground floor, she swiftly pops the lid and slips a single pill into her mouth, swallowing it dry with practiced ease.

Then she locks the bag and returns to her seat beside the fireplace for a few more seconds—but the warmth no longer reaches her.

CHAPTER 2

DESPITE RICHIE'S INSISTENCE THAT THERE'S ROOM BENEATH THE UMBRELLA, the eldest Campbell boy is content to trot a few steps ahead of them. The storm that deposited them on the island so unceremoniously has passed over, but it is still raining lightly.

"You'd think the wee barra enjoys getting saturated," Richie mutters to George, eyeing the boy with concern as the drizzle turns his blond hair a dirty brown and soaks into his thick woolen jumper. "Maybe he's not altogether there."

"Or maybe he likes the rain," she says dryly. "Honestly, Rich, are you so old that you've forgotten what it's like to enjoy little things— Oi!" She snatches at the umbrella he's angled away, brushing off the fat droplets that landed on her forehead and cheeks. A woman exiting a shop ahead shoots them an alarmed look, then draws her hood up and hurries away.

"I was reminding you to enjoy the little things," Richie says solemnly, then peers through the drizzle at their surroundings. "It's a funny little place, isn't it? Quaint."

George ducks her head to look out from under the umbrella. Quaint might be one word for it, but it's not a pretty street. With only the seawall between the stacked stone shopfronts and the harbor to protect their walls from the salty air and relentless ocean spray, every surface—from the crushed stone road underfoot to the slate roof tiles—has been stained the same shade of weathered brown, though splashes of the original paint—off-white, rusty red and just more brown—are faintly visible where some persistent owners have scrubbed hard at the timber doors and window frames. The air is thick with the odor of seaweed and fish.

Navigating potholes large enough to catch paddling pools of rainwater, they pass a glass-fronted butcher, a bakery that doubles as a grocer, and other buildings with darkened windows and an air of disuse. Ahead, a man with ruddy skin smokes a cigarette, his eyes following them as they approach. Richie nods a friendly greeting.

"Inspectors," the man grunts, nodding back.

Richie looks at George, bemused. "News travels fast."

The road begins to slope gently upward, and the buildings get smaller and squatter. The rain has carved deep lanes into the dirt, the water carrying sticks and leaves down to the bottom. Long grass is waging a war to reclaim the path.

Richie nudges her. "If you had to pick a spot for the most important building in the village, where would you put it?"

George follows his gaze and snorts. "As close to God as it can get?"

The brooding clouds form a sinister backdrop to Eadar's surprisingly large stone church. A dominant presence on the skyline, it must offer a commanding—all-seeing—view over the community. A weathered iron crucifix juts into the sky from atop the steeply pitched roof. Remembering the religious imagery in the Campbell home and the way Cecily had toyed with the crucifix around her neck, George wonders if Sunday Mass is Eadar's most popular social event.

It surprised them both that Eadar had remained a Catholic community in the staunchly Protestant northern Hebrides. No doubt the island's isolation had helped it escape the Reformation.

She looks back down the hill at the tiny building that is the village's only grocer. "Gives you an insight into their priorities, eh? Oh—I think that's the post office up ahead."

Cecily's son has stopped halfway up the hill and is pointing at a whitewashed building with a cluster of notices stuck on the inside of the windows.

Richie sends the boy running home as George ducks under the awning. Most of the notices are handwritten—someone's cat is missing, others offer bicycle repairs and laundry services. A lone printed notice with a color picture she recognizes catches her eye.

"Rich."

He joins her at the window, closing the umbrella and shaking it off. "Ah. There he is."

They spend a few moments looking at Alan Ferguson's young, handsome face on the funeral notice, even though they've both looked at this very picture hundreds of times over the past three days—George has a photocopy tucked into the briefcase in her right hand. Wispy strands of dark blond hair frame his slim face, and his lips are parted to reveal a significant gap between his two front teeth. Rather than detracting from his looks, this small imperfection only adds to Alan's striking appearance; George remembers Richie observing that Alan looked like a charming pickpocket from a black-and-white film.

Another picture of Alan flashes into her mind, this one a close-up of that mouth. Metal hooks stretch the full lips back. One of those front teeth is missing, the other snapped jaggedly in two. The gums are deep purple and torn open. The whole jaw is a bruise and too far to the right.

Richie gestures for her to precede him. They enter the post office with the tinkle of metal chimes, passing a worn wooden letterbox with a symbol carved into the wood. They're greeted by a muted smell of aged paper and a low hum from a small heater that valiantly pushes stale air toward them. The space seems to be equal parts post office, library, community hub, and historical society. Apparently, the posters in the windows haven't just been placed there to be visible from the street—there's simply no space left on the walls to hang them. Large maps of Eilean Eadar and the west coast and isles of Scotland hang alongside photos ranging from sepia to full color, and framed newspaper clippings reveal recent examples of Eadar making the mainland headlines. October 1959 boasted a RECORD HADDOCK HAUL OFF COAST, and the past eight winners of the LEEK PIE COMPETITION have been immortalized beside a rack of yellowing worship pamphlets and wicker baskets of well-thumbed books. None of the articles reference the lighthouse. George suspects that's on purpose.

Eyeing the heater, Richie rewards its efforts by unzipping his rain jacket a few inches. He's wearing a crisp shirt and tie beneath a dark gray jumper. Knowing that beneath her own coat is a gaudy jumper her nan gifted her for Christmas last month, George doesn't follow suit.

There's a counter against the far wall with a closed door behind it. On top of the counter is a stack of books tied with thick string, a bulky computer monitor beside an older model satellite phone, and a tarnished silver bell. Richie looks at George hopefully. She lifts a shoulder.

The bell's ring is sharp, drawing an impish grin from Richie. He returns to her side as they wait for someone to emerge through the rear door, which is why they're both caught off guard when the door to the street flies open behind them.

"Inspectors, *fàilte*! Thank the Lord you made it through that drizzle."

The woman who enters with a waft of cold air is both tall and solid, the top half of her face obscured by a broad waxed rain hat. She moves with a youthful energy that's unexpected given the long salt-and-pepper braids that swish across her chest. She is carrying a large basket in the crook of her right elbow, and the way she's leaning to the left suggests the contents are weighty. She holds a ceramic pot with a fitted lid to her chest, and a leather satchel bounces off her hip as she strides across the room.

"Sorry I wasn't here to greet you," she says cheerfully, rounding the counter and depositing her items on the top. "I had to collect a few more things for the basket, and then I watched your colleagues head off back to the mainland." Doffing her hat to reveal lively brown eyes, she smiles at the detectives. "I hope you weren't waiting long."

George steps forward. "Are you Ms. MacKinnon?"

"To the children, aye. To anyone over the age of sixteen, I'm Kathy. Are you DI Lennox or Stewart?"

"Detective Inspector Georgina Lennox," George says, emphasizing the first two words out of habit. "My partner there is DI Richard Stewart."

Kathy chews the inside of her cheek as her eyes run over George's face. "I didn't expect you to be so young."

George works to keep the irritation from her features; she's spent years perfecting an outward expression of cool boredom when someone measures her age against her rank. It's exasperating when a colleague does it; with civilians . . .

She forces a smile. "I have a good moisturizer."

It's a joke George has used many times before, and Richie throws her a sympathetic look. But it has the intended effect on Kathy. After her peals of laughter subside, she nods toward the windows.

"It's a shame the clouds won't budge. Eadar is breathtaking when the sun is shining. I hope you'll get to see it yourself by the time you've finished your wee investigation."

She slides over a thick ledger from beside the phone and opens it to a page that is divided into columns and rows, tiny handwriting filling the top third. "Will you be needing a ride back to the mainland tomorrow? I'll have to check the schedule and see which crew heads that far east on a Wednesday."

"No need," Richie says. "Our people will return for us on Sunday morning."

Kathy glances up. "You'll be here for five nights?"

George looks at Richie, then to Kathy. "Was this not communicated to you over the phone?"

"Your man on the other end said it'd be a couple of days, but I thought . . ." She chuckles. "I think you'll find you won't need that much time to get around. Just this afternoon would have sufficed."

"Aye, well, the days are short this time of year, and we don't want to rush anything," Richie says smoothly. "It's important that we learn everything we can about Alan."

Kathy's eyes become shiny, and she retrieves a box of tissues from below the counter. "It's terrible," she whispers, pressing a tissue to her nose. "A bright boy robbed of a bright future. I'm a friend of Catriona—his mother. Lord knows it was an awful shock to her. To all of us. In such a small community, every loss is a devastating blow, especially when it's from suicide. I was with Catriona when she found out." She swallows thickly. "I can still hear her screams."

"I can't imagine," Richie says honestly. "I'm a Glaswegian lad, born and raised. There are more people living on my street than there are on this whole island."

"We have one butcher, one church. One post office." She smiles sadly. "Everyone knows everyone and their mother and granda and sister and uncle. The only new faces come when a delivery arrives or one of the lads brings a girl home from the mainland and marries her."

"That's what Mrs. Campbell said."

Humor sparks in her eyes. "There are three Mrs. Campbells

on Eilean Eadar, but I assume you mean Cecily. Lovely girl. Used to work with me in here, sorting letters and such. She's become so much a part of the fabric of the place, I sometimes forget that she started as a mainlander."

"Is that an important distinction?" George asks. Her tone only just walks the line of politeness, and Richie flicks his eyebrows at her.

To her credit, Kathy doesn't retreat from the question. "We've a long history of our cries for help being ignored by the mainland, so we've learned to rely on each other. But when you make the choice to settle here properly, we welcome you with open arms." Her lips turn up in a smile. "Once you've seen Eadar in the sunshine, you'll be out there deciding if you want your bedroom window to face the church or the lighthouse."

As the last word leaves her mouth she falters, and the shine returns to her eyes. She glances toward a small framed picture beside the computer. George follows her gaze. It's an image of a man with one arm slung almost casually around a crucifix. Curly handwriting declares him to be St. Andrew.

"Mrs. Campbell informed me that a few of the fishermen headed out on their boats, despite the weather," George says.

"Aye, and damned fools for it. Just the one boat went out today. Left a little after three in the morning, like they do every day." She closes the ledger with a snap. "We have eleven trawlers in total, and each carries around five men. And women," she adds, with a meaningful nod at George. "Our girls have been getting out there for years. Started during the Great War and never stopped."

With a population this small, George guesses that women working on the boats is less about equal opportunity and more about necessity. "When are they expected back?"

Kathy taps the ledger. "If they're not dropping off a haul on the mainland, everyone usually signs back in by sunset. But this lot will likely head back around that time tomorrow." She pauses, then chuckles. "I'm sorry to disappoint you, but I'm simply the postmistress. I receive information and pass it on. What people do after that is their business. Now"—she slaps her hand on the counter—"you'll be wanting your keys. Give me a moment; I put them down here somewhere."

Richie sends George a pointed look as Kathy stoops to retrieve a plastic sleeve with a wad of papers stuffed inside. She's familiar with that look—it's an invitation to switch who is leading an interview. It's just a coincidence that it often arrives at the same moment her patience begins to thin. She thought she'd been doing a good job of keeping her expression smooth; the pill has muted the throbbing in her head, which is normally the cause of her irritability. But George steps away without protest and begins a casual circuit of the room, examining the pictures and posters.

Richie rests his hip against the counter. "Young Cecily informed me that should I have any general queries, you're the first person I should ask."

"Oh, I don't know about that," Kathy says in a tone that suggests otherwise. "I just like to be helpful, run little errands, make sure everyone's got food on the table. You know, if I had a pound for every person who's said, 'Kathy MacKinnon, you're a lifesaver,' I'd be a lady of leisure instead of the postmistress."

Richie's easy laugh earns a deep giggle from Kathy in response. George listens as Richie continues the interview she started so gently that Kathy doesn't seem to realize it's happening.

"I'd wager not much happens around here without you knowing," he says.

"Oh, it's essential to keep track of when people are coming

and going in my line of work. If I'm not here to receive a delivery from the mainland, it causes all sorts of trouble—it could be baby formula or medication."

"I get the impression that people trust you with more than just their mail."

"It can be hard to find an open-minded ear in a small town. People know I can keep my mouth shut." She smiles proudly. "Something said in confidence to Kathy MacKinnon never sees the light of day again."

Richie says something in response that makes the woman giggle again.

Rolling her eyes, George stops at a large map beside the door. From above, the island of Eilean Eadar looks like a swollen kidney with craggy divots carved into the perimeter. The topographic details indicate a shallow beach along the inner curve of the kidney, above which is the narrow harbor. Someone has neatly printed YOU ARE HERE in red marker. With her fingers George walks the path between the words across wavy lines that indicate a steep climb to where their accommodation supposedly awaits. The idea of walking up and down that hill every day for the rest of the week isn't a prospect that fazes George, though she's certain Richie will have a different outlook.

Her finger sweeps over a dense patch of woods in the middle of the island and lands on a black dot on the southeast coast: LIGHTHOUSE. Her eyes chart the distance between the village and the black dot.

"Being the postmistress for a whole village is quite a responsibility," Richie is saying.

"It's not as hard as you might think," Kathy replies. "I have some of the young ones run the letters when my knee plays up, but to be honest, we don't get that much post. There's only two hundred and seven of us on this rock; if you want to tell someone something, you need only stand on your front step and yell."

"Two hundred and six."

Both Kathy and Richie look over at George; Richie quizzically, Kathy as though she'd forgotten George was in the room. "What's that, Inspector?"

"There's two hundred and six people living here. Unless you already subtracted Alan Ferguson from the total."

There's an awkward silence.

"Aye," Kathy says finally, a hand pressed to her pink neck. "Two hundred and six. Quite right." Then, as if a cloud has passed over the sun, she brightens abruptly. "I'm sure you're both dying for a lie-down and a hot meal. Let me show you to Auld Sam's."

It takes thirty minutes to walk back through the village and up a winding dirt path to reach Samuel Nicholson's croft on the hill. Thankfully the rain has stopped at last, but the mud is treacherous underfoot.

"The sun won't be showing its face anytime soon, though," Kathy remarks, puffing lightly. Her breaths fog in the frigid air. "Look how thick those clouds are. We're in for more rain today."

George shifts the strap of her duffel bag to her other shoulder with a wince. Being a police officer requires a certain level of fitness, but carrying two heavy bags uphill while treading carefully is testing even her endurance.

Remarkably, Kathy hasn't even broken a sweat, despite the fact that she's still carrying the ceramic pot and basket, which contains their provisions for the night.

"Does it ever snow here?" George asks, looking around. The rolling hills are currently a patchwork of fresh mud, wiry grass, and scattered stones that have been bleached white by the salty wind. She can't imagine how a change in seasons could bring life to such a bleak place, but perhaps Kathy is right about the transformative powers of sunlight.

"Only occasionally, because of the Gulf Stream," Kathy says, falling into step with her. "But I found a report about a snowstorm so heavy that even the lighthouse's lantern was obscured." After a moment, she quietly adds, "The keepers were very anxious."

George glances at her sideways. "How do you know that?"

"When the lighthouse was in use, the resident keepers kept logbooks."

She nods, pressing her lips together against a wave of questions.

As if appreciating her restraint, Kathy continues unprompted. "They complained about the rain and the cold, and celebrated the odd burst of sunshine, but there's one entry from, oh, I think it was October 1918, where they describe how thick the snow was falling. It says that two of the men stayed up in the dome all night, brushing down the windows with a broom so that passing ships could see the light." She pauses, looking up. "I believe their words were, 'Snow falls on Eadar like a blanket.'"

George hesitates. "In 1918?"

Kathy's expression changes. "This island has been populated on and off for millennia—did you know that?" she asks, her tone bitter. "Found tools in the ground dating back to the Iron Age. Pottery, too, and artifacts from when the first settlers from Ireland arrived here, and from later when the Vikings arrived. But you'll never see us in the history books for all that. It'll always just be that bloody story."

"I don't know much about it," George hedges. "From what I've read, it seems like people have taken liberty with the facts over time."

Kathy's lips tighten. "What has your reading told you?"

"Just that the lighthouse was decommissioned in 1919, shortly after the last three keepers, um . . . disappeared. I believe it was two older men and a boy of around nineteen."

"So far, all true."

George takes that for permission to continue. "I read that the keepers weren't locals. They were part of a rotation around these outer islands, and replacements came every three months. But when the replacement crew arrived, the keepers were gone. And the way things were left was"—she hesitates again—"odd."

Kathy sighs. "Two oilskin coats hung by the door, and there was fresh oil in the lamps and a fire dying in the grate," she recites, like she's reading from a shopping list. "The crew asked all the locals where the keepers had gone, but nobody knew. It was as if that morning all three of them had woken up and vanished in the rain. Is that what they say on the mainland?"

George shrugs, trying to downplay how much she absorbed from the online forum. "Maybe they had an argument and one of them tossed the others off the cliff, then escaped on a boat. Or they were lured into the water by sirens, or driven mad by some insidious island spirit."

Kathy huffs a laugh. "Do they not suspect the locals?"

"I'm sure that came up." It had actually been one of the main theories, accompanied by speculation about the savage and backward residents of an island barely grazed by civilization, but George isn't game to tell Kathy as much. "If that's the case, maybe the keepers caused some trouble in the village," she says lightly. "Maybe they weren't good men."

"Aye, well. It can be hard to tell sometimes."

"So you have the logbooks? I would have thought they'd be in a museum."

"Someone would actually have to come here to get them." She brightens with an idea. "Would you like to read them? The paper is thin, and some sections have been rubbed away, but there are lots of fascinating bits and pieces about the island. What things were like back then."

"Oh, uh . . . sure." She can't think of anything she'd rather do less than thumb through delicate dusty tomes, but she's certain Kathy would take the rejection personally. "Do you think it's the story that keeps people away? Or something else?"

"Well, the distance doesn't help. But a few of us are campaigning for change, trying to encourage tourism. It's an uphill battle with some of the older folks, but we're making progress."

George's hair lifts in a ribbon of wind, sending a shiver down her spine. She claps a hand to her head and smooths the curls down around her ears. "So what do *you* think happened to them? The keepers."

Kathy sighs again, a plaintive sound. "I suspect it's the same thing that's brought you here now."

They walk in contemplative quiet for a moment.

"So, you're the postmistress, tour guide, and local historian?"

"A community like this only survives because everyone takes on a few jobs. Even our priest works on the boats from time to time." Kathy looks sideways at George. "Though I suppose being a police inspector in the city must keep you quite busy. You probably see more tragedy in a day than we do in a decade."

George wonders if Alan Ferguson's death is their tragedy of this decade. "I'm sure I get about as much time off as you do," is what she decides to say aloud.

They stick to lighter topics as they continue up the never-ending incline, Kathy asking increasingly personal questions that George expertly evades. Having left the tourist-heavy center of Edinburgh to cut her teeth as a constable patrolling the streets of Glasgow, George is used to deflecting unwanted attention. Despite the uniform, civilians and colleagues alike presumed that her youth and pretty face made her either fair game or a pushover. But as time passed, and she clawed her way up through the ranks, she learned that changing their minds wasn't as simple as proving her worth—sometimes you had to strike first. The only thing that stops a bully is throwing the first punch.

"Are you married?" Kathy asks.

George channels her irritation into a sigh. Even if she wasn't at work, it would be an inappropriate question for a complete stranger to ask. But either Kathy's lack of experience with law enforcement is showing, or she's used to stepping over personal boundaries like they're drawn in chalk. Regardless, Kathy's genuine interest is so different from the leering faces she's used to that she begrudgingly answers in the negative.

And regrets it immediately.

"I'll have to introduce you to a few of the young men in the village," Kathy says eagerly. "All very responsible, reliable, and never say no to a hard day's work."

"That won't be necessary." Or wanted.

Kathy's expression suggests she's affronted that George isn't interested in a line-up of Eadar's eligible bachelors, but she lets it go as she turns to call back down the hill. "How are you going, DI Stewart?"

Richie's cheeks and nose are bright red from both cold and exertion, and his cheery attitude has vanished sometime in the last thirty minutes. "How far away is this bloody house?" he pants, loosening his tie as he draws level with them.

"Just around the next bend," Kathy says encouragingly.

Despite Richie's weak protests, they slow to his pace for the final stretch, and soon spot a low hand-thrown stone structure that has clearly been subjected to many halfhearted renovations over its life. By virtue of its kingly position, Samuel Nicholson's croft has escaped the fate of its ocean-side kin. The stones are weathered but not deteriorated, the color off-white rather than brown. Small windows with frosted glass are set high into the walls, and a chimney sticks out of the thick thatched roof at a slight angle. To the rear is a small shed.

"You'll want to get the fire going right away," Kathy says as they approach the front door. "I got one of the lads to stack some wood beside the fireplace, and you've got more in the shed just there. Once you start the fire, don't let it go out."

She unlocks the flaking wooden door, preceding them into the croft. Richie follows her in immediately, but George lingers outside for a minute.

Despite the miserable weather, the view from the top of Nicholson's hill is . . . well, nicer than she expected. From this position she can see the whole island: to the left is the village, where every chimney smokes relentlessly; straight ahead are several fenced paddocks that abut the dense copse of woods she saw on the map; and all the way across the slope to the right is the lighthouse, standing solitary on the cliff edge. And in every direction she turns is the sea, crushed slate and white foam, seabirds taking to the sky now that the rain has stopped. George is surprised to note the lack of salt in the air that lifts her hair again; it smells fresh and clean, untainted. She fishes her phone from her pocket, but with a sinking feeling sees that, even though she's standing at the highest point of Eadar, the reception flickers between one bar and SOS.

"Come on out of the cold, Inspector! We're lighting the fire."

Filling her lungs once more, she turns for the door—and notices something carved into the lintel above her head. Rocking up onto her toes, she sees that a small double spiral has been carved painstakingly into the timber, the even circles speaking to a steady hand. It looks old, put there by Samuel's father or grandfather, perhaps. She wonders if it's a family crest, or if someone had just been bored one day.

The tour of the interior takes less than a minute. The entire residence smells of wood smoke and dust, clouds of which are stirred up as they move through the space. Kathy shows them a small bedroom with a low double bed, a tiny bathroom "with proper plumbing" that George has to bend her knees slightly to enter, and a sparse area that Kathy describes generously as "the great room," which combines the kitchen, dining, and sitting rooms. A window above the sink faces out toward the woodshed. The only furniture is a scarred timber table with two chairs and a squashy two-seater couch. The only decoration is a large hand-carved crucifix on the wall.

"Samuel didn't entertain much," Kathy says in the silence concluding their tour.

It takes three attempts to persuade Kathy to leave—she insists upon showing them how to light the tricky stove and pointing out the tiny generator that provides electricity. George lets Richie handle the negotiations; the pressure in her head is returning, sooner than expected. She leans casually against the arm of the couch and tries to keep her face smooth.

Kathy finally heads out the door with the promise of returning the following day—"To make sure you've survived the night," she says.

"They clearly aren't used to talking to police," Richie says, watching from the doorway as the postmistress lopes back toward the village. "If someone said that to me back home, I'd take it as a threat."

"Or a warning," George adds, surreptitiously pressing her thumb to her eyebrow.

CHAPTER 3

GEORGE AND RICHIE'S PLAN FOR THEIR FIRST DAY ON EADAR—AFTER ARRIVING in the early afternoon and settling into the croft—involved introducing themselves to Alan's mother before the sun went down. But the heavy downpour Kathy predicted keeps them indoors, and by the time it eases, darkness has fallen over the island.

"In hindsight," Richie says, as they find themselves slumped over Samuel Nicholson's ancient table, stifling yawns and spooning the last dregs of stew directly from the pot to their mouths, "we were probably a little overambitious for our first day."

"To be fair, it's only four thirty," George points out. "It just *looks* like midnight. What do you suppose this is?" She peers at an unidentifiable protein on her spoon.

"Eh?"

She jerks her chin toward the front of the croft, to the paddocks beyond. "I saw a few sheep grazing down there, but hardly enough to feed the village. They must bring in supplies from the mainland."

Richie suppresses a burp. "Probably—'scuse me—fish. I don't think the sheep are for eating. They sell some wool, remember? They have a butcher, so perhaps someone keeps other livestock—pigs, or chickens. Or they get meat delivered from the mainland." His face expands with a huge yawn. "Lord, there's something about a sea journey that I find exhausting. But I think we should stick to our plan: introduce ourselves to Alan's mother and ask her some questions before we call it a day."

George groans at the thought of traipsing back down that

hill in the dark. "She probably knows we're here. Probably already knows our names, too."

But Richie is insistent. "It'll start us off on the right foot with her. Go on, get your boots on."

They manage to make their way back to the main street without any broken ankles, and Richie is in a far better mood heading downhill than he was going up. George finds that her impression of total darkness was exaggerated; though the sun is long gone, the blue-gray clouds still allow enough of a glow to filter through for her to take in her surroundings. It helps that many of the windows are alight, a wash spilling onto the street to illuminate the road and the faces of people passing by. Richie flags down a couple of teenagers to ask for directions to the Ferguson home, and they point up past the post office. He smiles as they murmur a polite farewell and continue on.

"People here are friendlier than we were led to believe, don't you think?"

"Kathy might have something to do with that. She said a few people have unofficially started a campaign to encourage tourists to visit the island." As they walk past the row of darkened buildings, she adds, "Not sure how much luck they'll have, though."

"They've got the raw beauty of the Outer Hebrides working in their favor." He breaks off to greet a woman walking toward them. "Good evening," he says.

"Inspector Stewart, Inspector Lennox," she replies, with a shallow nod for each of them before continuing past.

At George's frown, Richie asks, "You really don't like it? I'm starting to feel like a celebrity."

"I don't like people knowing my name until I know theirs."

He snorts. "People trust who they know. If someone is closed off to you, why would you open up to them?"

"Is this lesson complimentary, or is there a subscription I need to cancel?"

A wide smile splits his face. "Just saying, you attract more flies with honey, Lennox. You'll learn that when you've been doing this job as long as I have."

As they leave the lights of the main street behind them, they both take out their torches to guide their way up the incline that leads toward the church. Turning right at an intersection brings them to a gable-ended croft with a covered porch. There's a weak light above the front door that flickers every few seconds. Grass is overtaking the small round pavers that guide them to the door, at the foot of which sits a large, lidded cooking pot. George stoops to investigate the contents as Richie pulls a cord attached to a tarnished bell.

"Fish," she notes without surprise. Stowing her torch, she picks up the pot and stands. "It's still warm."

"Maybe she's popped out," Richie mutters, peering through the front window. "Or she's not up for visitors."

They wait a minute, then Richie rings the bell again. There's no movement from within the house, not even the twitch of a curtain.

George starts lowering the pot back to the ground. "I'll check the back. She might—"

"What do you want?"

They whirl around. A rail-thin woman in her mid-forties with deep smoker's lines stands at the corner of the porch, one gardening glove on and the other clutched in her bare hand. She wears soft trousers and a jumper that looks like it used to fit but now dips below her sharp collarbones.

Richie recovers quickly and steps forward, switching off his torch. "I'm DI Richard Stewart, and this is DI Georgina Lennox. We're looking for Catriona Ferguson."

"Well, you've found her." Pushing a few silvery blonde hairs back off her forehead, Catriona looks at them with resentful eyes. "You know, I've already answered your lot's questions. Even had Kathy send photos."

"Yes, and thank you for doing that," Richie says with a polite smile, "but we've been sent by the Crown Office. We just have a few questions, if you don't mind."

"Lots of people have questions, Inspector," Catriona replies quietly. "The answers to most of them lie with God alone."

"Still," Richie says after a moment, "if you have a few minutes to speak with us . . ."

Catriona's eyes drop to the pot George is holding.

"It was on the step," George says. "It's still warm."

Catriona's mouth thins. "I wish people would stop bringing me food. I can cook for myself. I lost a son, not my hands." She looks past them out to the road, then nods toward the side of the house. "Come on, then."

They exchange a quick look before following her, cautiously stepping over objects half hidden in shadows: a neatly coiled hose, a punctured bike tire, and a variety of empty flowerpots. The backyard is illuminated by a bright spotlight over the back door, and it looks as rough as the front, bordered by battered plants with a few weeds encroaching onto a muddy lawn. There're two chairs on the grass and a full ashtray on a table between them. Rainwater has pooled on the seats.

George nods toward the lawn. "Doing some evening gardening, Mrs. Ferguson?"

"Mm. It's been raining hard and the weeds are soaking it up. Have to pull them out at the roots before they do too much damage." She pauses to drop her gloves at the door. They land beside a pair of gumboots crusted in dried mud, too big for Catriona. "Wipe your feet. Please."

They step into a tiny kitchen that reminds George of her grandmother's house in Edinburgh, an interactive relic from another era: timber benches worn smooth by time, green cupboards, and a smell of cigarette smoke that seems to seep from the walls.

"You can put that on the stove," Catriona says to George, who's still clutching the pot. "I suppose I'd better eat it or I'll hurt someone's feelings. Was there a note?"

George checks, then shakes her head.

"I'm sure Kathy will know," Catriona says with a small sigh. "Tea?"

———

They settle into a sitting room right off the kitchen. Soft fabrics offset the coldness of the stone walls; there's a thick carpet beneath their feet, and if the couch George and Richie are sitting on was deep-cleaned it would sell for a mint at a vintage showroom.

Catriona sits stiffly in a cream paisley armchair, a coffee table dividing them. The arrangement of the seats indicates she's entertained many visitors in this same configuration. Probably a lot more than usual in the three weeks since Alan's death.

A crucifix hangs above a framed photo of Alan on the wall, the glass glowing in the warm lamplight.

Richie leans forward and rests his teacup on his knee. "First, Mrs. Ferguson, I just want to say on behalf of myself and DI Lennox that we're terribly sorry for your loss. I have two girls of my own just a few years older than Alan. It's something no parent should ever experience. We're not meant to bury our children."

Catriona's chin bobs. "Aye, well. That's the deal you make with God when you bring a child into the world. He has His reasons." Like Cecily, Catriona wears a small silver crucifix around her neck; she brushes her spindly fingers against it as she speaks.

"Is Alan's father around?" Richie asks.

"Not since Alan was nine."

"And you raised him out here all on your own?" Richie whistles, impressed. "You're an unsung hero, Mrs. Ferguson."

But Catriona waves away the praise. "I didn't do it alone." She nods toward the front window to the village below. "People come when they're called."

George withdraws her notebook. "We just have a few questions, Mrs. Ferguson."

"We'll take this slowly," Richie adds, and George knows he's directing the words at her, even though he smiles at Catriona. "If you need to take a break at any time, just let us know."

George dips her chin in acknowledgment. "We'd like to discuss the day Alan died. Could you walk us through your movements?"

"Movements? You mean, you want to know what I was doing?"

"As much as you can recall."

"Why?"

"It's procedure, ma'am."

Catriona opens her mouth, but before she can begin a sharp knock on the front door makes her jump. "Oh," she says, as if struck by a sobering thought.

Richie rises. "Shall I get that for you, Mrs. Ferguson?"

She hesitates, then nods. "Tell him to come in."

Richie disappears into a narrow hallway and returns a few moments later with a tall, solid man in tow. Gray hairs sprout from his temples, and he's dressed like a suburban dad in a thick navy jumper and jeans. He could be a few years younger than Richie—though he certainly moves like someone of more advanced years, limping significantly on his left leg.

"Sorry I'm late, Catriona—I found myself on the receiving end of one of Gordon MacKinnon's war stories, and you know how they seem to get longer every time. Inspector Lennox . . ." He extends his hand toward George. "James Ross. It's a pleasure to meet you finally. The village has been buzzing with the news of your arrival. I feel like I'm the last one on the island to actually clap eyes on the both of you."

George grasps his hand. "Well, you've actually found us in the middle of an interview, so if you wouldn't mind . . . ?"

Ross blinks, then looks at Catriona.

She glances down at her hands, folded in her lap, then addresses George. "I guessed you'd come to see me tonight, Inspectors. Father Ross offered his support."

A thread of her conversation with Cecily comes back to her, and she raises her eyebrows at the man. "You're the priest?"

Father Ross grins, revealing a set of even teeth. "Do you need to see my credentials?" He hooks a thick finger into the neckline of his jumper and pulls it down enough to reveal the clerical collar underneath.

"I see. And how did you know we were with Catriona now?"

"Someone told someone told me," he says with a laugh. "That's how word usually travels here. I can leave, though, if there's anything you need to discuss with Catriona privately."

"We're just going through the details of the day Alan was found. If Catriona has asked for you to sit in, then it's fine with us," Richie says.

George purses her lips but doesn't argue as the priest settles himself into an armchair at Catriona's side, massaging his left knee with a grimace.

"Please, don't let me interrupt you further," he says.

Feeling inexplicably ruffled, George turns back to Catriona. "So . . . could you tell us about that day, Mrs. Ferguson? Start from when you woke up."

Catriona's expression is vacant for a moment, then she casts her eyes around until they land on a cigarette case on a side table. She plucks one out, puts it between her lips, then strikes a match. After a steadying inhale, Catriona begins.

"I woke up at three a.m.," she says, her voice quiet but clear. "Had a cup of tea, got dressed, and let myself into the bakery at three forty; it was my day to open up. Sally MacGill came in at four thirty. I had six loaves in the oven and two dozen rolls rising by then, so she took over while I had a break. Sat on the steps outside. Smoked. Looked at the stars."

George jots down some notes, even though she hears Richie scribbling rapidly beside her. "And it was just Sally and yourself for how long?"

"I was still on my break when Andy Fraser came over. He's got a wee baby now, and he'd been up half the night. Then came Linda Campbell, the elder Ross-Nicholson girl, my sister-in-law and her children—and then Kathy popped in. Asked me to come by for a tea when I could. I told her I'd be round when Sally could look after customers without worrying about the ovens."

"What time did you get there?"

Catriona shrugs, tapping the ash off her cigarette. "At the same time as our delivery man arrived, just after six. Kathy went out back to make the tea, so I chatted with him for a few minutes. That's when Sally ran in, all pale and shaking like a leaf."

A short silence follows in which Catriona takes two long draws of her cigarette, and George and Richie wait. Father Ross listens with his head bowed.

"It was the last thing I ever expected to hear," she says, pausing to send a mouthful of smoke up to the ceiling. "Who kills themselves on a Wednesday?"

From there, Catriona's grasp on the timeline becomes less firm. She recalls falling into Sally's arms when her legs gave out, followed by some blurry words and wails. There was the sensation of being pressed against the chests of many different people, so many sets of arms holding her close and then releasing her into the next. Everyone had been preparing for Mass; Catriona said it seemed like the entire population had gathered around her.

"There were some people at the lighthouse already—word traveled faster than my legs. Someone tried to hold me back, but Father here made them give way. And there he was. My boy. Lying on his back, arms by his sides."

Her eyes are shiny; she squeezes them shut.

"I knelt down in the mud beside him," she continues in a whisper, "and I brushed the hair away from his eyes, and I kissed him here, like when he was small." Her hand rises to brush a spot between her eyebrows, the same fair shade as her son's. "It was the only part of him that wasn't damaged."

When she finally looks at George, the mistiness has evaporated. "I didn't know the delivery man had radioed the coastguard while we were up at the tower, so it was a shock when they came to take him away. I thought it was all done after they gave him back a week later and we buried him, and I could get on with my grieving. But then someone from the Crown Office called a few days ago to tell me they're sending some *city police* to talk to me." She mashes the cigarette stub into the ashtray.

Richie smiles apologetically. "Thank you for going through that with us, Mrs. Ferguson."

She nods once, then lights another cigarette. "Is that all you wanted to know?"

George looks over her questions. "Were you close with your son, Mrs. Ferguson?"

"I believe so, aye."

"Any concerns with his mental health?"

Catriona looks at her blankly.

She tries again. "Had he seemed out of sorts recently?"

"He was a happy child, then a happy teenager. He liked studying. He was clever."

Father Ross shifts in his seat; when George looks over, he's rubbing his knee again.

"We saw his reports," Richie says. "A very intelligent boy. And he was homeschooled, I believe?"

Catriona makes an affirmative sound around the cigarette. "All the teenagers here are."

"We don't see much sense in sending them off to the schools in Stornoway, or some boarding school on the mainland," Father Ross interjects. "Not when they can complete the same coursework at home."

"And after high school?" George asks. "Surely some of them want to leave the island to pursue higher education."

"Alan had sent off a few applications for universities on the mainland," Catriona says, nodding. "I was trying not to badger him about it. He was nervous. Started snapping at me when I asked if he'd had any acceptance letters."

"How would he have reacted if he'd received a rejection? Might that have upset him?"

Catriona shakes her head. "Kathy sees all the post come through, and she said nothing arrived for him."

"Maybe it came in an e-mail? Did he have a computer?"

The priest chuckles awkwardly. "There's only one, and it's at the post office. We rely on that and the radios on the boats for any communication. Our dear Kathy passes on messages."

The lack of mobile reception is one thing, but two hundred people sharing a single computer? No privacy for browsing the web, placing prescription orders, buying gifts . . . George can't discipline her face back to neutrality fast enough, and the priest's smile widens.

"I know that must seem very strange to you, Inspector. Living in the city, with all that technology at your fingertips. But we've learned to go without many things, and we always manage just fine."

"Good for you," is all she can think to say.

"Did Alan have a job?" Richie asks.

"Aye, he was working up at MacLeod's," Catriona says.

George's pen is poised over the notebook. "Who?"

"Alisdair MacLeod. He keeps the sheep."

George makes a note of that. "Did Alan like working for him?"

"He's not friendly, but he's not unfriendly either. Likes his own company, which I don't have a problem with. Some do."

"What was the nature of Alan's work with Mr. MacLeod?"

"Tending to the sheep, I suppose. But if there wasn't much to do, he'd get a day of work on someone's boat."

"Was he meant to be working the day he died? Either on the farm or the boats?"

Catriona hesitates, then nods. "On the farm. He was supposed to be there all week."

"Did he have friends at work?"

"I don't know."

George looks up with a slight frown. "Really?" Given how small the community is, she finds this surprising.

"I'm not the type of mother who feels the need to pry," Catriona replies, a new edge to her voice.

Richie leans in again. "We're just interested in learning how Alan was spending his time, and who he was spending it with."

Catriona appears to have forgotten the cigarette in her hand; the ash has started to build up. "Alan didn't have much interest in the other kids. He was friendly, but preferred his own company. He had a girlfriend at the end of last year—Fiona Bell. But that only lasted a few months."

Richie jots the name down. "Do you know why they broke up?"

Catriona looks over at Alan's photo and sighs. "I heard that he was caught with another girl. I don't know who, before you go asking. I doubt Fiona knows either, or that girly would have copped the same black eye that Alan did. Fiona's father was a champion boxer," she adds by way of an explanation, then throws an apologetic look at Father Ross.

He catches it and smiles. "It's not adultery until marriage. And Alan was just a boy; we were all young once." The priest turns to Richie. "Fiona does a few shifts here and there on the boats, but she takes after her da. She's over on the mainland every other weekend for fights. Junior champion four years running. We're all very proud of her."

"I see," Richie says mildly, shooting a glance at George. "Do you think Fiona might still be upset about the way things ended?"

Catriona shakes her head. "She came to see me the day after, saying how sad it all was. That's what you're going to hear a lot of as you go around asking your questions," she says, her voice suddenly hard. "Nobody disliked Alan, and he never hurt anybody."

The priest stretches to place a comforting hand on Catriona's arm. "It's not for us to know God's plans, Catriona. We must simply endure the task of accepting it. Remember Proverbs 3:5."

George looks between them, confused. "What's Proverbs 3—"

"*Trust in the Lord with all your heart, and do not lean on your own understanding,*" Richie says. He gives George a nod then says, "I think we'll leave it here for today, Mrs. Ferguson. Thank you for your time."

"Actually, if you don't mind," George says quickly, as she gets to her feet, "there's one more thing I'd like to see."

———

When George was fifteen, a girl at her school passed away after a long battle with cancer. The school organized a fundraiser to help the girl's parents pay for the memorial, and after the final amount had been tallied they asked for volunteers to deliver the check. George's best friend at the time was head girl and had known the girl who died, so she put her hand up for the task. George went along for moral support.

It was awful, of course. The parents couldn't stop crying, even when they were attempting to smile or passing around cups of tea. George already felt uncomfortable hugging the father with his quivering chin, but that feeling skyrocketed when they were ushered into the dead girl's room to "say good-bye." Even at fifteen, she felt a deep sense of discomfort when she looked around; the parents hadn't touched a thing—not even the unswallowed pills on the bedside table and the wrinkle in their daughter's pillow. It was as if they were expecting her to arrive home at any minute.

In stark contrast, but just as discomfiting, is the room where Alan Ferguson slept for eighteen years. The tiny rectangular space with its low, sloped ceiling could be a motel room for all the warmth and personality it holds. The single bed is crisply made, a blue coverlet folded neatly at the foot. A bare timber desk sits beneath a small window, the shades half drawn. There are no pictures, no posters, no markers of teen passion or rebellion anywhere.

"Did you . . . ?" Richie trails off, eyes traveling across the barren surfaces with barely contained disbelief. "Have you tidied up a bit?"

"Some of the ladies came to clear it for me," Catriona says from her stiff position in the hall.

Despite the fact that Alan's essence seems to have been scrubbed entirely from the room, Catriona's body language makes George feel like she's intruding on a sacred space.

They exit through the front door this time, Father Ross waving from the armchair. The sun has well and truly set now, and the world beyond the reach of the porch light is as dark as the bottom of a well. As they walk down the path, George half turns to raise a hand in farewell, but Catriona's arms stay firmly crossed over her chest.

Then the priest calls her back into the house, and as they start back onto the dirt road, George swears she hears the lock turn.

———

Once they're out of sight and earshot of the house, George and Richie both click their torches back on.

"Well that was interesting," George says.

"I know. I thought out of everyone here, she would be pleased to see us."

"You would think. But it seems like there was a deadline on grieving. He's only been dead for three weeks, and they've already cleared out his room."

He considers. "With so few workers, they probably can't afford to have someone falling to pieces. Death happens, but people still need bread."

They turn left at the intersection and start walking back down toward the village. The path is still a little slippery from the rain, especially where the mud is thin over half-buried stones. Richie keeps his beam concentrated on the ground, guiding their tentative steps, and George sweeps her own torch through the darkness ahead. As they make their way carefully toward the main street, George's replies to Richie's musings get shorter. Each step is sending a jolt up her spine, a lash of lightning all the way into that sore point in her skull, and she has to make a concerted effort not to groan. Luckily, she knows her partner doesn't need encouragement from her; he tends to think aloud, ideas and suggestions falling into place like train tracks before him.

So when he abruptly stops speaking, she looks at him curiously.

"What are you—"

"Shh."

He can't see her raised eyebrows, but he correctly senses her irritation. The hand that finds her shoulder is both an apology and a restraint—his steps slow, then angle slightly off the path. Even when they come to a stop in the wet grass he doesn't speak, and the sudden prickling along the back of her neck tells George to keep her mouth shut, too. She follows his lead as he directs his torch up the hill, back the way they just came, but even with both beams concentrated in the one direction, the light is quickly swallowed by shadow.

As the two of them stand side by side in the dark, Richie's warm hand still clasping her shoulder, George's hearing sharpens, taking over for the lack of sight. And then she picks up what Richie had caught moments earlier.

Footsteps. Quiet, unhurried. Getting closer.

But from which direction? Richie clearly thinks they're coming from up the hill—he's still aiming his torch back toward the Ferguson house.

"Maybe we forgot something?" she whispers, and Richie grunts, then startles her when he calls, "Who's there?"

There's a sound of a foot scuffing against earth—but it comes from *behind* them. Both George and Richie whip around, and their fused torchlight lands on a woman carrying a large woven basket on her hip. She yelps, squinting in the sudden glare. "Put that down, you great galoot!"

George laughs as Richie exhales, a little shakily, and directs the torch to her feet. "Apologies, ma'am," she says. "We didn't mean to startle you."

Even in the dimmed light, George sees the shock flash across the woman's face, followed swiftly by understanding. "Oh, it's the mainlanders," she says, as if making an aside to a companion, though as far as George can tell it's just the three of them on the path. "You know, you half blinded me there," she continues, blinking theatrically.

"Aye, you probably don't need these things to make your way around," Richie says, raising his torch a fraction. "Must know the paths like the back of your hand."

Her irritation gives way with a chuckle. "Some people use them, or lanterns. But you get used to the dark when you're in it long enough."

She bids them good night and turns left at the intersection, heading inland. George, unnerved by how quickly her figure is swallowed by the night, tightens her grip on the torch.

"Would you get a look at me," Richie says as they start walking again, "scaring the life out of the locals on our first day here. Though I could have sworn I heard someone coming from . . ." He looks over his shoulder toward where the woman has just vanished. "I've been in the city too long, I suppose. Not used to how sound works without anything to bounce off."

George hears his embarrassment. "I didn't even hear her coming to begin with."

"Aye, well," he mumbles, "I just don't want either of us to be caught off guard again."

Again.

Did he mean to say that? Or had the word slipped out? Because there was only a single event in recent history when one of them was caught off guard, and it ended with blood and bone and a scar behind her ear. Despite the chill, her face feels very hot all of a sudden.

Richie's voice breaks the silence. "I wonder if the pathologist who examined Alan factored in farm work when they recommended the case to COPFS," he says thoughtfully.

"What?"

"Could explain the bruises."

She scoffs, the heat in her cheeks leaking into her tone. "Are you suggesting a sheep grew fingers and used them to grip Alan's arm so hard it left marks?"

She feels more than sees Richie frown at her, unimpressed as always with her sarcasm. "Not even the pathologist could conclude that they were fingerprints," he points out.

"But *we* know they are," she pushes, and feels a rush of vindication when Richie doesn't argue. "And they were unusual enough to warrant an investigation."

"Unusual doesn't equal homicide, Lennox. Teen deaths are almost always recommended for investigation, suspicious or not. And even if it wasn't suicide, it could have been an accident. Maybe he and some kids were messing around on top of the tower. He lost his balance, they tried to grab him, but . . ." He clicks his tongue. "Now, Ross—why did his name sound familiar?"

"The coastguard's report mentions him. He was one of the few who gave a statement when they came to collect Alan's body."

"Oh, that's right. And who found him?"

"Someone called . . ." She mentally flips through the pages of her notebook. "John MacNeil."

"Let's add him to the list," Richie says, then tuts. "And if this is what the sky looks like at five thirty, then we'd best be getting an early start tomorrow."

The conversation dwindles as they pass through town and begin their second ascent of the day up to Nicholson's croft. George could attribute the silence to Richie's tiredness—she has to suppress a yawn herself as they dig their toes into the soft ground—but after a few minutes of quiet broken only by the squelch of mud, she knows he's doing exactly what she's doing: listening for footsteps in the dark.

CHAPTER 4

A LOW GROAN MAKES HER LOOK UP FROM THE SOAPY WATER IN THE SINK. Richie is standing in the living area, looking down at the couch with quiet despair.

"I'm sure it won't be too bad," he says, sinking one knee into the cushion and wincing.

She dries the last mug and hangs the tea towel on a hook beside the tap. "Take the bed. I'm going to stay up a while longer and look over my notes."

Despite his tiredness, his eyes are sharp on her. "You feeling okay?"

"Fine," she replies evenly. "You?"

He ignores the attempt at a diversion. "How's your head? Any pain?"

"Head's okay, but I *can* report a new pain in my arse . . ."

He holds up his hands. "All right, all right, I'm just checking. You know I have to." His eyes slide to the side of her head, and she sweeps her hair forward. An embarrassing knee-jerk reaction, made worse by the pitying looks it usually triggers from people who know what she's trying to hide. And Richie is no different, his expression softening into something that makes her want to keep brushing her hair forward until it covers her entire face. Even so, for a second she considers telling him about the headaches and the wave of vertigo she experienced on the boat. But after eight long months of specialist appointments and desk duty, she bites her tongue.

"You don't need to worry about me, Rich." At his raised eyebrows, she adds testily, "Look, do you want the bed or not?"

After a very halfhearted argument over the sleeping arrangements, less than twenty minutes later George hears a rumbling snore through the bedroom door. She crouches beside the hearth and drops two large logs in, stoking the fire until the flames are high. The familiar smell and prickling heat on her skin remind her of the holiday cottage her family rented between school terms, her dad threading marshmallows onto long sticks for her and her sister to toast over the fire.

Her family had very different reactions when she told them she'd been assigned to an investigation on one of Scotland's most remote islands.

"When you say you're traveling for work, it's supposed to be to Dubai or Sydney," Jane said, her smirk evident even over the phone. "I thought being promoted to inspector would come with a little more glamour."

Her parents' response was one of gentle concern.

"Are you sure you're up for that, love?" her dad asked. "It's only been eight months . . ."

Her mam's voice wobbled. "And what if you need a doctor? You'll be hours away from a decent hospital."

But George had been petitioning her superintendent for months to get back to real detective work, though this determination backfired when the Crown Office and Procurator Fiscal Service's request with Alan's file attached was deposited on her desk three days ago.

"It's probably just a suicide," Superintendent Kylie Cole said, sliding her glasses down her nose and peering over them. She had summoned George and Richie to her office to talk over the case. "We see a lot of them among those wee islands out west. The isolation and rain drive them batty. But he'd just turned eighteen, so COPFS requires us to look into it."

"And you really think sending two DIs is a good use of the force's time and resources?" George asked, gesturing to Richie. He was sitting with the file open in his lap, reading the pathology report thoughtfully.

Cole leveled a warning look at her. "Watch yourself, Lennox. Your new title still has the plastic on it. And it'll be good experience for you. You've never worked a case off the mainland."

"Because nothing happens out there. Those islands are medieval time capsules with a population of relics."

"So, you get to spend a few days in a picturesque coastal village. Consider it a paid holiday." Sensing George gearing up for further protest, the superintendent looked at Richie. "Give us a minute."

Richie left the room without comment, handing George the file. Cole then removed her glasses entirely. "Now, I want you to listen closely and without interruption. Can you manage that? If not, then you clearly need to spend more time as a DS learning your place."

Gritting her teeth, George nodded.

"Good. Because you seem to have forgotten that when I assign cases, I do not invite a debate. *Yes*, you and Stewart are good detectives, and *yes*, this might very well be open-and-shut. But it's your first case as a DI, *and* it's your first case since the incident, so treat this as an opportunity to show me that you can handle it, and I'll consider giving you more complex assignments. Understood?"

George's mind raced with a hundred arguments, but she swallowed them with effort and nodded again.

Cole smiled broadly. "Great. Get out."

But as George reached the door, Cole spoke again.

"Are you *sure* you're up for it, Lennox? There's no need to rush back. Not after what you went through."

The softness in her voice sparked a resentful fire in George. "The doctor cleared me."

"That's not what I asked."

"I'm fine," she said quickly. "I'm ready."

After a long look, Cole nodded. "Once you've confirmed suicide as the manner of death, we'll advise the Crown Office to close the case. Then I'll know you're really back."

With the promise of real cases on the horizon, George asked Cole to arrange for their departure to Eadar as soon as possible, before hurrying back to her desk to start researching Alan Ferguson and the tiny island he called home.

Now, after depositing her duffel bag next to the musty couch which is to be her bed for the next five nights, George carries her briefcase over to the table. Flicking back the clasps, she extracts every document they've gathered relating to Alan and his eighteen years of life. George is disheartened to see how few there are. She entertained a vague hope that the documents might have multiplied just from being in the place where he died.

There's the minimal autopsy report detailing every crack and cut the pathologist had observed on Alan's body, and eleven accompanying photos secured by a bulldog clip. There's his N5 home learning report showing top marks, only one unwelcome B in biology among a sea of As; the same subject that George struggled with in secondary school.

She takes out her notebook and re-reads the notes she's made. So far, they consist mostly of questions, and there's only so many times she can stare at them, seeing as they're already committed to memory.

With Richie's snores becoming more and more of a temptation, she slides two pill bottles from the inside pocket of her briefcase and shakes out a pill from each. Even without the labels—which she peeled off before leaving home this morning—

she can tell the tramadol from the zolpidem. Both pills are oblong, but while the former is white, the latter has a pinkish hue. They sit side by side in her slightly trembling hand.

The couch looks comfortable enough with Cecily's donated blankets and a pillow Richie had insisted she take from the bed. Even though she's taller than Richie, she knows his back wouldn't have survived the night out here. She loads a few more logs on the fire and slides beneath the blankets.

With the assistance of the zolpidem, it doesn't take long for sleep to claim her—despite a sweet smell of damp rising from the couch cushions. The flickering firelight turns the darkness purple. It reminds her of the note on the autopsy report that her superintendent had mentioned.

Bruising inconsistent with impact trauma.

George watches the flames lick up the logs, turning them from brown to white to black, until her eyes close.

———

She's not sure how many hours have passed when she stirs awake. All that remains of the fire are a couple of glowing logs, casting a weak light that can't compete with the shadows in the room. Aside from the occasional crack from the fireplace, the only sound is the tail end of a breeze, a plaintive sound that fades to a whimper as she twists on the couch, one hand patting along the floor for the familiar outline of her phone. When she locates it, she turns the torch feature on and shines it over the back of the couch.

With so few furnishings it's easy to detect if anything is out of place, but nothing looks amiss. Her ears pick up on tiny man-made sounds: the hum of the small refrigerator, the distant drone of the generator outside. But beyond that . . . She rubs at her eyes, as if clearing her vision will sharpen her hearing. It doesn't help; either that or there's nothing *to* hear, because beyond the two machines, the island is completely silent. No calls between nocturnal animals, no grass stirring. It's the kind of quiet that is like a held breath; the kind of stillness that feels like eavesdropping. As if the island is waiting for someone to disturb the peace.

She yawns. If someone is mad enough to run about outside at night, good luck to them—it certainly won't be her. She turns off the torch, letting the coaxing fingers of sleep drag her back down into the depths.

———

The next time she wakes, she knows exactly who's to blame. A loud smash and a stream of hearty curses propel George from deep sleep to painfully awake in seconds. The culprit is Richie, who apologizes profusely for the rude awakening as he delicately collects shards of the mug he knocked off the table.

She scrubs at her eyes, feeling her pulse thump wildly in her neck. "You could have just tapped me on the shoulder."

"I was going to have a cup of tea ready before I woke you up," he says forlornly. "How'd you sleep?"

"Fine," she says through a yawn. "Being beside the fire makes it worth the twist I'm putting into my spine. I think the wind woke me up at one point—did you hear anything?"

"Not a peep. But I was knocked out as soon as I hit the pillow." He rolls his shoulders. "Somehow that mattress is both too hard and too soft. And I shudder to think how it got that way." He refills the kettle and jerks his chin toward the bathroom. "Go get dressed and I'll get another tea sorted."

She doesn't bother waiting for the ancient hot-water system to kick in, instead splashing her face with icy water. She shimmies into a pair of trousers, then eases a soft black turtleneck over her head. Glancing into the mirror, her eyes are drawn to the line of pink scar that starts behind her left ear and disappears into her hairline. She runs a finger over the raised skin dispassionately, the roughness triggering a twinge of disgust in her stomach. Turning her back on the mirror, she pulls the neck of her top up and lets her hair swing forward over her shoulders.

By the time she emerges, Richie has piled the case documents to one side and set out two steaming mugs and a plate of toast.

"It's like we're at a bed and breakfast," he says, poking through the basket Kathy had left. "Would you like jam or honey?"

"What kind of jam?"

"Blackcurrant."

She pulls a face. "Honey."

"Big day ahead," Richie says, sliding the jar to her. "We'll have to stop at the post office first thing, we need to borrow their satphone to check in with Cole. And I was thinking this afternoon we should stick some of this up on the wall." He nods at the notes. "I brought Blu-tack. I reckon it'll hold on the stone."

"Let's hope we have some more notes to add to the collection by the end of today," George says, sipping her tea to chase a metallic taste from her mouth. "You're sure you didn't hear anything last night?"

"No. You said it was the wind?"

She presses the rim of the mug to her bottom lip, enjoying the warmth. "I *think* so. But then, afterward, it was . . . quiet."

Richie laughs. Replaying her words in her head, she laughs, too. "You were probably right last night—noises are different here. I'm just used to living on a busy street."

"Mm, no cars tearing up the road, no music blasting, or dogs barking." He smiles, letting his eyes close. "These people have no idea how lucky they are to live here."

CHAPTER 5

IT'S A DIFFERENT KIND OF COLD THAT GREETS THEM WHEN THEY STEP OUTSIDE.

"It's brighter today," Richie observes, then looks down at the path ahead of them with distaste. "But I'm guessing rain isn't far away."

Looking up at the sky, George isn't so sure. Though it's overcast, the white glow emanating from the clouds makes it seem lighter than yesterday. They trudge down the hill, trying to avoid the muddy slicks that could send them tumbling down to the village. She relays Kathy's offer to introduce her to the village's bachelors, making Richie cackle. "Could you imagine living here?" she asks. "Doing the same thing every day, the same routines, same faces, same stories?"

"You're describing my ideal retirement. I'm planning to call it a day as soon as I turn sixty," Richie says. "That'll round me up to a forty-year career on the force, and I imagine I'll have had quite enough of it by then. I've been planning it all in my head for years. I'll cut a cake, make a grand speech, let you weep over me for an hour or so, then I'll hop in the car Jenny will be idling on the street and take off into the sunset. The next time you'll hear from me, it'll be inviting you to the grand reopening of the country pub I've taken over."

"Does Jenny know about this yet?" George can easily summon the image of his wife's face creased in loving consternation, an expression she often wears around Richie.

He bats the question away. "I've got three years to work out how to pitch it to her— Oh, hello!"

Startled by his abrupt change in tone, George follows Richie's gaze to where a lithe older man moves through the paddocks parallel to them, cutting a path through a handful of grazing sheep. He looks over at Richie's greeting. Thick gray hair brushes the shoulders of his quilted vest, long legs sheathed in muddy trousers. His face is weathered but striking; George's mam would probably find him handsome.

"We've come from the Nicholson place," Richie calls, highly skilled in small talk. "Was cold overnight, eh?"

The man looks from Richie to George then back again, and he says nothing.

Richie points toward the sky. "But a better day ahead than yesterday, I'm hoping."

Nothing.

"I'm DI Stewart, and this is DI Lennox," Richie persists. "We're here about Alan Ferguson. Did you know him?"

Neither their titles nor Alan's name seem to land with the man. Without a flicker on his lined face, he continues on through the paddocks. A few of the sheep trot after him.

Richie turns to George. "Couldn't shut him up, eh?"

"Do you think that might have been Alisdair MacLeod?"

"Oh!" Richie looks back at the man's retreating figure. "I suppose it could be. Good catch, Lennox."

The main street is livelier than yesterday. They're met with curious eyes and murmured hellos—some locals going so far as to correctly address George and Richie by name. Richie continues to find it delightful, but the unearned familiarity still disquiets George.

The metal chimes as they enter the post office to find that this time Kathy is behind the counter.

"Good morning," she says brightly. "I was just about to head up your way. How did you get on?"

"Fine, fine," Richie says. "Actually, we were hoping to lean on your hospitality a wee bit more. May we use your phone?"

"Of course," she says, sliding the satellite phone across the counter. "Do you need me to look up a number?"

Richie suppresses a smile. "No, no, got it saved in my head."

Kathy's obvious disappointment is palpable. But as they quietly wait for the line to connect, she whips around to face George with renewed enthusiasm. "I've got those books for you, Inspector! I'll just go fetch them."

She turns and hurries through the door behind her as Richie raises an eyebrow at George. "What books?" he whispers.

"No idea," she mouths back.

Richie's eyes crinkle with amusement, but his expression shifts as a tinny voice comes through the receiver. "Hey, Lucy, it's Richard. Can you pop me through to the boss, please?"

Quick footsteps herald Kathy's return, and the postmistress places three thick tomes on the counter. "Here you go, Inspector."

George eyes them cautiously. "What are these?"

Beside her, Richie has started speaking in a low voice.

"The keepers' logbooks," Kathy says in a tone that makes it seem like that should have been obvious. "You said you wanted to read them."

Their breathless conversation as they hiked up to the croft yesterday comes flooding back. "Oh, did I? I mean, I did. Wow." George reaches out to touch the top one, the tattered brown leather of the cover feeling surprisingly soft beneath her fingers. "Oh, wow," she repeats with more sincerity. "They're so . . . old."

"Over a hundred years," Kathy says proudly, opening the book to the first page. "Look—you can see where they've written their names."

George peers down at the spot Kathy's short fingernail indicates. In faded black ink are three names: *J. Smith, D. Wilson, T. McClure.*

"This is them. This is *really* them."

"Mmm. The poor souls."

George turns the pages carefully, scanning the first few entries. "They wrote in the logbook every day?"

"Without fail. Observing the weather, recording the names of ships that passed and if they were going east or west. They even mention what they ate for supper," she says with a chuckle.

"I see that," George says, having just winced at the words *salted mutton.* "And is there anything to indicate what might have happened to them?"

"If there is, I'm sure you'll find it, *Inspector.*"

George laughs awkwardly. "Not sure I'll have time for two separate investigations."

"Just as a bedtime story, then," Kathy presses. "I really think you'll get something out of them."

George makes a halfhearted sound of agreement. Richie joins them, having wrapped up the call.

"Shall we head out?" he says. "Oh, what have we got here?"

"I'll tell you on the way," George says, sensing Kathy gearing up for another explanation. "Have you got a bag I can put these in, Kathy? We've got a bit of a walk ahead of us."

———

It takes them almost half an hour to reach the lighthouse. Kathy had pointed them toward a shortcut that meant they wouldn't have to go back up toward the croft and skirt around MacLeod's farm.

The dirt track starts from the very bottom of the main street, beside the Campbell house, and George hears playful shouts and squeals from inside as they pass. The route forks almost immediately—to the left is the skinny strip of beach they saw from the boat, to the right a path that almost immediately angles upward along the cliffs. It's along this right-hand path that George and Richie trek, exchanging puffs of conversation as the path snakes relentlessly toward the top. She carries the logbooks in a woven bag, the weight stretching the fabric; they bounce against her thigh with each step.

At Richie's insistence, they pause when they reach the crest. There's just a narrow line of long, scratchy grass between the path and the relatively short drop to the beach below. The view is impressive, but George's eyes are drawn to the right, to the eastern border of the dense woods. With the sea breeze whistling in her ears, George wonders how deep into the woods you can get before the sounds of the ocean are blocked out completely. She notices a break in the tree line up ahead, and when Richie recovers his breath sufficiently for them to continue on, it's revealed as the start of a spindly track. She figures it must lead to the farm, cutting right at some point.

A few people pass them on their journey, acknowledging their presence with a smile or familiar greeting. There's only one strange interaction: a balding man carrying three dead rabbits over his shoulder grips the arm of the thin teen beside him when he sees them, stepping off the path entirely to let George and Richie pass. She looks back at the pair curiously and sees the boy doing likewise. But their respective companions recapture their attention, and the moment passes.

The lighthouse where Alan Ferguson was found dead sits alone at the southeast tip of Eadar, with only the sky and squalling seabirds for company. Nearby is a low peaked building: the ruins of the keepers' cottage, now a mere shell after more than a century of neglect and exposure to the wind and rain. But the tower itself still stands, solid and resistant to the worst that the Atlantic has thrown at it. The rough white stone and rotting windowsills are stained brown, giving the impression that something vile has been oozing out of the tower for generations.

George and Richie circle the cottage once, peering in through those windows that aren't obscured by muck or threadbare curtains. The hinges are crusted in coppery rust, and more than one pane is shattered—by the elements or vandals, George isn't sure. It appears that neither Kathy nor anyone else has volunteered to maintain this place; knee-high grass and weeds compete for dominance all the way up to the walls.

On the far side of the lighthouse the ground dips slightly, a shallow cavity now filled with thick mud and a small pool of dirty water. Richie skirts the mud delicately, but George pauses.

"Rich."

"Mm?"

She nods at the puddle. "You think this is where he landed?"

Richie blinks, then examines the ground again with renewed interest. "Catriona said she found him lying in mud . . ."

Their eyes travel up all forty-two feet of the tower. The stain fades the further up it goes; the stones that make up the top third of the tower may still be their original color. A thin railing encloses the glass-walled dome where the great lantern once burned. She can hear the railing rattling in the wind. Nausea stirs in her stomach.

Richie blows out a long breath. "What a terrible place to die."

Gladly bringing her gaze to ground level, George silently agrees. The view from the croft made Eadar look nice because everything was at a distance. It's only when you get up close that you see the cracks.

"All right, I'll be back in a minute."

She frowns. "Where are you going?"

Richie nods upward, toward the top of the tower.

Swallowing back her nausea, George strides after him. "Let's get up there, then."

He throws out a hand to block her. "No, you keep looking around here."

"You can't go up there alone. We've got no idea how stable that railing is."

"Exactly, and if it's loose then we can confirm that accidental death is a possibility."

"And you want to find that out the hard way?"

"It's a one-person job, Lennox."

"Oh, enough!" she says sharply. "You don't have to . . ." She exhales, sending her frustration down into the earth like an electrical current. "I said it back in Glasgow: I won't be sidelined."

His eyes are soft. "I just don't want you to push yourself too hard."

The pity in his tone hits her hard and painfully. "You don't get to decide which parts of my job I can handle, Richard."

She can tell he bites his tongue on a retort, and he maintains his silence as he nods toward the tower. Straightening her spine, she follows.

Eight months ago, George and Richie were called to investigate the death of a seventy-year-old woman in her two-story maisonette. From the way she was lying at the bottom of the stairs, it could easily have been a trip and fall situation. But neighbors mentioned hearing violent arguments between the woman and her adult grandson, who was living with her at the time.

As Richie nudges open the door of the lighthouse and switches his torch on, George is taken back to the night she first entered Margaret Villo's residence. She'd been informed where she'd find Margaret, but George had always felt a thrumming current of electricity in the unnatural stillness of a murder house that seemed to lead her where she really needed to go. And on that night, it drew her like a magnet past the body and up the stairs to a bedroom.

Peering into the rectangular void of the lighthouse doorway, George waits for that old feeling to trickle through her veins, the buzz that whispers, *Look over there*—but it doesn't come. Another integral part of herself that was stolen by the Villo case.

"Do you think anyone's here?" she asks, the memory making her voice reedy.

Richie doesn't seem to sense her tension. He cups his hands around his mouth. "Hello? Anyone up there?"

His voice bounces off the curved walls, but no response comes. Richie raises an eyebrow at her. "Stay sharp anyway."

Stepping into the darkness after Richie, George turns on her own torch and sweeps it across the entry. It's about five degrees colder than it is outside, and the muted light from unseen windows offers no warmth. The ceiling is high above the door but rapidly slopes down to where the spiral stairs begin on the right.

"Best prop that door open; I don't think we're going to have much light until we reach the top."

They start the climb, Richie's light directed upward as George points hers at their feet, the two of them retracing Alan Ferguson's final steps.

Richie was right about the lack of light. Their two torches barely keep the shadows at bay between evenly spaced windows that are so small George doubts she could squeeze through them, even without her thick coat on. There are alcoves that Richie theorizes used to hold candles or lanterns.

"Now arriving at the first floor," Richie says with the same intonation as a railway announcement. The way his voice echoes gives the impression that the room they've entered is cavernous, but as they direct their lights around, they see it's just a small, bare space. The single window has long since lost its glass; whenever the wind blows, dust stirs on the white stone floor.

"Look at the scorches on the stone," George says, pointing out a wide black mark on the ground by the window. "Do you think whoever was tending the light cooked their food here? The ventilation must have been awful."

"Everything about this job would have been awful," Richie mutters. "You couldn't pay me enough to sit in a tower shivering all day and night. Do you think that's welded to the wall?"

George follows his finger to a crucifix hanging on the wall to the right of the window. "They're probably terrified to take it down."

They proceed up the stairs to the second floor to find a room identical to the one below. There's nothing on the walls here, but there's a rusty trough shoved against the wall. Even that makes the space feel claustrophobic. She wonders how three grown men navigated this cramped space without losing the plot.

Then again, maybe that's exactly what happened.

The next flight of stairs ends in bright daylight. Richie precedes her up a narrow ladder through a hole in the ceiling, which turns out to be the floor of the domed watch room. The small circular space is dominated by the ancient shell that once housed the lantern. Today it's a bin for old tools, beer bottles, and broken furniture.

It's almost impossible to see through the lower windows with all the grime that has built up over the years, but George scans the room and spies what she's looking for. It takes two hands and considerable effort, but she finally slides back a rusted iron bolt and opens the door out onto the gallery. Even before she steps outside, her heart is galloping and her mouth dry. She places the logbooks carefully on the floor and grips the door-frame, knowing that if she lifts her fingers they'll be shaking.

"Lennox?"

She knows he wants to ask if she's all right, or tell her she can stay inside, but Cole's words echo in her head.

Show me that you can handle it.

"I'm lighter than you," she says, only the slightest wobble to her voice.

He knows better than to argue again.

The gallery feels firm enough beneath her feet but she doesn't take it for granted, clutching the inside rail with a white-knuckled grip. The wind seeks out the gaps in her clothes with precision, making her teeth chatter. She tucks the ends of her hair into the collar of her coat to stop it whipping against her face and concentrates on taking steady, even breaths as her stomach rolls. She orders herself not to look directly down.

The view from the top isn't as grand as the one from the hill, but it's easy to see the Nicholson croft up to the left. A thin trail of smoke wafts from the chimney.

"Our fire is still going," she calls out to Richie, but as she turns to hear his response, a movement on the hill catches her eye. She glances back, scanning the croft and the area around it, but only the smoke disturbs the stillness.

She returns to her task reluctantly. The distance between the railing she's clutching for dear life and the one that runs around the outside of the platform is just over three feet, but to her thumping heart it feels like a mile. Inching her feet to the middle of the gallery, she stretches a shaking hand she hopes Richie can't see. Her fingertips reach the cold rail, and she gives it an experimental shake. The squeal of the metal makes her breath catch.

"Lennox," Richie says in a high voice. "You're giving me palpitations."

Her vision is starting to swim. The pounding in her chest has gained an echoing pulse in her head. How long has it been since she took her meds? She had to move quickly this morning, waiting for Richie to use the bathroom before slipping them out of the case.

"I'll make my way around," she says loudly, gritting her teeth against the throb behind her eye.

"There's no need for that, just *look* around."

She ignores him, focusing on her fingers so hard that everything in her peripheral vision—including the drop below—blurs. To an observer it must look like she has a limp, the way she's keeping all of her weight on the foot closest to the wall. If one of these rails was loose, all it would take is one strong gust of wind and she'd be plummeting to the grass below. The thought triggers another wave of nausea, but this one she can't suppress. She gags, dropping into a crouch, pressing her body to the inner wall.

The gallery vibrates with footsteps and then Richie is sliding an arm around her waist.

"Come on, Lennox. Let's get our feet on solid ground, eh?"

———

At Richie's insistence, George spends a short time at the base of the lighthouse with her head between her knees.

"It's just vertigo," she says again. "I've had it since I was a teenager."

Richie squats beside her, the logbook bag slung over his shoulder now. "Less talking, more breathing."

She glares at him from under her eyebrows. "Would you stop looking at me like that?"

"Like what?"

Like you're worried about me.

Like I can't handle this.

Like I'm about to break into little pieces.

"From what I could tell, the railing is old but secure enough," she says instead. "Unless Alan was sitting on top of it and toppled over, I don't think an accident is likely."

"Could have been up there with friends, drinking, mucking about."

"Except Catriona said he didn't spend much time with other kids."

"True. Okay, so he's lonely, everyone knows he cheated on his girlfriend, and he's worried about whether he's going to get into university. He was scared and sad and felt like his ticket off the island wasn't coming. Perhaps Cole was right about suicide being the likeliest option."

George raises her head finally, relieved that the movement isn't met with any dizziness. "It's an option, for sure. But why do it up there?"

"What do you mean?"

Batting away his extended hand, George gets to her feet. There's only a slight wobble in her knees as she stalks forward until the only thing between her and the plunge to the ocean is a semicircle of rocky dirt. The air seems to crackle this close to the edge. She braces herself to shuffle closer and peer down. One hundred and fifty feet below, the waves crash and recede over jagged rocks at the base of the cliff. A jump from here would mean certain death.

"If you're going to kill yourself by jumping off something, why not do it here?" She turns to Richie, who has reluctantly joined her, and gestures toward the edge. "The tower is high, but not *that* high. If he'd landed differently he might have survived. Some broken bones perhaps, but alive."

"People who are in that frame of mind aren't always thinking clearly."

"Clearly enough to climb three flights of stairs and struggle with that bolt."

"If he'd made the decision to end things there, the determination might have been enough."

George chews her lip, scanning the horizon. "Maybe."

Richie tugs his beanie down. "Let's get the hell away from this tower," he says with a shiver.

She doesn't resist—she isn't sure if it's rising vibrations from the waves pummeling the cliff face below or if her legs are still unsteady, but as she stood on the edge of Eadar just now, it felt like the island was trembling.

They follow another dirt path along the southern edge of the woods, planning to return to the croft for a bite to eat. The incline starts easy but quickly gets tough; however, Richie is in better spirits with the knowledge that lunch awaits them at the top. As he chatters away George's eyes are drawn to the woods on their right. The sunlight, already struggling to break through the thick cloud cover, is having an even harder time penetrating the canopy. Walking more than a few steps into the woods would plunge you into shadows—a darkness that only deepens as the knobbly trees grow more densely together.

A sudden movement brings her to a stop. She retrieves her torch and shines it into the voids between trunks.

"Lennox?"

She shushes him. "I thought I saw something."

Richie joins her, and they peer into the darkness together for a few seconds. "These are very old trees," he says after a few moments, then his voice changes, affecting an academic tone. "Very few islands out this way have trees at all. Mostly due to the rough weather and peat bog expansion, though some theorize that the Vikings destroyed any woodland they found to prevent islanders from building boats." He looks at the trees curiously. "I wonder how these managed to escape the ax."

"Inspectors!"

The shout comes from an uncharacteristically out of breath Kathy, who is jogging toward them with a large carrier bag bouncing off her shoulder. A tall man follows behind her, one long stride equal to two of Kathy's.

"There you are," she calls. "I've been all over! Where have you been hiding?"

"We've just come from the lighthouse," Richie says, sounding bemused by her accusatory tone. "Now we're heading back for a bite."

"Oh, perfect. I just dropped off some more food, now that I know you're staying longer."

George raises an eyebrow. "You ran all the way down here to tell us that?"

The other woman nods earnestly. "And I wanted to introduce Lewis. He's our resident odd-jobs man—you can thank him for the hot water at Auld Sam's croft. When he saw how many deliveries I had to make today he volunteered to accompany me. Lucky he's not married or his wife would wonder what he was doing in the fields with me all day." Kathy does a terrible job of winking subtly at George.

The man called Lewis steps forward, pushing shaggy blond hair off his forehead. Freckles dot his nose, cheeks, and forehead, giving him a boyish appearance—but with the pale scruff across his jaw and neck, George suspects he's at least her age, maybe even older. "We have to give the old folks something else to gossip about," he says, setting Kathy off in a fit of giggles. "Lewis MacGill."

"I'm sure you know our names already," George says, grasping the hand he extends.

He smiles knowingly. "We're glad you've come, Inspectors. Alan clearly needed help. I just wish we'd noticed that he was in trouble before things got this far."

A hitch in Kathy's breathing captures their attention.

"Sorry," she says. "I just—I can't stop thinking about Catriona. How much pain she's in, and for no good reason."

Richie pats her back. "Come on, come have some lunch with us. My stomach has been rumbling for an hour."

She gives him a watery smile and allows Richie to turn her back up the hill. Lewis falls into step beside George.

"So, Inspector Lennox. What did you do to deserve this?"

She frowns at him. "What do you mean?"

Lewis gestures at their surroundings. "It's not exactly Ibiza."

"It's certainly not what I was promised in the brochure," she says dryly, then nods toward Kathy. "She's really torn up about this."

"She and Catriona are best friends," Lewis explains. "But when something like this happens, it hits everyone hard. Coming from a population this small, every loss feels . . ." He blows out a long breath. "We all hear it when a baby cries at night, you know? The women gather when there's sickness in a house. And when someone dies, everyone grieves."

"Mr. MacGill, I'm wondering if—"

"Lewis is fine."

"Mr. MacGill," George repeats pointedly, "has anything like this happened before?"

"People jumping off the lighthouse? Or . . . do you mean suicide?"

"It would make sense if it had. Living in each other's pockets, the isolation from the mainland. And no matter where you stand, all you see is ocean. That must get to people."

"I'll admit that this place is sorely lacking as a tourist destination, but it really is a good place to live. People here care about each other. We share what we have, especially if the delivery hasn't come in on time."

Sensing a "but," George waits.

"Of course, it's not perfect," he says reluctantly. "We have the same problems as anywhere else."

She shoots him a questioning look. His laugh clouds in the frigid air. "Oh, you know what I mean. There's politics, there's gossip. Lord, there's gossip," he repeats darkly. "There's always someone whispering about something. Making assumptions. Pointing fingers."

"Is anyone whispering about Alan's death?"

Lewis's jaw clenches. "Of course. It was just so . . ." He looks back at the lighthouse. George follows his gaze. From this distance it looks perfectly white again, no cracks in sight. "So violent," he finishes. "It wasn't a quick death, was it?"

She slides her hands into her pockets, pursing her lips as she weighs up whether she should tell him, whether he can handle the brutality. "The official cause of death was suffocation. The report says he likely landed on his front, then managed to roll over. Blood pooled in his throat, but he was unconscious by then. He choked."

Lewis's freckles are stark against his pale cheeks. "So, he was alive for . . . what? A minute, two?"

"Closer to five." George hesitates. "I always wonder—when someone tries to take their own life but death doesn't happen instantly—I wonder if they regret it. If they're hoping help will come."

Lewis exhales shakily.

She keeps her eyes on the tower, giving him a moment to compose himself; it took her years to build compartments in her mind to hold these kinds of realities.

But what Lewis says next surprises her.

"If I died like that . . . I'd like someone to know what happened at the end. There should always be someone who knows what your last moments were like." His big shoulders lift in a shrug. "It feels important, doesn't it?"

She thinks about that, watching the soft ground swallow her boots. "Yes," she says finally, "it does."

After a quiet moment, Lewis looks up at the sky. "Let's get out of this rain."

"It isn't raining."

He just shoots her a knowing look and lopes up the hill.

———

The first drops land as they reach the croft. Kathy is back to her bubbly self and puts a new pot of stew—fish again—on the stove. As they wait for it to heat up she lists more of Lewis's personal qualities in an unconvincingly casual tone. Richie smirks at George over his cup of tea. She shoots him a glare that has more to do with her intensifying headache than annoyance, but there's no way to extricate her pills without being noticed. She just clasps her shaking hands behind her back until Kathy hands her a steaming bowl.

George and Lewis surrender the two chairs to Richie and Kathy, and with the couch still made up as her bed, they take their stew outside. Steam rises off the surface of their bowls. The raindrops are heavy but slow, splatting against the impacted earth around the croft and sending dirt spraying out like land mines. In the paddock below, MacLeod's sheep call to each other plaintively.

Lewis squats under the eaves with his back against the wall. George watches him from her perch on the doorstep.

"Among her many roles, is Kathy also the village matchmaker?" she asks, trying to distract herself from the pain behind her eyebrow. It shows how desperate the islanders are to maintain their population that even police are considered fair game to be paired off with locals.

He groans, and George is relieved that he seems to find Kathy's efforts as uncomfortable as she does. "It's not just her—

everybody has a go. People who have been married no more than two days start getting on my case, asking me who I've got my eye on, telling me it's time to settle down."

"I thought Kathy could be using me to break up a bad match."

"Surely that church over there tells you our stance on adultery? And divorce," he mutters, rolling his eyes.

"It's hard not to notice it."

"It's a reminder to be on our best behavior. I suppose religion is one reason for the push to get married, but it's not the main thing."

George gestures with her spoon for him to continue.

"It's silly," he says around a mouthful of potato. "Old fears run deep here, and there's this ridiculous assumption that if you're not married, you might pack up for the mainland and never come back. They're scared of losing a good worker. Kathy's got the best of intentions, but she doesn't take no for an answer." His pained expression twists into a challenging grin. "Unless you're looking for a sea change?"

George pulls a face.

His grin widens. "Didn't think so. Is your family back in Glasgow?"

"Edinburgh, actually, but I've been based in Glasgow for a few years now. My parents didn't want me to leave home, but then my sister took the heat off me by moving to Dubai for a job. Is your family here?"

He nods. "My parents and all my cousins."

"You must be close."

"I get along with my cousins, sure. My parents . . . we coexist." His tone doesn't welcome further questions, and he changes the subject abruptly. "How old are you?"

She narrows her eyes. "Why do you want to know?"

"Because I can't tell."

His tone seems innocent enough.

"I'm twenty-eight."

"Oh. You're younger than I thought."

Perhaps she was wrong. Her mind is already generating a dozen withering responses that will put Lewis back in his place, targeted barbs that have felled more hardened men than him.

"Not because you look old," he says in a rush. "Your face just has a lot of character. Like you've been through some things."

Her indignation fades. "Being a police officer isn't just traffic stops and shoplifting," she says. "I know officers with ten, twenty years under their belt who have gone out on a call one night and quit the next day. What they saw, the things that happened to them, made all the good they'd done in their careers meaningless."

The way he's looking at her makes her tense, as if the scar behind her ear has somehow moved to the center of her forehead.

"But you're still here," he observes.

George schools her face into neutrality, quelling a rising urge to check her hair. She's hardly going to prove to Cole that she's ready for tougher cases if she can't even talk about–

"What happened to you?"

She stabs her spoon into the bowl. "I was injured on the job a little while ago."

"Badly?"

She lifts a shoulder. "Nothing that couldn't be fixed."

"You didn't consider calling it quits?"

"Never. I'm too good at what I do."

Lewis looks out across the hills. "Let's hope so. How much longer are you here for?"

"Five days, including today. We're getting picked up on Sunday morning."

"That's a long time," he says, sounding impressed. "Have you spoken to many people yet? About Alan?"

"Not yet, but we will. In situations like these, everyone holds a small piece of the puzzle. It's just a matter of collecting the pieces so we can fit the whole picture together."

"You want to know why he killed himself."

"Of course."

His eyes flick to hers. "Or you want to know *if* he killed himself."

Her stomach tightens. "What makes you say that?"

"You're here, for starters. That's strange."

"It's standard procedure."

"Is it?"

George realizes that Lewis didn't answer her question earlier. "Has anyone on Eadar ever taken their own life before?"

"As far as I know Alan is the first one. For the most part, people are happy here." He scoops a piece of haddock into his mouth.

George nods thoughtfully as she pictures Alan's crushed and bloody lips pulled back into that grotesque smile.

"Actually, there is one thing about this island that makes me very unhappy," Lewis says into the stretched silence.

"Fish stew?"

He nods gravely. "Fish stew."

———

Again, it takes some time to coax Kathy out the door.

"You promised we'd have these deliveries done by two," Lewis says, taking the carrier bag from her shoulder and slinging it over his own. "I've got other jobs to do, and I don't want to be doing them in the dark."

"Oh, fine, fine," she says, allowing herself to be drawn outside. "I'll pop back over tomorrow morning to see if you need anything," she says to George and Richie.

"No need to come all the way up here," Richie says. "We know where to find you."

Her lower lip juts out. "If you say so." She waves and follows Lewis down the path.

George hears her voice carrying across the fields until she's out of sight. She and Richie retreat indoors and allow themselves a few moments of silence.

"She would make an excellent criminal," Richie says. "Nobody would put their hand up to interrogate her. Learn anything interesting from him?"

George flops onto the couch, letting her eyes close for a moment of relief. "The general consensus is that it was suicide, but he says Alan is the only person who's killed themselves in living memory. Makes me wonder if one of their only luxuries is willful ignorance."

She cracks an eyelid and looks longingly toward the corner where her briefcase leans against the wall. Richie's chin starts to turn, following her gaze.

"He said people are talking about it," she says quickly, bringing his attention back to her. "We need to find out what they're saying behind closed doors."

"Well, there's only one way to do that."

Swallowing a groan, George hauls herself up. "Get behind a closed door."

"Speaking of, you left this one open."

"Eh?"

Pulling his gloves on, Richie jerks his head toward the front door. "Kathy had left the food on the table before coming to find us."

Thinking back to their departure that morning, George shakes her head. "I swear I locked it. Look." She fishes the key from her pocket and holds it up.

Richie shrugs. "Just telling you what she said."

But his nonchalance seems crafted when he holds out his hand. "Maybe it's a tricky lock," he says lightly, and after a moment she presses the key into his palm.

As he pulls the door closed behind them, George catches one last glimpse of her briefcase. When Richie turns to fuss with the lock, she takes a long, shaky breath.

CHAPTER 6

"FATHER ROSS? CAN WE SPEAK TO YOU FOR A FEW MINUTES?"

Eadar's spiritual leader seems taken aback by their presence on the doorstep, but he is cordial enough as he invites them through the looming double doors of the island's house of worship. As he leads them down a wide carpeted corridor to his office, his left foot drags slightly behind the right.

"A boyhood injury," he explains at Richie's query. "I'd hoped for an illustrious rugby career, but a mistimed tackle tore my ACL. One poorly done surgery later, and this limp is what I'm left with. Theology was a fallback plan."

"You have enough players here for a competition?"

He chuckles. "My father let me join the rugby club in Stornoway, so I spent most weekends over there. Then, after my injury, I studied abroad for a few years and did a bit of traveling." He turns to look at them over his shoulder, smiling wryly. "I figured I should learn a little more about the world before I tried to guide people through it. Then I came home to take over from the previous priest. It was a seamless transition. Helped that he was also called Father Ross."

"Uncle?" George guesses.

The priest nods. "We tend to keep things in the family around here."

They pass an open door. A group of children, their ages ranging from five to twelve, sit at low tables in a large classroom, plucking colored pencils from communal tins and hunching over workbooks that are clearly homemade. George recognizes Cecily Campbell's middle child at the nearest table, a young girl with a single blonde plait running down her back. The babble of joyful conversation bounces around the room. Posters on the wall depict cartoon versions of Jesus, Moses and the Commandments, Noah and his Ark, with both English and Gaelic descriptions. A dark-haired woman in a long skirt floats between the tables offering comments and guidance. She sees them at the door and smiles at the priest, but her smile slides from her face when she clocks George and Richie beside him.

"Who are they?" a young boy asks, staring at them with a pencil poised in his hand.

"That's the police," Cecily's daughter announces matter-of-factly. "They came to my house."

"*Our* house!" Her older brother, the one who had walked them to the post office, stands up to wave at them enthusiastically.

A boy sitting beside him frowns. "My da said we weren't supposed to talk to—"

"All right, that's enough chatter," the teacher says loudly, but George hears the kids continue to whisper as the three move past the schoolroom.

The priest's office is surprisingly small, considering the size of the church. Bookshelves line two of the walls, filled with different versions and bindings of the Bible. George guesses that the collection must span generations. The remaining walls are hung with religious posters, children's artwork, and framed photos.

George drops into the seat Father Ross indicated, beneath a child's wobbly depiction of snarling dogs, and Richie takes the seat beside her. A narrow desk separates them from the priest, and it takes George a second to realize what's so odd about the layout.

"I don't think I've seen a desk without a computer in years."

Father Ross chuckles as he settles into his own chair. "All a priest really needs is a pencil, paper, and a winning personality. I can always run into the village if I need Kathy to order anything in." He folds his hands on the desk. "Now, let me begin by thanking you for coming all this way. I wish your first visit to our home wasn't in such tragic circumstances."

"Well, Alan's death was deemed unusual enough to warrant our involvement," Richie says gently.

"And it sits heavily on my mind and heart. Losing a member of our community to suicide is . . . well, difficult for people to understand. For hundreds of years this island has battled storms, poverty, and fires, and we've lost loved ones to the sea. We've survived it all by holding true to our beliefs. Faith in God, in the world He created for us, is our foundation. When one of our members falters, I'm left with the task of reassuring my flock and praying for forgiveness from the one I couldn't save."

George raises an eyebrow. "Flock? Does that make you the shepherd?"

"The analogy feels appropriate."

"Was Alan Catholic?" Richie asks.

"He attended church with everyone else," Father Ross answers carefully. "It can be difficult to tell with some of the younger members of our community if they're attending for their faith or for the social aspect. I do feel for them—the only other gathering space with good heating is the pub, and that certainly isn't the place for impressionable young people to get to know one another. I try to encourage people of all ages to avoid the pub altogether, but it's difficult when the owner sits in the front pew and eyeballs me throughout the entire service."

"Did you ever get—" George begins, but a knock at the door interrupts her.

A tiny woman with a white cloud of hair sticks her head in.

"Will you be needing anything, Father? Tea? Coffee?" She

turns a warm smile on George and Richie. "Anything for the inspectors?"

The priest looks at them questioningly, but they shake their heads.

The woman smiles again, her eyes lingering on George. "My grandson is about your age," she notes. "Are you—"

"Thank you, Mary," Father Ross says swiftly. "I'll come and find you when the inspectors have left."

With a disappointed twist to her lips, she closes the door behind her.

"As I was saying," George resumes through gritted teeth, "did you ever get the impression that Alan was struggling with anything?"

"I believe he was quite intelligent and that he'd received excellent marks for his N5s. But he was a teenager, on the cusp of becoming a young man. I'm sure there were things he kept secret, just like anyone else."

"On an island this small, surely secrets don't stay that way for long," George remarks, remembering what Lewis had said about gossip. "Neighborly disputes, stolen glances . . ."

Father Ross frowns. "I don't appreciate the implication of adultery happening on my watch, Inspector. The members of my congregation are good, God-fearing Catholics."

"I've seen plenty of God-fearing people get themselves tangled in all manner of situations that contradict the teachings of their faith."

The priest doesn't balk, his chin rising defiantly. "You won't see it here. The people of Eadar are pious and, most of all, obedient."

George gazes at him, forcing her lips into a polite smile.

Richie, clearly aware of the static building in the air, intervenes. "Do you offer confession?" he asks.

"Not in the traditional sense. We don't have a stall, so it's just these two ears"—he points—"and an exceptional poker face." He shakes his head sadly and says, "Unlike many of the islanders, including some of Alan's peers, Alan never sought me out as a confidant."

"Has anyone unburdened themselves to you recently?"

"I assume you're not about to ask me to break the Seal of Confession?"

"It is of interest to our investigation if anybody has mentioned Alan in the past few weeks," George says.

Father Ross looks at her as if she's said something stupid. "We have all shared our shock and grief, of course. There has been anger, too, from people who believe Alan interrupted God's plan for his life. Ultimately, people have been seeking me out to ask what signs they missed that led to this, and what they should be looking out for among their own family and friends."

"Did anyone talk to you about Alan in the weeks or months leading up to his death?" Richie asks. "Did anyone notice him behaving strangely or getting into any disagreements?"

"No," Father Ross says firmly, "which is why his death was such a shock."

George glances at her notebook. "Would you say that the general consensus from people you've spoken to is that Alan took his own life?"

Father Ross's eyes widen. "I wasn't aware there was an alternative theory."

"We're just keeping an open mind," Richie says. "So, to the best of your knowledge, and from your own observations, Alan displayed no signs of distress in the lead-up to his death?"

"Correct." The priest shifts in his seat, flexing his injured leg. "But then again, happy people don't kill themselves."

George shakes her head. "Not in our experience."

"Mrs. Ferguson said you were already at the lighthouse when she got there," Richie says. "Did someone come to fetch you?"

"It was Alex Thomson. When he told me what had happened, I left for the lighthouse immediately."

"What time was that?" George asks.

"I was preparing for the morning Mass, so perhaps . . . just after six?"

According to Father Ross, he moved as quickly as his weak leg would allow him while Alex filled him in: John MacNeil had been out setting rabbit traps when he spotted a body at the base of the lighthouse. He got as close as he dared, but when he realized Alan was dead he ran to MacLeod's to raise the alarm. Alex was another worker who split his time between the farm and the boats, and he'd been in the paddocks that morning.

"A couple of MacLeod's farmhands returned to the lighthouse to wait with the body, another went for Catriona. Alex came to find me."

Richie pushes his own notebook across the desk. "Could you write down the names of the farmhands for me?"

The priest takes the notebook and plucks a pen from a ceramic cup full of pens and pencils. "Alex and I went up there on our own," he continues as he writes. "MacLeod's lads had already checked Alan over, but I felt for a pulse anyway. Just to make sure, I suppose. I can still remember how cold his skin was. It was like touching a stone that has been sitting at the bottom of a river." He pauses, looking at them. "Alan wasn't in there anymore."

George is struck by how well he has articulated a sensation she knows so well, from investigating so many deaths. Beside her, Richie nods grimly.

"I should have gone to Catriona as soon as I heard. Without any police of our own, the burden of delivering bad news often falls to me. Unfortunately, the news reached her before I could." He shakes his head, disappointment deepening the lines around his mouth. "I was told that she went to pieces in the post office.

Frightened the life out of the delivery man from the mainland, but thank the Lord he was able to get the authorities here so quickly."

George knows that the coastguard is often required to assume the role of first responder when called to these outer islands, acting as rescuer, paramedic, and occasionally even law enforcement.

Richie asks a few more questions about the days following, and whether anything remarkable happened at the funeral. Other than it being a somber day, Father Ross didn't observe anything strange—"except that MacLeod didn't come down."

George looks up. "Alan's boss didn't attend the funeral?"

"Alisdair is one of my more . . . challenging lambs. He worships God in his own way, and keeps to himself." This description, along with the one Catriona provided, makes George even more confident that the taciturn man they encountered in the paddock was Alisdair MacLeod.

Richie slides his eyes to George, then claps his hands to his knees. "I think that's all we need from you today, Father. I'm sure we'll be by with more questions over the next few days."

"Anything you require, I'm at your service."

George flips back a page as she walks to the door. "Can you tell us where we might find John MacNeil? We'd like to hear his account of the day."

Father Ross grimaces. "Ah . . ."

Richie and George exchange another look. "Is there a problem?" Richie asks.

"No, no," Father Ross says hurriedly. "But I think it would be best if I accompany you. John is a single father, and his son is . . . well, neither of them are used to hosting visitors. He'll appreciate a familiar face."

"Are you planning to be present for every interview we conduct?" George asks mildly.

The priest blinks at her. "Only the ones I'm needed for. But do let me know if that becomes a problem for you, Inspector."

As he leads them back down the corridor, Father Ross comes to an abrupt stop. "Oh, I didn't show you!"

Turning right instead of left, they arrive at another set of light timber double doors. He pushes them open and waves George and Richie in.

The church smells of clean carpet, wood polish, and an inescapable mustiness. The vaulted ceiling reaches high above their heads, with exposed rafters likely to blame for the pervasive shower of dust. Ten long pews extend on either side of a wide aisle. Two women and a man shuffle along them, chatting casually, collecting hymnbooks or wiping down the seats. The conversation falters as soon as they spot George and Richie, and they've stopped talking entirely by the time the priest closes the doors behind them.

Either Father Ross doesn't notice the tension or he's choosing to ignore it—he calls out a cheery greeting to the trio, who have stopped midway through their tasks to stare. They're prompted back into action by the priest's presence, but they move stiffly, as if they're trying to keep George and Richie in their peripherals. George is a little affronted by their wariness; it's as if she and Richie were dangerous animals they dare not turn their backs on.

Richie's whistle captures her attention, and she follows his gaze to the peaked window on the rear wall of the apse. "That's a sight that reaffirms your belief in God," he says.

Father Ross beams. "Beautiful, isn't it?"

George has to agree. The building's placement on top of the hill offers more than just a reminder to be on your best behavior; with the window positioned just yards away from a steep drop to the ocean below, the striking division of sea and sky must create a dramatic backdrop for Father Ross's sermons.

"Some of the Hebridean islands held on to the Catholic faith when the Protestant wave swept across the country," Father Ross says, joining Richie at the window.

"I was wondering about that," Richie says. "Perhaps being so far out kept Eadar off the radar?"

"Perhaps," Father Ross agrees lightly, "though I also suspect they didn't consider our congregation large enough to be worth the effort it would take to quash us. And look at us now—centuries later, and we've never changed our ways."

He looks incredibly proud of this fact. Richie looks a little perturbed.

"We've kept most of the original timber," the priest continues, oblivious to Richie's reaction, "and we've made necessary improvements over time as we had more access to materials from the mainland. But this window has always been here." He smiles wistfully, running his hand along the frame. "It's certainly helped me to find perspective in dark times. A reminder that just as He crafted the sky above and the ocean below, He placed us all here on this little lonely island for a reason."

There are aged crisscrossed beams all the way along the ceiling from the door to the apse. Looking up at them as she wanders back toward the entrance, George notices that a double spiral has been carved into the beam that's in line with the back row of pews, the symbol facing the floor. "What is this symbol?" she asks, beckoning the men over. "There's one above the door at our croft."

"And at the post office," Richie says. "On that gorgeous old letterbox out the front."

One of the cleaners, a middle-aged woman with tight curls who is holding a sheaf of papers to her chest, looks up sharply. Father Ross chuckles. "You're earning your title, Inspectors."

George isn't certain whether he means to sound so condescending, or if preaching has bled into every aspect of his personality. "It seems pretty pagan for a Catholic community," she says bluntly.

Richie shoots her a warning look, but the priest seems unbothered.

"I suppose it must seem unusual to a mainlander," he says. "The old ways aren't so dutifully kept over there. But Celtic culture predates Christianity by twelve hundred years at least. Just because we adopted the latter doesn't mean we abandoned the former. And since becoming the island's priest and inheriting the responsibilities that come with this position, I've come to see that the two go hand in hand." He gestures to the spiral. "It was here long before I arrived, and long, *long* before we got carpet and heating."

"What does it mean?"

It's not Father Ross who answers.

"It represents a balance between two opposing forces. Birth and death, creation and destruction, light and dark."

George turns to look at the curly haired woman quizzically. Her expression is intense, the papers clutched to her chest in a tight grip.

"Not that we'd expect anyone from the mainland to understand that," she adds, her lip curling back over crooked teeth.

George looks at Richie, who seems equally taken aback by the venom in the woman's voice. "I don't think we've been introduced. I'm DI Lennox—what's your name?"

Instead of answering, the woman looks past George to Father Ross. George turns in time to see the priest nod minutely.

The woman sounds annoyed as she says, "Angela Fraser."

"And what exactly do you think I wouldn't understand, Ms. Fraser?"

"That His world is one of duality, and it is not for any of us to question. We must perform the roles we have been given in the dark, and make peace with it come sunrise."

George struggles to keep a straight face. "I think I can wrap my head around that."

Angela jerks her head toward the window and the ocean beyond. "Then you know that we have no need for your presence here."

"I think that's quite enough, Angela," Father Ross says lightly. "The inspectors are just doing their jobs, as must we all." He points to the papers in her arms. "You can give those to Mary when you leave."

Anger flashes across the woman's face, but she hurries off.

Father Ross smiles apologetically. "We're a passionate lot, here on our little rock. I think what she was trying to explain is that folklore isn't the opposite of religion. Both require faith, practice, and sacrifice." He nods up at the symbol fondly. "That's why the two can exist in harmony on Eadar."

George and Richie don't linger much longer. Father Ross walks them to the entrance. There are a few people milling around Angela Fraser in the foyer, who is furiously whispering in Gaelic. George spies a familiar face among them: Cecily Campbell is there, her daughter hanging off her leg. She catches George's eye and, checking to see Angela's back is turned, flicks her gaze to the ceiling in exasperation.

Zipping her coat up against the cold, George looks back at the priest. "Are you angry at Alan for what he did? It goes against your faith, after all."

"No," Father Ross answers, worming his hands into his pockets. "I just feel guilty for not intervening earlier. Maybe he could have been guided back to the right path."

"Does everyone believe Alan—his soul, I guess—is in hell now?"

From the way he peers at her, George senses that he's trying to figure out if she's being sarcastic. Her neutral expression seems to mollify him, and when he speaks she hears the ringing voice of Eadar's shepherd.

"*For I am certain of this: neither death nor life, nor angels, nor principalities, nothing already in existence and nothing still to come, nor any power, nor the heights nor the depths, nor any created thing whatever, will be able to come between us and the love of God, known to us in Christ Jesus our Lord.* That's Paul in Romans 8:38–39."

His lips part in a true smile that touches his eyes. "In short, regardless of the sins he accrued in life, I believe that Alan's soul is being cradled tenderly in the palms of Our Lord. And that's what I encourage everyone else to believe."

CHAPTER 7

THE LIGHT OUTSIDE HAS CHANGED. DESPITE THE CLOUD COVER, GEORGE CAN tell that the sun is sinking toward the horizon.

"Should we head back up to the croft?" When she doesn't get a response from Richie, she glances around.

He is looking at something over the far side of the rise. "Come and look at this, Lennox."

Eadar's well-tended cemetery is on the side of the hill overlooking the ocean, a swept path leading up to a side door in the church. A low stone wall creates a border between the island's living and dead.

"That's a view I'd happily die for," Richie says.

With the harsh calls of circling seabirds in her ears and the roar of waves pummeling the cliffs below, George isn't sure she agrees, but she follows Richie through the low gate to look around.

Though many of the crumbling headstones George passes in the first row certainly reflect the number of years that have passed since they were erected, it's not long before the etched dates stretch back decades rather than centuries.

"MacKinnons, Campbells, some MacLeods," she mutters, descending a short set of cut stone steps to the next row. "They weren't kidding about needing mainlanders to marry in," she calls to Richie. "There are about five surnames in rotation."

"Kathy's probably got a family tree hung up in the post office." Richie bends to inspect a crumbling stone. "*Taken by ill-*

ness," he reads aloud with a tut, then leans over the next stone. "*Lost at sea*. Must be an empty grave."

"Fishing is a dangerous profession, I guess."

"We might know a little something about dangerous professions."

George thinks back to their dramatic arrival on the island. "I'd hoped that drowning would be further down on our list of professional risks. Hey, I found Samuel Nicholson!"

Richie weaves between the plots to join her. Nearby, a brave gull swoops down to perch on a headstone, observing them with beady eyes.

"Mr. Nicholson," Richie says, stooping to be at eye level with the headstone, "thank you for letting us stay in your home."

George puts her lips to Richie's ear and croaks, "*I died in that bed.*"

Richie glowers at her. "Have a modicum of respect for the dead, DI Lennox."

She scoffs and points at the dates on Samuel Nicholson's headstone. "If I die when I'm ninety-three years old, I won't be lingering around my grave to make sure people are being polite."

But her humor evaporates as they turn the final corner and see freshly disturbed earth.

It appears that Alan has had plenty of visitors in the two weeks since he was laid to rest. There are several paper cards, obviously handmade. Three candle stubs huddle together, the wicks unlikely ever to hold a flame in the wind. A small bouquet of flowers leans against the brand-new headstone, freshly picked and tied with coarse string. The yellow petals are bright against the dirt. George wonders who is managing to grow such bright blooms in this soggy, sunless place.

Richie rights a card that must have been knocked over by the wind, then carefully retreats to the base of the muddy rectangle.

"It's always hard to see birth and death dates that close to-gether," he says, then glances up at the church. "What did you think of that?"

George follows his gaze, her eyes drawn to the crucifix looming over them. "Ross sounded genuinely sad. He seems to think it was a failure on his part."

"I suppose it was." Then, in response to George's querying look, Richie adds, "I understand why he'd take something like this to heart, given that it's his job to protect the spiritual well-being of the community. It's a rather grim indication that peo-ple are slipping through the cracks." He stares down at the headstone quietly, then grips the top and bows his head. His lips move silently, and George knows that he's praying. Finally, he straightens and nods at her. "Let's go spin a web."

Without waiting for an answer, he threads back through the stones toward the gate.

But George hesitates. As her fingers brush the top of Alan's headstone, a sudden breeze lifts her hair and sends more cards tumbling from the grave. She steps nimbly over the dirt to gather them up. A few have *With Sympathy* and other condolences printed in neat hand on the front, and George opens one to see what kind of messages a teen suicide elicits from the people here.

But the top card is blank inside, as is the one beneath it. She sorts through the others, but they're all devoid of personal mes-sages. Perhaps there isn't anything one can write in these cir-cumstances; perhaps *With Sympathy* says it all.

A prickling sensation creeps down her spine, and with the cards still clutched in her hands, she looks around the cemetery, the land beyond the wall. There's Richie, just exiting through the gate. A couple of squealing kids chasing a third down a dis-tant slope. A boat entering the harbor, figures moving around in the cabin. There's nobody going in or out of the church, no one coming to chastise her for wandering through the cemetery—but *there*. Movement in a little window beside the side door.

The swish of a curtain settling back into place.

Trying to ignore the growing unease in her gut, she plucks a fist-sized stone from the ground beneath the shrubs. Returning to the grave, she makes a neat pile of the cards and puts the stone on top to weigh them down. Then she hurries after Richie.

They don't talk much on the walk back up to the croft, breaking the silence only to ask the occasional question or confirm something Father Ross said.

A pair of men at least two decades older than Richie are ambling down the hill toward them, taking their time on the steep decline. Their faces seem to be set in permanent scowls, and George wonders if it's from a lifetime of squinting into the horizon or because they've spotted the police detectives. Though they'd largely been treated with warmth and politeness, the confrontation with Angela Fraser confirmed that not everyone on Eadar is comfortable with their presence. Still, when Richie raises a hand to the men, they return the gesture and mutter a greeting in Gaelic.

But George eyes them cautiously; she could swear she saw movement up here when she was at the top of the lighthouse. Could the islanders be curious enough about their investigation to poke around the croft when George and Richie are out?

The unease she felt at being watched in the cemetery has lingered. She told Richie about it, but he didn't seem surprised—of course people were curious about them, he reasoned. Still, as she waits impatiently for him to retrieve the keys, she scans the windows and doorframe, looking for signs of forced entry. Her eyes are drawn to the spiral on the lintel, and as Richie slides the key into the lock she reaches up to trace it with her fingertip. The wood feels soft, eroded by decades of exposure to the elements—until it doesn't. She yanks her hand back with a hiss.

Richie, startled, looks at her with concern. "You all right?"

She examines the thin splinter in her forefinger before bringing it to her mouth and tugging the shard out with her teeth. A tiny drop of blood pushes through the skin. She holds it up to him, and he rolls his eyes.

"I think you'll survive."

Sucking on her finger, she follows him inside.

Richie heads straight to the fireplace to coax the hot coals back into a flame with some fresh logs. That done, they shift the furniture away from the only blank wall in the croft. Then, armed with index cards and Blu-tack, they start building their web.

Dinnertime comes and goes, and the sky outside the window is inky black by the time they've constructed the timeline of Alan's life and death as they know it so far. It's sobering to see how many gaps are yet to be filled.

Before speaking to Father Ross that afternoon, they spent some time going door to door through the village. Most of the residents were surprised to see them on their doorstep but were helpful enough, willing to share what they knew—which, according to the wall, really wasn't much.

"I think we should hit MacLeod first thing," George says from her perch on the table. The pressure in her head has doubled over the past few hours, but Richie hasn't left the room long enough for her to dash to her briefcase. "I want to know what kind of work Alan was doing, who his workmates were. And why his boss didn't come to the funeral."

As he crouches beside the fire with his hands wrapped around a mug, Richie's eyelids begin to droop. He rubs his face roughly before nodding. "Okay, MacLeod first. And then our next priority is John MacNeil, but apparently we'll need the priest to chaperone."

"I wonder if that's really for Mr. MacNeil's benefit."

"Another theory?"

"It's percolating. He said something I've been wondering about."

"Mm?"

She opens to a blank page in her notebook and draws a rough map of Eadar. "Lighthouse here, MacLeod's in the middle, main street here." Along the main street she draws three Xs, two close together and one set slightly apart. "Alex Thomson runs from the farm straight to the church to get Ross," she says, dotting a line to the furthest X, "and then they rush back."

"Quite the artist, Lennox."

"Shut it. Now, Ross said he assumed one of the other farmhands had gone to tell Catriona." She plants her pen back on the rectangle representing MacLeod's farmhouse. "Alex Thomson and this other unidentified worker would have had to travel the same path to the village, but the worker would have stopped in at the bakery"—the pen circles the first X—"and then, when they didn't find Catriona there, Sally went to get her at the post office"—another circle around the second X—"where Catriona heard the news and left for the lighthouse." She draws a sharp line between the two points and tosses the pen down with a clatter. "So how'd Ross get there before her?"

But Richie is already shaking his head. "She said she was overcome by the news, remember? She collapsed. I assume she didn't leave for the lighthouse right away."

George stares at the map intently, then groans. "Well, shit."

He chuckles. "You think the priest had something to do with his death? I know he rubs you the wrong way—"

"I never said that."

"—but I don't think he's picking fights, with that leg," he finishes firmly.

"Hm," George muses, then looks to the autopsy report on the table. With her left hand, she lines up her fingers on her right arm. "One, two, *three* small circular bruises evenly spaced on the top of his bicep, and one underneath. I wonder what could have caused them."

Richie does the same with his own fingers, squinting at his bicep with a frown. "Aye, well. That I can't argue with. And we'll keep it in mind as we ask our questions, but you're jumping between theories like a flea at a dog park, Lennox. Keep . . . *percolating*, but don't let your theories influence procedure." His authoritative tone is weakened by a loud yawn. "I'm turning in. You should, too."

"We've only got four more days here," George says, pulling the COPFS request toward her. "I'm not worried about getting my eight hours."

"Some of us need more rest than others," Richie says with a sniff. "But you're going to be useless to me if you're strung out from no sleep and going around in circles with the only information we've got." Sensing another protest, his voice becomes sharp. "Argue all you like, Lennox, but we both know that you're still recovering from your fall."

After a loaded silence, Richie waggles his finger at her. "Go to sleep. That's an order from your superior."

"We have the same rank now."

"Superior in age. And beauty."

With that, he steps into the bedroom and closes the door.

George waits until the light spilling under his door is extinguished before she slips from the table and tiptoes to her briefcase. The sleeping pill is the first to slide down her throat, assisted by a gulp of her cold tea. But the painkiller is halfway to her mouth when Richie's door suddenly opens.

There's no disguising the action; their eyes meet as her cupped hand reaches her mouth.

She swallows the pill quickly. "They're just for headaches."

After a beat, he nods. But then her heart starts to thump as he approaches, prying the bottle from her fingers. Even without the label, his eyes widen with recognition as he looks at the pills inside.

"Tramadol? These are strong. You're taking these for headaches, you said?"

Some simmering emotion is rising into her throat. "They were prescribed," she says, surprising herself with her heated tone. "By the doctor."

She isn't sure why she added that last part. From the way Richie's eyebrows pull together slightly, he clearly isn't sure either. But she can't stand to have him look at her again like he had at the lighthouse—the way everyone who knows looks at her now: with concern and pity and doubt. So with a quick glance to check that the other pill bottle is properly tucked back in its pocket, she snatches the tramadol back.

"How long have you been taking them?" he asks, watching as she tosses the bottle into the case and closes the lid.

She ignores him, snapping the locks shut.

"I've taken those before," he persists, following her as she carries the case toward the couch. "After I came off a motorbike, about ten years ago. But the doctor only gave me enough for a couple of weeks. Your accident was *months* ago."

"Are you saying you know better than my doctor?"

"No, George, it's just I know taking them too long increases the risk of dependency."

"Which I've obviously discussed *with my doctor.* So unless you've been hiding a medical degree up your sleeve, you can keep your opinions to yourself."

Richie falls silent as she slides the case beneath the couch and climbs under the covers. She doesn't care that she's still wearing her clothes; she just pulls the blankets up to her chin and turns her back to him.

He takes a breath, shuffling on the stone floor. Then he crosses to the bathroom and closes the door behind him.

Half an hour later, with Richie back in his darkened room, George has rolled over to watch the flames. The adrenaline from the argument must have delayed the sleeping pill's effect—rest feels frustratingly out of reach.

Richie's snoring rumbles through the wall like distant thunder. One of George's ex-boyfriends snored terribly, and it was a contributing factor—if not the main one—to their eventual split. She'd wondered if the reason they'd stayed together so long was because she'd never actually slept beside him for so much of their relationship; either because she was working night shifts or because she'd stumbled to his guestroom when she couldn't take the noise. It was certainly easier to sleep alone, but the sensation is starting to chafe. For the past eight months, *ease* has been forced on her from all angles. Gentle exercise, reduced responsibilities, quiet dinners where her friends apologized for clattering their cutlery.

I'm not broken, she wanted to scream at Cole, her parents and friends. *I can think, I can move, I'm all right!*

But it's hard to convince people that you're whole again when they've seen you smashed to pieces.

A tear forms in the corner of her eye. It's warm as it rolls down her cheek to soak into her hair. She doesn't bother wiping away the trail it left behind—the heat from the fire soon dries her skin. Though when she feels more tears threaten to spill, she sits up and presses her fingers into her temple, her cheekbones, along the line of her jaw. She really needs to get it together, or Richie will think she's losing the plot.

Maybe she can blame the island—it might have sent people mad before.

She looks over at the dining chair that has the bag containing the logbooks hanging off the back. Sleep clearly isn't coming anytime soon—maybe Kathy's bedtimes stories will be useful after all.

Crossing to the table, George slides into the seat and withdraws the logbooks. The timeframe that each book covers is written on the inside cover in black pen, so George assumes these additions are Kathy's doing. She chooses the oldest one, from the men's first month on Eadar. The pages feel brittle between her fingers, the edges curling inward. She presses her nose against the paper and inhales, enjoying the slightly sweet smell, before beginning to read.

The first few entries are mostly written in ink, but every now and then someone has come in with a pencil. It makes deciphering the cursive handwriting even harder because those letters and lines have been erased over time. There's evidence of Kathy's journey through the books tucked between pages: a piece of scrap paper, a frayed ribbon, a large safety pin. She wonders if Kathy was marking something worth noting or just continually losing her place.

A relatively legible section dated 17 September 1918 is the work of J. Smith. It describes a morning of duties: cleaning, chopping firewood, fueling the lantern. He expresses his distaste for the previous night's supper in such vivid detail that George laughs aloud. He then goes on to write:

Once again Wilson did not sleep well, did not rise on time for his watch. The weather disturbs him; the gale is fierce, and he fears the roof will cave. He is young, and has not been this far west before. Despite my reassurances, his countenance sours the longer we are here. I pray that a break in this terrible weather will settle his nerves, for he is becoming more un-pleasant with each passing day. McClure is losing patience.

That last line sobers her a little. There are no further mentions of Wilson's attitude problem or McClure's irritation in this section, but considering a popular theory is that one of the keepers snapped and turned on his companions, the suggestion of conflict piques her interest. She turns the page eagerly, but a strange sound makes her look around.

Richie's snores have taken on an odd tone; they've grown longer and more drawn out. After a few seconds, she realizes the sound isn't actually coming from the bedroom—it's coming from outside. She moves slowly toward the door, her ears straining in the space between Richie's rumbling breaths. However, by the time she reaches the door, the sound has died out completely. Shrugging, she takes a single step back toward the table.

The sound starts up as if it had been waiting for her back to be turned. And for a moment, she can't process it. Surely it's not possible—they're on a tiny island in the middle of the ocean. But even as she struggles with the logic, the sound echoes across the hill again.

The stone beneath her feet tilts. She sways, throwing out a hand to steady herself. The pill is finally kicking in, bringing with it a creeping drowsiness. She makes a beeline for the couch and sinks down, drawing the blankets up to her chin. George's last cohesive thought before she sinks into a dreamless sleep is that, if what she heard is real, there is more to fear on Eadar than brutal storms and isolation. And now she has another question on her list.

Why has nobody mentioned the wolves?

CHAPTER 8

TRY AS SHE MIGHT TO CONVINCE HIM, RICHIE DOESN'T BOTHER TO CONCEAL his skepticism. "Tell me," he says, "did the wolves swim over, or charter a boat? Besides the very salient fact that there hasn't been a wolf in Scotland for a thousand years."

"Don't be an arse; I know there can't be actual wolves here. I'm just telling you what I heard."

He was already showering when she woke up, and the temperature between the two of them was frosty when he entered the kitchen. But as they started to talk over breakfast, George felt the beginnings of a thaw.

Hiding a chuckle behind his cup of tea, Richie checks his watch. "Assuming we aren't snatched up before we reach Granny's house, we'll need to stop in at the post office again today." His cheeks flush. "I forgot to call Jenny yesterday."

As they gather their things and head out the door, George starts to wish she'd kept the strange sound to herself. Especially after he caught her—no, not *caught*. Caught implied she was doing something wrong. A doctor *had* prescribed those painkillers. And he said that she should continue taking them until the headaches stopped. But that's beside the point; as long as she keeps her shattered pieces glued together, she doesn't owe anyone an explanation as to how she's managing it.

The howling was probably the wind, she thinks as they head down toward the farmhouse at the bottom of the hill. Maybe this was the sound that woke her on the first night—maybe it's the same thing that caused Wilson, the young lighthouse keeper, so many sleepless nights. As if to confirm this likelihood, a breeze stirs through the paddock, the long grass rippling. If she were to view Eadar from above, she thinks the tiny island would blend seamlessly into the choppy sea.

A handful of farmhands are dispersed throughout the paddocks, some mending fences, others refilling water troughs or distributing feed. A young woman at the top fence line scrunches her face with effort as she holds a timber post upright, two other farmhands stretching a piece of wire between it and another post. All three glance over as George and Richie walk past.

George's mouth is already pulling into a tight smile, anticipating a too-personal greeting or at least a wave, but she receives neither; instead, her smile is met with three identical expressions of undisguised hostility. Beside her, Richie appears oblivious, prattling on about wind direction and tides as the woman moves. Holding George's eye, she slowly leans over the fence and spits onto the grass.

Shocked by the unexpected act of aggression, George doesn't realize Richie is waiting for a response from her until he repeats her name loudly.

"What?" she says, tearing her eyes from the trio behind them.

"Just asking your thoughts on Alisdair MacLeod," Richie says, peering at his notebook. "If that was him yesterday, what are the chances he'll have more to say today?"

"Uh . . ." She drags her thoughts back to the task at hand. "Based on the descriptions we've heard so far? You can take the lead on this one."

Richie pulls a face but resigns himself to being the one who raises his fist to the door of MacLeod's farmhouse. It's an old stone building not unlike their own croft, though obviously maintained by more capable hands. The windowsills have recently been painted a dark green, and the garden beds are neat. George has grown so used to the muted color palette on Eadar that the pops of purple and yellow flowers take her aback.

George looks up and nudges Richie; there's a double spiral above this door, too. He widens his eyes and mouths, "Spooky."

As Richie knocks again, she steps away to survey the rest of MacLeod's property. There's a small yard between the house and a couple of sheds, one much larger than the other. A bicycle leans against the wall of the smaller one, and a pitchfork is sticking out of a pile of soiled hay in a wheelbarrow. A farm-hand appears from around the corner, bending to grab the bar-row's handles.

"Excuse me?" George calls out. "Is Mr. MacLeod around?"

The man almost drops the wheelbarrow in surprise, then points up the hill toward an approaching figure.

She nudges Richie. "You don't see that in the city."

Richie follows her gaze and he whistles, impressed. "If he was thirty years younger, you'd be swooning. Hell, *I'd* be swooning."

The two of them watch in awed silence as Alisdair MacLeod—confirmed now as the rugged man they met yesterday—strides toward the farmhouse from a distant paddock, sleeves rolled up to his elbows, a fully grown sheep slung across his shoul-ders and several more trotting along behind him. The sheep on his shoulders bobs along with his movements, seeming per-fectly content to be transported this way. George guesses by the sheep's bulk that it must be around her own weight, but Ma-cLeod doesn't seem to be struggling at all, muscular forearms gripping the sheep's lower legs to keep it from sliding off.

As MacLeod reaches the gate, his gruff voice carries across the yard to George and Richie.

"Stay back!" he shouts at the trailing sheep. "Back, you dumb bastards."

He successfully closes the gate behind him without any escapees and moves toward the larger shed. After sharing an impressed glance, the detectives move to intercept him.

"Mr. MacLeod?" Richie calls. "Can we talk with you for a few minutes?"

MacLeod's eyes narrow at the sight of them, but he jerks his head and continues on into the shed. It has a nice smell, a mixture of straw and old leather and animal. As her eyes adjust to the semi-darkness, George realizes this shed is actually a barn. Half-walls divide the space into four stalls. Three are bare, swept dirt floors with small piles of straw caught in the corners. The final stall has been covered in a thick bed of fresh straw. There's a water trough and a bucket of mixed grains. It's into this stall that MacLeod deposits the sheep, lowering it gently to the ground.

"Is it sick?" George asks, drawing closer.

MacLeod rises and pulls his shoulder blades back with an audible click.

"Cut her leg," he grunts, shaking out his hands. George notes the streaks of dirt and blood on his white shirt. There's more blood on the sheep's front left leg, and she winces when she sees the deep cut.

"How?"

He shrugs. "They're sheep. It happens." He reaches for a strip of clean fabric that's draped over the door of the stall and efficiently binds the sheep's leg. It bleats once as MacLeod pulls the knots tight, but otherwise seems calm. He stands, brushing straw from his knees.

George inches closer again. "Can I . . . ?"

MacLeod doesn't say yes or no, only watches her expressionlessly as she reaches out to pat the sheep's head. The wool is shorter here, but still springy under her fingers. The sheep sniffs at her wrist with interest, its breath warm against her skin.

Richie shakes his head good-naturedly as she steps back, privately delighted. She's never touched a sheep before.

Once he's certain the sheep can reach the food and water, MacLeod closes the stall door and walks straight past them out to the courtyard. They tag along behind him all the way to the farmhouse. He pauses at a side door to kick his heavy boots off, and glances back at them. "No shoes inside," is all he says before disappearing into the house.

George grins at Richie and gives him a thumbs up. He scowls and bends to unlace his boots.

The interior of MacLeod's home is as minimalist as the man himself. The door they enter through takes them into a small mudroom and beyond to a narrow hallway. MacLeod points them to the left, taking himself off to the right to "get the shite off my hands."

Two leather armchairs dominate the center of the living room. A low bookshelf holds a collection of paperback novels, their covers worn. A ceramic sculpture of a soldier in ceremonial tartans sits on a side table next to a framed photo of a couple with a young child on the woman's lap. The era of their clothing suggests they're MacLeod's parents. George examines the child's wide eyes and open mouth, trying to find a trace of the grim-faced man who just let them into his home. It's hard to see a resemblance. There's no art on the wood-paneled walls, though the extra layer of insulation has George and Richie removing their thick coats within a minute.

They linger in the living area as MacLeod steps around the corner and into his compact kitchen. A counter separates the spaces, and George sees that the wood paneling continues into that room. She hasn't seen this much wood in any of the houses they've visited so far; the church is the only other building that seems able to afford that luxury. Managing the flock must bring in a tidy income.

"Tea," MacLeod says, already reaching for the kettle.

Realizing it was a question, Richie hurries to answer. "Not for me, thanks."

"I'll take one," George says, earning a surprised glance from Richie. She smiles placidly, and the realization lands on his face a second later—she's more than happy to drag out this encounter, knowing he's taking the lead.

With a scowl, Richie approaches the counter. "Have you always lived here, Mr. MacLeod?"

He makes a sound of affirmation as he fills the kettle. "Family farm."

"And do you live alone?"

"Aye."

He sets the kettle on the stovetop to boil then disappears from sight, reappearing a second later in the living room. As he looks between the two of them, the first sign of discomfort appears on his face in the form of a crease between his silvery eyebrows. "You can sit."

George takes one of the armchairs. It's the type of chair that tries to swallow you whole if you make the mistake of settling in, so she perches rigidly on the edge. MacLeod sinks into the other chair with a quiet groan.

"Is this going to take long? I have a lot to do, and the days are short."

"Not long, no," Richie assures him. "We'd just like to ask you a few questions about Alan. We're told he worked for you in the months leading up to his death."

MacLeod blinks slowly but doesn't respond.

"Is that correct?" Richie prompts.

"Is what correct?"

"That Alan worked for you. It's a yes or no question."

"It didn't sound like one."

"Was Alan working here at the time he died?" Richie says,

his voice uncharacteristically strained. It isn't often that his natural charisma is challenged.

"Aye."

"How long had he been working here?"

"Three months."

"Did he have friends? A girlfriend?"

MacLeod stares at him. "That's none of my business," he says, an unexpected flint in his voice.

Richie makes a low sound of impatience. "You're not in any trouble—we're just trying to get a clearer picture of Alan's life."

"Then you've come to the wrong person," MacLeod replies in the same level tone. "I paid him to do a job, not to be my friend. I don't give a shite what people do in their own time, so long as they don't waste mine."

A whistle in the kitchen quickly builds to a screech. Mac-Leod pushes out of the chair to attend to it. The half-wall doesn't allow for even a whispered conversation, but George has decided to show mercy and makes a *switch* gesture to Richie before MacLeod returns with two mugs. He hands one to her before settling back into his chair. She notices with bemusement that he didn't ask her how she took her tea; weak and milky is what she's been given.

"You're right, Mr. MacLeod," George says. "You were his boss, not his friend. So, let's focus on that side of things."

With his eyes on his mug, MacLeod makes a vague gesture. George takes it as an invitation to continue.

"You sell wool to the mainland?" she asks.

"Mm. I've a micro-flock in comparison to mainland farmers, but it's premium quality, and I sell enough to pay the bills."

"And to pay your employees," she says, nodding to the fields. She recalls the faces of the three who'd stared her down, and her stomach tightens. "You must be supporting a fair few families on the island."

He shrugs. "Work needs doing. Can't do it on my own."

"And what kind of work do they do for you?"

"Fixing fences, shearing, moving sheep about. Chasing down strays before they wander off the cliff."

Richie clears his throat, apparently ready to re-enter the fray. "On the day of Alan's death, what time did everyone start work?"

MacLeod rubs his jaw, rasping against the stubble. "Sheep needed to be moved to a new field that day. They would've started at four, I s'pose."

"Then would it be fair to assume they were all present and working by four thirty?"

He grunts in affirmation.

"Do your employees get along with each other?" George asks.

"Never heard otherwise."

"So can you think of a reason why nobody let you know that Alan hadn't turned up for work that morning?"

MacLeod doesn't answer.

"Is it possible they didn't notice he wasn't there?" Richie suggests. "Your property covers a fair bit of ground."

"Maybe," is all he gets in response.

"Did he have a habit of being late to work?" Richie asks.

"Nobody ever complained about him to me."

"Did *you* have any issues with Alan as a worker?"

MacLeod makes a low *humph* sound in his throat. "He couldn't tell one end of a sheep from the other when he started. Forgot simple orders. Head in the clouds, that one."

"If he wasn't a good worker, why did you keep him on?" Richie asks.

The farmer sips his tea. "What else is there for kids to do? If they're not working, they're bored. And boredom breeds strife."

"Did Alan get into any strife?" George asks.

"Like what?"

"I'm just wondering if Alan could have found himself on someone's bad side."

MacLeod shifts forward in his chair. "What would make you think that?"

"He had injuries."

"I imagine you would after falling all that way."

George chews the inside of her cheek, considering how to approach this next part. Fortunately, Richie steps back in.

"Alan had some strange bruises," he says. "Ones that don't quite line up with a fall. We aren't certain what caused them"—he cuts his eyes toward George, a reminder—"so we're just asking all the questions, seeing if we can make sense of those injuries. Could something have happened here at work?"

"I don't tolerate fighting on my land. Other than that, it's like I said: none of my business."

"An accident?" Richie suggests. "Surely working with livestock comes with hazards."

"Maybe. Depends where he was hurt."

"What do you mean?" George asks.

MacLeod fixes her with a condescending stare. "A sheep isn't going to be leaving marks above the waist, unless you're stupid enough to lie down next to one."

"Perhaps not a sheep, then," Richie says, reclaiming MacLeod's attention. "Are there other tasks that might result in a couple of scrapes, maybe a few bruises?"

"It's a farm," he says, turning that condescension on Richie now, "not some cozy shirt-and-tie job. It's hard going most of the time." MacLeod raises his cup to his lips, not fast enough to cover a smirk. "If you can't handle a few knocks, you will not last long in this place."

"What happens if people can't?" George asks. "Handle it, I mean."

His eyes flick to hers over his mug. "I imagine they have a

very rough time of it. Our world is a harsh one, Inspector. I hope you don't linger long enough to find that out."

"Well, even if I did," she says, keeping her expression mild, "sounds like you'd stay quite clear of it."

A glint comes into his eye. "Aye. None of my business."

She purses her lips thoughtfully, then glances at Richie and nods.

"Thank you for your time, Mr. MacLeod," Richie says on cue. "We'll let you enjoy the rest of your break. And if you remember anything . . . well, we're neighbors for the next three days. You know where to find us."

As they make their way to the door, movement outside the window catches George's eye. A sheep grazes its way along the fence line, the woods an ominous presence on the horizon.

"Do you have any issues with predators out here?" she asks abruptly.

"What do you mean?"

George gestures outside. "Your flock being out in the open like that. Anything ever try to take a bite out of them?"

He shrugs. "There aren't many dogs on the island, and those who have them know better than to let them wander this far. And everyone knows I keep a shotgun close by." MacLeod's lips pull back from his teeth in a savage grin. "Anything—or *anyone*—comes sniffing around this farm, I'll happily send them on their way with a bite taken out of *them*."

CHAPTER 9

"I DON'T LIKE HIM."

Richie laughs. "And I'm sure that'll keep him up at night."

They're passing through the gate that leads out to the main path, the croft up to the left, the village down to the right.

"He didn't care at all that one of his employees—one of his *neighbors*—just died," George continues heatedly, glancing back at the farmhouse with disdain. "And if something *was* going on with Alan and another worker, he'd prefer to keep his nose clean instead of doing something about it."

"And what's wrong with that? He's their employer, not a referee."

"If you and I were fighting, Cole would step in."

"You and I fight all the time, and Cole is more than happy to let us duke it out on the pavement." Before she has a chance to retort he continues, "You heard the man: it's none of his business what goes on in people's personal lives."

"Why are you defending him? He was pissing you off, too."

"He's certainly not a model witness, but we're the ones who knocked on his door. He has no obligation to be *nice*. And I'm not defending him," he says, eyeing her disapprovingly. "I don't like him, Lennox, but I don't *dislike* him either. Maybe when you get to my age, you'll realize nothing is ever that black and white." After a pause, he adds, "It is strange that none of the other farmhands told him that Alan hadn't arrived. Or maybe they didn't care. If Alan wasn't any good on the farm, maybe he was more use when he stayed away."

"Maybe. If it were me, I'd be a bit pissed off if someone was earning the same wage for doing less work."

"That's because you're a selfish, nasty creature."

She rolls her eyes. "Can you imagine trying to hold a grudge in a place this small? It'd be impossible to stay angry with someone when they're your boss, your cousin, and your hairdresser."

"And when Kathy is inserting herself into the fray, getting into everyone's business." He looks at her from the corner of his eye. "What was that in there at the end?"

"What?"

"About the sheep. You don't actually think you heard wolves, do you?"

"I'm not imagining things," she says, more sharply than she intended, "and I know it was just the wind. The question just came to mind."

"All right," he says. "I'll head to the post office now to phone Jenny. Let's meet at the church in"—he checks his watch—"one hour so that Father Ross can take us to John MacNeil. Don't wander too far. And don't get gobbled up by the wolf."

She flips her middle finger up.

Watching his figure retreat, she considers heading back up to the croft to transfer her notes to their web. But she estimates that by the time she made it all the way back up and filled in more of the timeline, she'd need to rush to get to the church.

Suddenly she realizes there is something she can do in the meantime—especially now that Richie isn't watching her. She takes off at a quick walk, following the fence around MacLeod's property. A few sheep in the back paddock raise their heads as she passes, their lower jaws moving rhythmically, before returning to the grass.

Now heading back downhill on the far side of the property,

George strives to look more casual as she approaches the first line of trees, aware of the farmhands still mending the fence.

Though the sun is making a brave attempt to peek through the clouds, the temperature hasn't shifted up the dial at all since yesterday—but as the ground beneath George's feet transitions from grass to decaying leaves and soft undergrowth, a chill slides down her neck like the brush of a cold finger.

The trees branch out quite low to the ground here, like clawed hands rising from the earth. The trunks are deep brown and draped in velvety green moss. It reminds George of the lighthouse and shopfronts, how they are similarly covered in dirt and salt. It seems like everything on Eadar is masked in some way.

A few more yards into the trees, and George wrinkles her nose. Something is rotting nearby—a dead animal, she guesses, judging by the familiar smell of decomposition. She scans the ground as she moves off the path, stepping tentatively around stones and fallen branches covered in piles of leaves. The last thing she wants right now is to sink up to her ankle in the rib cage of one of the island's natives. But although she spends several minutes looking, she can't find a telltale tuft of fur or feathers to track back to a corpse.

"Are you lost?"

George jumps, turning on the spot. When she locates the speaker, the flash of fear heats into anger. "You shouldn't sneak up on a police officer, Mr. MacGill!"

Lewis stands a few yards away, a bag slung over one shoulder. "Who's sneaking?" he asks, approaching her. "*You* were the one who gave *me* a heart attack. I thought I'd stumbled across one of the fair folk."

"Fair folk? Oh, you mean a fairy?"

Without warning, Lewis claps his hand over her mouth.

Her body reacts instinctively, muscle memory taking over. In three quick moves, Lewis is on his knees on the damp ground and George has his right arm twisted behind his back. Blood pounds through her pulse points, aggravating the one in her temple.

"What the *hell*?" she growls.

"Sorry!" Lewis gasps. "I wasn't trying to—it's just . . . *they* don't like being called that."

Nonplussed but satisfied that she could plant him into the earth if he tries something like that again, she releases Lewis and steps back. "Father Ross wasn't kidding," she says tightly as Lewis pushes up to his feet. "As if Catholic guilt wasn't enough, you've also got myths and legends to keep you all in line."

"Do you know how many Celtic traditions and stories Christians have stolen? Makes it easy to be scared of both." He looks around, rubbing his shoulder. "You're a ways off the path. Where were you going?"

"Nowhere. Following my nose."

He shifts his weight, leaves rustling beneath his feet. "And what'd you find?"

"Nothing," she answers honestly.

He breathes out a laugh. "Better luck next time, then. Come on, I'll show you the way out—there's something you *have* to see."

She follows Lewis as he leads the way back to the edge of MacLeod's paddocks. She is indeed surprised by what she sees: a decent gap between two clouds has allowed the sun to finally break through. As soon as she steps out from under the canopy of trees, George feels the weak rays working their way through her clothes. She raises her face, basking in it. Beside her, Lewis is doing the same.

"Everyone goes a bit mad when the sun comes out," he says, tilting his chin from side to side. "Suddenly we're all walking around with no coats, making plans to go down to the beach, asking Kathy to order in sun cream. Then thirty seconds later, the clouds roll in again and it's back to reality."

"You know, you could always just move to a place that isn't constantly on the verge of a record-breaking storm. Go a few thousand miles"—she pauses, calculating the sun's position in the sky, then points—"*that* way, and you'll be in North America."

"I did travel for a few months, when I turned eighteen," he says. "I've seen a wee bit of the world."

"And you chose to come back." She wonders if it's clear in her tone that she's questioning his sanity.

"Of course. It's home, right? You miss it after a while. Besides, there's too much to do here."

She raises an eyebrow, not sure if he's joking, and for the first time notices what he's wearing. "That is a very red hat."

He tugs on the earflaps, flipping one to show her the fur-lined interior. "Do you like it? I thought if ever I was swept off this rock by a large wave, this is the color I want to be wearing when someone comes looking for me." He snorts. "They'll have to move fast, though. I can't swim."

George stares at him. "You know where you live, right?"

"On a rock surrounded by water? Aye." He shrugs defensively. "A few people—parents, mostly—have campaigned the council to take the little ones to the mainland for a few weeks for lessons. But as for the adults . . . none of us ever learned."

She is distracted from the staggering revelation that he can't swim. "Did you say the island has a council?"

"Hasn't anyone told you about that?"

"You're about to."

He chuckles. "The council is made up of some of Eadar's oldest residents—the ones who still have their wits about them. And a few who don't. They meet every week to decide what we spend money on, settle disputes between neighbors, all that boring stuff. Most of what they do is harmless, but like I said, some of us are campaigning for change."

"They're not keeping with the times?"

Lewis rests his elbows on the fence. "Oh, they are—it's just that it's their time they're keeping to. There's a long list of requests they've said no to."

George leans beside him. "So it's you, Kathy . . . who else is on Team Progress?"

"Most people, I think. But they're too scared to say it."

"Why would they be scared?"

Lewis's expression clouds. "Nobody wants to rock the boat."

"But things are already changing. I can hear it in your voices." Seeing his puzzled look, she explains, "The older people I've spoken to in the last few days have such thick accents. But you, Cecily Campbell and her kids, all the younger people—you sound more like mainlanders."

This observation seems to delight him. "All part of the plan for progress. More people spending time on the mainland, allowing the kids access to music and films and books. Small steps, but . . ." He shrugs, then nods to the trees. "What were you doing in there?"

"Killing time before I meet Inspector Stewart. He had to make a phone call, and we can't get reception anywhere on the island. Which reminds me," she says, hopping down lightly and setting off for the path, "I should get going. See you."

"Wait!"

She turns.

Lewis nods toward the woods. "Don't go in there on your own."

"Why not?"

He waves her off. "I'll tell you next time we see each other, all right?"

She considers pressing him for details now, but she checks her watch, swears, and starts jogging toward the village. It's only when she gets to the main street that she realizes she never asked Lewis what *he* was doing in the woods.

CHAPTER 10

"YOU WANDERED OFF, DIDN'T YOU?" RICHIE ASKS, ARMS CROSSED. THE CHURCH looms behind him.

"Calm down, I'm only twelve minutes late. Ross know we're here?"

"Just getting his coat. He already told John we'd be coming by."

"Great. Phone call went okay?"

"The connection was crackly, but I got through to Jen. Apparently the rain has been nonstop back home. Poppy's flat flooded, so she'll be with us for a few weeks." Richie looks cheery despite his eldest daughter's bad luck. "Ness isn't thrilled about sharing a room with her sister again, but it'll be very nice having all my girls under the same roof."

Richie has never troubled to conceal his affection for his family; she doesn't even know if he can. Back when they first started working together as DS and DI, her wariness of senior officers and their belittling tactics made their first few weeks strained, to say the least. But after hearing Richie speak so lovingly about his family, friends, and former colleagues, she gradually let down her guard. Sometimes when she's listening to him put his feelings into words with such unforced ease, she pictures herself as a lizard and Richie as the sun-warmed rock beneath her.

She shakes her head. "I just don't think there's enough money in the world to get my sister and my dad to share a ceiling again. They love each other," she insists, as if she hasn't complained to Richie for years about her family's incompatible communication styles, "but it's not an easy relationship."

"Aye, well. Sometimes it's easier to love someone in short bursts."

"Like me."

"Aye, like you," he says seriously, but his eyes sparkle with humor. "I'd love you *far* more if you'd stop showing up at my home."

"Tell your wife to stop inviting me, then."

"It's too late for that," he grumbles. "She seems to think you're our ward."

George smirks. Jenny has said as much to her during her—admittedly frequent—visits to the Stewart home for birthdays, holidays, casual midweek dinners. According to Jenny, George's loving relationship with her parents didn't count because they lived in a different city; in Jen's eyes, George was an orphan who needed claiming.

The front door of the church swings open and Father Ross emerges. A long black woolen coat is fastened tightly across his chest, and he winds a scarf around his neck as he approaches them. "Did you see the sun come out?" he asks excitedly. "It was only for a short while, but it was glorious."

"I was making a phone call," Richie says. "I'll try to catch the next one."

Father Ross laughs. "They're like solar eclipses. You might be waiting a while."

The priest chats easily with them as he leads the way to John MacNeil's house. Happy to have someone to make small talk with, Richie takes on the lion's share of questions Father Ross directs their way. However, their conversation is interrupted frequently by passersby calling out to the priest, who returns the greetings with smiles and nods.

Their path takes them back toward the village, past the Ferguson place and the post office, turning up a laneway just before the Campbells' home. Father Ross comes to a halt in front of a narrow house and rests his hand on a thigh-high green gate. Weeds poke out between the iron posts.

"As I said yesterday, John can be a bit . . . stand-offish to new faces. You'd best let me make the introductions."

They walk up the short path and wait as Father Ross knocks on the door—two sharp raps. Footsteps approach immediately. George counts the distinct sound of three different locks being turned before a short, balding man in his early forties fills the doorway. He eyes George and Richie suspiciously, and she realizes that she and Richie passed this man on the clifftop track yesterday.

"John," Father Ross begins pleasantly. "This is DI Lennox and DI Stewart."

John's mouth thins. "I already told you people what happened."

"They won't stay long," Father Ross assures him, pressing his palm to the door as if he suspects John is about to slam it shut.

After another measured look at the two police officers, John grunts and steps aside. "Down on the right. And keep your bloody voices down."

George freezes on the threshold, Richie almost running into her. "Is someone else in the house?" she asks warily, her heart picking up speed.

She feels Richie tense at her back, then he skirts around her to take the lead position.

Before John can answer, she hears soft footsteps approaching. A pale hand curls around a doorframe and then a pair of big, dark eyes are peering at her.

Father Ross looks at John. "I thought you said he'd be with Sarah."

John's jaw tightens. "He didn't want to go."

Father Ross looks at John for another beat, then chuckles good-naturedly. "Stubborn as always."

George barely hears the exchange, her pulse only just quietening in her ears.

Richie angles his head, smiling warmly. "Hello."

The boy—George puts his age at fifteen—doesn't answer, but he continues to peer at Richie and George with undisguised curiosity.

John puffs out his chest, an indecipherable challenge on his face. "That's my son, Calum." His voice becomes surprisingly soft. "It's all right, Cal."

The dark eyes flick to him.

"They're just here to talk to me. You can stay in your room." John's face shifts as he turns back to them, and his voice resumes its gruffness. "Make this quick."

They follow John to a cramped dining room with a small table and four chairs. The kitchen is visible through a wide arch, and George sees dishes stacked high on a drying rack. The rest of the space looks immaculate.

John drops into a chair with a sullen expression, thick arms crossed over his chest. George and Richie take the seats opposite, and Father Ross settles into the final seat, looking nervous. His gaze barely leaves John's face, and George wonders if he's trying to warn John to drop the hostility.

It doesn't seem to work.

"I already told the other ones all this," John says. "The first lot who came."

"Yes, we've read the statement you made to the coastguard," Richie says. "We just need a few more details from you."

John looks to Father Ross sharply. "What else do they want to know?"

Richie opens his notebook to a dog-eared page. "Your name is John MacNeil?"

"Are you really going to waste my time with questions like that?"

Father Ross extends his hand to clasp John's shoulder. "They're just doing their job, then they'll be off."

John shrugs him off. "John MacNeil, forty-one. Do you need my birth certificate? The time of my last shite?"

George is pleased that Richie took the lead on this interview. She'd taken pity on him with MacLeod, but after his snarky comment about her being late, she's happy to watch him squirm.

Richie forces a smile. "In your statement, you said you discovered Alan's body at around five a.m. What were you doing out there at that time of morning?"

"Checking traps."

"What kind of traps?"

Father Ross pipes up. "We have a small and pesky rabbit population. With no natural predators on the island, their numbers can get out of hand quickly. John makes sure that doesn't happen."

"So, you work for the village?" George asks, unable to help herself.

John glares at her. "It's not charity. I'm a tradesman."

"Oh, like Lewis MacGill?"

If John's expression was peeved before, it's thunderous now.

"No," he says curtly, "not like fucking MacGill. I actually get my hands dirty, instead of running around all holier than thou, telling people what to think."

George wonders if Lewis is aware of MacNeil's animosity toward him.

"There's a lot of work involved in keeping the island running smoothly," Father Ross says cheerily. "We each contribute in our own way. Even Calum works as his father's wee apprentice." The priest gives John a knowing smile. "Keeps the lad out of trouble, doesn't it? Otherwise he gets into all sorts of mischief."

John just scowls at the table.

"Was Calum with you the day you found Alan?" Richie asks.

John shakes his head. "He had a bug. I made him stay in bed."

"And you were checking traps when you came across Alan's body?"

"Aye. I'd set a few at the bottom of the lighthouse. They get lost in the grass, so my eyes were on the ground when I walked up. I almost fell over him."

"And when you found him, he was already deceased?"

John fixes Richie with a disdainful look. "Aye, he was dead. I could tell as soon as I looked at him. Face all mashed in like that, and cold as ice."

"How did you know it was Alan?" George interjects.

"Eh?"

"I've seen the pictures. His face was a mess, bruises and swelling. I wondered how you knew who it was."

"Who said I did?"

"Catriona wasn't asked to identify the body," George says. "Half the village knew who'd jumped off the tower before anyone told her. Were you able to recognize him?"

John looks at her evenly. "It's a bit of a blur. I can't really remember much of that day."

George smiles. "You've been doing well so far."

He just stares at her.

"Okay," Richie says, breaking the stand-off. "Did you see anyone else around or in the lighthouse?"

"No. I knew MacLeod's crew was in the fields. I ran across to tell them."

"Do you remember who you spoke to?"

"Like I said, it was a blur. Someone went into the village."

"Can you remember who—" Richie begins, but stops as a head peers around the dining room door.

John catches the movement and he starts to rise.

"All right, Cal? You need something?"

Calum MacNeil's big eyes flick between George and Richie curiously.

"I'll call for Sarah," Father Ross says, already starting to stand, but John beckons Calum closer.

The boy takes a few tentative steps, then scurries to his father's side. Across the table, George watches Father Ross's brows draw together for a moment before smoothing out again.

John wraps a protective arm around his son's waist, watching the boy's expression closely. "Okay, Cal?"

Calum nods once, his gaze raking over every detail of George and Richie; their faces, hair, clothing, notebooks.

"Hello, Calum," Richie says. "I'm Inspector Stewart. How old are you?"

"He's twelve," John says immediately.

George hides her surprise, casting her eyes over Calum's tall frame. As if sensing her appraisal, Calum meets her gaze. She smiles. One corner of his mouth lifts in response, then he looks at the table shyly.

"Do you handle Calum's schooling, Mr. MacNeil?" she asks casually.

"Aye. And there's Sarah Mackay. She comes by a few times a week to help me out. Clever girl. And Calum likes her."

Indeed, Calum looked up at the sound of Sarah's name, his eyes running over everyone's faces again.

"Can he not stay here on his own while you're working?" Richie asks.

"He gets . . . restless when he's inside for too long," John says, shooting an indecipherable look at Father Ross. "If I don't bring him with me, he wanders off. He's interested in the world around him, people. Tries to understand why they do the things they do. I've tried to tell him . . ." John shakes his head, but it's more in wonder than consternation. "He knows right from wrong. He's smart, too, Sarah says. Smarter than me, but that's not saying much. But you mean well, don't you?" He gently touches his forehead to Calum's shoulder, then looks at the detectives as if daring someone to comment on the soft gesture.

But George leans forward. "Hi. I'm George. I'm from the mainland."

Calum responds with a bubble of laughter.

"Well, my full name is actually Georgina," she explains, guessing what made him laugh, "but I think George suits me better. Richie thinks so, don't you?"

"Oh, aye," he says, enjoying the boy's amusement. "Georgina doesn't suit you at all. It's far too dainty."

She ignores the jibe. "Have you ever been to the mainland, Calum?"

"No," John interjects.

"Does the lad speak for himself?" Richie asks lightly.

"He's shy," is John's curt reply.

George keeps her eyes on Calum. "We're here to learn about Alan Ferguson. Did you know him?"

Before John can interject, Calum nods.

Remembering that Cecily had said she was keeping her children in the dark, George asks tentatively, "Do you know what happened to him? To Alan?"

Father Ross scratches his chin. In the quiet house, the sound pricks at George's ears. It pulls Calum's focus entirely; he turns his head to stare at the priest.

Then John growls, "Of course we do—the foolish man went off the tower."

"Man?" George echoes. "He was barely eighteen."

John's eyes fill with anger and a surprising amount of distress. "Seeing as I'm the one who dug the grave," he says shakily, "I know I didn't bury a *child*. I wouldn't—I . . . I *couldn't*—"

Father Ross reaches to grasp his shoulder again. Not acknowledging the touch, John speaks through gritted teeth. "Are we done here? I need to make Calum's lunch."

Richie starts to rise. "I think that's all we—"

But George interrupts. "Mr. MacNeil, I'm not sure what kind of resources you have access to from here, but there are organizations on the mainland that could offer you some assistance."

John stills. "What are you talking about?"

She almost chickens out, but as Calum gazes worriedly between their faces, obviously feeling the tension, her resolve hardens. "There are . . . groups," she says slowly, like she's approaching a bomb with a pair of pliers. "People who can support Calum as he gets older. If he's such a curious kid, maybe one day he'll want to get out and see more of the world."

But she may as well have been stomping through a minefield. John pushes to his feet so fast that his chair scrapes across the floor.

"I don't know what tree you're barking up, but it's the wrong one," he hisses. "Cal doesn't need anything except me."

Then he leans over the table, his reddening face less than a foot from George's. She braces, refusing to retreat even as spittle hits her face. "And if I hear you're running your mouth off about Calum out there, the next grave I'll be digging is—"

Father Ross's voice cracks like a whip. "*John.*"

With just one word from the priest, the bomb is defused. John gasps. "Sorry, Father," he mumbles, reaching out for Calum's forearm—to soothe himself more than his son, George suspects. "I just—may I—I need to make Calum's lunch and get on with the rest of my jobs."

The priest just stares at him, a coldness in his eyes that George hasn't seen before; she can tell by Richie's face that he too has noted the shift.

Eventually, Father Ross's face relaxes into one of parental disappointment. "It's your own home, John. You may do as you wish."

John doesn't move right away; he seems to be waiting for more definitive permission. When it isn't forthcoming, he steers Calum out of the room. Heavy footsteps march down the hallway, and a door slams.

An awkward silence stretches out; George leans back in her seat as Richie stares open-mouthed at the doorway.

Eventually, Father Ross clears his throat. "Shall we?"

CHAPTER 11

AS SOON AS THE GATE SQUEAKS TO A CLOSE BEHIND THEM, RICHIE GLOWERS at Father Ross. "While I feel for his situation, he just threatened my colleague."

The priest looks at Richie beseechingly. George gets the feeling it's an expression he doesn't have to wear often. "It's my fault," he says, looking back up at the house. "I thought I'd be able to manage him better. Please understand, he's under an enormous amount of pressure. His wife moved back to the mainland a few years ago. Calum is all he has."

Richie is about to argue, but George shakes her head. "What was he saying about digging graves?"

"Oh—he maintains our little cemetery. When the need arises, he picks up a shovel."

George frowns. "And his son helps?"

"Hinders, mostly. John spends most of his time keeping Calum out of trouble. A sweet boy, but burdensome. He's . . . well, you saw."

Richie's lips thin. "He's what?"

Father Ross huffs in exasperation. "I mean that . . . Calum *isn't* shy. He's always sticking his nose into things, or dragging poor Sarah around by the sleeve to look at whatever's piqued his interest that day. He understands everything, sometimes more than people are comfortable with. He just doesn't *talk*."

George and Richie exchange a look, and she asks, "Do you have a doctor here?"

"Oh, well," the priest begins, leading them back toward the main street, "we had a resident GP, but he fell ill himself and had to move to Stornoway to be closer to a hospital. That was two years ago. The position has been open since then."

"What do people do when they're sick?" Richie asks, stunned.

"Hope they get better?" the priest says with a weak smile, then quickly adds, "Of course, they'll go to Stornoway or the mainland if it's something serious."

"Has the council contacted the NHS about this?" George asks. "Or there's an organization called the Scottish Rural Medicine Collaborative that might be able to assist. Perhaps you can raise it at the next council meeting."

Father Ross comes to an abrupt stop. "You know about the council?"

"Someone mentioned it in passing."

After a moment, his face becomes contemplative. "Well, I'll certainly present the opportunity at the next meeting, but it's not exactly a tempting post for young doctors. We may have to wait until one of my flock meets a doctor on the mainland and lures them back here."

"I think you should insist," she presses, not willing to let it go. "If Calum needs more support than his father or Sarah can offer, then your council should be doing everything they can to help. And as someone who wields considerable influence in this community, you should be pushing them to do it. There are probably many people on Eadar who would benefit from more interaction with the mainland."

Father Ross smiles. George feels the chill of it. "Perhaps at the end of your visit here, Inspector, you could compile a list of all the ways in which we could improve our lives here on the island."

As they turn onto the main street, the priest is again besieged with eager greetings from residents. He receives the attention warmly, seeming to have boundless time and patience for all his parishioners. George, still rattled by the glares of MacLeod's farmhands earlier, can't help but wonder what people are really thinking when they turn polite smiles on her and Richie. Given the way word spreads here, it wouldn't surprise her if they already knew about their abrupt ejection from the MacNeil home.

"As DI Lennox noted, you're a popular man," Richie says to the priest when they are alone again. "People respect you."

Father Ross shrugs, but he seems pleased by the observation. "It's a smart idea to stay on your priest's good side. Speaking of which"—he raises his chin, a challenge—"will I be seeing you both at Mass tomorrow? Seven a.m. sharp."

"I don't think so," George says quickly. "We get started quite early."

"Oh? Inspector Stewart managed to find the time this morning."

George blinks, turning to Richie. "You went to the church?"

He lifts a shoulder, unbothered by her surprise. "You know I go back home. Father Ross saw me out walking and invited me in. Didn't mind that I'm a Protestant."

The priest chuckles. "We don't check your membership at the door. The more the merrier, as far as I'm concerned."

"Thank you for the invitation," George says, "but it's not for me."

Father Ross smiles indulgently, like she has said something childish. "Church is for everyone."

"I'm not a Catholic or a Protestant," she insists, taking a step backward. "I'm not anything, actually."

"You don't need to have religion. You just need to have faith."

"Well, I'm a little short on that, too."

"Then perhaps you were sent here to learn more than just Alan's story, Inspector." He bids them farewell and takes off toward the church.

George waits until he's out of earshot before turning to Richie. "Why didn't you tell me?"

"About going to the service? It's not something we talk about normally, Lennox, so why would it be any different here?" He shrugs. "Let's head back to add these new time frames to the wall. And then I'm thinking we should track down Alex Thomson."

"We should have asked Ross where he lives. Though I'd be very happy not to have to talk to him again. He gives me the creeps."

Richie laughs.

"What?"

He starts counting on his fingers. "You don't like MacLeod, you pick a fight with John MacNeil, and now the priest gives you the creeps. Is there anyone on the island who you do like, Lennox?"

"Only you, at the moment, but that's not saying much." Over his shoulder, George sees a familiar figure entering the bakery. "Actually, there's another candidate. I'll find out where Alex lives. Meet you back up at the croft in a bit."

As Richie walks off, George pulls out her notebook and leans against the bakery wall. She jots down some takeaways from the interview with John and Calum, but a nagging feeling takes her thoughts in a different direction.

It's true that she and Richie don't discuss his faith, but it's not because it's a taboo topic between them. After working together for the past four years and Jenny's insistence on folding George into their family, there aren't many subjects that are off limits. She knows that Richie doesn't like to push his beliefs on anyone, not even his daughters—Vanessa stopped attending church with the rest of the Stewarts when she was a teenager, and now makes a bored face at George when the others say grace before meals. And he's never asked George to participate in that, or invited her to Christmas or Easter services, even when he knew she was coming around for lunch or dinner afterward.

She suspects the real reason they don't talk about it is that he has picked up on her bewilderment at his ability *to* believe. Richie's career surpasses hers by decades, but even she has witnessed things that have made her question her own understanding of the universe. For Richie, who has seen more than she has, to still believe in a higher power—and to take *comfort* from that belief? Sometimes her bafflement shifts into something closer to anger, and perhaps it's this that Richie refuses to address. After so many years in the job, he's better at picking his battles than she is.

When Cecily emerges from the bakery she is occupied with juggling paper-wrapped items in her arms and doesn't spot George right away. But when she does, she breaks into a smile. "DI Lennox!"

George stows her notebook. "Hello, Mrs. Campbell."

"Oh, call me Cess," the other woman says. "Mrs. Campbell is my mother-in-law, and the less I have in common with her, the better." She smothers a yawn. "Excuse me."

"Of course." Taking in Cecily's rumpled appearance, George asks, "Rough night?"

Cecily huffs a weary laugh. "My littlest was up with bad dreams, and since it's just me on duty, I was going back and forward. Mary Thomas was just telling me that I should call some of the women over to perform spells on him."

George shakes her head. "Spells? As in, magic?"

Cecily makes an irritated sound. "Some kind of cure for the evil eye. Because everyone knows that children don't just have nightmares because they're *children*." Her voice is heavy with sarcasm now. "No, it has to be a curse or a malevolent spirit that's keeping him—and me—up all night." She throws these last few words back at the bakery; George presumes they're meant for Mary Thomas. "I'm desperate for another cuppa. Here," she says, tipping a few of her items into George's arms, "you help me carry these and I'll make you the best cup of tea you'll get any-where on this rock."

They make their way down the street. "How have you been finding things here?" Cecily asks. "The weather is tragic, isn't it?"

"I think I've spent most of my time either walking or shiver-ing. Usually at the same time."

"Oh, I know. I'm still not used to the cold, and I've been here so long that I'm almost part of the furniture."

A woman with cropped red hair who's holding a cloth-covered plate is walking ahead of them, headed toward the har-bor steps. George is surprised to see so many people in heavy boots and thick jackets walking along the quay, carrying buck-ets and dragging nets to a small storage shed. Of course, there must be more to running a fishing operation than just going out on the boats.

A shout goes up. "You stop right there, May MacGill!"

The redhead plants her feet on the top step. "Don't be ridic-ulous!" she hollers back.

A graying man trots up the steps toward her and takes the plate. "Ridiculous to you, maybe, but I've seen a boat go down and another splintered against the rocks after their captains walked by a ginger lass." His stern expression morphs into a grin, and he musses her hair.

She dances back with a scowl, kicking out at his shins.

"Keep that hair away from the boats, Miss MacGill, and

we'll keep bringing your supper home," he calls as she stalks back toward the shops, shaking her head.

Another man, indistinguishable from his cohort in identical knitted hats and high collars, has been watching the exchange. He glances toward George and Cecily and waves. She assumes the gesture is meant for Cecily but returns it all the same. The man immediately drops his hand.

Cecily, who hasn't seen this interaction, is already springing up her front steps. George looks up toward the Campbells' front door—then further up still. "Oh, you've got one, too."

"Eh?" Cecily cranes her neck, peering up at the double spiral above the door. "Oh, that? It was here long before I moved in; I don't even notice it anymore. I wish I could say the same for the other original features. Tilted floors, foul wallpaper, a bathroom window that never quite closes . . ." She rolls her finger to indicate that her list of complaints goes on for a while. "Come inside, Inspector. At least the old place stays warm."

The last time George was in the Campbell home, Cecily rushed her straight upstairs. Today, she is led down a narrow hallway into the cozy kitchen. It's shabby but neat, with yellow cabinets and well-used appliances. The air smells faintly of fish. George wonders if all the houses along the harbor smell like this, or if it's the curse of being married to a fisherman.

George tries to imagine what her flat back home would smell like to a stranger. Exhaustion and frozen dinners, probably. The little one-bedroom place is a copy-and-paste job of the other nine flats on her floor, each with its own little balcony—though signs of habitation are more evident on theirs than hers, which is bare but for the bunting wrapped around the railing. Her friends threw her a surprise welcome-home party when she was discharged from hospital, but one incredulous look from her sister sent them scrambling to bring the plates and drinks inside.

After relieving George of the parcels, Cecily points her to a seat at a scratched table. A ceramic jug in the center holds a bunch of fake lilies.

"I should have told you before I dragged you all the way here that I only have loose-leaf," Cecily says, filling an electric kettle at the sink. "That okay?"

"I don't think I'm in a position to be picky."

Cecily chuckles. "Choices are very limited here." Setting the kettle to boil, she unsheathes a knife from a wooden block and starts carving a deep brown loaf of bread.

There are sheets of paper covered in drawings on the floor, colored pencils scattered around. George bends to retrieve some. She looks through them, enjoying the insane caricatures. She thinks she recognizes the church and Father Ross, an underwater scene, a shaggy dog running around the lighthouse. "Which of your kids is the Picasso?"

"Eh? Oh." She snorts. "She's a Picasso all right. If you can't already tell, the purple thing with arms coming out of its head is me."

"I assume these small goblin-looking creatures are her siblings."

"So I'm told. And if you look on the roof, that's Donald. He was up there fixing the chimney a few weeks ago, and it clearly left an impression."

George is certainly impressed with the artistic license. Donald is mostly green, with a toucan beak for a nose and spiky brown hair that looks like a bird's nest. He's holding a hammer in one hand and a small brown rectangle that George assumes is a brick in the other.

"Have you got a photo of Donald so I can compare the likeness?"

"Oh, uh . . ." Cecily looks around the kitchen and frowns.

"Not in here. I've probably got some upstairs. But this is spot on, trust me. Especially the nose."

George points to a small figure poking out of a wall. "Did she get the dog right, at least?"

Cecily frowns. "The what?"

George turns the drawing toward her. "There. That's a dog, right?" She shuffles through the other drawings, pointing to the shaggy brown shapes with pointy teeth. "It's the same one in all of these, look—here in the window, on the doorstep. Does one of your neighbors own it?"

After a quick glance, Cecily shrugs. "Lord knows. She probably just saw it in a book." The kettle clicks. "Milk?"

"Just sugar, if you've got it."

"I do now," she says, patting one of the brown parcels. "The delivery came in this morning." She sighs wistfully. "That's one of the things I miss about home—being able to run two minutes down the road and find everything you need. It's a hell of an adjustment to make when you have to plan your life around a fortnightly delivery. You have to be a real romantic to move to the Western Isles—or a total lunatic."

George leans back in her chair. "I can't imagine being brave enough to make that choice. Especially at such a young age."

"I know! What on earth could Donald have said to persuade me to leave my whole life behind?" She ponders, then shakes her head. "Wouldn't work on me now, whatever it was."

"What did your family think when you told them you were running off with the fisherman's son?"

"I'm sure you can imagine," she says, loading all of the tea items onto a tray and bringing them over with the bread. "They knew I had a crush on him, but they thought it would fade when I went off to college. Unfortunately for them, I believe in asking for forgiveness rather than permission." She grins slyly. "The ring was on my finger and my bags on his da's boat by the time they knew what was going on."

"They never suspected what you were planning?"

She rolls her eyes. "Donald almost ruined everything about six times—can't keep a secret to save himself, that man. Gets all worked up if people ask him too many questions, then completely buckles under the pressure. I had to handle all the talking, made him keep his mouth shut anytime my parents brought up the future." She jerks her chin at George. "Five minutes with you and he'd be singing every song he knew."

George laughs. "And it was never an option for Donald to move to the mainland?"

Cecily scoffs, digging a knife into a dish of butter. "You're joking, right? Nobody who's born here leaves. They come out of the womb with an anchor chained to their ankle."

"How traumatic for the mothers."

"And I've done it three times. Lord willing, I won't do it again."

Remembering the Virgin Mary picture upstairs, George approaches her next observation delicately. "Father Ross spent some time studying on the mainland. He must have returned with some . . . modern opinions."

"With a total population of little more than two hundred people, the general attitude isn't overwhelmingly pro-choice," she says dryly. "And Donald wants more—has dreams of building an armada of Campbell boats to sail the high seas with."

George frowns. "Do you have access to birth control, at least?"

"It's a lot harder to get without a doctor around. And the last one had a seat on the council, which has its own priorities. We all stockpile medicine and first-aid kits, and the council let a few of us take a course on the mainland. It wouldn't worry me so much if it was just me and Donald to look after, but the kids . . . ?" She sighs, and picks up the teapot to pour. "The things we do for love, right?" A new glint comes into her eye. "Speaking of, I heard a rumor about you."

"I've been here three days. How is that possible?"

"Word is you've been spotted with Lewis MacGill. Kathy won't rest until you've popped out the first baby." She slides a steaming mug toward George. "The only way you'll escape her is by getting out of here as quickly as you can. Though you would have tall, beautiful children."

"Don't you start. And you should all leave Lewis alone. Let him find love in his own time." A thought occurs to her. "What's the consensus here on, er, non-heterosexual relationships?"

"You think Lewis is gay?"

"I don't *think* anything. I'm just wondering whether it's even an option."

"Father Ross teaches from the same Bible his uncle did, and the Ross before him. It says that desires aren't sinful until they become actions. But here, just thinking the wrong thing can get you in all kinds of trouble." She looks down, her fingers steadily tearing a piece of bread apart. "I haven't been able to talk to someone like this in years. Like I'm a real person, with thoughts that matter. Not just Donald's mainland wife who's here to diversify the bloodlines."

George isn't quite sure how to respond to all of that, so she just says, "I'm sorry," and they sit quietly as George blows a cooling breath on her tea.

"Ooh," Cecily says, the sadness in her voice replaced with humor. "You're about to get a letter."

"Excuse me?"

She points at the surface of George's mug. "According to my mother-in-law, if you see a tea-leaf floating in your cup, it's a sign you're about to receive a letter." She snorts derisively. "One of the many superstitions these people live by."

The distinction doesn't escape George's notice. "You don't?"

Cecily fixes her with a wry look. "I have enough to worry about without throwing signs and symbols into the mix." She takes a bite of the bread, chewing slowly. "I heard you spoke to Catriona," she says, her voice thick. "How is she?"

George searches for the right words. "She seems very resilient."

"Well, she's had to be." Seeing George's obvious confusion, she adds, "Because of her husband. Did she not tell you?"

"Tell us what?"

"Oh. Well, he died, too."

"*What?* How?"

"I don't know the whole story. When I first arrived here, I basically got handed a job at the pub. Within a few weeks I was working almost every night, and Iain Ferguson would always be there, on the same stool in the corner. I poured that man so many pints." She blows out a breath. "I didn't know until after he'd died that he'd been enjoying a drink too much and for too long. I'm not sure if it was his heart or his liver that gave out first."

"That must have been awful for Catriona. And Alan."

Cecily nods. "Iain was always flirting with us girls behind the bar. It was harmless; he just wanted to get a smile out of us. I heard Alan had his da's charm." She yawns, and glares down at her tea accusingly.

"How much longer are you parenting solo?"

"I don't know. Apparently there's something wrong with the engine. That's what they radioed in, anyway." Anger flares in her eyes. "If I find out they've treated themselves to a boys' trip to the mainland, so help me . . ."

"Has Donald done that before?"

Cecily stares into her cup. "Can I tell you something? Off

the record, or however that works? It's just not the kind of thing I'd want to get around the village."

"You need a set of mainland ears for a minute?"

She nods gratefully. "It's just . . . I get so *lonely* when Donald is away. People are nice to me, they include me in things, but I can tell that they're more comfortable when I walk into a room on Donald's arm." Her fingers curl in toward her palms. "I've given nine years and three children to this island, and they're still withholding their verdict," she says resentfully, "and at any minute they could just decide my time is up here and break my family apart."

"Have you told him how you feel?"

Cecily snorts. "Sure. In the five minutes he spends at home between the boat and the pub. It's like he doesn't look at me anymore, you know? Or if he looks, he doesn't see the girl from the shop that he fell in love with; he just sees this dowdy house-wife who always has something to complain about when he walks through the door."

Her voice breaks, and she presses her hand to her mouth. "I never thought I'd become this person," she says, her voice trembling. "And I feel like I've betrayed him."

"Betrayed him? By growing up? I'm yet to meet the man, but I imagine he doesn't look like he did at seventeen."

Cecily gives George a watery smile. "He's got some gray hairs in the back. I haven't told him yet. But he goes to the mainland so often, and for so long . . ." Without seeming to realize it, she begins to spin the slim gold band on her ring finger.

George tentatively makes the leap. "Do you think there's another woman?"

Surprisingly, Cecily barks a laugh. "No." Then she sobers. "I mean I . . . I hope not. I gave up so much to be here with him." She gazes toward the front door, though George is sure she's seeing far beyond it, to the harbor and slate-gray sea. "What would you do," she asks, "if you found out your partner was cheating on you?"

"The uniform is usually a good deterrent."

"But what would you *do*?" she presses. "Would you walk away? Or would you stay and fight?"

George bites her tongue on another joke; Cecily's eyes are shining, and she hasn't blinked in a while. "I'd like to think that I'd fight."

Cecily is silent for a moment, then whispers, "I would, too."

"Well," George says in a rallying tone, "that's the first thing you ought to tell him when he walks through that door. Remind him who's holding down the fort at home and that he can't just disappear for days on end when he's got a wife and children who need him." George reaches into an inner pocket and withdraws her card. "And if you ever need additional support, or just someone to talk to, I want you to call me. Even when I'm back on the mainland. Okay?"

Cecily accepts the card. "Thank you, Inspector Lennox. It's been a while since I could . . . There's just . . ." She lowers her voice conspiratorially. "You can't *talk* to anyone here. Not about anything real. Not without it being heard by the wrong person."

"Well, you can talk to me. And you can call me George."

Cecily's lips quirk. "I take it that means you're not about to arrest me for anything?"

"Not yet." Then she remembers the original purpose of her visit. "But you can help me with something."

CHAPTER 12

IT'S A STROKE OF LUCK THAT RICHIE DECIDED TO WANDER OVER TO THE NARrow beach to look around while she was chatting with Cecily—she catches him at the base of the path back to the croft. She can imagine the complaints she would have to endure if she'd told him she'd found out where Alex Thomson lives after he'd already kicked off his boots.

The directions Cecily gave George take them up the hill toward the church. Three kids are gathered just off the path on a rare patch of flat grass. They're noisy, laughing and shouting at one another as they play a breathless game of piggy in the middle.

Richie is uncharacteristically quiet. "Why'd you let him get in your face like that?" he asks abruptly.

"Excuse me?"

"John MacNeil. Back at his house, when he was shouting at you. He could have hurt you, but you didn't back off. Didn't try to de-escalate."

She looks at him sideways, thrown by the direction of his thoughts. "You really think he would have hit me? In front of you? In front of his priest?"

"You didn't know what he'd do. That's the point."

The disapproval in his tone makes George's hackles rise, but her retort is interrupted by a chorus of shouts. One of the kids has overshot a pass, or it was lifted by the wind, and the ball is bouncing down the hill toward them. She darts off the path and intercepts it.

"Here," she says, holding it out as the pursuing kids draw level. "Almost bounced right back into the village."

But nobody moves to take it from her.

"Here," she says again, taking a step toward them.

All three shuffle away.

George stills. Is this part of the game? "Shall I just . . . throw it to you?"

When none of them respond, she tosses the ball with enough of an arc that they have plenty of time to react. But the middle child leans away, as if avoiding something contagious. The ball bounces off a rock and picks up speed as it rolls all the way down the hill.

"Why'd you do that?" she asks, nonplussed.

"We can't talk to you," the blond boy in the middle says.

"Why? Because I'm a police officer?"

"Lennox!"

Richie is waving her back. She holds up a finger to tell him to wait. "Why didn't you take the ball?"

"It's got bad luck on it," the boy says.

George frowns. "Bad luck? Because I touched it?"

But the boy simply grabs his friends by their arms and tows them away.

Richie calls again and she hurries over to join him.

"What was that about?" he asks, shifting his scarf further up his neck.

She just shrugs. "More anti-mainlander bullshit."

———

Where they turned right at the intersection to go to Catriona's house, they now turn left, heading further inland. There are several stone houses along this road, though the distances between them grow the further they walk.

"Don't you think it's odd that Catriona didn't mention her husband's death when we interviewed her?" George asks after filling him in on her chat with Cecily.

"Perhaps she didn't think it was relevant."

"She didn't think that Alan losing a parent might be relevant to a *suicide investigation*?"

"I think that depends on what kind of parent Iain was. How do we know which one is Alex's?" Richie is looking at the houses they're passing.

George scans the front yards, recalling Cecily's directions. A flash of color catches her eye. "That's the one."

Out of all of the battered and bruised houses they've seen on Eadar thus far, Alex Thomson's house, a hand-thrown stone building with a ramshackle patio wrapping around the front, is the closest to dilapidation. George can tell that it hasn't seen a hammer and nails in years. It has the same thatched roof as their own residence on the hill, as do the crofts on the neighboring properties—she wonders if upgrading the buildings outside the village is a council decision or a reflection of each owner's economic status. Even though the village center isn't pretty, the houses have roof tiles, at least.

They pick their way through the overgrown lawn, stepping over discarded bicycle parts and broken furniture—including the warped red lawn chairs Cecily had told George to look out for—and make their way to the front door. Her eyes flick up to the eaves; as expected, a double spiral has been worked into the wood.

George knocks, and they both lean in to listen for sounds inside. A strained hum suggests an old fridge or freezer sits close to the door, but otherwise the house is quiet.

Richie purses his lips and reaches out to knock again. "Mr. Thomson?" he calls. "Are you home?"

With no response forthcoming, they find the only window that isn't obscured by curtains. It shows a tiny kitchen with rubbish strewn across the benches, dirty dishes stacked in the sink, and a tiny wooden table shoved against a wall. George cups her hands over her eyes, trying to make out the items on the table: an ashtray, a plate with half a piece of toast, and a chipped mug.

Wading through knee-high grass, Richie yelps when his foot comes down on something that squeaks, and a rapid ripple through the grass indicates a quick getaway. "Lennox," he says with barely concealed impatience, "I don't think he's home. And I really don't think he's going to tell us anything that we haven't heard already."

She doesn't reply, and he lets out an exasperated sigh. "Do you think John's lying? If he'd had something to do with Alan's death, why would he raise the alarm himself?"

"Makes him look less suspicious?"

"What's the motive? He said he didn't really know Alan. And I think he's kept busy enough with Calum." Richie ducks under a sagging washing line that's strung between the roof and a pole, a ripped gray t-shirt and some undergarments hanging limply from it.

As George bends to pass beneath the line, she notices something. "Rich."

When he turns back George holds up one of the shirt sleeves, her finger hovering above several faded, rusty splotches.

"Could be wine," he points out. "Mud. Hair dye. Ink."

"Could be. Could be something else, too."

Richie tuts. "If only we had a warrant."

He starts walking back toward the road. George hurries after him.

"Okay. What if we got one?"

"To test a tiny stain on the shirt of a man who is not a suspect in a case that is not currently labeled a homicide?"

"We've been here three days, Rich, and what do we have to show for it?"

"We're doing our job: talking to the people who knew him, asking questions, building a timeline . . ."

"And we're still no closer to figuring out the manner of Alan's death."

"Probably because we already have it," he says, exasperated. "We had the answer before we even left home."

She throws up her hands. "If you thought that way, why didn't you help me when I asked Cole for a better case?"

"Because I'm not sure you can handle anything more."

She can tell he regrets the words as soon as they leave his mouth.

"Lennox," he says quickly as she turns on her heel, "wait—that came out wrong."

She strides back toward the road, taking grim pleasure in the pained sound of him tripping over another hidden piece of junk.

"It's not because I don't think you're good, Lennox. I know what you can do; I've seen it firsthand."

"Sure. You just don't think I'm capable anymore."

"Not when you're tossing down opioids like they're lollies."

As if in response, the pain behind her eye pulses mockingly. She knows she should take it as a warning to calm down, to slow her racing thoughts, but the rush of sensations has her fingers inching toward the pocket where she stashed a pill this morning. With gritted teeth, she keeps her hand by her side.

"If you didn't think I could handle this, you should never have agreed to come," she throws over her shoulder. "You should have told Cole that you didn't want to go into the field with a partner you didn't trust."

"I did."

The twist of the knife. It brings her to a rocking halt.

He at least has the grace to look apologetic when she turns to face him. "After you left her office, she called me back in. She asked if I felt comfortable going out with you, if I thought you were ready."

"And you said no."

His eyes are beseeching. "George—I know you. We've worked together for years. We've seen awful things, the most horrendous acts of violence that people can inflict on each other. And I've seen you take it all in your stride. But what happened that night . . ."

A chunk of the ice that's hardening around George's heart slides down to her stomach.

"I'm not blaming you for what he did," he says, moving toward her slowly—like a zookeeper approaching a tiger with a twitching tail. "That kid was so twisted up on meth that he couldn't remember his own name, and I know if I'd gone into that room first, it would have been me lying in that driveway."

"But it wasn't," she snaps. "It was *me.*"

"Because *you* didn't wait for me," he says, his own temper rising. "Because you didn't *think* before you acted on an impulse."

"That used to be what you liked about working with me."

"Yes, right up until you nearly died!"

"So you agree with Cole." *With my parents, my sister, my friends.* "You think it's too soon."

Richie rubs his forehead as if he too has a headache. "The reason you're alive today is because you're a fighter. I always knew you'd come back to work, and trust me when I say that there is nobody else I want to do this job with. We're partners, George. We're supposed to have each other's backs." Richie pauses then says, "But how can I trust you to have my back when you won't be honest with me?"

She freezes. Has he guessed what the missing label meant? Or does he know about the sleeping pills, too? Her pulse is in her ears and it's saying *strike first strike first strike first.* There are venomous words on her tongue and it's only with huge effort that she swallows them. They burn her throat.

"I was cleared for duty," she says finally. "So even if you doubt *me*, you can at least trust that."

Her words don't have the desired effect; she sees sadness mix with the disappointment on his face. Almost as if he'd seen the truth in her eyes and wished she'd let it erupt.

He just says, "A doctor can't know what you don't tell them, George." He takes a deep breath. "We have a few more days here. We'll do what we came here to do, but I hope you also use the time to think about what happens when we go back. Okay?"

The poison churns in her abdomen.

"Okay."

CHAPTER 13

BY THE TIME THEY REACH THE CROFT, THE TENSION FROM THEIR ARGUMENT has eased somewhat—but not the pounding in her head. It's like the bluntness of Richie's words are bouncing around inside her skull.

Candor is something George has always appreciated about Richie. It's also the rumored reason why he's never achieved a rank higher than DI, despite having served more than three decades on the force. And while she knows she should have been honest with him, she can't deny a pang of frustration that he won't take her at her word. These headaches and dizziness—the lingering reminders of a severe head trauma—are manageable, and she *is* managing them. Even if she's had to find the solutions herself.

He's not wrong about the case, though; of course, Alan's death is most likely a suicide or an accident, and they could get to the end of their time here no closer to knowing the reason behind it. Cole isn't weighing her future based on whether she unearths a homicide on Eadar, but still . . . there's something about closing Alan's file with the easy answer—even if it is most probably correct—that's nagging at her.

Richie retrieves the key from his pocket, then sniffs. "What is *that*?"

"You're going to need to be more specific."

He takes a step back, peering at the ground around the front of the croft. "It smells like something's gone off."

She inhales deeply, then recoils. It doesn't smell quite the same as what she encountered in the woods, but it's undeniably the reek of something rotting.

"I miss home more and more every day," he mutters as he goes inside.

A basket of fresh bread and a sealed pot await them on the table.

George rounds on Richie. "I *told* you I locked the door yesterday."

"Maybe it *is* a tricky lock," Richie protests, looking down at the key in consternation. "Regardless, we'll have to tell her that she can't just let herself in. And surely we should be paying for all this food."

"It does seem slightly unethical to be accepting free meals from these people." She sniffs the contents of the pot and replaces the lid quickly. It's not *the* bad smell, but it's not a pleasant one. "If it's a bribe, it's not working."

"Did you bring any food from home?"

She mentally searches her bag. "I think I have breath mints?"

Richie returns to digging through the basket. "I think we'll have to accept the bribes. Oh, what do we have here?" He withdraws two unlabeled dark glass bottles and holds them up to the light for inspection. "Cider, maybe? Or an ale?" Richie checks his watch then shoots an impish look at George. "Are we off the clock?"

Having a drink halfway through a case is not Richie's usual style; she suspects he's more interested in melting the last few icicles between them before they call it a night.

"It'd be rude not to."

His smile falters. "When did you last take a . . . ?"

"Not since this morning." She gives him a thumbs up. Overdoing it, maybe.

They carry the dining chairs outside and dig the legs into

the grass. Richie uses the heel of his boot to work the bottle tops off, passing one to her. George sniffs it warily. Richie, sharing her caution, takes a tentative sip.

"Oh," he says in surprise, going back for another. "That's a wee heavy!"

She peers down the neck. "Really? I've never tried one."

"It's the finest Scotch ale, in my humble opinion," he says, looking fondly at the bottle. "Lord, I haven't had a home-brewed heavy in years. You know, this ale was one of the first drinks I ever had. I think I was . . . fourteen, maybe? It put hairs on my chest." He smacks his lips and makes a sound of pleasure. "Proceed with caution, Lennox. This is the day you become a man."

They sit in comfortable silence for a while, looking out over the swaying grass. The sun peeks from between the clouds long enough for them to watch as it's swallowed by the dark and hungry sea. In that instant, Eadar transforms from picturesque to desolate—green hills turn to gray mountains, the earth comes alive with invisible scurrying, and distant lights from the village beam through the darkness like glowing eyes.

"I've been thinking about what Father Ross said."

"Which thing in particular?" she asks. "There have been several comments of note."

"The first time we were at the church, he said the island hasn't evolved for centuries. I thought he just meant their faith, which is unnerving enough—things that made sense a thousand years ago don't hold water today, and rightly so. And I can't tell if it's diligence or obstinance that's fueling their grip on tradition." He looks down at his bottle, swirls the dregs thoughtfully. "But then he was so uncomfortable talking about Calum. And then so flippant about having a doctor on the island."

"And Cecily said she and some of the others needed to get council permission to take first-aid courses."

He nods, frowning. "It makes me wonder how they feel about . . . deviations."

"You mean, what happens if they're not Catholic, neurotypical"—she recalls more of her conversation with Cecily—"and heterosexual?"

"Yes, exactly," Richie says, and then he tips his head back to swallow the last of the wee heavy. "Just a thought."

The sky is a deep blue when he starts complaining about the temperature drop and heads inside. She goes to follow him, but her gaze falls on a section of long grass beside the front door. Some of the blades are bent, as if something heavy has passed through. She follows the trail, treading carefully to where it ends beneath the kitchen window. With darkness falling outside, the interior of the croft is lit up like a Christmas display.

From this angle, someone would have a clear view of the main room, the doors to the bedroom and bathroom, the evidence wall. And the couch where George sleeps.

The islanders have been so openly curious about their presence here—not just because they're police, but because they're from the mainland. It wouldn't be surprising if some inquisitive kids had crept up here to look around. She squints at the evidence wall, wondering how much someone could even read from this distance. The picture of Alan, definitely, but as for their handwritten notes . . .

Richie raises an eyebrow when he watches her awkwardly clamber onto the counter with one of Cecily's thin blankets, wedging the fabric into the gap between the splintery timber that frames the window and the stone. It doesn't feel very secure, but it'll do for now. "I should have thought of that earlier," is all he says.

They justify their early dinner by spending an hour writing out their day's notes and adding them to the wall. They throw ideas and questions back and forth for another half-hour, but it feels to George that it's more to kill time than to actually pursue anything; she can tell that Richie's still sorting through the thoughts he'd voiced earlier. As the minutes go by, her leg starts to shake.

Still feeling wide awake—a sensation that would be cured by one of those little pills in her bag, her pounding head solved by the one in her pocket—George is staring unseeing at the web of information when Richie says good night. She grunts out a reply as the warped bedroom door closes with the sound of protesting timber, and seconds later she hears the bed frame squeak.

She can only hold herself still for a few more seconds before she digs her trembling fingers into her pocket, slipping the pill between her lips. She's not sure how much longer she could have kept this headache under wraps; hopefully she's caught it before it turns into a fully fledged migraine. Padding to the sink, she twists the tap and cups her hand under the stream, bringing water to her mouth again and again until she's panting.

Clinically, distantly, she is aware that the intervals of time between taking a pill and needing the next are getting shorter. That the trembling in her hands isn't fading as the pain does. She knows she has a long way to go to get back to the shape she was in before the Villo case, before the injury, before the months of recovery, but continuing to slog through paperwork behind a desk isn't the solution—for her, it's not even an option.

Her fingers go to the scar behind her ear, feeling around its perimeter. She knows it's not as large as her mind bullies her into thinking, that it's only visible when her hair is pulled back into a ponytail. But Richie saw the mess of blood and hair and scalp ripped open to the bone that night, watched helplessly as the paramedics loaded George into the ambulance on a stiff spinal board, her neck swallowed in a brace, her upper body soaked red.

She'd read his statement. He hadn't seen the incident, had only just arrived at the residence when he heard her scream. By the time he'd sprinted up the stairs to the bedroom, George had already fallen from the narrow balcony, and her blood was running down the driveway to the street.

No. Not fallen.

Everyone had told her it was a good thing she couldn't remember the incident. But George pored over witness statements, official reports, her medical files, trying to weave the threads of her story into something she could recognize, something that made sense of it all.

Even now, with the pain beating a slow retreat from her skull, nausea swirling in her stomach and the scar rough beneath her fingertips, she wonders if—just like Lewis's campaign to make Eadar a tourist hotspot—it's a lost cause.

Her thoughts drift back to the logbooks. The howling wind last night had distracted her from reading more about the friction growing between Wilson and McClure. She told Kathy she wouldn't have time to look into the keepers' disappearance, but with nothing more to add to the wall . . .

She settles onto the couch this time, the fire bright enough to read by. The next few weeks of entries are patchy, entire paragraphs lost to water damage or greasy fingers. What she can decipher is a little disappointing—they really did have to report *everything*, and most of that is incredibly boring. She finds the entry about the snowfall in the second book, Kathy having marked the page with a speckled brown feather. She had quoted Smith perfectly: *Snow falls on Eadar like a blanket.* George cringes at the thought of the island getting any colder than it is now.

After another half an hour she has only learned three things: McClure has the worst handwriting, Wilson writes the least, and all three of them are getting sick of the wind.

A yawn hits her, and she is about to give up on McClure's latest scrawled entry when a word catches her eye. Shifting closer to the fire, she starts reading the section carefully from the top.

Woke to a fierce cold. Suspected Wilson failed to bolt door again, but discovered broken window in kitchen. Large rock on floor. Second time this month—both just days after the Catholic came to call. Smith has gone to solicit wood and nails from Mr. I. MacLeod to board the window. Wilson still out.

The tension between McClure and young Wilson is still apparent—and she isn't sure whether "Wilson still out" means asleep or wandering the hills—but all that fades in comparison to this new information. Two windows had been smashed, and McClure clearly doesn't suspect a gust of wind. George reads further, now looking for specific words, and soon finds what she's looking for.

Wilson writes:

Sent to collect parcel, stopped at the Catch for a dram. The Fenian priest hailed me, entreated again for us to attend services. I made no reply—I drained my glass and departed. Mam would be proud.

"Nothing has changed there," she mutters. She wonders if the priest back then was also a Ross; if so, she admires Wilson's restraint. But if these repeated rejections of the priest's invitations are linked to the rocks being thrown into the keepers' cottage, as McClure hints, then is it possible that petty vandalism could have escalated into something more violent?

She leans back, rubbing her strained eyes. Why is she even bothering with this? Kathy would have told her if there was explicit evidence pointing to the locals; or if she had wanted to protect the island's reputation from further damage, why give her the books at all? George already has too many questions jostling in her mind about Alan's death; she can't afford to keep adding new ones to the mix, and about a case she's not here to solve.

The conclusion is simple, if a little sad. When they leave on Sunday, she'll return the books to Kathy with an apology: the mystery of Eadar's last lighthouse keepers will have to remain just that.

———

She manages to coax a steady stream of water from the taps above the tiny bathtub, and though the pipes start to shake a few minutes into the process, the end result is a steaming bathtub that she slips into gratefully.

Being immersed in hot water makes her realize how much the cold had leached into her body; the abrupt transition to warmth actually pains her joints before it eases them. She spends the first five minutes willing herself not to launch out of the tub, and her perseverance eventually pays off.

Having left a decent fire going in the other room, George feels confident enough to wash her hair. It has suffered from three days under a beanie, pressed flat against her skull without fresh air or shampoo. She loosens it with her fingers and, taking a deep breath, lets herself sink beneath the surface.

When she's clocked off for the day, the first thing she does when she gets back to her flat is jump into the shower. The physical act of washing away the day was a recommendation from a fellow constable back in her early days of policing, but what George loves most about this ritual is tipping her head beneath the pounding water until it clogs her ears and the sounds of the outside world are muffled. Those precious few moments of near silence bring George a sense of peace that's been hard to come by naturally in the past few months.

Being immersed in the bath is having the same effect on her. Already she can feel her thoughts slowing down. She stays like this for a long time, raising her nose above the surface to draw long breaths. When the water becomes lukewarm, she pulls the plug and steps out onto the cold stone.

It's a few minutes later, when she's combing out her towel-dried hair in front of the fogged mirror, that she hears the howling again.

She freezes, all the work the bath did to relax her undone in an instant. The howl lasts about eight seconds before cutting off abruptly.

Wrapped in a towel, she sprints on quiet feet to the small window beside the front door and tugs the curtain aside. The flicker of the firelight against the glass makes it impossible to see anything out there. It's no use; if she wanted to investigate the source of the sound, she'd have to go outside. And she's not crazy enough to do that.

With a resigned sigh she turns, leaning back against the door—and her heart stops.

The makeshift curtain has fallen down. And there's a wolf at the window.

For a moment, she's overwhelmed by pure, primal terror before she realizes that what she's looking at is a human figure wearing a snarling wolf *mask*. Riding the flood of adrenaline, she flies into the kitchen with the intention of grabbing a knife, a heavy pan, anything she can use to defend herself. Apparently startled by her movement, the figure takes off. And even as her heartbeat fills her ears, she hears the distinct sound of footsteps pounding around the side of the croft.

The fear she felt only moments earlier is replaced by anger. Did this creep really think she'd be scared by a silly mask? A shirt is pulled over her head and her feet are shoved into pants and boots before she fully thinks out what she's doing. Pushing her arms through the sleeves of her coat, she goes to the block of knives on the kitchen counter and draws out a sturdy cook's knife. With trembling hands, she slips it into a deep side pocket.

Shooting one final glance toward Richie's door—under which his snores leak—she heads out to hunt a wolf.

CHAPTER 14

REGRET HITS HER AS SOON AS THE WIND FINDS HER DAMP HAIR. CURSING AT herself for forgetting her beanie and gloves, she scrambles to pull up the wide hood of her coat and cinch it tightly around her chin. A jumper and socks would have been smart, too. She's also conscious of the irony—two nights ago, she thought that anyone going outside at night must be out of their mind, and yet here she is, shivering under the open sky.

The moon is days away from being truly full; however, it throws a decent amount of light across the paddocks. As she scans the hills, looking for movement, something in the distance catches her eye.

A light is on in the lighthouse.

Even with the extra time it took her to throw on her coat and shoes, she doubts the person at her window could have made it all the way over there. But they certainly had enough time to disappear over the crest of the hill and into the village. With her adrenaline ebbing, she realizes there's no way she can catch up with them now.

But the light in the lighthouse window indicates someone is there right now. Considering the building is derelict, it's strange. She measures the distance between the croft and the lighthouse, calculating if she can make it there fast enough to cover the exit before the person inside could leave. At least her approach will be muffled by the long grass and waves smashing the cliff below.

She moves swiftly, and the parts of her body that aren't exposed to the elements are feeling a bit warmer by the time she reaches the lighthouse, though her nose and fingertips are beginning to burn. Panting clouds into the air, she steps back to gaze up at the tower. Her eyes roam from window to window until she locates the light about two-thirds of the way up—the second floor. She pats the pocket that doesn't hold the knife, then swears; she left her torch back at the croft.

A combination of the weak moonlight straining through the windows and her left hand on the inner stone wall takes the danger out of climbing the first flight of stairs. She pauses at the first floor, peering up the next flight. The soft glow from above is steady; a lantern, perhaps, rather than a fire.

"Hello?" she calls. "Is someone up there?"

She counts three heartbeats of silence.

Then the light goes out.

The fear that crackles through her limbs like lightning could power a thousand torches. In the terrible stretched-out seconds following the plunge into darkness, she strains her ears for sound as her eyes slowly adjust. Whoever is up there has turned off the light for a reason: they don't want to be seen.

As if taking her thought as a challenge, footsteps cross above her head toward the stairwell. George feels her way to the nearest wall to stand flush against the stone, then slides her hand into her pocket and retrieves the knife. Her fingers are numb and clumsy around the handle.

"Police," she calls, making her voice hard. "I am armed. Announce yourself and come down the stairs slowly."

She thinks she hears them breathing, perhaps the crack of a joint as they shift their weight anxiously. Could they be holding a weapon, too? Is the barrel of a gun trailing through the air, its owner waiting to pick up a sound that would indicate her position?

For what feels like an eternity, there is no sound, no movement. The silence stretches so long that George wonders if her opponent has decided to wait her out till dawn. With the galloping horse in her chest and the pressure returning to her head, George knows she's incapable of standing motionless for hours in a freezing tower.

But the other person breaks first.

It starts as two tentative footsteps that swiftly become a frantic beating down the stairs. Impulsively she throws herself around the corner and onto the landing between the two sets of stairs, hands raised, blade pointed to the ceiling.

"Stop!" is all she has time to say before a body sideswipes her, sending her staggering against the inner wall. She grunts at the impact, but before she can recover, the door slams with a bang.

Rubbing her shoulder, George crosses back to the tiny window, desperately trying to force her head out so she can see which direction her assailant is running, but the opening is too narrow. With a frustrated yell, she yanks herself back into the room and runs down the narrow stairs.

Clouds have rolled in and the moonlight has dimmed. The temperature is no less forgiving than it was earlier as she comes to a skidding halt in the long grass. The wind has calmed, but still the grass shifts as if it's teeming with invisible creatures. Though she casts around for another minute, she knows immediately that her search is hopeless. Whoever was skulking around the lighthouse has been embraced by the darkness. She curses and kicks out at the ground, the energy that's zinging through her body demanding a release. It's far too dark to return to the lighthouse, and even with the knife gripped in her now clammy hand, George remembers her fear on the dark staircase.

Reluctantly, she searches for the path that runs up from the woods to the croft. She's so focused on finding the path, she doesn't see the man emerging from the trees until he flicks on his electric lantern and holds it aloft.

The knife is already slicing upward through the frigid air before her eyes register the face. Even when the recognition hits, she doesn't lower her arm. Especially when she sees the long barrel of a shotgun slung over his shoulder.

"Mr. MacLeod? What the hell are you doing out here?"

The lantern throws deep shadows beneath MacLeod's thick eyebrows and broad nose, but she can still tell that he's shocked to see her. "Could ask you the same. It's late."

"Lucky for me, I'm a DI," George says frostily, "so my questions get answered first."

He grunts. "Some sheep got loose."

She eyes the gun, tempering her tone. "And you're just wandering around in the dark looking for them?"

"Aye. Could get hurt." His eyes flick to her hand. "Are you going to stab me?"

"Are you going to shoot me?"

"Why would I do that?"

Measuring his expression, George lowers the knife. "Don't you know how dangerous it is to be wandering around in the middle of the night?"

"Not afraid of anything at my age."

"Yet you carry a gun."

"You've not heard the sounds a sheep with a broken leg makes. Can't sleep?"

She eyes him, trying to decide if he's telling the truth, or whether he's the one who was watching her through the window.

"I'm a bad sleeper in general. But that's not why . . ." Her gaze is drawn back to the lighthouse. She can just make it out in the dark, a smudge of gray paint against a black sky.

"What did you see?" MacLeod asks suddenly.

She bites the inside of her cheek. "Did anyone run past here a few minutes ago?"

"No," he answers, but he turns in a slow circle to survey the landscape. "Where from?"

"The lighthouse," she says, wishing he was facing her so she could read his reaction. By the time he twists back around, his expression has been wiped clear.

"Kids," he grunts with certainty. "They get pissed up there."

George tries to recall the moments she was locked in that tense stand-off. Without seeing the person it's impossible to guess their age, but even so, her other senses had been working in overdrive to form a picture of the scene. Is it possible that her imagination had leaped into action, too? Could it have been a teenager up there, scared they'd been busted with the booze they swiped from their parents' liquor cabinet? The threatening presence, the painful silence—had that actually been a terrified kid, the only weapon in their hands a half-drunk bottle of wee heavy? The weapon in her own hand feels ridiculous now, and she's glad it's too dark for MacLeod to see the heat rising in her cheeks. Unfortunately, that warmth doesn't extend past her chin; she blows air into her free hand, fingertips tingling again.

"It's only going to get colder," he says abruptly, then gestures toward the hill. "I'll walk you up."

"You don't have to do—"

"I need to look for my sheep, too."

He takes off, angling to the left. With one final glance at the lighthouse, she jogs after him and realizes he's led her to the path.

"How do you think the sheep got out?" she asks as she draws level.

He makes a sound she translates as, "Not sure."

"Have you lost sheep before?"

"Aye. Through broken fences, gates left open. The daft things keep their eyes on the grass right up until they're dropping into the ocean."

"That's horrible."

"And a waste of wool."

An idea occurs to her. "Did Alan ever let any sheep escape?"

MacLeod grunts. "Once. Dumb animal fell down the steps to the beach. Broke its legs. Made the boy put a bullet 'tween its eyes to remind him not to make that mistake again."

"You must have been angry with him."

He doesn't answer, so she presses again. "Is that why you didn't attend his funeral?"

Even in the shifting light, she can see him glance at her. "Who told you that?"

"Is it not true?"

Silence falls between them for a while as they tackle a particularly steep section of the hill. She watches him from the corner of her eye, remembering Richie's pep talk from their first day on Eadar about earning people's trust with honesty. "Someone was at my window tonight," she says. "That's why I was out here in the first place."

"And you were going to confront them."

"To *talk* to them."

"You know what they say about curiosity, Inspector."

She hums, but he speaks as if he reads the direction of her thoughts. "I was busy," he says gruffly, "the day of the boy's funeral. And as the bloody priest well knows, I do not come when I'm clicked at."

The lantern throws flickering shadows over their faces like they're huddled around a campfire. It deepens the scowl lines around MacLeod's mouth, makes him look even wilder than he'd been earlier. But whether it's the dig at Father Ross, or the fact that he'd saved her from stumbling around in the dark, George is suddenly struck by an intense desire to *trust* him.

"Are your sheep really missing?" she asks, a tinge of desperation in her voice.

The scowl softens, and MacLeod sighs. "Aye, and I'd like to find them and get back to bed before the sun comes up. I know that you should do the same." At her quizzical look, he adds, "You look like shite."

She surprises herself by laughing. It's been a while since someone has spoken to her so bluntly.

They've arrived at the crest of the hill, but she hesitates just in front of the door to the croft. MacLeod stops with her, and waits.

"I heard something," she admits. "It sounded like . . . well, it sounded like a wolf. And I know that's not possible. But it's what I heard."

"You think that person at your window was howling?"

She hadn't considered that; but she shakes her head. "It doesn't sound like a person."

He looks at her squarely for a long moment. "There *are* wolves on Eadar, Inspector. They just walk on two legs."

Before George can ask his meaning, he jerks his chin toward the door. "Go on inside now. A change is coming."

As if on cue, an icy breeze stirs the grass at their feet. Shivering, she moves for the door—but then MacLeod grabs her arm.

"What?" she hisses, whipping her head around. "What is it?"

MacLeod's eyes are wide as they flick across her, across the front of the croft. "That smell."

She sags slightly. "Oh, *that*. I have no idea, but I swear it's getting worse."

While she didn't expect him to laugh, she thought he might relax a little. But he remains tense as he releases her arm and starts sweeping the lantern across the ground and around the doorway.

George frowns. "What are you looking for?"

He doesn't answer, just continues his methodical movements, sniffing the air like a bloodhound. Wondering if she should warn him off going inside, she almost jumps when his head snaps up. He raises the lantern above his head, staring up into the eaves that overhang the door.

"Ach," he says in a low voice laced with disgust, then reaches up to a shadowy ledge just under the lintel. Watching on in confusion, she recoils when MacLeod retrieves a small cloth bag, stained and sodden and the obvious source of the bad smell.

"What is that?" she asks, trying not to gag.

"A dirty trick," he responds, and before she can protest, he opens the bag.

Despite the new wave of the putrid smell, George's curiosity drives her forward to peer down into the bag herself.

Soaking into the fabric are two or three purple and black eggs, broken, the slimy texture bringing another rush of bile to her throat. But it's the other item in the bag that draws her attention; the thing that MacLeod slowly withdraws.

"Is that a doll?" she asks, baffled by the figure made of crudely twisted straw.

"Of a sort," MacLeod says. "It's a curse."

"A *curse*?"

MacLeod looks around suddenly, as if expecting the owner of the bag to show up, demanding its return. Then, without a word, he shoves the figure and the bag into George's hand.

"Burn them," he orders. "Throw it all into the fire as soon as you get in." He glances over his shoulder, peering into the dark. "Go now, while I'm here."

Confused, and more than a little rattled by the discovery of the sinister little bag in the roof and MacLeod's erratic behavior, she heads for the door. But before she enters, she looks back at MacLeod. "Good luck finding your sheep."

Something shifts in his expression. Before she can interpret it, he nods sharply. "Good night, Inspector."

Slipping inside, she bolts the door behind her and hurries to the sink, fixing the blanket back into place as best she can with her stiff fingers. Then she makes a beeline to the fireplace, shedding her layers until she's crouched beside the flames in just her underwear. She inspects the straw figure, turning it over in her hands for any identifying features, but it's just a simple human-like doll made of straw. No obvious sex, no indication of who made it or why it was in a bag full of rotten eggs that had been shoved into a crevice above their front door. She wonders if it was there before she and Richie arrived, or if some of the kids just wanted to play a gross prank on the two visiting mainlanders.

"Good try," she mutters, tossing the doll and the bag into the flames. They are immediately consumed, and the bag gives off a brief but awful smell as it burns. Although her eyes water, she keeps them trained on the figure; it is only when it has completely dissolved into ash that she relaxes.

It takes a long time for her body to warm up—time she spends thinking about the tumultuous events of the past hour. When she's thawed enough to pull her pajamas on, she crosses to the table and selects four blank cards. When she's finished writing, they read:

PERSON AT KITCH WINDOW. WOLF MASK. RAN TOWARD THE VILLAGE

PERSON AT L.H. TEEN(?) RAN BEFORE ID

A.M. OUTSIDE. MADE A.F. KILL SHEEP. "BUSY" D/O FUNERAL

STRAW DOLL + ROTTEN EGGS—PRANK??

As she takes the cards to the evidence wall, Richie lets out a particularly loud snore. She looks at his door, thinking. Two incidents in one night, then uncovering the stupid joke with the doll and eggs—all because she went out on her own. This is not the kind of behavior that will get her back in his—and Cole's—good graces.

A few minutes later, George is curled up beneath the heavy blankets and watching the cards join the ashes of the curse in the flames.

CHAPTER 15

HAVING BEEN TOO NERVOUS TO DISAPPEAR INTO A MEDICATED SLEEP, GEORGE is up and pulling on her clothes as soon as the first light of dawn breaks.

Making an effort to rug up properly this time, she slips out the front door with a beanie pulled low over her ears. Her breath clouds in the air, now mercifully free from the sulfurous reek of rotten eggs. She pauses to slide on a pair of gloves, looking out over the island.

There's something so insulated about early mornings, even from the top of an island in the middle of the sea. It's as if everything and everyone is emerging from a bout of shyness—the birds are tentative in their calls to one another, and the sound of the water lapping against the cliff is muted, giving her time to adjust to the new day. A break in the clouds allows the sun to paint the eastern sky with streaks of pale pink and gold, and she is momentarily struck by the effect it has on Eadar.

What was last night a scene from a nightmare is this morning a sleepy storybook village. Smoke rises lazily from chimneys, the frosted tips of the grass shimmer, and even the ocean is calm.

Can Alan Ferguson really have been so miserable here that he felt his only way out was death?

On her third trip to the lighthouse in as many days, she feels a deep sadness at the knowledge that this could very well have been the path Alan trod in his last moments. He wasn't warm, held, and comforted. Though legally an adult, Alan was just eighteen years old—a kid in George's eyes, a whole decade younger than her. At that age she was surrounded by people who were still figuring out what they wanted to do, who they wanted to be. She's always considered herself fortunate to have known that she wanted to join the police force as soon as she left school, but even now—*especially* now—she isn't sure if being a career cop is what she'll want in five, ten, fifteen years' time. And the realization that she has options makes her heart break all over again for Alan.

At eighteen, there shouldn't have been any pressure on him to decide what he wanted to do for the rest of his life. He should have had time to move and grow, make decisions and mistakes. He should have had a safety net of people to catch him long before he climbed up that cold tower. Whatever Alan could have been is now nothing more than imagination and regret.

Wanting to avoid cutting through the dewy grass, George continues along the dirt track that takes her the long way to the lighthouse entrance. Remembering MacLeod's spectral appearance the night before, her eyes flick to the woods. Even the trees look less threatening in this morning light, sunlight streaming through gaps in the canopy in soft golden beams that touch down like searchlights. She wonders if the farmer found his missing sheep, or if they became the latest residents of Eadar to fall to their death.

———

"Hello? Anyone up there?"

Her voice echoes up the stairwell. She takes the first flight slowly, announcing her presence twice more before she hits the first landing. It's hard to believe what happened in this room only hours earlier. She tries to picture what she must have looked like—huddled against the wall, hair still dripping down the back of her neck, knife clutched in her hand. Evidence of their flight has been captured in the dust on the floor; though there's an absence of defined footsteps, she can see a disturbance on the landing where the fleeing person pushed her aside.

It's no easier defining a footprint on the stairs as she proceeds to the second floor. The patches in the dust could just as easily be hers or Richie's footsteps from their initial visit two days ago. But as she enters the second room, she sees something that she and Richie definitely weren't responsible for.

"Damn," she mutters. Lying on its side beneath the window is an empty bottle of bourbon bearing a label she recognizes from back home. She gingerly picks it up by grasping the bottom of the neck between her gloved fingers, then rolls her eyes at herself. As if fingerprinting is even an option. Or a necessity.

It's exactly as MacLeod said—some kid snuck in here with a bottle to drink in peace and had the shit scared out of them when they heard her voice in the darkness. If she weren't so disappointed, she'd find it funny.

There's something else on the floor. George picks up the piece of paper and examines it. It's been softened with overhandling, crisscrossing lines indicating the numerous times it's been folded. One side of the page is blank, but on the inside is a hasty scrawl.

Look for the candle.

She scans the floor, the windowsill, the staircase, but there isn't a single candle. Is it a quote? A code? She wonders if the kid dropped this last night, or if she and Richie simply missed it during their first visit. Speaking of which . . . Richie will be stirring soon, and she knows he'll be worried when he doesn't find her on the couch.

However, her sleepless night is catching up with her already, and she slides down the wall to sit beneath the window. Markings on the sill catch her eye. She leans closer, struggling to discern some of the wonky initials that have been scratched into the aging wood. And it's with a surprised laugh that she realizes she's reading, with differing degrees of legibility, what could be the entire history of Eadar's sweethearts.

It's clear that this tradition has spanned many years—some of the scars are much older than others. A few couples have filled in the letters with pen or marker, making them stand out against the flaking paint. She traces a faded *H and J* encircled in a heart, an *O&M*, a fairly recent-looking *D+A* wedged between a fresh *S+T* and an ancient *K.P.* Her lips tug when she finds multiple *C+D*s, the sharp angles of the *C* hinting at the same amorous author each time. The sight of these small acts of passionate vandalism keeps the smile on her lips. No matter where you are in the world, the urge to declare love comes out in the same beautifully juvenile way.

Now the cold has officially reached her skin, and she clambers to her feet. With one final look around, she trots down both flights of stairs and lets the door swing closed with a heavy thud.

The kettle has just started to whistle when Richie emerges from the bedroom, his hair sticking up like a crest from the back of his head. He blinks at her, his hands tucked in his pockets.

She stares at him. "You packed a dressing-gown?"

"I like my creature comforts, Lennox. What are you doing up so early?" He withdraws one hand to check his watch.

"Went for a run. Oh, I found out what was causing that weird smell. Someone had shoved a bag of rotten eggs into the roof."

He laughs, a shocked sound. "What? Why? Some kind of prank?"

She remembers MacLeod's face when he found the bag and the straw figure inside, his explanation of its intention. "I think it was meant to make bad things happen to us."

He pulls a face and looks around. "What did you do with it?"

"Chucked it in the fire. But maybe we should ask around today, see if we can figure out who put it there?"

Richie rubs his forehead roughly, then he heads into the bathroom. "Just jumping in for a quick shower."

"I'll have a cuppa waiting. Hey, be careful getting in," she calls as the door closes behind him, "just in case the curse worked. Don't want you breaking a hip."

He doesn't dignify her warning with a response.

Less than ten minutes later he returns to the kitchen, and by that time George has the table set with two plates, all the remaining spreads from Kathy's basket, and two cups of tea.

"You went for a run?" Richie asks as he sinks into a chair. "Couldn't sleep?"

"Got a few hours," she answers honestly.

He looks guilty. "You should take the bed for the last two nights. It's not fair for you to be doubled up on that couch the whole time."

She waves away his suggestion with her toast. "It's not the couch. And it's not . . ." She gestures to her head. "I was just restless. Besides," she adds smugly, "out here, I'm closer to the fire."

He grunts. "Yes, I do feel a chill creep under my covers in the wee hours of the morning. But then I put on my bed socks and fall straight back to sleep."

"You're too young to say so many elderly things in one sentence."

"I choose to take the compliment from that, so thank you,

Lennox. Although, these gray hairs beg to differ. But at least they mean I'm still here."

"And I'm sure Jenny isn't complaining. She has a thing for silver foxes."

His eyebrows fly up. "When did she say that?"

"At your birthday dinner," she says, hiding a smile behind her mug. "She, Poppy, and I were watching you throw a royal tantrum over the pizza oven—"

"Now, hold on, that oven was *brand new* and I hadn't quite figured out—"

"And she sighed and said, 'At least he's starting to look like Iain Glen.' Then she made me and Poppy go help you."

Richie's face has gone comically blank. "Iain Glen?" he repeats, one hand sweeping absently through his hair, tugging at the strands. "Well, that's just . . . just . . ." He straightens up, squinting at the cards on the wall. "What's the plan for today?"

Generously ignoring his pink cheeks, George rises with her tea and crosses to the wall. "We should talk to Fiona Bell, Alan's ex-girlfriend. Catriona said Fiona had no hard feelings toward Alan at the time of his death, but their relationship ended on bad terms. Plus, she's the same age as him—she might have more insight into what he was like in the years leading up to his death."

"Agreed. And I had a couple of thoughts as I was getting into bed, so I'd like to meet with Catriona again to ask a few more questions."

Remembering what Cecily told her about Catriona's husband, George is also keen to speak with her. She finishes her tea in two large gulps, ignoring how it scalds her throat. "Let's get going, then."

Richie gestures at his plate, offended. "Let a man finish his toast, would you?"

"We've only got two more full days here, Rich. Bring it with you."

Grumbling as he pushes back his chair, Richie snatches up his plate. "You'll give me leave to change out of my pajamas, yes?"

———

If she hadn't confirmed her name, George might have assumed that the woman who opens the peeling brown door of the house next to the butcher was Fiona Bell's mother. Her square face seems to belong to someone far older than her alleged eighteen years, the effect not helped by the crooked nose and sagging brow bone of a boxer. A yellowing bruise along her jaw suggests that Fiona recently competed in a match. George wonders if the scowl on her face is for them, or something left over from a defeat.

"What the fuck do you want?"

It's for them.

"I'm DI Stew—"

"I know who you are," she interrupts, fixing the twisted strap of her sports bra. "I asked what you want."

Richie blinks. "We want to ask you some questions about Alan Ferguson. I understand you two dated for a while."

"Yeah, ages ago," Fiona says, crossing her thick arms. "What's that got to do with anything?"

"Can we come in?" George asks.

Fiona grits her teeth as she looks between the two of them, then leans out to look up and down the street. "Fine," she mutters, stepping aside to let them pass. "You've got ten minutes, all right? Then I'm meeting my da for training."

They follow Fiona down a narrow corridor. The Bell boxing legacy is clear from the photos on the walls showing generations of square-faced men with their hands raised in a fighting stance or held above their heads in victory. The latest photos are in color and show younger versions of Fiona, often bloodied and bruised, holding golden belts that shine in the camera's flash.

Fiona bypasses the small kitchenette and steps outside into a tiny courtyard. A glass table has been shoved all the way against the left side of the fence, two legs creating deep divots in the barren flowerbed. There's a skipping rope on the table. Without preamble, Fiona picks up the rope and whips it over her head. Despite the uneven pavers that threaten to snag the rope, she doesn't miss a beat. The wide arc of the rope and limited space in the courtyard push George and Richie back into the doorway. George decides to conduct the interview with one foot in the kitchen.

"I want to assure you that you're not in any trouble," she says. "We're just trying to get a better understanding of what Alan was like, and why he might have taken his own life."

"Well, like I said," Fiona responds, an edge to her voice that could be annoyance or exertion, "we dated ages ago."

"How long were you together?" Richie asks.

The rope loops over her head. "Three months?"

"In that time, or afterward, did Alan ever mention having trouble at home or with friends?"

"Dunno. We didn't talk much. Too busy doing other things." She fixes Richie with a look that dares him to ask for clarification.

He doesn't, but George accepts the challenge. "You and Alan were sexually active during your relationship?"

Fiona shoots her a look that says *duh*. "Besides, we live in this shithole. There's not much else to do here other than fish, fight, or fuck."

"Any issues during your relationship?"

"Like what?"

"Sexual relationships aren't always smooth sailing."

Fiona pulls a face. "Do you really need to know all that?"

"It might help us get a better picture of Alan's frame of mind after exiting his relationship with you," Richie says.

"Exiting the relationship," Fiona snorts, still skipping at a consistent pace. "Makes it sound like my vagina is a Tesco."

God, George really wishes she could laugh. Beside her, she can tell Richie isn't sure whether to be amused or horrified.

With an exaggerated sigh, Fiona lets the rope go slack. "We didn't argue 'cos we didn't talk that much. I was—am—away a lot for matches." She pauses. "I think that's what he liked about me."

"That you weren't around?" Richie asks doubtfully.

"That I knew the world was bigger than this fucking rock. Not many other people here seem to get that. But I get it, and I'm actually doing something about it." She falls silent, and her brow furrows. "Alan got it. He was trying to leave, too."

Until now, George has been honestly wondering what it was about Fiona's personality that Alan was attracted to. But hearing the maturity in Fiona's words, she understands that to someone like Alan—who wanted more from life than silence and sea spray—Fiona's determination would have been inspiring.

"So, what happened between you two?" Richie asks.

The scowl returns to Fiona's face. "We didn't have any issues until I found out he was fucking some other girl. Then we had a massive fucking issue. I hit him," she says without shame. "Smacked him in his cheating mouth."

George struggles to keep her expression even, but it's not from stifled laughter anymore. "You assaulted him?"

"He deserved it. And it was either going to be me or Da, and trust me, he was relieved it was me. And I was pre-training, so he got off easy."

George senses that a lecture on battery wouldn't do much good here. "Who was Alan sleeping with?"

"Never found out. Lucky for her."

"Why? Would you have hit her as well?"

Fiona opens her mouth to answer, then she narrows her eyes. "Can I be arrested for saying what I wish I'd done?"

"I'm certain DI Lennox and I get the picture," Richie says tightly. "Do you have any theories as to who the young lady might have been?"

"Whoever she was, she wasn't from here."

This piques George's interest. "You think she was a main-lander?"

"Probably. Alan went there with some of the fishing lads. They stayed the night, and a few weeks later someone told me they'd heard some interesting sounds coming from Alan's room." She looks at Richie's notebook with a smirk. "I'm not a DI, but even I can connect the dots."

"So you confronted him?"

Fiona scratches her jaw, wincing as she presses too hard on the bruise. "Yep. He didn't try to lie about the cheating, which I respected, even though I was steaming. He said he wanted us to give it another go, that the thing with the other girl would never work out. Think he said she had a fella back home. But it was all over as soon as I heard what he'd done." Her chin rises defiantly. "You get one chance with me, and if you fuck it up, we're done."

Despite Fiona's obvious distaste for their presence, George is actually starting to like her. "Is that the attitude you take into the ring? We've been told you've got a bit of a reputation on the mainland."

At that, Fiona's face transforms from her signature scowl into an expression of genuine pride. Suddenly the smashed fea-tures suit her. "I've got a reputation across the entire UK, love. Fiona Rings the Bell," she says in a booming voice, "that's what they call me, 'cos I'm always the last one standing." She eyes George appraisingly. "You look like you could throw a punch. And take one."

George recalls Lewis's shocked expression when she planted him into the ground the day before, but tries not to look too outwardly pleased with Fiona's assessment. As Fiona starts coiling the rope, George steps closer, away from Richie. "Did he have any close friends? Someone he might have spoken to about how he was feeling?"

But even before Fiona even answers, George knows what she's going to say.

"Nah, he was more of a thinker than a talker. I guess that's what I liked about him." She squints as if trying to remember. "He'd tell me *some* things."

"Can you remember what?"

"Uh . . . I'm sure he talked about his ma, if they were getting into it over something. His schoolwork, but he knew that shit bored me. Talked about whatever odd jobs he got pushed into doing on the boats. I do remember him complaining about one of the lads down there, always had some annoying job for him to do." Fiona makes a face. "But normal, boring shit, y'know? The stuff you say when you're zipping up your trousers."

"What can you remember about the day Alan died?" Richie asks, edging into the gap George has vacated.

Fiona rolls her eyes. "Well, it was fucking awful, wasn't it? Me and Da were training and my ma came in yelling and crying her eyes out. Da went up to the lighthouse to check if it was true. I wanted to go, too, but Ma was going to pieces. She really liked Alan, despite it all."

"Your family didn't hold a grudge against him?" Richie asks.

"We didn't hang out anymore, but like I said, I'm barely here. And probably won't be for much longer—there's a manager on the mainland who's trying to get me into the US circuit. And when that call comes, it'll be a one-way trip."

Richie seems surprised. "You wouldn't want to come back?"

"Fuck no. Why would I?"

"It's your home, isn't it?"

She opens her mouth, then shakes her head. "If anyone has told you that they're happy here, they're lying through their fucking teeth, all right? This island is a prison, only you don't know if you're a prisoner or a guard until someone hands you a uniform."

Before George can even process that sentence, Fiona checks her watch. "And that's ten minutes."

CHAPTER 16

FIONA EXITS WITH THEM, SNAGGING A SPORTS BAG FROM INSIDE THE FRONT door before pulling it shut behind her.

There are a fair few islanders out today, ducking into shops or down side streets. A group of young girls hunch over something on the ground by the harbor steps, then shriek when one rises with the skeletal remains of a fish pinched between her thumb and forefinger. An elderly couple smile indulgently at the girls, leaning into each other as they look out over the boats.

Something feels strange about the scene, then George finally puts her finger on it. There's no sense of urgency to their pace. It's so unlike the rush of the city that it seems to George as if they're all moving in slow motion.

"Catriona mentioned that you dropped by to see her after Alan died," Richie says, and George drags her attention back to the task at hand.

For the first time, Fiona looks a little self-conscious. "It's what you do, isn't it? When someone dies? I mean, it wasn't her fault he lost his mind." She looks at her watch again.

"When's your next fight?" George asks.

Fiona grins. "Next Thursday in Fort William. You should come. Kathy's got the flyer in the window." She jerks her thumb up the hill in the direction of the post office. "I'll sign it for you when I win." She breaks into a jog, heading toward the path to the beach.

"Well," Richie says, retrieving a hanky from his pocket. "She's a charmer."

"I wouldn't want to go toe to toe with her. I'd throw in the towel as soon as I saw her walk in."

Richie hums in agreement. "What did you think of her story? The breakup sounded quite amicable, apart from the punch."

"Maybe that's just the island's justice system," George jokes, then glances back at the Bell home. "How about this mysterious mainland girl?"

Richie groans. "I'm not spending the next twelve months hunting down a hypothetical homewrecker who could be living anywhere on the west coast of Scotland."

"But it's another piece of the puzzle," George insists. "What if he fell in love with this mainlander? According to Catriona, Alan didn't date anyone else after he and Fiona broke up. What if he actually *was* seeing someone?"

"You think he was carrying on a long-distance relationship?" He considers this for a moment, then turns to her with a serious expression. "Do you think Kathy let him use the satphone, or were they sexting via smoke signal?"

She looks at him, impressed. "How do you know what sexting is?"

"I'm old, but I'm not *dead*," he sniffs, then glances in the window of the butcher. "Think we need to start fending for ourselves?"

She joins him at the window, cupping her hand on the glass to see inside. "I'd kill for anything that isn't fish. But how fresh do you think this meat is?"

As they debate the pros and cons of the different cuts of meat on display, footsteps approach from the right. She expects to hear them step off the path to go around them, but when the person maintains their course directly toward George, she turns just in time to see the clenched fist swing toward her face.

The knuckles of a bony hand connect with her cheekbone. She staggers back into the glass, which thankfully holds. A ringing sound fills her ears and she gasps more from shock than pain, raising her hands to cover them.

The assailant—an old man with a bristly beard—pursues her, already cocking his arm to strike again, but Richie darts in front of her and catches the man's forearm in a tight grip.

I'm fine, George barks at her racing heart. *I can think, I can move, I'm all right.* She hisses as pain ripples up from her cheek to her forehead. Richie's shouts are muffled beneath the ringing; all she can hear are her own hitched breaths. She works her jaw, pressing her tongue against her teeth. Satisfied that none are loose, and relieved to not feel any dizziness setting in, she launches forward to offer backup to Richie. But it's clear that he doesn't need it.

Up close, she observes that her attacker is wizened, with cloudy brown eyes and sagging jowls. His ropy arms indicate a past life of hard labor, but his limbs are racked with tremors now. It becomes less about Richie restraining him and more a struggle to hold the man up—the punch seems to have used up all his energy. She hurries to his other side and helps Richie lower him to the steps at the butcher's entrance. By now the butcher has pressed his face against the window, peering down at them with mouth agape. A handful of islanders who witnessed the attack have frozen in place, staring in shock. Further away, the handful of fishermen who were working down at the harbor have crept closer and stand in a silent huddle on the steps.

"What on earth were you thinking?" Richie asks, crouching down beside the man with one hand still gripping his arm. "Why have you gone and done something foolish like that?" He glances at George, concerned. "How you doing there, Lennox?"

She nods tightly, averting her eyes so that he won't see the remnants of fear in them. "I'm just glad it wasn't Fiona."

The man wheezes, his thin chest rattling visibly with the effort. His eyes flick between their faces, across the street, up to the sky. George wonders if perhaps his mind isn't all the way there, and the expression on Richie's face confirms he's thinking the same thing. She looks around at the bystanders and singles out a tall man wearing a baby sling, an infant snoozing against his chest. "Excuse me—what's your name?"

The man seems startled to be addressed, but takes a small step forward. "Andy."

"Andy, can you tell me who this is?"

Andy looks at the man in disbelief. "It's Spud."

Richie frowns. "Spud?"

"Stephen Mackay—Spud, we call him. He owns that orange boat down the end." Andy bends down as far as the sling will allow him, trying to get in Stephen's eyeline without coming too close. "What've you done, you silly bugger?"

Stephen either doesn't hear Andy or he's too exhausted to respond.

"Does he do this often?" Richie asks, cautiously loosening his grip on Stephen to peer into his eyes, checking the pupils.

Andy looks around at the others who have gathered, none of them daring to come closer. "I didn't even know he was . . . like this. He stopped coming out on his boat months ago—Harry just said his joints have been bad."

Stephen's head droops suddenly, and George places a hand under his chin to support his neck. "We need to get him inside," she mutters to Richie, then to Andy says, "Where does he live?"

Andy points a few doors down from Fiona's home. "Down there, with his grandkids."

"Do they look after him?"

He looks down at the quivering man crumpled in Richie's arms, and a strange look passes over his face. "We didn't know he needed looking after."

Based on the power behind his punch, George is taken aback by how easy it is to lift Stephen to his feet. If Richie wasn't here, she thinks she could have carried Stephen into his house on her own. But Stephen has regained some strength in his legs, swaying on the spot while George and Richie loop their arms around his waist. As George wraps her other hand around his wrist, Stephen's glassy eyes suddenly focus on her. She feels his body tense before he even opens his mouth, but she tightens her grip before he can pull his arm back.

"Get away," he shouts in a quavering voice, thrashing weakly. "Mainland scum!"

"Delightful," Richie remarks sourly. "Come on, Mr. Mackay, let's get you home."

Stephen resists, trying to tug his arms free, and snarls something in Gaelic.

"Did you catch any of that?" George asks Richie.

"Not a word," he mutters. In a louder voice, he says, "We're just taking you back inside, Mr. Mackay. Can you tell me if you're on any medication, or have you had anything to drink today?"

Stephen just continues to rant in Gaelic, and she figures it's probably fortunate that she doesn't understand what he's saying. As the old man draws a rattling breath, she hears Richie mumble to himself, "Remember why you love this job."

As they approach his front door, a teenage girl flies out, her long red hair pulled back in a high ponytail. She looks around frantically, and when she sees Stephen suspended between George and Richie, her eyes widen.

"Granda!" she shouts, flinging herself forward. "What's happened?"

"Your grandfather just assaulted my colleague," Richie says sternly.

The girl blinks up at Richie, tears welling. "I'm so sorry, it's all my fault. He was calling out for tea, but I had a paragraph to go on my essay and I just wanted to get it finished before I went downstairs." She turns her watery eyes on George. "Are you all right, Inspector? He didn't mean it, I promise. He just gets upset if nobody comes when he calls."

Her eyes dart to the inquisitive islanders who are still watching. George follows her gaze and is surprised to see how stony some of their expressions are . . . and some, George notes, are looking at Stephen with shifting glances of unease, as if he were a rabid dog whose bite they feared.

George lets the girl take over supporting her grandfather, going ahead to hold the door open so that the three of them can maneuver through the narrow entry.

A musty smell saturates the space, and the further they stagger into the house, George realizes why. There is stuff *everywhere*—newspapers, furniture, piles of books, and boxes of tools and mechanical parts. They deposit the old man into an armchair in a cluttered sitting room. Within seconds, Stephen's eyelids are fluttering closed.

"He'll be all right now," the girl says, though her tone is subdued. "Can I, um, get you both something to drink?"

But George doesn't want to risk Stephen waking up and seeing unfamiliar faces. Her throbbing cheekbone is a testament to the fact that he is unpredictable, and stronger than he looks. "Richie, fancy making some tea?"

Richie nods. "Kitchen this way?"

"Turn right at the end of the hall," the girl says, perching on the arm of her grandfather's chair. "What did he do?" she asks George, looking down at him with a trembling lower lip.

"Aside from send me flying, shouting mostly. He seemed quite upset to see us."

The girl looks at her guiltily. "I'm so sorry, miss—I mean

Inspector." She dips her head. "He's not violent, I swear. He just gets upset sometimes. Normally I'm there to calm him down, but today . . ." She sighs. "What . . . what did he say?"

George looks at the girl's youthful features, the premature worry lines on her forehead, and feels a deep wave of empathy for her. "I didn't understand much of it, but there was nothing that I'll take to heart. Are you looking after him on your own?"

"My brother helps, but he's out. It's just bad timing that I have assignments due this week."

"Are you still in high school?"

She shakes her head. "First year at university. I graduated early."

"Really?" George studies her for a moment. "Are you Sarah Mackay?"

The girl stares at her. "How did you know that?"

"We spoke with Mr. MacNeil yesterday. He said you were very clever."

Sarah's cheeks flush, bringing new freckles into view. "Oh, well. I try quite hard. You have to, if you want to be accepted into any of the big universities. There's a few of us doing it remotely, like me." Her words are lower, faster now. "I know a couple of kids want to move to the mainland, actually *go* to university there. Or to England. Maybe even *America*."

"You didn't want to do that?"

Sarah's smile slips, and her eyes cut toward her slumbering grandfather. "Oh, no. I—I'm quite happy to keep studying from here."

George's stomach sinks, regretting the question. "John also mentioned that you help him out with Calum," she says quickly.

"Oh, I just love Cal," Sarah says with a tender smile. "He's always got something new to show me from his wanderings."

"Are you able to communicate with him?"

Sarah nods, then her lips tug to the side. "Well . . . you've met him. I usually understand what he wants, because we've spent so much time together. And even when I don't understand, he's so patient with me. He just waits until it clicks."

"It must be hard for you, looking after Calum and your grandfather at the same time."

"Oh, I wouldn't say I'm looking after Granda," she says quickly. "He's very capable, very strong. He just gets bothered by little things."

Richie pops his head into the room. "How does Mr. Mackay take his tea?"

"Black with three sugars, thanks."

"And you?"

A pink tint warms Sarah's cheeks again. "Oh, um. One sugar, with some milk. Thank you, sir."

With a wink at George, Richie retreats again.

"We didn't introduce ourselves," George remembers. "That's Inspector Richard Stewart, and I'm Inspector Georgina Lennox."

Sarah smiles sheepishly. "Everyone knows your names."

How could she forget? "You can call me George."

Sarah's lips turn up at the corners, but they droop again as her grandfather lets out a low moan. Sarah reaches to feel his hands, then pulls a blanket off the back of the armchair and drapes it over his lap.

"A few of the people outside seemed surprised to see your granda acting this way," George says, keeping her tone light. "Is this behavior new for him?"

After a hesitation, Sarah nods. "Only in the last few months, really. We lost my grandma last year, and he hasn't been the same since. That's why Harry is lying about the boat. My brother, Harry," she adds, seeing the query on George's face.

"What do you mean he's lying?"

Her fingers twist in her lap, and she lowers her voice. "Harry told him that the engine needs a new part. We were worried about him getting out there on the water, and it would just be Harry there to calm him down in front of all the others."

"You don't go out there with them? Because of your studies?"

"Oh, no," she says matter-of-factly, then flicks her ponytail. "Because of *this*."

"Because of your hair?" But as she says it, she remembers the strange interaction she observed on the harbor steps the day before: the red-haired May MacGill prevented from nearing the boats.

"Yeah," Sarah says, her tone as serious as it was when she discussed her studies. "Ginger hair is a bad omen to fishermen."

"I swear I've seen men down there with red hair."

"Men are okay. It's just the girls who cause trouble."

"Jesus," George mutters, then says louder, "What else are we good for, I suppose?"

Sarah splutters a laugh, and though she looks far more relaxed now than she did when they first entered the home, the circles under her eyes are dark. It makes George wonder: if Sarah and her brother are looking after Stephen, who's been looking after them?

"It's just you and your brother here?"

"Yeah, but it's fine," she says in a rush, correctly interpreting George's scrutiny. "Granda's looked after us our whole lives, and now it's our turn. I don't mind at all."

"Have you considered asking some of your neighbors for help? I'm sure Kathy would—"

There's a glint of panic in the girl's wide eyes. "Oh, no— Granda wouldn't want anyone else helping him. He feels more comfortable when it's just me and Harry."

George looks out into the hallway. "Is Harry due home soon?"

"I don't know. He just got home from a long trip yesterday, so he's catching up with some people."

George wonders if the elusive Donald Campbell is among the returning party—she hopes so, for Cecily's sake.

Richie returns with two mugs. He places one down on a low table beside Stephen's chair, then hands the other to Sarah. "Here you go, miss."

"I'm really sorry about Granda," she says again. "He wouldn't have meant to hurt you, I promise."

"But it doesn't change the fact that he did," Richie says gently. "What is it about us mainlanders that gets him so riled up?"

Sarah takes a sip of her tea and shrugs. "I don't really know. He's been that way for as long as I can remember. The older folks have a lot of pride in the island, how we've survived."

Richie nods, though he doesn't seem convinced.

Stephen stirs, groaning again. Immediately Sarah is on her feet, her tea forgotten. "You should leave," she says in a whisper. "He'll only get upset again if he sees you in here."

George rises. She has a feeling that bringing the law down on Stephen will only end up punishing Sarah, and she doesn't want to make the young girl's life any harder. They allow her to push them toward the door, but George pauses in the doorway.

"Can we drop in tomorrow? I'd like to see if we can help."

Movement from within the house distracts Sarah, but she nods rapidly. "Okay," she whispers. "Good-bye, Inspector Stewart; bye, George." And she ushers them out.

They both stare at the door for a moment—George's gaze drawn irresistibly to the symbol she knows she'll find above the frame—then Richie glances at her curiously. "George, eh?"

"People like her get to use my name," she says, frowning up at the double spiral before backing away from the doorstep. "Jesus, what kind of a chance has she got at a career off this island if she's a full-time carer for her grandfather? And then there's Calum. If she does eventually go to a mainland university—or she graduates and gets offered work elsewhere—he'll lose one of the only two people on this island he can communicate with."

"I know," Richie says, "but that's a problem for later. How are you feeling? Your face is swelling."

"It's fine. I just hope Fiona didn't see what happened. She said she thought I could take a punch."

He doesn't let her brush him off. "Pain? Dizziness? Head injuries after a TBI can set off—"

"TBI? Look at you, Doctor Stewart."

His jaw clenches. "I spent two days learning all the words associated with a brain injury," he says flatly. "Two days wondering how many words *in general* you'd remember when you woke up—if you woke up at all. So I don't appreciate the tone."

Shame reaches a clammy hand into her chest, squeezing her lungs. She averts her eyes, unable to meet the hurt and frustration in his.

"Sorry. I promise—" No, she can't lead with a lie like that, not after his honesty. "It hurts, but I'll be fine. No permanent damage. Aside from my pride." She smiles reassuringly.

It takes a few long seconds, during which he appraises her expression and measures her truthfulness, before he beckons with his chin for her to fall into step, and they move on.

The people who witnessed the altercation with Stephen Mackay have dispersed. It's unclear if word has already spread about the incident and the fact that she was assaulted—there are certainly more eyes on them than usual as they walk back down the street—but George knows that the news will have made it to every house by sundown.

As they approach the butcher again, Richie tells her to wait so he can step inside. Lingering by the entrance, she tries to catch her reflection in the grimy glass. She runs her fingers over her cheek and grimaces at the lump that's already formed. She hopes it won't bruise too badly. Her parents were already worried enough about her coming here; she doesn't want to show up to her mam's birthday dinner next Tuesday with a shiner.

A crisp wind sweeps across the street from the water, and she turns her sore cheek toward it. Who needs an ice pack when you've got the frosty Eadar air?

Down at the harbor, people have returned to their work. One of them hauls a coil of thick rope across to the small shed and disappears inside; another sits on an upturned crate running a fishing net through his hands, checking for holes. Even at this distance, George thinks she recognizes him as the one who waved at Cecily yesterday.

She glances in the window. Richie seems to have ensnared the butcher into a conversation which, judging by the man's blank stare, seems to be one-sided. Figuring she has a few minutes before he's even close to choosing a cut of meat, she crosses the street and heads down the stone steps to the quay.

There are only five or six fishermen working on the half-dozen or so small trawlers moored along the inner wall of the harbor, and they see her coming: elbows are dug into ribs, chins jerked in her direction. A few call greetings as she passes, which she acknowledges with a wave. The man twisting the net through his hands doesn't look up at first, though when it becomes clear that she's stopped beside the crate he's sitting on for a reason, he looks up.

George suspects that, like Fiona Bell, this man is much younger than his weather-beaten face suggests. Children seem to grow up quickly here. Though she guesses a life on the water, battered by wind and sun, is responsible for the broken capillaries in this man's cheeks and nose, the deep lines beside his mouth and eyes. A faded scar runs through his left eyebrow, which is now raised as he looks her up and down, the damage to her cheek catching his attention only briefly.

"No comment," he says, returning his focus to the net.

She grins; the movement sends a crackle of pain through her cheek. "I'm not a reporter."

"Doesn't matter."

"You waved yesterday, right?"

"No."

Appraising him again, George wonders if she's misidentified the man. They're all wearing the same clothes in the same faded colors with the same hardened faces. "Regardless, I'm sure you know why I'm here."

"Aye," he grunts. "Going around asking questions about what happened, upsetting Catriona. And that there with Spud. Never seen him like that before you got here."

"We're not here to cause problems. We just want to find out why Alan did what he did."

He looks up at her again, now with open suspicion. "I already told you, no com—"

"How about you let me ask a question first?" she asks, irritation flaring. "Then you can decide if you've got an answer or not." After a long moment of sullen silence, she proceeds. "Let's start with your name."

The silence stretches so long that she guesses it's his new tactic to avoid engaging with her. But she sees him check their surroundings with a furtive glance, and when he sees there's no one in earshot he mutters, "Ewan."

"And your surname?"

He glares at her, and she holds up her hands. "Fine. No surname necessary."

One of his hands, toughened by a life of hard labor, moves delicately under the net until it reaches a spot where debris has caught in the rope, forming a knot. He bends down to retrieve a small knife from the ground and works delicately to free it.

"Did you ever work with Alan?"

His hands still on the rope momentarily. "Saw him around."

"Did you ever speak with him?"

"I don't know."

"You don't know if you ever spoke to the boy who just died?"

"He didn't come out on the boats that much. He had the farm job, and Catriona was making him concentrate on school, too."

"How many times did he go out, would you say?"

Ewan growls as the knife slips out of the knot. "Maybe three or four," he says through gritted teeth, rethreading it.

"And when he was out with you, did you ever hear . . . ?" She trails off, checking that nobody is hovering too closely. She drops to a crouch beside him. "Did anyone ever talk about Alan seeing someone on the mainland?"

The sudden ferocity in his expression makes her muscles tighten. She won't be caught off guard for a second time today.

"Who told you that?" he demands. The knife is now clenched in a white-knuckled grip.

She keeps her eyes on it as she says, "Someone said they thought it could be why he and his girlfriend broke up."

"They broke up because he didn't—" Ewan cuts himself off with a sharp breath, shaking his head.

"Didn't what?" She bites her lip then takes the risk, shuffling minutely closer to Ewan. "Didn't . . . love her?"

She hears his next breath, the catch in his throat.

"Did he love someone else?" she presses. "Was it . . . *is* it someone you know?" It's a gamble, but she has nothing else to go on. "A sister? A friend?"

Something stormy—angry, resentful—darkens his face. "How the fuck would I know?"

"They wouldn't be in trouble," George says softly, trying to counteract his anger. "And neither would Alan, all right? So what if he cheated? He was just a kid."

"He wasn't a kid," Ewan snaps. "He was a grown man, and he knew what he was doing."

Trying to keep up with Ewan's erratic train of thought, George nods along. "Okay, yeah. You're right, he was an adult. And if he did something wrong," she hedges, "then it makes sense that people would be upset with him."

"You finished with that net?"

George and Ewan both look up to see a couple of men standing beside the first boat, watching them. One of them takes a step forward. "I'd like to catch some fish in it sometime this century."

"Bugger off," Ewan shoots back.

The man calls out again, this time in Gaelic, and Ewan returns his attention to the net with renewed vigor.

"So . . ." George says, sensing the eyes still on the two of them, "you were saying?"

She thinks he isn't going to answer; the moment drags on longer than is comfortable, and she is wondering if she should repeat the question or abandon the interview when he finally mutters, "Things would be much better around here if everyone just minded their own damn business."

"Lennox!"

Richie stands at the top of the quay steps, a paper-wrapped parcel in one arm, a net bag hanging from the other. He makes a gesture to ask if he should join her, but she shakes her head. Based on the tense set of Ewan's broad shoulders, she knows she won't get anything else out of him today. "All right, well . . . thanks for your time, Ewan. If you remember something, or if there's someone you think I should talk to, please come and find me."

He just grunts, and she heads for the stairs. Before she climbs them, she looks back over her shoulder to see Ewan has abandoned the knife and is now yanking savagely at the knot with his hands.

CHAPTER 17

"WHO WAS THAT?" RICHIE ASKS WHEN GEORGE JOINS HIM UP ON THE STREET.

"One of the fishing crew. I think he knows who Alan dumped Fiona for, but he got pretty worked up when I pressed for a name."

Richie peers over her shoulder, frowning. "Think he's protecting someone?"

"Don't know. But it makes me wonder how severe the consequences for adultery are. He was a bit all over the place—I couldn't keep up with him, to be honest." She looks at Richie's laden arms. "What've we got here?"

"Couple of steaks courtesy of Harold the butcher, and Kathy spotted me through the window and passed on this." He peers down into the net bag. "She rattled off what's in there, but I can't remember a thing. And she got angry when I offered to pay for it."

"It's either aggressive hospitality or straight-up aggression with these people, eh?"

Richie grunts in agreement. "I also gently requested that she not go into the croft without one of us present. She seemed genuinely surprised when I brought it up."

"She tried to say she hadn't done it?"

"No, she was just taken aback that there might be somewhere on this island that she isn't allowed to go. Luckily, she'd already handed the goods over, or I suspect we might have gone hungry today. Now, let's get up to Nicholson's and have a proper look at your face." When she starts to protest he cuts her off. "No, shut it," he says. "It's a workplace incident and we need to write up a report. Revisiting Catriona can wait till this afternoon."

She reluctantly agrees, shooting the sun a threatening look. They've been limited in their ability to interview people by how short the daylight hours are here, and there are still so many people to speak to before the police launch returns to pick them up—even if it's just to confirm what they've already surmised about Alan.

They start walking toward the path that leads up the big hill, which takes them right past Cecily's house. As they approach, the front door opens and Cecily appears holding two steaming mugs. She looks their way and her gloomy expression brightens into a wide smile.

"Hello, you two! Where have you just come from?"

Richie holds up his parcels. "Getting some supplies, among other things. How are you, Mrs. Campbell? Any word from your husband?"

"No, and he'd want to have a brilliant reason for it. Join me for a cuppa?" She nods toward the two in her hands. "A couple of the lads down by the boats begged me for a hot drink, but they can wait a while longer."

"Thanks for the offer," George says, "but we're heading up the hill."

"All right. Stop by later, though." Suddenly her eyes go round. "What *happened*?"

If the building throb in her cheek is indicative of how it looks, George isn't surprised by Cecily's reaction.

"Hazard of the job," she says briskly, feeling an urge to protect Sarah Mackay's privacy.

Cecily comes down the front steps to get a closer look and winces. "That's going to be nasty tomorrow," she says, and

George's heart sinks. "May I? You can see my first-aid training in action."

"Good idea," Richie says before George can decline.

Handing him the mugs, Cecily prods at George's cheek softly, moving in a widening spiral around the lump. George's eyes water traitorously.

"Hmm. There might be a fracture. You're a bit clammy, too."

"I'm fine," George says quickly, trying to convince both Cecily and Richie. "I'll just put a cold cloth on it."

"A cloth?" Richie holds up the parcel of steaks. "What do you think these are for?"

Cecily wrinkles her nose. "I can do better than both those options." She disappears into the house and returns seconds later with something wrapped in a checkered tea towel. "Return it to me later. Donald will need it when I'm through with him."

———

At the base of the hill, Richie allows George to take the bag from him without protest. The resentful look he gives the incline ahead makes her laugh, then wince from the resulting pain.

"Kathy asked us to join her for dinner tonight at the pub," he says as they begin the climb. "How do you feel about a steak lunch?"

George whistles through her teeth. "I don't think I should commit to anything that requires vigorous chewing right now."

Over the next couple of hours, the pain grows from a localized throb to a full-head pulse; so much that she wonders if Cecily was right and the blow fractured her cheekbone. Having violently resisted Richie's attempt to press one of the steaks to her face—"Well, you're not going to eat it, are you?"—she lies on the couch with her eyes closed, holding the ice block Cecily gave her to her cheek. One of her legs is bent off the couch, and her foot taps against the floor in an irregular rhythm.

"For a little old man, he's got a hell of an arm on him." She moves her jaw and groans as the pain shoots down her neck.

"Did you take the painkillers I gave you?"

She pushes herself up into a sitting position. "Not yet. God, my whole head is thumping now."

"You don't think you have a concussion, do you?" Richie asks, hovering at the arm of the couch. "Let me see your eyes."

"My head is fine—it just feels like my heart is in my mouth." She pops two painkillers from the foil packet and slips them between her lips. "These will help."

They won't. Her tolerance for pain medication is way too high for these supermarket pills to make a dent.

She gulps down the water Richie has fetched for her then reaches for her boots, hoping her partner doesn't notice the tremor in her fingers. "Right, let's go."

But Richie holds up a hand. "No, no—you're done for today."

She stiffens. "Excuse me?"

"Lennox, you were assaulted. You have to rest."

"I was clipped by a confused old man with bony hands." She shifts the ice block and suppresses another groan. "It's not like I was stabbed."

"I don't care. It's protocol." He sinks into a chair and pulls his own shoes toward him. "I'll have to let Cole know. They never tell you how much of this job is paperwork, do they?"

He reaches for the report they already filled in, after some debate over whether she's sustained a "cheek injury" or "head injury." George argued ferociously against writing the report at all, worried that it might affect Cole's decision about her readiness to return to work.

"I'll let Kathy know we won't be coming to the pub tonight," he says.

"Rich, a banged-up cheek might bench me from investigating for one afternoon, but it's not going to keep me from another meal."

He chews his lip, considering. George knows how much Richie loves pub food; she hopes this will work in her favor. "We'll see how you're feeling when I get back," he says finally, crossing to the door. "As long as you stay put until then. Got it?"

She makes a show of lying down again, then gives him a thumbs up over the back of the couch. The sound of his chuckle reaches her a second before the door closes behind him.

As soon as she hears the crunching of his footsteps fade, she sits up and opens her briefcase. The shaking in her hands makes it hard to separate a single pill from the mix, but eventually one lands on her tongue and she swallows. She feels it slide all the way down her throat, dry and uncomfortable, yet she heaves a relieved sigh. She just has to distract herself until the painkiller kicks in . . . which is how she finds herself reaching yet again for the logbooks.

When she skips ahead to the third and final volume, the tone of the entries starts to change. The men report clumsy mistakes, more oversleeping—even by Smith and McClure—and Wilson admits to being reprimanded after an argument with some locals ended with punches thrown. As the last entry grows closer, it becomes evident from the deteriorating quality of the handwriting that all the men are struggling now. Even Smith's comparatively wordy reports are brief—some days he doesn't even mention the tasks he's completed or whether any ships passed by. Yet despite the lack of description, George can *see* it. The lack of sleep making them clumsy, irritable; the tension and bickering between colleagues; and the prickling sensation of being observed, like the island itself is watching their every move.

And when she gets to one of Smith's final entries in late November, her breath catches in her throat.

> *Wilson cries. McClure will not speak. Rain, waves, thunder. Lightning turns night to day. We are surrounded. And then there is the howling.*
>   *It is inside our heads.*
>   *It is inside us.*
>   *It is inside.*

"Jesus," she mutters, slamming the book closed. Goosebumps have erupted on her arms, and she hauls the blankets over her to combat the shiver running down her spine. Those poor men—exhausted, rebuffed by the community, and stuck here until the boat arrived with their replacements. A rescue that wouldn't come in time.

Though the eeriness of Smith's words reverberates in her mind for a while longer, the last few nights of interrupted sleep creep in with the silence. The fire burns high enough to keep the chill outside the walls, and as the pain and agitation retreat, her eyes close.

"George?"

She wakes with a jolt, sitting upright instantly and almost bumping heads with Richie.

Richie yelps, leaping away from the couch. "Good Lord, woman," he thunders. "You sprung up like a demon."

She groans, her mouth dry and hot. She prods the inside of her swollen cheek with her tongue and winces. "Ugh. What time is it?"

"Just after five," he says, still clutching at his chest.

She raises her wrist and squints at her watch, the face swimming. "You've been gone for three hours?"

"An hour of that was with Kathy alone," he says darkly. "I got pulled in for a lecture on the whole history of Eadar, but I had to cut her off when she got to the turn of the twentieth century. She told me I should read the logbooks, too—if I could pry them away from you, of course," he adds with a grin.

She scowls. "You should—they complained about the howling, too. I know it's the wind," she says quickly, getting in before he can mock her again, "but it really scared them." *And me*, she thinks, remembering the disturbing tone of Smith's last entry. "Did you talk to Catriona?" she asks, happy to change the subject.

"She wasn't home, so we'll go past in the morning. But I ended up doing a few more doorknocks, and then Father Ross invited me up for tea." He crosses to the kitchen and starts filling the kettle. "I asked him about Iain Ferguson," he says over the hollow sound of the water hitting metal. "I understand why Catriona might have avoided the topic. Apparently he was a mean drunk. There were rumors that he was hitting her, but she was doing her best to cover it up."

This surprises George. "Only rumors? Isn't the island motto 'Everyone Knows Everything'? Why wouldn't someone intervene?"

Richie shrugs. "We've seen it before, haven't we? The victim is too scared or embarrassed to ask for help, and the people who suspect are too nervous to call it out." Coaxing a flame to life on the stove beneath the kettle, Richie leans back against the bench. "Have you looked in a mirror lately?"

"Is it bad?"

"I imagine it's going to get worse, but it's already not pretty."

She gets to her feet and heads to the bathroom. "What time are we meeting Kathy?" she asks over her shoulder.

"I said I had to check on you."

George leans over the tiny sink to look in the mirror. "Whoa."

"You won't be winning the title of Miss Eilean Eadar tonight, I'm afraid."

With a shaky forefinger, she prods the shiny lump on her cheekbone. It's about half the size of a golf ball, and the swollen skin around it has an unnerving purple streak within the red. "It doesn't even look cool."

Richie appears in the doorway. "Yes, it does," he protests. "You look very cool. So tough. Like an action star." He taps his chin thoughtfully, then snaps his fingers. "Like Sigourney Weaver. Do you know who that is?"

"I'm not *that* young. I'm sure this won't draw too much attention tonight."

The kettle starts to whistle, pulling Richie back to the kitchen. "Oh, word has already got around."

"And how many of them cheered when they heard?"

"A good third. But the rest were very concerned for you. We don't have to go out."

"No, it'll be interesting to see a lot of them in one place, especially after they've had a few drinks. Also, I'm very hungry and the thought of leftover fish stew is turning my stomach."

George chases away the lingering tiredness in her limbs with a shower, leaning away from the feeble spray to keep her hair dry. The tension she almost successfully eased from her muscles while lying in the bath last night is back. Angling her shoulders one at a time into the stream, she digs her fingers into the muscles beneath the skin. It's nice to focus on a pain other than the one in her face.

Not wanting to use up all the hot water, she steps out and dries herself quickly. Her regular uniform of thermals, jeans, and as many top layers as possible while still retaining the use of her arms will have to do for the pub tonight, but at least she'll blend in. And her mission for tonight is to remain unobserved; it's her turn to watch them.

But she catches her reflection in the mirror and is reminded that fading into the background tonight might be more difficult than usual. She wishes she'd packed some concealer.

Richie is still getting dressed when she enters the main room. She takes the opportunity to swallow another proper painkiller, chugging down the remainder of her water just as his door opens. She smiles, maybe too brightly, because she swears his eyes flick to her briefcase, now locked and in the corner again. But he doesn't say anything as they step outside.

The sun must have just slipped below the horizon. A low rumble reaches them from way in the distance.

"Is it supposed to rain tonight?" she asks. "We've still got Cecily's umbrella."

"It's coming tomorrow. About six different people warned me as I walked through the village that there's another huge storm off the coast." He buttons his coat up to his chin. "Come on, before the cold gets into my bones."

CHAPTER 18

SINCE NONE OF THEIR RESPECTIVE TOUR GUIDES HAD POINTED OUT THE PUB during daylight hours, George wonders if they'll need to knock on someone's door to ask for directions. But as soon as they step onto the main street, George realizes it won't be necessary. A lively melody stretches out from a narrow alley like a crooked finger, beckoning a steady flow of people within like the Pied Piper. Richie and George join the procession.

The music and a hubbub of voices are coming from a neat, whitewashed double-story building at the end of the alley, the windows ablaze with warm yellow light.

Richie nudges her. "Is it just me, or is this place the most well-kept building we've seen on the island?"

It's certainly not far off. Tucked down this side street and sheltered from the sea salt and relentless wind, the pub—named the Wulver's Catch—looks warm and inviting. A wooden sign hangs above the door with a painting on it that George can't see from this angle, but she can clearly make out the double spiral carved into the lintel. She doesn't bother pointing it out to Richie.

They're swept through the doors among a spirited group. As they enter the main room, Richie claps his hands together. "Perfect," he says, a grin lighting up his face.

The pub is cozy and crowded, voices overlapping and laughter booming over their heads. The music is coming from a small stage at the back of the room, currently occupied by a woman with graying hair and an older man with a fiddle. Her lilting voice weaves through the room effortlessly, even without a microphone. As George listens, she recognizes a folk song she learned at school.

Tall tables dot the swept stone floor, and a fire roars merrily in a large stone fireplace against the far wall. A long U-shaped bar divides the main room, on the far side of which are a few rough timber tables where the food is served. George spots many familiar faces—people they've spoken to or simply passed in the street—but there are plenty of strangers mixed into the crowd. When these people lock eyes with her, she is reminded by their curious expressions that she's the stranger here.

"Water?" Richie says into her ear.

"A beer, thanks." She ignores his disapproving look and taps her head. "No concussion, okay? I'll find us somewhere to sit."

She turns on her heel and makes her way through the crowd until she finds an empty table in the pub's back corner. It's on the far side of the room from the fireplace, which she assumes is the reason nobody is occupying it. Still, she feels eyes on her as she slides onto the seat. More than one person did a double take as she passed by.

Even this far from the fire, it isn't long before George feels warm enough to shuck off her heavy coat and lay it on the seat beside her. Richie appears not long after with a wine in one hand and a beer in the other, a basket of beer nuts balanced in the crook of his elbow.

"I ordered some food as well," he says, sinking into the seat opposite her. "Haddock makes up eighty percent of what's on offer, but everything is battered and served with chips so I figured you wouldn't mind me deciding for you."

"You made the right call." She angles her glass toward him. "Slàinte."

He knocks her glass with his own. "We don't usually do a

pub meal until we've closed a case. Feels strange to be here when we're still poking around." He takes a sip and smacks his lips. "Ah, well. We'll just have to do it again when we get home."

"We're definitely going with suicide, then?"

"I haven't seen anything to suggest otherwise. And don't look at me like that, Lennox, because neither have you." He holds up a finger as she opens her mouth. "I'll never tell you not to trust your gut. But a homicide needs evidence, and we've got nothing of the sort—because . . . ?"

"Because maybe there isn't any," she says resignedly.

"We'll go over what we've got tomorrow," he says placatingly. "And even if Father Ross hates the idea, I think we should put together a list of services that might improve the standard of living around here. We can send some information for John regarding the support he can get for Calum, too. What do you reckon?"

She takes a long pull of her beer. "Sounds like a plan."

Their food arrives surprisingly—worryingly—fast. It's as delightfully monochrome as every pub meal George has ever enjoyed, both battered fish and thick-cut chips an appealing shade of golden brown and glistening with oil.

"They don't even bother with salad," Richie says, looking at his own meal with glee. "Fantastic!"

It's easy to fall into their usual rapport as they eat—George flattening each bite with her fork to minimize the ache in her jaw when she opens it too wide—and she starts to feel surprisingly at home in their corner, with the normal sounds of a busy pub around them. They could be sitting in a booth at their regular back in Glasgow, a two-minute walk from the station. A favorite among their colleagues, that pub is always full of officers either celebrating a guilty verdict or drowning their sorrows.

Looking around at the assortment of people, George remembers what Father Ross said about the pub being the social hub of Eadar. People of all ages—definitely some on the young side of legal—are packed into the two halves of the room, crammed around tables or standing shoulder to shoulder at the bar. A few elderly patrons pick at their own fried fish, their conversation drowned out by a crowd whose faces George recognizes from the quay, along with some others who must be from the crews that went out today. Andy has his arm around a curvy blonde woman, the baby cuddled to her chest. Around the other side of the bar, a rowdy group of about fifteen people shout and drain their drinks in unison, then start shoving each other toward the door. George watches them with interest until her view is blocked by Kathy, who has suddenly materialized beside their table.

"You came!" she crows, then leans toward George. "My, DI Stewart wasn't kidding, you poor thing. You said Stephen Mackay did this?" At Richie's nod, she clicks her tongue. "I'll need to have a stern word to that man tomorrow."

"I don't know if that would be entirely helpful," George says quickly. "But his grandkids might benefit from someone checking in on them every now and again."

Kathy nods seriously. "I'll pop over tomorrow and get the lay of the land."

"I think Sarah would appreciate that. She seems like a good person."

"Oh, one of our best. She's destined for big things, that girl, and I just know she'll bring it all back home with her." Spotting their empty glasses, she snatches them up. "Same again?" Barely waiting for a reply, she slips back into the crowd, where she's enthusiastically greeted by everyone she passes.

Richie shakes his head, amused. "I've never seen someone so completely satisfied with their lot in life. Have you?"

"No. I'm a bit jealous, to be honest." She looks around the room again, this time focusing on the architecture. "I think you're right—this might be the best-looking place in the village. I wonder when it was built?"

Richie cranes his neck to look at the ceiling, the bar, the layout. "It's pretty traditional. I'd say around 1910, 1920."

"Kathy said there's been a community here for hundreds of years, and it's a fishing village. I don't think they waited until the 1900s to build the first pub."

They bicker until Kathy returns with their drinks, including one for herself. She slides in next to Richie, who turns to her. "Settle something for us. When was this pub built?"

Kathy's face falls slightly as she says, "1917." She takes a sip from her pint.

Richie pumps his fist.

"Was there another pub before that?" George presses, unwilling to concede.

After a pause, she nods. George immediately regrets mimicking Richie's victorious gesture when Kathy adds, "The original pub burned down. This one was built on the same spot."

"Oh, what a shame," Richie says. "That would have been a real piece of history."

"It was a shame indeed." Something catches her eyes, and her face brightens. "Oh, there he is! Over here, Lewis!"

Lewis, his head visible above the crowd, locates Kathy's voice and heads their way. When he spots George and Richie, he frowns down at Kathy. "I should have known you didn't just want a chat."

She widens her eyes innocently. "We can find our own table, if the inspectors' presence bothers you."

George starts to make room for him, guessing how this debate will end. She's right; as Kathy demands Richie's attention, Lewis folds himself onto the bench and places a pint on the table beside hers.

"Off duty?" he asks, nodding to her glass.

"In theory." She nods at Kathy. "Seems like she never takes a day off."

The last notes of a jaunty song fade out and applause fills the air. George turns to see the musicians taking a bow, the fiddler signaling to the barman for a drink.

Lewis sucks in a sharp breath. She jerks back and finds him looking at her cheek.

"I heard about Stephen," he says. "At least tell me you got him back."

"Did I hit the small, confused old man? No, I managed to keep my need for vengeance in check."

"Oh? I didn't know you had that restraint in you, given the way you put me on my knees yesterday."

She shrugs. "Serves you right for coming at me like that. You're lucky you look like a woodsman from a fairy tale, or I would have done some serious damage."

Lewis plucks at his wool-lined coat self-consciously. "At least I took the hat off tonight."

"Maybe you'll finally have some luck with the ladies here."

"Remind me when you're leaving again? I'm looking forward to the insults leaving with you."

She chuckles, taking a sip of her beer. "Sunday."

He nods thoughtfully, one finger tracing the lip of his glass. "How goes the investigation?"

She glances at Richie, wondering if he's got one ear tuned in to their conversation. "I think we're on the cusp of confirming what we already suspected."

"You think he did it to himself?"

"There's no indication of anyone having a grievance with him. He was private, but nobody noticed anything off about his behavior." She shrugs. "But then again, you never know what people are really thinking."

A muscle jumps in Lewis's jaw; he brings the glass to his

lips. "That's fair," he says before taking a long drink. "You could say that of a lot of people around here."

She raises her eyebrows.

He resumes playing with his glass, rolling the base in a circle on the table. When he speaks, the words come out in a rush. "You're born here, right? You're born, and everyone knows who your ma and da and grandparents and cousins are right away. And when you're a kid you do homeschooling, but it's mostly running wild, climbing cliffs, chasing birds and rabbits, running up and down those hills with no responsibilities. But then you get older and when you're not busy with school lessons you're at church learning about God and the saints and all the ways you're going to disappoint them throughout your life. Then you're told that the island needs three things to survive: security, money, and children. And the expectation is that you'll stop with school and go to work so you can contribute all three." He looks up, his eyes on hers. "You see what I'm getting at? It's hard to know what someone really thinks when they only have one option."

George's chest feels heavy. "But you left."

He stares into his glass. "I tried," he says quietly. "But there's something about this place that drags people back."

"You said you missed home."

He tilts his head, as if regretting his earlier choice of words. "I missed the home I knew as a child. I thought . . ."

"What?"

"Maybe if I came back, I could show the younger ones that they have more options."

She watches him swallow the rest of his beer in a gulp. "Your parents must have been happy you came back," she asks, striving for a lighter topic. But it doesn't work—Lewis looks even more morose.

"You'd think," he says with a dark laugh. "My ma didn't take too well to my time off traveling, and Da . . . well, she's the mouthpiece for that relationship. Da and I work together on odd jobs every so often, but let's just say that I'm not asked around for dinner much."

"And they're damn fools for it," Kathy says fiercely, clearly having eavesdropped on their conversation. "There are too few good men in this world, and your parents raised a great one. It boils my blood when parents turn their children away over such trivial things."

Lewis gives her a small smile. "Who needs parents when I've got you, Kathy? You're my biggest champion."

Kathy gives him a stern nod. "Don't you worry, I chip away at your ma every time I drop her letters around. If she keeps being stubborn, then maybe her packages start getting lost in the sea crossing."

Her deadpan expression draws a laugh from all of them, and as they shift into a group conversation, George is surprised to find she's actually enjoying herself. At Richie's request, Kathy happily continues her gossip-filled history of the village that he'd cut short earlier. After she finishes explaining that there's been a pub on the same spot they're sitting in since the seventeenth century, Richie asks, "Do you know how the original pub burned down?"

Kathy and Lewis exchange a loaded look.

"What?" George jokes, now on her third beer and feeling warmer than she has all week. "Is the memory of losing the entire island's supply of wee heavy in one night too painful to recall?"

But neither of them laughs.

Lewis sighs. "It happened long before I was born, obviously—before my grandparents were born, even—but we all know the story."

"The catch had been thinning for months," Kathy says.

"Empty nets piling up on the quay. The world around us was at war, and too many of our men had been called away to fight. Our remaining people pulled together as much as they could, but there was no denying that we were starving, and precious little help was coming from the mainland." Kathy's mouth turns down. "And there were some people who just couldn't take it."

"They left the island?" Richie asks.

"A few families did," Lewis says. "Those who stayed behind considered it a huge betrayal. But if loyalty means watching your loved ones slowly starve . . . well, I know what I would do. And then there were some who stayed who really should have gone."

Kathy picks the story up again. "The pressure got to people. And in the case of Broddy Cameron, well . . ."

"It drove him mad," Lewis finishes.

The logbooks flash in her mind, the keepers' increasingly scratchy handwriting, mirroring the malignant spread of their paranoia.

George glances at Richie, who shakes his head—he hasn't heard that name either. "Who's he?"

"He worked at the pub," Lewis says, then adds, "the original one. But he's the reason this one had to be built."

Richie leans forward, cupping his chin with his hand. "What happened?"

"The only evidence I've been able to find is correspondence between the council and the priest of the day," Kathy says. "They mention small things—Broddy was seen pacing his garden at night, got into fights with men he'd known his whole life. He stopped coming into the village, refused to go to church, and barricaded the door against the priest when he came by to coax Broddy back. Nobody knew what to do about him. He wouldn't listen to reason."

Richie tilts his head. "It sounds like a fairly understandable response to living with famine, not to mention a world war."

Kathy looks at Lewis. "I can never say the next part."

"A storm was rolling in one night, and a few people's dogs were sensing it," Lewis says. "But Broddy couldn't stand the barking, so he took a knife and went around to each house to shut them up."

"It spurred the village into action," Kathy continues, her voice wobbling. "Unfortunately, they did the only thing they could think of."

George cringes in anticipation. "It's going to be awfully medieval, isn't it?"

Lewis pauses before a sip. "Is chaining a man up in Mac-Leod's barn for three weeks medieval?"

Richie groans, his forehead dropping into his palm, and George feels a little nauseous with the knowledge that she's been inside that barn. Had she been too distracted by the sheep to sense the misery trapped in those walls? Or had generations of MacLeods worked their fingers to the bone scrubbing them clean?

"It was desperate times," Kathy says quickly, "and they couldn't afford to have someone running around out of their mind. It had been almost eight months of hell. Two people starved to *death*. They made sure Broddy got as much food as they could spare. He was treated with as much kindness as they could spare, too. But they had to be tough. This island has always had to look after itself. Since the first folk arrived here we've looked after our own. When the safety of the community is threatened, something has to be done. It's our way, and we've done it for almost a thousand years.

"And then one day, *finally*, the luck changed. The boats went out one morning and came back that night with full nets.

And the next day, same again. And every other day that week." The corners of Kathy's lips turn up. "Letters say they sang in the streets, they thanked God, and they all finally *ate*."

But then her face drops again, sending a coil of apprehension into George's stomach. When she doesn't resume speaking, Lewis continues.

"They held a celebration. A big party. The whole village turned up." He sighs deeply. "So that means there were about a hundred and fifty people crammed inside the old pub when Broddy Cameron broke free and made his way to the storeroom underneath it. Nobody knows how he got out of the barn, or what he was looking for. They're not even sure if he dropped the candle on purpose, but regardless of his intention, the effect was the same. The room was filled with timber barrels and impregnated with three hundred years of alcohol. The place went up like a bomb."

"Did everyone get out?" Richie asks, eyes wide.

"Almost."

"How many didn't?"

Lewis exhales heavily. "Twenty-two, including Broddy himself. So many lives lost in one night, all because of one man. Can you imagine what a loss of that scale feels like? Or what people might do to make sure it never happens again?"

"Hopefully they started with not locking people up for weeks on end," George remarks.

Lewis looks at her pointedly. "They didn't think they had any other options."

"It's why we're all so close," Kathy interrupts. "For centuries we'd looked after ourselves. Kept our community safe from things that threaten us from without and within. There were old ways of keeping the peace. Ways that have been forgotten on the mainland. But memories here are long. What happened that night with Broddy showed why the old ways are still vital. A reminder to hold our neighbors close. To protect each other at all costs. Even if it's from ourselves."

Lewis reaches over and squeezes her hand, and she smiles tightly. "And that's enough wine for me," she says with a shaky laugh, sliding away from the table.

"Shall I walk you home?" Richie asks.

She shakes her head. "But come by for a tea tomorrow." She waves at them then slips into the crowd. Lewis watches her leave, his expression sad.

"Who does the matchmaker go home to?" George asks.

"Nobody. Her husband was thrown off a boat during a storm about twelve years ago."

"Did they have children?" Richie asks.

He shakes his head. "They never figured out which one of them couldn't. It just never happened. That's why she's the third parent to every stray on this rock." He sighs heavily. "Another round?"

"Best not," Richie says. "We're back at it tomorrow."

George excuses herself to use the bathroom, stopping at the bar to ask for directions. Based on what she knows of the man, it's a surprise to see MacLeod hunched over a stool with a glass of whisky cupped in both hands. Though not typically one for conversation, he seems especially unapproachable tonight, but that hasn't stopped a man of similar age attempting to engage him in a slurred back-and-forth. She wishes she could ask him if he learned who put the curse in their roof, but she gives Mac-Leod the gift of ignoring his presence as she's directed toward the dining room.

The bathroom is tiny, with only a dim light overhead. Her foot taps to the muffled music, and as she washes her hands in the steel basin, her ears prick at the sound of a collective groan.

214 — LAURA McCLUSKEY

If she were back in her normal pub in Glasgow, she would have associated the sound with whatever sports game was playing on the TV at the time. But there are no TVs here. And when she hears the slap of bone against skin, she hurries out the door.

In her absence, a fight has broken out in the center of the room. She looks toward their booth, but both Richie and Lewis are gone—likely somewhere in the teeming mass of bodies surrounding whoever is involved in the fray. It's hard to make out what the two fighters are shouting above the sounds of the crowd, but apparently someone steps over the line because the next sound George hears is another punch landing.

"Police, let me through," she yells, shoving her way through the ring of onlookers who are enthusiastically lending their voices to the din. She spots Lewis trying to do the same thing from the other side, and when she finally breaks through to the open space, she finds Richie already there. He spots her with relief as he struggles to contain a purple-faced MacLeod, his arms outstretched toward the man George saw talking to him at the bar.

"What's going on?" George shouts to Richie, who shakes his head in bewilderment.

MacLeod roars something in Gaelic at the drunk man, spit spraying from his mouth. Blood oozes from a fresh split in his opponent's lip, and the man sways on his feet slightly as he pursues MacLeod across the floor, elbowing past restraining hands to line up a retaliatory punch.

George throws herself in his path and shoves him back into the arms of the crowd. "Don't even think about it," she orders, bracing herself for his second attempt.

It comes fast; the man rallies, throwing himself forward with a snarl. She blocks him again, but this time she twists one of his arms behind his back.

Lewis abandons crowd control to lend his strength to

Richie as MacLeod renews his efforts to choke the life from his assailant, who starts to cackle wildly. He only resists a little as George forces him to turn around, marching him forward until she can shove him into a group of people on the edge of the ring. Ewan is among them; he has blood dripping from his nose. George guesses he was part of an unsuccessful attempt to break up the fight before she arrived.

"I strongly advise you to get him out of here before I have to put him in handcuffs," she says to the crowd, and to Ewan she says, "You all right?"

He waves away her concern, his eyes shifting awkwardly. She can empathize—she was also caught off guard by a punch from an old man today.

The group exchange glances, some clearly questioning whether they need to follow her orders. But then a freckled woman with cropped hair seizes the drunk man's collar and tows him to the door and the others quickly join in, Ewan included.

Now that the shouting has stopped, the bar is strangely quiet. Lewis mutters into MacLeod's ear in a low voice. George watches the fight drain out of MacLeod's body.

"Come on," Richie says, gripping MacLeod's shoulder. "I'll walk you home, man." He shoots a look at George. She responds with a small nod—missions assigned.

The crowd parts quietly to let MacLeod and Richie through, and she and Lewis are left standing in the middle of the circle. In the strained silence that follows, George turns on the spot and meets as many eyes as she can.

"Someone want to tell me what that was about?" she asks in a tone that expects answers. So much for being off duty.

A few people cast their eyes to the ground while others just meet her gaze blankly.

Lewis crosses his arms over his chest. "Don't make her ask again."

An older woman with tightly curled black hair steps forward. "They were just drunk, Inspector."

"What were they arguing about?"

There's some more reluctant shuffling before the barman pipes up. "Iain Ferguson."

George frowns. "Why?"

"MacLeod was a friend of Iain's. He didn't like what Bill was saying."

"Which was?"

The barman hesitates, but a slurred voice near Lewis chimes in. "That Alan was just like his daddy."

She spins to confront a woman with glossy eyes and a half-filled glass of white wine halfway to her lips. "What do you mean by that?"

The woman shrugs, the movement causing her wine to slosh. "Something wrong with them, eh? In *here*," she adds, pressing a hand to her chest before raising it to tap her temple, "and *here*. Bill said we shouldn't have let Iain breed."

There's an angry hiss from someone in the crowd; George finds more than one person is glaring at the woman. George shakes her head, then winces when pain pulses behind her eye—the last thing she needs is another drunk mouthing off and starting a fight. "Can someone tell me where Bill lives?" she asks.

The barman finds his voice again. "I wouldn't bother, Inspector. He'll likely be drowning his sorrows now and wake up with nothing more than a headache and foggy memories."

"But he might want to press charges against Mr. MacLeod."

The barman laughs, as do several others. "That's not how we handle things around here."

She wants to push further, but the pain-free window of time she bought herself with the beers and the pill is clearly about to elapse. "Okay," she says finally. "Get on with your night, then."

The barman signals to the singer and the music strikes up again. The rest of the crowd disperses, and soon only Lewis is left standing with her in the much emptier room.

"Do you know Bill?" she asks him.

He pulls a face. "Enough to avoid him when he's had a few. The man's got a death wish." At George's raised eyebrow, he adds, "MacLeod looked like he wanted to kill him."

Her thoughts flash to Richie, walking through the dark with MacLeod. She hurries back to the booth to fetch her coat. "I'm heading out."

Lewis follows her. "I'll come with you."

"You don't have to leave."

He shoots her a stern look. "I'm walking you home."

"That's really not necessary."

The next look he gives her makes her wonder if that's true.

———

The night air hits George like a slap. She makes an audible sound of dismay and Lewis looks over, his eyes zeroing in on her bruised cheek. "You okay?"

She fastens her coat as high up her neck as possible. "I just don't think I'm designed for this climate."

"Best batten down the hatches tomorrow, then. Big storm coming in from the northeast."

His words trigger a blurry memory, a snatch of conversation that she can't fully recall. She thinks that someone down at the harbor who'd greeted them when they first arrived had mentioned something about northeasterly winds.

Lewis withdraws his red hat from a pocket and offers it to her, then puts it on his own head when she declines. There are a few people lingering around the pub's entrance; most are huddled around cigarettes, their cold breath twining with the smoke.

A solid figure with a familiar gait is hurrying down the alley;

the light from the pub finds the lines on his strained face. His eyes are locked on the door of the pub.

"Father Ross?" she calls.

The priest jerks to a halt. "Evening, Inspector. Lewis. That looks nasty," he says tersely, indicating her face. His tone suggests he already knows what happened, which is confirmed when he adds, "I'll be encouraging Mr. Mackay to make a full apology in the morning."

"I wasn't planning to press him for one. That family has enough on their plate."

He smiles tightly. "You've certainly taken the time to acquaint yourself with our people."

"Keeping tabs on me, Father?"

"Not well enough, apparently. I'm terribly embarrassed that a guest of Eadar was treated so poorly. You've seen the uglier side of our community, and I can assure you it won't happen again."

"Don't worry about it." She cocks her head. "What are you doing here? I didn't pick you for a regular at the pub."

His tense expression returns. "I heard there was an incident."

"It's broken up now," Lewis says calmly. "They've both gone home to sleep it off."

"Who?"

The corners of Lewis's mouth turn down. "They were drunk, it wasn't anything serious."

"*Who?*"

Lewis sighs. "Bill Thomson . . . and Alisdair MacLeod."

Father Ross scowls. "I thought I made it very clear to Bill that he was to stay away from Alisdair after last time."

"If it were that easy, I'd be out of a job," George says.

"Perhaps it's different where you're from, Inspector, but when I tell someone to do something, they do it." His stern expression gives way to weariness, and he nods at them both. "I'd best go find Bill and remind him of that fact. Good evening."

He marches back the way he came, moving as quickly as he can with his injured leg.

Lewis watches him depart with a tight jaw. "Bill's about to have the fear of God put back into him."

"What's Ross going to do? Patronize him into submission?" The sarcasm sours as a question occurs to her. "What *do* you do with people who break the law here? I've been in that barn. Didn't see any shackles."

"We don't need shackles. People just do what they're told. And if they don't"—he gestures to Father Ross's retreating figure—"he gets involved."

"How? Orders them to love thy neighbor, and then what? Everyone just goes back to playing nice?"

"Something like that."

"What a utopia," she mutters, tucking her chin below her collar.

A ribbon of icy air steals through the alley and sets something swinging above her head. She glances up. The wooden sign is moving slightly, making an ominous creaking sound as it sways back and forth on its hinge. She takes a step back to look at the painted illustration on it.

This time it's shock that steals her breath.

The sign for the Wulver's Catch features a terrified fish in the jaws of a hulking creature with jagged teeth and wild eyes.

Lewis follows her wide-eyed gaze and snorts. "Nothing gentle about this place, eh?"

He sets off down the street, but George is slower to follow. Her eyes are still drawn to the creature that's about to crush that fish between its long, bared teeth.

It's a wolf. And she's seen it before, staring in the kitchen window.

As she starts to call Lewis back to ask him about the wolf, loud shouting reaches them from the main street. The two of them exchange a wary look before she jogs to catch up with him. As they round the corner they see a rowdy group of people at the end of the street, hurrying past Cecily's home and turning left onto the track that leads down to the narrow beach.

"Where on earth are they going at this time of night?"

He looks concerned. "I don't know. There's nothing down there except sea. But with a storm coming in, and if they've had a few drinks . . ."

The group has already disappeared around the bend. George turns to Lewis. "Remember when you asked if I was having a night off?"

Darkness envelops them quicker than George expected; leaving the street and stepping onto the gritty track feels like being swallowed by a shadow. The only indications that they're moving in the right direction are the sweeping beams of torchlight and the diffused white glow of the lanterns up ahead. Even Lewis, at her side, is barely visible in the cloud-obscured moonlight. She glances back at the warm, firelit windows of the Campbell home and hopes that Richie has left MacLeod's and returned to their croft to coax the fire back to life.

"Do you know Donald Campbell?" she asks.

"Do you really need to ask that?"

"Do you know him *well*? You must be around the same age."

He sighs. "Yes, I know Donald. No, we're not close."

"Why not?"

"Are you friends with every person your age back home?"

"The difference being that I live in a city with a population of approximately . . . three thousand times yours."

He concedes a laugh. "Just because there're only a few of us doesn't mean we have to get along. I have my friends, and Donald . . . well, he keeps it simple. Got his wife and kids, and the lads on the boats." He pauses. "Used to get into fights a bit, I remember that now. Seemed to say the wrong thing to the wrong blokes. Always had a black eye or a fat lip, and someone glaring at him from across the pub. But that hasn't happened for years—not since he brought Cecily over. I think she learned to keep him muzzled, lest he say something stupid. Probably got his mates to keep an eye on him, too." He looks at her curiously. "Why are you so interested in Donald?"

She just shrugs; Cecily had told her about her struggles with Donald in private, and she's not about to betray her trust. "Should I bother asking if you know much about Alex Thomson?"

"Alex? Works on the boats. He's got a kid on the mainland, and he visits her a few times a year. I think he's over there now, actually," Lewis says, then chuckles. "He and the mother aren't together, but he's been trying to get them to visit here."

"How's that going?"

"Well, his daughter is almost four and hasn't set foot on Eadar once. What do you think?"

George laughs, but it's tinged with annoyance. *Damn.* Richie was right about Alex not being home. And as much as the loose end irks her, Richie is probably right about the other thing—Alex would probably just confirm both John's and Father Ross's accounts of the day Alan's body was found.

They follow the path down to the pebbly beach. Nestled under the headland that separates the beach from the harbor there's some shelter from the waves. It's about as calm a stretch of water as the island offers outside the protection of the harbor's breakwaters. After just a few minutes, they realize that the group up ahead have come to a stop and the people have formed a rough circle with their lights reflecting off the beach's wet pebbles. High spirits or drunkenness keep their feet shifting, elbows digging into one another's sides, shouts and laughter carried into shore on the wind.

"It's looking a little pagan," George whispers. "Should I have brought a goat?"

"I thought you were bringing the knife."

George is about to retort when the thick clouds part enough for the waning moon to cast a glow over the beach. She recognizes some of the faces as belonging to people from the loud group who had exited the pub before Kathy and Lewis arrived.

"Oh, they're pissed," Lewis groans. "They'd better not be planning to go in. I really don't fancy going after them."

"So you can drown, too? Good idea."

Lewis looks over her shoulder, up at the cliff behind them. George remembers walking that path just the other day, looking down at the exact spot where she's standing now. She hadn't noticed from above, but there's a rough set of stone steps cut into the lowest section of the cliff.

A glow appears at the top of the stairs, and with it comes a group of four or five people huddled close together, their steps jerky. George can't figure out what is making their collective movement so awkward as they stagger down the steps to the beach. They're greeted with an enthusiastic roar from their friends on the beach, and a few break off to assist the newcomers with their burden. Though there's nothing she can put her finger on, there's something about the odd movements, the drunkenness, that's making her apprehensive. "Can you see what they're carrying?"

Lewis shakes his head. "We'll have to get closer."

Before they can move, a shrill, inhuman cry reaches their ears. The hair on the back of George's neck rises.

"What the hell was that?" she asks sharply.

Lewis has gone still. "Oh, God."

"What? Lewis, what is it?"

"One of the old fishermen has been in their ear," Lewis says, his tone unexpectedly harsh. "Got them all riled up with stories."

"Stories about what?"

Instead of answering, he takes a step backward. "We need to get MacLeod."

But George starts heading toward the group as if there's a hook around her waist. "What are they doing?"

"Inspector..."

The two groups have met, and together they begin walking toward the water.

George breaks into a jog. She hears Lewis curse, then the crunch of footsteps along the stony beach as he follows.

The icy water is around the group's calves now, eliciting shocked laughs and squeals. Some carry lanterns still, the light bouncing erratically off the foamy waves that reach for their knees.

George and Lewis draw level with them on the shore, watching their backs as they stagger deeper into the water.

"They're going to kill themselves if they keep going," she says in disbelief.

"Not themselves."

His tone makes her body tense. "Why did you say we needed to get MacLeod?"

"Because his gun would be very handy right now."

It's then that another squeal rises from the group, and one of the people in the center cries out in pain and falls, copping a mouthful of water as a wave breaks over his head. The movement creates enough of a gap for George to finally lay eyes on what they've been struggling to carry.

Upside down and bucking wildly is a clearly terrified sheep.

George takes off toward the water at a sprint. Her first few steps in the swell are smooth, but the deeper she gets, the harder it is to move with speed. Even with anger radiating outward from her chest, she's not immune to the icy water—within seconds her teeth are chattering.

"Hey! Stop!"

A waist-high wave sends her breath gusting out. It appears the group didn't hear, or they're simply ignoring her. They're wrestling with the sheep again, too many hands making their efforts clumsy. They can't seem to decide how best to hold the animal to . . . what? George isn't sure what the next part of this ritual is, but she's certain it doesn't end with this sheep being returned to the paddocks.

A decision is made, and the mob holding the sheep repositions itself. A few of the onlookers raise their lanterns, shouting encouragement. With their faces so close to the light, they don't see George wading through the inky water toward them. She's relieved; it means she's able to break through the first ring of observers without resistance.

"Oi," she shouts again, panting. "What the hell are you doing?"

"Fuck off," someone says gruffly, and another calls, "Who *is* that?"

George elbows her way through to the inner knot of people. It's not easy; even though the bottom shelves gently here, the choppy waves are relentless and they're now a fair way from the beach—she recoils when the water splashes against her neck.

"Stop this right now," she snarls.

A shaggy-haired man scowls over his shoulder. "It's the bloody cop," he slurs, buffeted by another wave.

"This is none of your business," another shouts, struggling to keep his grip as the sheep kicks out.

Seeing the hardness—and glassiness—in their eyes, she's reminded of her time pulling night shifts when she first arrived in Glasgow. Alcohol makes people unpredictable, especially when they're in groups. She knows she needs to be very, very careful.

The water is so deep here that it's not only the sheep that could drown if the mob turns on her.

She just has to buy enough time for the cold water to sober them up. Planting her feet on the seabed as best she can, she drives her shoulder into the nearest person, a girl who squeals as she staggers back. George takes her place and gets a good grip on the fleece around the sheep's neck.

The shaggy man glares at her. "Bugger off, cop. This doesn't concern you."

"Sure about that?" She hopes her chattering teeth aren't undermining her authority. "You know that cruelty to animals is a criminal offense, right?"

A few of the onlookers exchange glances, but the shaggy man clenches his jaw. "It's *tradition*."

"Whatever your tradition is, it gives you no right to break the law. Now get back to the beach."

"'S for Gentle Annie," a girl to George's left inserts, her eyes unfocused.

"Who?"

"A weather god," a new voice says.

Lewis pushes through the onlookers to stand beside the shaggy man. "And one who's only remembered by people who are three sheets to the wind."

"She's sending a big one, MacGill, can't you feel it?" the shaggy man says fiercely. "Some of the old boys think we'll take a beating."

Lewis scoffs. "The harbor has been hit plenty of times before, Malcolm. It's still standing."

But the man—Malcolm—persists, his eyes fixed intently on Lewis. "My granda said if we send an offering to Annie, she'll pass us by. Come on, MacGill—do you want her taking one of the boats instead? Or one of us?"

"Don't get sucked in by silly old men telling tales. They're stuck in the past, but we're not," Lewis says, a ferocity entering his tone. "If we keep doing things the way our great-grand-parents did, then we're already dead."

He steps closer, putting his hand on the sheep's leg. It has gone strangely still; George fiercely hopes it's just exhausted, and not already dead. It stares up at the sky with mute appeal in its terrified eyes.

The scowl returns to Malcolm's face. "Has this bitch been in *your* ear, MacGill, filling your head with her mainland shite? Rules that don't apply to us out here?"

George laughs, even though her lower body has broken out in intense pins and needles. But Lewis doesn't see the humor. When he speaks, his voice is flintier than she's ever heard it.

"Let go, Malcolm. Or else Father Ross will be hearing about the show you've put on for Inspector Lennox tonight." He looks around at the uneasy faces, his expression as cold as the water. "All of you, get back to the beach."

There's a moment when George isn't sure which way things will go; in preparation, she readjusts her grip on the sheep and tries to steady her feet on the shifting ocean floor. But the icy water and battering wind has cooled their hot blood, and in pairs and threes people start peeling off. At Lewis's direction, those holding the sheep start carrying it back to the shore. When they reach the beach, Malcolm storms off, heading back toward the main street.

"Sorry," a woman whispers, before scrambling to catch up with Malcolm.

George and Lewis watch them go, both shuddering with the cold. Then Lewis sighs deeply. "Come on, Inspector. Let's get you both home."

CHAPTER 19

THEY WALK IN A TIRED BUT COMPANIONABLE SILENCE, LEWIS SAVING HIS breath as he tackles the stone steps with the sheep slung over his shoulders. Clearly island life builds a different kind of fitness; George's feet feel like they're encased in concrete, and there's a muted fire alarm wailing in her head.

"And I thought the most exciting part of my day was getting punched," she says.

Lewis huffs, readjusting the sheep as they reach the top of the stairs. "Hopefully that's the end of the evening's entertainment."

She looks to her left. "Did they come through the woods? I saw a little trail down there the other day."

Lewis does as much of a shrug as his cargo allows.

"If it's quicker, should we go back that way?"

He inspects the treeline, eyes flicking between shadows. Eventually he shakes his head. "Not worth the risk." Without further explanation, he starts off to the right, where the distant lights of the village can be seen.

"Oh, of course," George says, falling into step with him. "You don't want to run afoul of the fair folk. But down there, in the water . . . you told Malcolm that it was silly to believe in Easy Annie."

"Gentle Annie. And I would have said anything to keep him from sending this hefty bugger and its prize-winning wool to the depths."

George looks out to the ocean, the hungry waves high-lighted by a thin strip of moonlight. She hopes tonight was her first and last dip in that unforgiving water.

"So Gentle Annie controls the weather," she says, racking her memories, "the fair folk own the woods . . . what else is roaming these hills? Dragons? Elves?"

His head swivels as if to check the path is clear of mythical creatures. Then, breathing a little harder under the sheep's bulk, he answers. "There *are* ancient elves who live among the trees. There are stories of children all over Scotland who have found themselves lost in the woods, only for an elf to appear and show them the way home."

"Then how come you told me not to go into the woods? Sounds like they would have helped me out."

"Ah, but you're not a child. They'd be more likely to snap your bones and gobble you up. Or kidnap you and take you to the land of the *fae*."

"Christ," she mutters. "Any other creatures I should be wary of out here?"

"Hmm . . . have you ever heard of a wulver?"

She recalls the sign at the pub, the vicious imagery. "As in the Wulver's Catch? What is it?"

"Wulvers are gentle creatures who love to fish. An appropriate mascot for a fishing village, even though they mostly roam the Shetland Islands. Kathy thinks some northern fishermen brought the stories down with them when they hopped from port to port. And it's a story we've held on to."

"Why?"

"Because of what they symbolize. Wulvers have been known to share their catch with people who are hungry, those who can't fend for themselves. They represent peace, protection, kindness." His face darkens. "But they'll bite if provoked."

She can't help it; a laugh bursts from her lips. "You're mak-

ing all this up, aren't you? Just trying to scare the naive mainlanders?"

She realizes then that with everything that happened today,
she forgot to ask around about the bag of rotten eggs and the
doll. "Tell me, who do you think would have stuffed rotten eggs
into the eaves of the croft?"

Lewis lurches to a stop. "What?"

"Yeah, a little bag of rotten eggs, and a doll made of straw."

"Someone left a curse at the croft?" he interrupts, his eyes
wide. She realizes with a jolt that Lewis looks *scared*.

"That's what MacLeod called it, too," she says, a little nervously.

"MacLeod? What was he doing at your— Never mind," Lewis
says, his words coming fast. "What did you do with it?"

"MacLeod told me to burn it, so I did. He didn't explain why,
though. I presumed it was a lame prank."

"It's not a prank," Lewis says, and he twists suddenly, looking back the way they came. "Come on, we need to go."

"What? Lewis—wait!"

But he just beckons her on, the sheep bouncing on his
shoulders as he hurries up the hill. With a groan, she jogs after him.

"What is it?" she asks as she draws level with him. "Tell me,
Lewis."

"It's . . . I suppose you'd call it a curse for bad luck."

"Bad luck?" she echoes.

"Were the eggs broken?"

She nods.

He grimaces. "Definitely bad luck."

"Someone cursed the croft? Or cursed *us*?" She stares at
him, struggling to understand how he's saying all this with a
straight face. "Who would do that?"

"I don't know. Whoever it is, they don't like you very much."

Glancing up toward Nicholson's croft, she wonders if the person in the mask is responsible for the bag of bad luck. Then again, she hadn't imagined the venom in Angela Fraser's voice, or the hard looks she's received from other islanders. With a growing sense of unease, George wonders what other signs of ill will she's missed—supernatural or otherwise.

"Why, though? Are they trying to spook us? Or did they genuinely think it would work?"

Lewis's jaw is tight as he glances at her again. "I think they were hoping it would work."

After a moment, she huffs a laugh. "Whoever put it there is a bit late. My bad luck started a while ago. And I really don't think it can get any worse."

Lewis just groans as if she's said something very stupid. But all this talk about luck has reminded her of something. "Did people think that locking Broddy Cameron up made the fish come back?"

Lewis looks taken aback, then thoughtful. "I don't think so—it's not in any of the stories I've heard."

"And there's never any sense of guilt in the stories either? For what they did to him?"

"I think they felt justified after what he went on to do to them."

She bites her tongue against a rebuttal; after all, isn't it similar to the stance she's taken in the past? To strike first before someone has a chance to wound her? Nobody could draw an even line between what the islanders did to Broddy Cameron and her verbal takedowns of arrogant, sexist colleagues, but the comparison sits uncomfortably on her mind as they trudge on.

They arrive at the gate that leads to MacLeod's house. George can see that lights are on, but there's no indication if Richie is still inside. Looking up the hill, she can see a faint glow in the window of their croft, but that could be from the fire they left burning earlier tonight.

"All right. Give me a minute to pop this girl in the barn, then I'll be right back . . . Oi, wait!"

"You don't need to come all the way up," she says over her shoulder as she keeps walking. "I'll be all right from here."

"Seriously? After everything I just told you?"

His tone is shocked enough that she stops and turns. "I don't believe in any of that stuff, Lewis."

He fixes her with a stern look, hefting the sheep higher. "They might be stories to you, but people here live by them. Someone cast that curse because they want something bad to happen to you, Inspector."

"How is it possible, in this day and age, that you can all believe in those things? Curses, fairies, weather gods." *Any god,* she adds mentally.

"Because it's what we're taught."

"So you're saying that everyone just believes everything they're told?" she asks, condescension leaking into her voice. "No doubts, no questions? Even when that belief requires them to drown a living, breathing creature in the sea?"

"Yes."

"*Why?*"

Lewis goes quiet. "Because history has shown them that when people stop doing what they're supposed to, bad things happen."

Her fingers tingle; a stirring of electricity, or just her circulation returning. She isn't sure, but the prickling in her legs reminds her that hypothermia is not off the cards yet. She jerks her chin toward the sheep. "Get it somewhere warm."

As Lewis opens his mouth to argue, she interrupts with, "I'm a bloody police officer, Lewis. I don't need a bodyguard— from people or fairy tales."

She bids him good night and turns on her heel, striding up the hill.

———

The door is locked. She swears—Richie has the key. She considers her options, then trudges around the side of the croft.

The bathroom window is disturbingly easy to force open, though it's a little trickier to shimmy her torso through. She's a little ashamed at how hard she's breathing by the time she lands awkwardly on the bathroom floor.

She staggers to the hearth and collapses in front of it, placing another couple of logs on the coals and blowing on the small flame. As soon as it catches properly, she sets about the difficult task of peeling off her wet clothes. Coat, boots, and socks come off with some effort, and her trousers put up enough resistance that she's out of breath by the time she has them draped over a chair.

She pulls on a dry pair of underwear and a loose long-sleeved shirt, sorting through her duffel bag for trousers. Suddenly the hairs rise on the back of her neck. She jerks upright and looks around, only now noticing the curtain she rigged over the kitchen window has fallen into the sink.

The watcher has returned. And even though their eyes are hidden within the two dark eyeholes of the wolf mask, she can feel their gaze is fixed on her.

It's less startling than last time, but still enough to send her heart into her throat. But unlike last time, the person takes off as soon as they realize she's spotted them. It takes too long to force her sluggish legs into a run. She fumbles with the lock and bursts outside, rounding the side of the house just as the watcher, wearing oversized dark clothes and that ridiculous mask, makes it to the path.

"Hey!" she shouts as they disappear into the darkness. "Stop! I said *stop*!"

She runs as far as she can before a rock jabs into her bare foot. She stops and as soon as she does she's hit with a barrage of delayed discomfort. Her head is being pounded by a frantic gavel, her lungs are shrinking in the frosty air. And she's not wearing trousers.

That's twice now that the watcher has got away. She hasn't told Richie about the first incident, but she knows now that there could be more to this than just a prying islander. Sweeping a look into the darkness around her, she wraps her arms around herself for warmth and hobbles back up to the croft. "You better not have shoved any more rotten food around here," she mutters.

She pauses in the doorway, peering back into the night. If Richie is on his way up, it's possible the watcher will pass him. George's eyes are drawn to the spot where they vanished. But then something flickers straight ahead. A light, or her over-tired brain?

For a moment she thinks she's imagined it, but there it is again—the flash of a torch moving through the dark. Heading toward the woods.

Her hands rise to grip the doorframe as she leans forward, eyes straining to see something more. Then the light goes out.

She stumbles back through the door, her heart thumping. Sliding the lock home, she does her best to banish images of storm gods and elves from her head, then settles in to wait for Richie.

He arrives ten minutes later, during which time George has changed into her pajamas, set the kettle over a flame, and is pressing the ice block to her cheek.

"How'd it go with MacLeod?" she asks immediately.

He sighs heavily, shedding his coat. "He wasn't in the mood to talk, but that didn't stop me from trying."

"Did he tell you why he and Bill Thomson were fighting?"

"Kept that information to himself. Told me it would be sorted out soon enough. Of course I told him this could be construed as premeditation should anything untoward befall Thomson, but I thought his blood had cooled enough that it was safe to leave him alone." He crosses to the stove, reaching for the handle of the kettle.

"Already boiled."

He shoots her a grateful look, then sighs. "What a night, eh?"

Talk about an understatement. "It certainly took some interesting twists."

At her tone, his eyebrow lifts. "Such as?"

She relays the information she gathered from the patrons at the bar, how they bumped into Father Ross before following the kids to the beach. As she describes the moment she realized they were holding the sheep, his expression shifts from shocked to grim.

"Where the hell are we?" he mutters, dunking a teabag into a cup.

"Insane, right? And it took a lot of convincing to get them to bring the sheep back to shore—we were standing out in the water for about ten minutes arguing with them. It was all I could do to keep the thing's head above water."

"*You went in?*"

George blinks. "Yes."

His mouth drops open. "Into the *ocean?*"

"Were you listening to what I just told you?"

Richie points to the window. "Were you listening when I told you there was a huge storm coming? Why on earth would you take such a risk?"

She senses that "to save the sheep" will not be an acceptable answer. "Lewis told me none of the adults on the island can swim; only a handful of the kids can."

Apparently, this answer is worse.

"So, what was your plan if they went out too far?" he asks, his eyes blazing. "Were you going to pull them back in single-handedly?"

If she weren't so confused, she's sure her anger would be taking over. "Isn't that our job?"

He groans, a harsh sound. "This is what I'm talking about," he says, throwing a spoon into the sink. The clash of metal makes her jump.

"What?" she asks, bewildered.

"Trust," he breathes, his lips curling back from the word. "How am I supposed to trust you when you're taking risks like that? All it would have taken is for one wave to sweep some-one's feet from under them, one panicked kid to grab on to you and drag you under. Then you'd be gone, just like that."

"Then I'd be dead from doing my fucking job, Richie," she says, heat rising from somewhere deep in her stomach. "That's what I've been doing this whole time, while you've been chat-ting and having tea and going to church. *I'm* the one who's actu-ally gone out there to find answers, *I'm* the one getting punched in the street, *I'm* the one chasing down the creepy fucker who's been watching us through *that* window," she jabs her finger to-ward it, "while you were off failing to get answers from Alisdair MacLeod!"

"Are you done?"

His quiet tone is more effective than a bellow. The ensuing silence, punctuated only by the pulse in her ears and the anx-ious call of a seabird, is like being smacked by a bone-shaking wave. She buckles beneath its force, dropping onto the couch.

And the silence stretches, until finally Richie says, "Some-one was at the window?"

A lifeline. She reaches for it. "Yes, a couple of times. Wearing a mask. A wolf mask. I couldn't tell gender or age, clothes were nondescript."

"And you went after them. Alone." Not asking. Confirming.

The lifeline slips from her grasp.

Richie shakes his head; a movement so slight, she isn't sure if he's aware he's doing it. "Clearly you didn't learn a lesson from the last time you got cocky. I would have thought three months in hospital would have taught you that you're not invincible, but it seems you're not as smart as I'd hoped." He looks away, as if he can't bear the sight of her. "Hang the curtain again. Lock the door. Try to stay on this side of it."

And then he stalks into his bedroom, tea forgotten.

———

Two pills later, she lies on the couch and stares up at the ceiling. The window has been covered again, though she already knows the makeshift curtain won't stay put through the night. But hopefully the fact she sprinted out into the night half-dressed reminded the watcher that she will respond when threatened. Or that she is completely insane and would chase strangers into the night in her underwear. Either way, someone not to be fucked with.

She rolls over, turning her back to the fire. Though her mind begs for sleep, a rebellious voice hisses Richie's words back to her with every pound of the gavel on her skull. It thuds in time with the footsteps in her memory.

Up, up, up she climbed the stairs at Margaret Villo's maisonette, following that electric tug in her body to the landing. Looking left, right, letting her eyes travel over the doors that felt like potential answers to a riddle.

That one.

She sees her fingers press against the door, the one to the

far right, the bedroom that overlooked the street. It didn't oc-cur to her to wait for Richie or to call for any of the constables below.

No. That's not true. She considered it. And decided to go ahead anyway.

Blue and red lights bounced around the room as she in-spected the unmade bed that belonged to the twisted body at the foot of the stairs, cataloged the knick-knacks on the bedside table, peered out the narrow glass door that led to a Juliet bal-cony overlooking the street, before her attention was drawn to a wardrobe.

Electricity crackled up her spine; urgent, dangerous, dar-ing. *Look over there.*

And instead of confirming with the constable downstairs that they had swept the upstairs rooms, checked to make sure that *nobody else* was in the residence, George simply reached for the handle and pulled.

The next part is—always has been, and perhaps always will be—a blur. It's a confusing wave of senses, a jumble of images; there's fear and pain, wild eyes and body odor. And then there's glass shattering, flailing limbs, and blood, and then . . . there's falling.

In her memory there is no impact. Everyone says that's a mercy.

But she'd happily relive the moment her head hit the con-crete driveway over this new memory that she knows she'll never be able to shake—of Richie's disgusted face as he walked away from her.

This time, it's George who is surprised to wake and see a fully dressed Richie, his nose still pink from being exposed to the wind.

"I bought some fresh bread," he says, noticing her head rise above the back of the couch. "Thought we could make ourselves a nice breakfast."

His tone is neutral, no hint of the sharpness from last night. It makes her stomach tighten. "Did you hear the wind last night?" she asks tentatively.

He twists the tap, holds the kettle beneath the stream of water. "I did. Very loud indeed."

She waits for him to elaborate, to say, *And you're right, it does sound like howling.* That would be enough—he doesn't need to ask about the watcher, about the wolf mask, about whether she's thought about the possible consequences of her actions last night. But he just places the kettle on the stove and starts coaxing a flame from the burner beneath it. It's his unwillingness to concede—or just to simply *humor* her, for God's sake—that has her stalking bitterly to the bathroom.

In the mirror she sees the lump on her cheek has gone down a little, but it's still tender to touch. The deep purple bruise matches the streaks under her eyes from another restless night, despite the sleeping pill; she was kept awake by both their argument and the intensifying wind outside. As well as making the house creak in ominous new ways, the howling continued almost nonstop—to the point where George sacrificed having a pillow under her head in order to block it out. When she was still tossing and turning in the small hours of the morning, it started to feel like the sound had been sent specifically to torment her.

After doing what little she can to make her face less . . . just *less*, she joins Richie at the table. The lighthouse logbooks have been cleared to make room for plates and cutlery. There's a strange assortment of spreads and side dishes between their plates. George glances at the empty net bag that hangs from a cupboard handle. Her lips press together. "Something you want to tell me?"

Richie's eyes dart up to hers, and for a second he appears apologetic. But then he straightens his spine and looks at her calmly. "It's time we went home."

"What? We still have another twenty-four hours here."

He pushes back from his chair abruptly, crossing to the wall to slap their patchwork timeline. "There's a reason we're struggling to fill in these gaps, and my only theory is that it's because the story we're trying to pick apart is *the truth*."

She stays seated, but the challenge rings in her voice. "You can't tell me that you don't think there's something strange about this place."

He throws up his hands. "There's no law against being strange. They're a religious and isolated community that is largely ignored by the mainland unless it's to place a seafood order. They've been through storms and famine and tragedy without assistance, and they've survived by pulling together. All we're doing by digging into Alan's past is prolonging their grief."

Her teeth work furiously on the inside of her cheek. She can taste metal. "You called Cole."

Richie turns his back as the kettle begins to whistle. "A boat will be here midmorning, weather permitting. We're to wait at the post office."

She stares at him. "Is this because of last night?"

"You haven't been listening to a word I've said for the past five days, have you? Absolutely nothing has changed since yesterday, or the day before, or last week. That's the problem." He pauses, then his tone becomes strangely formal. "You've done some excellent work this week, DI Lennox. You've got a very promising future ahead, and I know you'll go further than I ever have—if you can learn where to draw the line."

In her mind, she splutters a hundred rebuttals: the wolf at the window; the blank cards at Alan's grave; the curse in the eaves; the way people keep speaking to her in cut-off sentences with cryptic wording. But every single retort dies on her lips, because . . . he is right. If she wants to climb the ladder, she needs to stop swinging off the rungs.

Swallowing her pride, she crosses to the couch and starts rolling up the blankets.

"Eat some breakfast."

"Not hungry."

For the next few minutes she shoves clothes into her bag haphazardly, pain pulsing in her cheek, her eye, behind her ear. Her careless packing style means the bag bulges out of shape too quickly, and she's still got shoes and toiletries to shove in. With a huff, she upends the overflowing bag on the couch and makes a beeline for the bathroom before she embarrasses herself by bursting into frustrated tears.

She grips the edge of the small basin. The cold ceramic feels good under her hot palms, but it's not enough—she turns the knob to send a steady flow of water from the shower and sheds her clothes before stepping into the bathtub and underneath the spray, the cold water making her gasp, raising goosebumps across her whole body. She stands under the stream for as long as it takes to force the emotion back below the surface of her skin, and rewards her new composure with a twist of the hot tap.

When she returns to the main room wrapped in a towel, her wet hair twisted into a bun, only a single plate remains on the table. Everything else has been washed and stacked neatly in the dish rack to dry. The rest of the food has been returned to the bag that now sits on the clean benches. On the plate is a piece of buttered toast with honey.

She can hear Richie moving around in his bedroom, probably packing. Sinking her teeth into the toast with a resigned sigh, George heads to the pile of clothes upended on the couch to do the same.

CHAPTER 20

THE RAIN BEGINS TO PATTER LIGHTLY AGAINST THE WINDOW AS THEY DIS-
mantle the evidence wall and line up their bags beside the door.
When she climbs onto the counter to pull down the blanket
covering the kitchen window, Richie halfheartedly offers to
make one final cup of tea. George declines. Why delay the inev-
itable?

The only thing quiet about their walk into the village is the
air between them. The storm is close—the clouds are thick and
the same bruised color as her cheek, and there's static in the air.
The raindrops are fat and falling faster, beating a frenzied drum
on Cecily's red umbrella. Even if they wanted to talk, George
doubts they would be able to hear each other.

They walk straight to the post office and enter in a graceless
tumble of wet coats and dripping bags. Kathy is behind the
counter feeding slips of paper into the old wooden letterbox
George noticed outside when they first arrived. Her eyes zero in
on their luggage.

"I wish you didn't have to leave early," she says miserably as
she shoves the rest of the slips into the box.

"We're needed on other cases," Richie says smoothly as he
places the bag with the logbooks on the counter. "You wouldn't
happen to have a towel back there, would you?"

Kathy nods, then pauses. "Did you finish them?"

"Sorry?" Richie asks.

But Kathy is looking at George. "Did you finish reading the books?"

"Oh, almost. Very interesting."

"Hm. Learned anything you'll take back home with you?" Her tone is light, but there's a strange gleam in her eyes. "Set some of those silly theories straight?"

George shrugs, glancing at the books. "Nothing I'd take to trial. The mystery remains." She forces a light laugh. "I found them a bit creepy, to be honest. It felt like I was reading ghost stories."

Chewing her bottom lip, Kathy just stares at George intently until Richie reminds her of his request. She heads into the back, leaving George and Richie standing in yet another uncomfortable silence. He checks his watch. "We've got about an hour to kill. I was going to ask Kathy for her input on the list of services we're putting together, if you'd like to help?"

"I'm going to return this to Cecily," George says, holding up the umbrella.

He nods, his mouth taut. "Give her my best."

She makes a vague sound of acknowledgment and heads back out into the rain. There's nobody out on the street, and it looks as though the shops have shut up for the day. The harbor is more crowded than she's ever seen it, with at least ten boats jostling against their fenders. The fishermen must have decided it was too dangerous to head out in the face of the approaching storm. If these hardy sailors are staying ashore today, George dreads to think what their journey back to the mainland is going to be like. Though perhaps the punishment of a rough crossing is a fitting end to this investigation.

Glancing out from under the umbrella, George sees a flash of lightning far off in the distance. It makes her move a little quicker, the stones crunching under her feet.

As she raises her hand to Cecily's door, raised voices drift through the wood. Cecily shouting at the kids, probably. She hesitates, not wanting to intrude. After an extended period of quiet, George lifts her fist again and knocks.

She has to knock a second time before Cecily appears. Her eyebrows are still pulled together from the argument she's been having, but her eyes widen when she recognizes George. She laughs, a strained sound. "DI Lennox on my doorstep in a storm. It's déjà vu."

George closes the umbrella. "I just came to return this and to say good-bye."

Cecily's smile freezes. "You're leaving?"

"Yeah, the boat will be here soon." George glances back up the road. The prospect of getting so thoroughly wet on the walk back to the post office without the umbrella, and then having to spend an awkward hour with Richie spurs her to turn to Cecily with a pleading expression. "One last cup of tea before I go?"

Cecily looks back into the house quickly. "Oh, um . . . of course. The kettle's just boiled." She pushes George ahead of her down the hallway, but pauses at the stairs and calls up loudly to the second floor. "You play nicely up there, all right? DI Lennox is here, and she won't hesitate to arrest whoever starts the next fight."

She rolls her eyes at George as she enters the kitchen. "Honestly, stormy days are my worst nightmare. This house is too small for five of us, and when they can't get outside to burn their energy they start bouncing off the bloody walls." She claps her hands. "Tea. Right." The kettle is quiet but steams as Cecily pours water into the waiting teapot, two mugs already waiting beside it. "How come you're leaving early? Did you discover something about Alan?"

"In a way. We're satisfied that there was no foul play. As for the reason . . ." She takes a breath, trying to keep the disappointment out of her tone. "Whatever it was that drove Alan off that lighthouse died with him."

"You did your best, I'm sure."

George grunts morosely, watching Cecily spoon tea leaves into the pot. "Did you ever sneak out to go drinking at the lighthouse?"

Cecily giggles. "Oh God, how did you find out about that?"

George doesn't want to explain her nighttime excursion and how she probably scared the life out of a kid up there. "I heard a rumor."

Cecily grins as she brings the steaming teapot and mugs over to the table. "It was something Donald and his friends had been doing for years, and when I arrived he took me along so I could get to know them. We'd get a little fire going in an old water trough someone dragged up from MacLeod's, but that tower gets bloody cold at night." A blush rises in her cheeks. "Then he and I started going on our own. When you're sharing a bedroom wall with your in-laws, and the older Mrs. Campbell bursts into your bedroom whenever she pleases, well . . . we found that our, er, marital activities were impeded somewhat." She shakes her head, though George can tell that time has softened her frustration into amusement. "We couldn't write each other notes—they'd just get read—so we came up with a system. I'd leave a candle burning on the bedside table and that would tell him where I'd gone. The sun would be well down before he'd even show up, usually covered in fish guts."

George laughs at the face Cecily pulls. "You were brave heading up there on your own. Lewis told me off for wandering around at night. He said an elf might snatch me up."

"Well, I'd only just turned eighteen. The elf might have thought I was still a child," Cecily says with mock seriousness.

George recalls Lewis's grim face, the fear in his eyes when

she told him about the curse. "I suspect Lewis was trying to scare me."

"Or warn you. Surely you know by now that this island has its fair share of skeletons."

"Mm. I heard about Broddy Cameron."

"Ah, the man who made it so bloody hard for me to be accepted by these people," she says irritably. At George's querying look, she adds, "Not only did he do . . . what he did, but he was born a mainlander."

"I didn't know that part." She prods her cheek absently, wincing. "As if they needed another reason to resent visitors."

"It's ridiculous," Cecily snaps. "These people have such limited sources of entertainment that they'll latch on to a vintage case of schizophrenia and hold it against everyone who isn't born here. On the one hand, they desperately need us to keep the population growing or they'll disappear off the map entirely, but when they do lure you over you're put under a microscope until they're sure you don't have crazy in your blood." She shakes her head, then looks at the clock. "Oh, bloody hell. I need to start making morning tea for those ratbags up there. I don't want to rush you out the door . . ."

But George is already standing, taking two quick gulps of tea. The warmth radiates out pleasantly from her core. At the front door, she reaches for Cecily's hand. "It was really nice to meet you. Remember, you have my card."

Cecily nods. "Thanks for listening to all my grumbling." She opens the door and cold air rushes in, making them both shiver. "And all the best back on the mainland," she says, eyeing the roiling sky with apprehension. "Enjoy being away from the madness that I, for some reason, chose to marry into."

Just as George is about to step out into the rain, a deep voice calls down from the top of the stairs, underscored by heavy footsteps.

"Cess, are you making that tea or not? I've been—"

Ewan freezes halfway down the stairs, wide eyes on George. His nose is swollen and purple, and there's a small plaster across the bridge. Clad in just a faded T-shirt, trackpants, and socks, he looks right at home.

George looks at Cecily, whose expression is a revealing mixture of alarm and guilt. "I didn't realize you had company."

Cecily's hand floats through the air and settles on her necklace. "Oh, uh, I was just patching up his nose. You found the bathroom?" she asks him brightly.

He blinks, shifting his gaze from George to Cecily, and shoves his hands in his pockets. "Aye, I did."

George's eyes flick down to his exposed forearms then back up to his face. "How are you, Ewan? That looks sore."

"A bit tender, aye," he says in a low voice, as if reluctant to admit it. "Nothing I haven't had before."

"Yeah, I see that," George says, then points at Ewan's muscular right forearm. "How'd you get those?"

"Get what?" Cecily asks, as she and Ewan peer down at his skin, at the two fading scratches running from his wrist to his elbow.

Ewan swallows, his eyes darting toward Cecily. "Work, I suppose."

"You suppose?" George bends forward to get a better look. The skinny scratches are almost healed, the skin already turning from pink to white. "They look like they would have hurt at the time."

Ewan just shrugs, ducking his head. "I suppose," he says again.

"Oh, I'm always patching up the lads," Cecily trills. "Between the fishhooks and the gutting knives, I basically run an A and E in here."

"Not sure if you can blame fishhooks for those," George says lightly. "They look like they came from fingernails."

Ewan's chin jerks up, and George sees that same violent storm of emotions start stirring behind his eyes that had been brewing during their first encounter. "What the fuck are you accusing me of?" he says, moving one step further down the stairs.

Cecily looks scandalized. "You mind yourself," she snaps at him, shooting a nervous glance at George before rounding on him again. "How dare you? Mouthing off to a *police officer.*"

At her reprimand, the storm in Ewan's eyes dissipates. He looks unsure of himself now, his hands fidgeting in his pockets. "Sorry," he mutters.

In a milder voice, Cecily says, "You can go wait in the kitchen. We'll just be a minute."

With a final look at Cecily, he slouches down the hall.

Cecily watches him leave, then slowly turns to meet George's eyes. There's a nervous twist to her lips as she whispers, "Please don't tell anyone."

"About his behavior? Or the scratches?" At Cecily's stricken expression, she asks, "Are they from you? From an . . . intimate moment?"

Cecily looks like she's about to throw up—she glances over George's shoulder toward the street, as if checking for eaves-droppers. "Accusations like that split families down the middle," she hisses, her eyes shining. "*If* someone suspected a married person of having an aff—of *anything* like that, the village would turn on them. They'd take the children, and they'd make sure the parent never saw them again." Her voice drops. "And I will *never* let that happen."

George raises a calming hand. "It's not what I'm here to investigate, Cecily. I won't tell anyone."

Cecily's gaze runs over George's face, as if trying to assess her sincerity, then she gives a wobbly smile. "Okay . . . Thank you, George."

Rattled by the direction their farewell has taken, George gives Cecily a nod and heads out onto the street. The door closes behind her, and immediately afterward the first growl of thunder ripples across the sky.

Without the protection of the umbrella, George is reduced to a soaking, shivering wreck within ten steps. She tries to hug the walls as much as she can, but it's no use. The weak light and heavy rain make it difficult for her to see anything further than twenty yards in any direction as she stumbles toward the post office. But she spots the flash of vibrant red exiting from a building up ahead and tracks its path with confusion. *What on earth is he doing?*

As another clap of thunder sounds over their heads, George takes off after the figure.

She catches up with Lewis at the top of the steps leading down to the harbor. "Oi!"

"Inspector?" he shouts, grabbing her shoulder as if to confirm she's real. "What are you doing out here? It's not safe!"

She cups her hands around his ear and speaks into it. "What are *you* doing out here?"

He jabs a finger at the boats. "Jack went to check his boat, but he hasn't come back!"

Asking who Jack is seems pointless. She follows the line of his finger, squinting against the rain. "Which one is his?"

He tries to answer, but another thunderous roar drowns him out.

"What?" she shouts.

Lewis gestures at her hopelessly, then forges on toward the stairs. The northeasterly storm is now sweeping waves straight through the harbor entrance, the swells surging up the stone seawalls and flooding the harborside. The moored boats are tossed against the walls like toys, with only their fenders preventing their hulls from splintering. Taking in the chaotic scene, George knows that following him would be stupid, dangerous.

But he followed her into the ocean last night.

With a groan, she takes off after Lewis.

The ocean is darker than she's ever seen it, even darker than the steely gray that heralded her arrival. The waves hurl themselves against the inner walls of the harbor.

George shields her eyes. The rain is coming down harder now, the clouds so low that it's hard to see where they end and the horizon begins. She searches along the quay for Lewis, praying he hasn't already been swept away by the water. It takes her a worryingly long moment, but finally she spots him making his way toward a blue boat moored at the far side of the harbor wall.

She pauses to let a wave crash in front of her. When the foamy water retreats, she pushes into a careful jog, slipping on ribbons of seaweed the ocean has spewed up. Thunder ripples across the sky again. The boom is so powerful that it vibrates in her chest, making her bones tremble from more than the cold. She claps her hands over her ears as she runs, dodging another surge that threatens to drag her into the seething waters of the harbor.

As she approaches the boat, she can see Lewis gesticulating wildly at someone onboard. A few steps closer and she sees a burly figure on the boat's deck—Jack, she assumes—swing his legs over the railing and jump back onto the quay. Lewis grips Jack's shirtfront and bellows into his ear, then sends him staggering toward her with a shove.

George eyes the distance back to the stairs then gazes out at the harbor. The storm is on top of them now, that much is obvious. And given the ferocity of the waves barreling through the harbor entrance, they need to get off the quay *now*.

"Come on!" she yells at the men, but her words are snatched away by the wind.

Jack is close enough that she can make out his ruddy cheeks, Lewis just a few yards behind, when a wall of water crests the top of the stone arms that guard the entrance to the port, surging across the harbor and smashing into the inner wall, catching the three of them at chest height. She experiences a second of weightlessness as she's thrown through the air, only to land with a bone-jarring thud on the rough stones of the quay. The impact knocks the air out of her lungs, but she manages to cling to the ground until the surging water retreats enough for her to get to her feet. The pads of her fingers are stinging; she holds up her palms and sees a layer of skin has been scraped from her fingertips, watery blood dripping onto the stone.

"Fuck," she pants, then looks up to see how the men fared. *"Fuck!"*

Lewis is only now getting to his feet, swiping salt water from his eyes.

Jack is gone.

Heart pounding anew, her head whips toward the water. "Jack went in!"

Lewis comes to her side, peering into the waves frantically.

"Please, *please* tell me he's one of the few who can swim," she says.

His silence is answer enough. The seconds feel like hours as they scan the maelstrom, until finally Lewis shouts, "Over there!"

She looks to where he's pointing. About thirty yards away, she can see Jack. Even at this distance she can tell he's in distress, hands clawing ineffectively at the water.

Her body moves before her brain can catch up. Her sodden coat hits the ground, and she pulls her hair back into a fist and secures it with a hair tie she finds in her pocket.

"Get a rope," she orders, kicking off her boots.

For a second, Lewis looks like he's going to protest, but then Jack's head disappears beneath the surface and his jaw sets. He sprints for the nearest boat and retrieves a long coil from the deck. She secures one end around her waist with a firm knot as he ties off the other end around a mooring post. Grabbing the middle section tightly, he nods at her, bracing his feet.

Without another word, George takes a deep breath and dives into the water.

Considering she was already soaked, the cold isn't too much of a shock at first. In fact, as the sound of the storm around her fades and her body slices through the water, she experiences a moment of peace similar to when she was submerged in the bath.

But then the currents try to stake their claim on her, and she's pulled into a disorienting spin. The water is so dark that she can't tell if she's closer to the surface or the sea floor. When her lungs start to burn, she blindly picks a direction and starts kicking, reassured by the tug of the rope around her waist.

Miraculously, her head breaks the surface seconds later. She draws in one huge, gasping breath, but the relief is short-lived as another wave barrels toward her. She ducks beneath it and is pressed into the deep, her legs working furiously to bring her back up through the water. Her chest is burning by the time she feels the wind on her face again.

She looks around for Jack, hoping her dive has brought her far enough from the seawall that she's not about to be dashed against it. To her relief, she spots him about ten yards away. Bracing for another wave, she kicks toward him.

Jack is exhausted; she can tell by his drooping eyes, the

slackness of his pale lips. He dips below the surface again, and her heart stops when he doesn't immediately reappear.

"Shit," she pants, kicking over to where she last saw him. Sweeping her arms through the water, her fingers knock against something solid and she grips it, hauling Jack up by his shirt. His eyes are closed now.

"Jack? Jack!" She curses and slides her arms around his chest, interlocking her fingers. "Now, Lewis—*now*!"

There's a strong tug at her waist and then they're being swiftly towed backward. It doesn't occur to her that they're moving faster than Lewis alone could manage, but then she feels multiple sets of hands grabbing at her arms, and she and Jack are hauled bodily from the raging harbor.

George collapses onto her hands and knees, shivering and panting. Someone kneels down beside her and pats her back tentatively.

"Are you okay, Inspector?"

The man's breathing is harsh with the effort of the rescue. The voice doesn't belong to Lewis.

"Catch your breath," Ewan continues, untying the rope from around her waist.

There's a tense exchange of voices. She glances over her shoulder to see Jack sprawled behind her, totally still. A handful of islanders have gathered around, their faces creased with worry.

"Is he breathing?" she pants.

A woman kneels, her hands fluttering over Jack's chest, face. "How do I . . . ?"

"You've got to be kidding me," George mutters, and shoves the woman aside. Her shaking fingers press into the soft skin of his neck to feel for a pulse. Fear squeezes her lungs but she controls it. It's a useless emotion in moments like this.

"Jack, can you hear me?" she calls, tapping his cheek firmly. "Open your eyes, come on."

She doesn't wait more than half a second before she begins compressions, only pausing to throw open his coat so that her hands can press directly against his sternum. She hums under her breath to maintain a steady rhythm.

Thirty.

Breath. Breath.

His lips are icy.

Thirty.

Breath. Breath.

More islanders arrive, their huddled forms sheltering her from the worst of the wind.

Thirty.

Breath. Breath.

"You can do it," a woman murmurs.

"Come on, Inspector," another says, his voice breaking on her title.

She barely hears them, counting in her head. *Thirty. Breath. Breath. Thirty. Breath. Breath. Thirty —*

A cough.

Warmth floods George's shivering body and she falls back as Jack splutters, sea water trickling down his chin. Under her direction, the islanders roll him onto his side, cover him with a blanket, and rub his arms and legs roughly.

An arm across her shoulders keeps her from slumping to the ground, another tucks a blanket around her. The rain hasn't eased, but it seems the ocean was satisfied with stealing Jack's breath for that long minute—the waves that shoulder through the harbor entrance now don't have the same ferocity as before.

By this time it seems like the entire population of Eadar is streaming down the steps, juggling umbrellas as they hand out towels and blankets. Father Ross pushes through the crowd, his mouth dropping open in shock when he sees the man on the ground.

"Jack!" he cries, dropping awkwardly to his knees. Jack is already starting to stir, his eyelids fluttering in response to the activity around him.

Gentle hands pull George to her feet, and someone wraps an arm around her waist and guides her toward the stairs. Dazed and moving robotically, she looks up at Ewan. He glances at her, his mouth a thin line—leftover tension from their last encounter, she guesses—but still he supports her until they get to the top of the stairs and are greeted with the open-mouthed stares of the islanders who couldn't squeeze onto the quay.

Richie winds through the throng with Kathy on his heels. His face pales when he spots George, and he rushes over. "What the hell happened?" he demands, his hands burning hot against her numb cheeks.

"She saved Jack Ross," Ewan says before she can even take a breath. She's grateful; her teeth are chattering too hard to speak.

"Ross?" Richie asks.

"Father Ross's nephew. He nearly drowned. But I saw Inspector Lennox go in after him, and only MacGill there to pull them both back in. She almost drowned herself, the waves were that big . . ."

The crowd shifts as Jack is carried up the steps on a board, Lewis holding one side. He flashes her a tired smile, which she thinks she manages to return. Just beyond them, George spots Cecily, her mouth agape as she takes in George's sodden appearance, Ewan's arm around her still. George nods, but Cecily seems too shocked to respond. Before Ewan can continue with the story, another set of hands press against George's back, and the crowd parts to let her through.

In an echo of her first moments on the island, she's ushered into the home of an elderly couple on the main street and pointed to the front room, where a fire crackles merrily in the grate. The woman, whose name George's brain is too foggy to recall, leaves her alone to undress and wrap herself in another blanket, her steaming clothes and boots hanging off metal hooks that have been drilled into the mantel. She sinks into the closest chair and lifts her feet up, pointing her toes toward the flames.

The woman shuffles in a few minutes later and presses a cup of tea into George's hands. Her fingers start to tingle as the warmth chases out the cold, and she drinks deeply. With a soft pat to George's head, the woman smiles and returns to the kitchen. George pulls the hair tie free with some difficulty, the strands tangled from the rough water.

A few minutes later there's a knock at the front door. The woman's husband shows Richie into the room, George's duffel bag and briefcase in his hand. He lowers them to the floor. "You all right?"

Her head hurts, her face hurts, and doing all those compressions has made her body feel like she's gone three rounds against Fiona.

"Just cold," she says.

She'd all but forgotten about the police launch that was coming to pick them up. She looks at her watch, but the water must have got into it; the second hand has stopped ticking. Surely no boat would be out in this storm, let alone trying to negotiate the harbor that had just done its best to kill her.

As if reading her thoughts, Richie laughs, a clipped sound. "No need to rush. A call came through just after you left. Our pickup sensibly refused to make the journey. Weather permitting, they'll be here tomorrow morning around ten, as originally planned."

They look at each other for a moment, then he finally cuts his eyes to the side. "I'm staying in the village tonight. There's a room above the pub."

She blinks at him. "Oh. Why?"

"Because I'm pissed off, Lennox, and I'd like a break from you."

Her mouth falls open. "You can't be angry at me for saving that man."

His fingers flex at his sides, squeezing into fists. "Do you remember our conversation last night, or what we talked about this morning? Because I'm starting to think that you've ignored everything I've ever told you."

She must have swallowed some sea water, because her stomach is churning. "Do you want me to spend the next thirty years doing the bare minimum just so I can end up like you? Stuck in a rank that's beneath me because I'm too scared to take a risk?"

Eyes blazing, he reaches into his pocket. A familiar rattling sound makes her next breath catch in her throat.

"That's if you last thirty years," he spits, withdrawing the tramadol—*and* the zolpidem. "But based on these, I'd say you won't last another three months."

For a moment she is speechless. Then—

Strike first strike first strike first.

"What the fuck are you doing, going through my things?" she snarls, pushing up out of the chair. The cup tumbles to the floor, shattering around her bare feet.

"I'll answer your question if you can answer mine."

She jerks her chin, a challenge.

"Why did you rip off the labels?"

"That's none of your fucking busin—"

"You see," he interrupts, shaking the bottles contemplatively, "I can think of two reasons. Neither of them is good. I'm just hoping you have a third which will mean I won't have to report you to Cole when we get back."

She can't think, can't answer. Her mind is screaming contradictory messages, telling her to attack, to hide, to run away.

"The first reason," he continues, still not meeting her eyes, "is that you've been seeing different doctors and getting them to write prescriptions for these, and you took the labels off just in case anyone saw that the names don't match up."

"That's not—"

"And the second reason," he continues, relentless, "and Lord, I hope it's not this one, is that you've been getting them from somewhere else entirely."

No no no no—

"You're wrong," she whispers.

"Fucking hell, George. *Please* tell me I am." Richie's eyes are sparkling. "I'm begging you."

And George says . . . she says . . .

The long silence that follows is cracked when the thin bridge of trust between them collapses.

"I thought . . ." He clears his throat, but his voice still trembles when he tries again. "You know, people said from the start that we were a bad match. My friends, colleagues I've known for decades, they saw you walk in with your sour face and your sharp tongue and they said they were *sorry* for me. Sorry that you'd been dumped on me. That I had to put up with you." He rubs a knuckle under his eye, his Adam's apple bobbing. "But I never felt that way. I liked you before you let me. And after that . . . I thought we worked well together. I didn't imagine that, did I? I taught you—I've *tried* to teach you—everything I know. About people. About patterns. About listening to everyone and everything and keeping an open mind. And I thought I'd done a good enough job. I was proud of myself—prouder of you." His expression darkens. "But that night at the Villo house, you proved just how much I'd been fooling myself. You didn't wait for me to join you, even though you were supposed to. You entered an active crime scene without checking if the building had been swept. You didn't tell anyone you were going in, either. Maybe you don't remember that part," he says in response to her furrowed brow, "but it's true. I asked everyone who was there that night. Because I wanted to know exactly what happened—to see all the checkpoints at which you should have made a different choice. And I've spent so much time trying to understand you, to figure out why you disregarded everything I'd taught you, when all I've really wanted to do is scream at you for being *so stupid*."

She can only describe the feeling flooding through her as horror—a frightening, overwhelming sensation that has a stranglehold on her voice. She can only stand there, a chipped statue from some ancient tragedy, as Richie scrubs a hand across his now damp face.

"I'm sorry, George," he says, a fresh tear following the groove of his nose. "I'm so sorry, because all I can think is that somewhere, somehow I must have let you down." With a sniff, Richie's eyes drop to the bottles in his hand. "And I've clearly failed you *again*."

"Rich," she chokes out, but there's nothing else she can say, no ugly truths her heart can bear the shame of imparting.

Richie blinks another tear from his eye, then he holds the bottles out to her. And waits.

Don't take them, a small voice murmurs.

George knows it's a test. He's got control of his expression now, but she can see something desperate in his eyes. Maybe it's his voice in her head.

But her body is begging her, too: begging her to ease its myriad aches and pains, to release the pressure in her head. So even though she knows she might well die from the shame, she tightens the blanket around her shoulders, marches up to Richie, and snatches the bottles from his hand.

His lip quivers, then he nods. "Nicholson's key is in the briefcase. Don't be late tomorrow, or the boat will leave without you."

At the door, he pauses one last time. "I tried to teach you about patterns," he says, his voice thoughtful and distant, "and another has just occurred to me. We keep failing each other." He smiles, and it's so, so sad. "What are we to make of that?"

And then he's gone.

CHAPTER 21

HER CLOTHES AND SHOES ARE STILL DAMP WHEN SHE GETS DRESSED, AND after apologizing to her host for the broken cup, she slips out the front door.

The atmosphere is strange; it feels like the island is in shock. The violence of the storm front hit hard, but the worst of the wind and rain passed through quickly. People move slowly, collecting pieces of debris that the wind tossed around, speaking to each other in low voices. She approaches the turnoff to the croft, her entire focus fixed on putting one foot in front of the other.

It takes Lewis three attempts to break through her fog, and it's only when he clamps a hand on her shoulder that she snaps out of her daze with a gasp of pain.

"Whoa," he says, holding up his hands. "Are you all right, Inspector?"

Her head is nodding before she can muster the words. "How's Jack? Where did you take him?"

"His house is just up the street. We warmed him up, got some food into him. He's asleep now."

"He really should go to a hospital."

"He should. But he won't."

With a sigh, she leans against the nearest wall, her legs quivering warningly. She wonders if she'll even make it up the hill. "Do you think we pissed off Gentle Annie last night?"

A smile tugs at his lips. "Don't tell me you've turned into a believer."

The memory of the betrayal in Richie's eyes makes her voice thick. "I'm not sure what I believe anymore."

He pauses, really looking at her now. "*Are* you all right?"

For a second, she considers telling him the truth. That her mind and body are a switchboard of pain, and all the lights are flashing. But if she couldn't be honest with the one person in her life who deserves it more than anyone, she's not about to dump it on a relative stranger.

It was a mistake to stop moving—the fatigue has well and truly settled into her muscles. She wobbles slightly as she pushes away from the wall.

"I'm really trying to be. See you around, Lewis."

She doesn't get far before Kathy catches her, proffering a heavy bag. "A few little bits for supper," she explains. "And I've popped the logbooks back in there. You really should finish reading them while you rest tonight."

"Thanks," George says wearily. Over Kathy's shoulder, she notices several women entering the Mackay home. "Is everything okay over there?"

Kathy's forehead crumples. "Oh, you haven't heard. Poor Stephen passed during the night."

It takes a few seconds for her words to sink in. George replays the events of yesterday over in her head. Yes, Stephen appeared to tire quickly after his outburst in the street, but nothing about his condition seemed life-threatening when she and Richie left. "How?"

Kathy shakes her head, her eyes downcast. "He wasn't in good health. It's terribly sad." She smiles grimly. "If there's one silver lining to this awful situation, it's that Sarah will have a lot more time to study now."

George isn't sure what her face is showing, but Kathy's expression becomes strangely fierce, and then she's pulling George into a tight hug. The unexpected gesture makes her body go limp, and she melts into Kathy's softness and warmth. A steady hand strokes her tangled hair.

Kathy's breath flutters against George's ear. "Jack wouldn't be alive if you'd made a different choice. And our people will remember what you did. And"—she hesitates, then squeezes George gently—"most will come to understand what has to happen next."

Her words sound reassuring, but George can't think of what she's referring to—and her brain is too sluggish right now to parse them for meaning. Steeling herself, she withdraws from Kathy's embrace, thanks her for the food, then starts the long walk up the hill.

———

The brown paper parcel turns out to be a thick cut of haddock, the pearly white flesh shining under the overhead light. The other items Kathy sent up look like they belong in the knapsack of a child from an Enid Blyton novel: some bread, a red apple, a slice of teacake, and a small wedge of hard cheese. It's the perfect amount to tide her over for the night before packing up her belongings yet again to join Richie at the post office.

Their last conversation replays in her head as she fries the fish on the stove, nibbling on the bread to tame the growling in her stomach. As she transfers the sizzling haddock to a plate and sits cross-legged in front of the new fire she's lit, she considers his words again.

Did she follow Lewis down those steps without considering the dangers? No—she knew things could go badly, which was why she tried to stop him from going down to the quay in the first place. It was a risk to follow him, sure, but a calculated one. She assessed the situation and did what a police officer *should* do: run toward danger. Help however you can. Protect people.

She uses her wrist to wipe away a few tears as she eats. She can't even begin to address all the tiny points of pain caused by Richie's words earlier—she physically recoils from the memory, curling up against the base of the couch with a blanket around her. She spreads her arms before the fire to catch the heat, like she used to do when she was a kid. Her cheeks are starting to feel a little too hot, but she can't bear to pull herself away when just hours ago she was soaked to the bone in the freezing waters of the Atlantic.

Her heart kicks up a gear at the memory of the overwhelming darkness she faced in the sea. It was all so confusing and overwhelming, feeling the waves tugging her limbs in different directions, the pain in her chest as her lungs screamed for air.

Sitting before the fire now, George presses two fingers firmly against her warm neck, concentrating on increasing the time between pulses. But that just reminds her of how she slammed her weight on Jack's chest over and over, and the sense of failure that began to creep in the longer he took to respond.

She wishes she weren't alone now. She wants her parents and her sister beside her. She wants her friends and her flat and the cafe on the corner that does a really great veggie burger and oily hot chips. For the first time this week, she desperately wants to go home.

As her breathing slows along with her pulse, George realizes that there is one benefit to Richie staying down in the village tonight. She looks over her shoulder toward the bedroom. He made the bed military-perfect before leaving this morning. The sight of it makes her aching body sag with relief. No more curling up on this little couch.

She rises and puts the kettle on the stove, intending to take a cup of tea to bed. As she waits for the water to boil, her eyes are drawn to the logbooks. Kathy was adamant about her reading to the end. She decides to skim through as much as she can before the kettle boils; after that, she's closing the books for good.

The last entries are dated mere days before the three lighthouse keepers allegedly vanished. As she reads, she is alert for hints about the men's mental state, any more comments on the tension between McClure and Wilson, but the overarching theme of their final days is exhaustion, as they are kept awake by a brewing storm and, of course, a *howling* wind. There are no further reports of issues between the men or with the locals. Impatient now, she flips to the final entry, which Kathy has bookmarked, but is disappointed to find only one line from Wilson that simply says: *Tasks complete.*

She huffs a laugh—*this* is what Kathy was so keen for her to read? What a waste of time; despite the increasing strangeness of the entries, she's no closer to understanding the island's biggest mystery. Idly she turns the piece of paper that Kathy used as a bookmark over in her hands.

It's a clipping from a mainland newspaper. A photo is accompanied by a short piece announcing that the previous year's largest catch was taken by a group of Eadar fishermen. The crew are all crowded together in an awkward semicircle in an attempt to ensure nobody is cut out. Running her finger over the grainy image, George recognizes some of the men from the pub the other night. She wonders if the infamous Donald is among them, and, as she scans the faces, one in particular strikes her like a lightning bolt.

Standing on the edge of the group, one arm placed stiffly around the shoulder of the man beside him, is Alan Ferguson. George has never seen this photo before, but she's seen other photos of him at this age. He'd be just on the cusp of eighteen.

Everyone else is lit up with their victory, arms slung around each other in a way that shows their familiarity, their camaraderie. But not Alan. Even in the slightly blurred photo, it's clear that Alan's mind is not on the win. His narrowed eyes are angled off to the right, cutting across the circle, looking in the direction of a tall man with dark hair. George peers at him.

The person Alan is staring at with such intensity is Ewan. And Ewan . . . Ewan is looking right back at him, his expression unreadable. George thinks of the storms she's seen brewing in Ewan's eyes, the roiling emotions he doesn't seem to know how to handle. It was only Cecily's admonishment that kept him in line today—but even after that flare of anger, he still came out in the storm to help Lewis haul her and Jack in. Kept his arm at her back in case she stumbled. A stilted kind of kindness she hadn't expected from him, based on their previous encounters. Perhaps it's this rough but genuine compassion that drew Cecily to him, Donald having more or less abandoned her. It reminds George of the conversation she and Richie had with Fiona the day before, when the young woman observed that Alan had seen something more in her than what showed on the surface, recognizing the compelling duality of her character.

The kettle starts to whistle; absently, she turns off the flame, looking at the photo again. Fiona also mentioned that Alan had a problem with one of the fishermen—no, not a *problem*. Just that the man had kept assigning Alan tasks on the boats. But that's how a job works, isn't it? No teenager likes chores, even when they're getting paid to do them. If Richie were here, he'd be rolling his eyes and telling her stories about how hard it was to get his daughters to pick up after themselves at home. He'd look at this photo and say, "Aye, that's a sulky teenager if ever I saw one." And George would agree—Alan does look a bit sullen.

George rubs her eyes. Staring so closely at the tiny, grainy faces is making her feel a bit nauseous. She replaces the clipping in the logbook and lets it snap closed, then turns to the sink to retrieve a mug.

And finds herself face to face with the wolf.

Again, there's the sudden atavistic terror before her rational mind takes over. Her heart pounding, she holds the wolf's gaze for several seconds. Then the figure raises a hand and crooks their finger. An invitation. A summons.

Come.

CHAPTER 22

SHE DRESSES AS QUICKLY AS SHE CAN AND SNAGS HER BOOTS FROM BESIDE the fire, her tiredness swept away on a flood of adrenaline. With the kitchen knife in an easy-to-access pocket and her torch in another, she says a regretful farewell to the fireplace and plunges into the night.

Though the storm has moved on, there's still an ominous sense of foreboding in the air. The clouds are a deep gray against the black sky, the moon obscured behind their thick cover.

The figure is waiting at the fence of the top paddock, on the side closest to the woods.

"Who are you?" she calls, keeping some distance between them.

The mask tilts, its wearer looking at her curiously.

She scans them for weapons, concealed or otherwise. Their hands hang straight at their sides, and their clothes are too baggy to reveal anything.

"Why have you been looking through our window?" she asks, taking a step closer. "Were you trying to see what we'd found out about Alan? Did you leave the bad luck charm in the roof? Or do you know who did?"

Again, no answer.

George dares another step; but she remains wary. In her head she can hear Richie saying *Risk risk risk* in sync with the beats of her racing heart.

In the end, the masked figure makes the decision for her. On her next step, they spin on their heel and fly down the hill toward the woods. George immediately gives chase, but the watcher has a head start.

Her legs don't hide their resentment as she pushes them faster, muscles quivering. She feels the rasp in her nose and throat as she sucks in the frigid air. But she ignores it, ignores everything except the fleeing figure.

And when they come to a sudden stop, she does too, panting, suspicious.

The figure looks back at her for a long moment, eyes hidden within the shadows of the mask. Perhaps measuring the distance between them, ascertaining their likelihood of escape. George's mouth is dry, her muscles taut, as she waits for the other person to make a move. Then with one final glance at George, they duck into the woods.

Something about that look stirs the electricity in George's stomach.

Risk risk risk, her heart reminds her.

She follows at a jog, making her steps soft as she approaches the trees. If the figure does indeed want her to follow, then they'll wait for her.

She rounds the far corner of the paddock and hurries down the narrow alley of long grass between the fence and the woods, scanning for a face in the shadows. When she reaches the approximate point where the figure entered the woods she pauses to catch her breath, peering into the darkness.

With a last desperate look back at the croft—almost hoping she'll see Richie illuminated in the glowing windows—she resigns herself to her decision. Fishing the knife and torch from her pocket, she enters the woods in pursuit of a wolf.

Having skirted these woods more than once, George estimates that they can't be more than two hundred and fifty yards across.

However, it takes her less than ten before she is forced to slow her pace and turn on her torch in order to navigate the twisted tree trunks and tangled roots that threaten to trip her.

She keeps the knife at her side for now, though her ears are straining for any sound with such intensity that it's starting to make her jaw hurt. She tries to maintain as straight a line as possible, but her first indication that she's moving on a diagonal is when she stumbles onto a path that is clearly man-made.

Nighttime sounds filter through to her from between the trunks, from the leaves above. Scurrying feet across a branch, a low hoot from a bird disturbed by her torch, a rustle as something—or someone—darts across the path behind her. She whips around, the knife raised, her heart beating an anxious tattoo against her ribs.

"Hello?" Her voice wavers; she tries again. "Where are you?"

Silence.

Is this a trap? With the knife held firmly in front of her, George moves forward with slow, deliberate steps, the blade pointed into the dark.

Her ears prick up at a new sound—a dull, repetitive thud that's coming from somewhere in front and to her left. Slowly, cautiously, she follows the sound. For a second she thinks there must be a gap in the trees that has allowed the moonlight to stream through. But as she edges closer to the source of the thudding, she realizes the light has the artificial yellow tone of a lamp. She clicks off her torch, able to navigate the last few steps without it.

There's a large clearing ahead, illuminated by the lamplight. A single ancient tree with a twisted trunk dominates the center, branches casting gnarled fingers of shadow over a series of stone cairns. The dim light plays tricks on her eyes, makes those shadows flex and reach toward her feet.

She keeps to the dark edge of the clearing until she has a

clear line of sight. Smothering a gasp, she slips the knife back into her pocket and steps out of the shadows into the circle of light thrown by the lantern.

"Mr. MacNeil?"

John spins, his eyes widening when he recognizes her. Despite the frigid temperature, sweat is pouring down his face, gathering at the neckline and underarms of the long shirt he wears. His jacket has long since been abandoned, slung over a nearby cairn. He holds a shovel in his meaty hands.

George takes a few measured steps forward until she's within the lantern's circle of illumination.

"What are you doing here?" he hisses.

She assesses the distance, his grip on the shovel, the obvious strength in his burly frame. "Is there a reason I shouldn't be?"

George does a quick scan of their surroundings, but it's just herself and John in the clearing. She checks the ground around him; nothing apart from what looks like freshly turned soil. No wolf mask in sight.

"What are you doing out here, Mr. MacNeil?" she asks again, her eyes flicking back to the shovel.

"Where's your partner?" he responds.

"He's coming," she lies easily, taking another step—not closer but to the side, keeping a distance between them.

But John shakes his head. "Go stop him, and lock yourselves up at Auld Sam's. Stay there until the sun rises. *Then get the hell off this island.*"

She cocks her head, even as her stomach tightens. "Am I in danger?"

"You will be if anyone finds out you were here."

"Why?"

"Don't ask more questions," he says. "Trust me: you're better off if you keep your mouth shut and walk away."

"Trust you?" Keeping her eyes on him, George points at the

shovel. "Are you going to tell me what you were doing, or will we have to question you formally?"

John makes a low sound in his throat. "You think you know it all. Sticking your nose into things that do not concern you."

"It's not every day I see someone digging a hole in the middle of the woods *in the middle of the night*. I wouldn't be doing my job if I didn't have a few questions."

"Keep them to yourself and you might make it off this rock in one piece."

She throws up a hand in frustration. "Mr. MacNeil, I didn't come here of my own accord. I was led here. Someone clearly wants me to know what's going on."

John frowns. "What the hell are you on about?"

"Someone was waiting for me at the croft tonight. Someone who wanted me to follow them here." As he stares at her blankly, she adds, "Someone wearing a wolf mask!"

Even in the weak lantern light, George can tell John has paled.

"Does that mean something to you? Who is it?"

But from the way John spins on the spot, peering into the shadows around him, she knows the answer.

She clicks her torch back on and flashes it into the trees. "Calum?"

There's silence, then—*there*, to the left. A shuffle.

But Calum doesn't emerge from the darkness until his father says, in a thick voice, "It's all right, Cal. You can come out."

And then he does come, timidly, each step chosen with great care. Not because he's afraid; he still wears the wolf mask—which she can see now is made from carefully carved and painted wood and fabric—and the narrow eyeholes seem to restrict his peripheral vision. John's throat bobs, and he doesn't speak as he waits for his son to reach his side. Then he strokes Calum's hair gently and whispers, "It's all right, son. You're all right." But the expression John turns on George says the opposite. It's tinged with a desperation that makes George shift back a step.

"He's come to the croft," she says, swallowing hard. "More than once."

John's jaw clenches. "He wouldn't have meant you any harm."

"I don't think so either. I think . . ." She looks at Calum, trying to see past the grainy mask to his dark eyes. "Did you want to bring me here, Calum?"

After a beat, the wolf's face dips in a nod.

John stares at Calum in a mixture of shock and fear. Then he turns to George, and his words tumble out in a frantic rush.

"You can't tell them—you can't say it was him." He takes a few unsteady steps toward George. "Please, Inspector," he begs, "don't tell anyone it was Calum who showed you."

"Showed me *what*?" she asks, advancing on him. "What *is* this place? What were you—"

A bolt of panic grips her as her foot sinks into the ground. She stumbles, now standing calf-deep in a depression of loose soil. The ground has been turned over here, the soft earth spilling over her boots.

A prickle of fear rolls down her spine as she takes in the shape of the hole she's standing in. She shines her torch at the ground around her.

"What . . . ?" she breathes, her thoughts scrambling to make sense of it. "Why . . . ?" Her widened eyes land on John. "Were you digging a *grave*?"

But even as John doesn't answer—she's not sure he can summon the words—she's digging her gloved fingers into the earth, tearing away the loose soil.

"Don't," John chokes out. "For all our sakes, *don't*."

George ignores him. She places the torch on the edge of the grave so that she can work with both hands now. The freshly turned soil comes out easily, and after a few minutes she's cleared a foot, nearly two. Despite the cold, sweat prickles at her underarms. Then her fingertips meet something firmer than the soil. Something solid, covered in . . . cloth? George brushes the dirt aside to reveal the frayed edges of a light blue blanket. She stares down at it, at the earth around her, at her knees, which she realizes are straddling . . .

"Who?" she demands, nausea rising in her gut.

"Please, please—"

"*Who is this?*"

John chokes on a sob, his eyes wide as he clutches at his son. "It's—it's Spud."

George blinks, peering down into the grave at the soiled blanket sticking out from the dirt; a sliver of color in this dark place.

"Why have you buried him here?" she asks. "Why—why not in the church cemetery, with all the others?"

All the others. Her stomach roils as she looks around the clearing with fresh eyes—at all the cairns. "Are these *all* graves? Why are they out here?"

His lips turn down as he gestures toward George's face, her injured cheek. "Because of that."

For a second, George wonders if she's going to pass out. The ground tilts sharply and the cairns are spinning around her. She throws out a hand to catch herself, a hand braced on the firm shape beneath the blanket. On Stephen Mackay.

With a sickened cry she clambers out of the grave on hands and knees, her breathing too fast. Everything is shifting beneath her and there's too much *pressure* in her head.

"I have to get . . . I have to tell . . ."

"No," John says, his voice high.

She tries to push herself up. "I have to get Richie."

Three heavy footsteps are her only warning; then John's hand is in her hair and he's hauling her backward. She shouts with pain and shock, her hands flying up to claw at his. He's speaking as he drags her, and above her own cries she hears him repeating, "I'm sorry, I'm sorry, I'm—"

"Let go," she shrieks, fumbling for the knife in her pocket.

"I'm sorry," he says again, and his voice is shaking with sobs, and then she feels herself falling for the second time. She lands with a dull thud, her scalp tingling, and she realizes with horror that he has thrown her into the shallow grave that holds Stephen Mackay's corpse. And as John picks up the shovel, his chest heaving, she knows he intends to make it hers, too.

"John," she says, her voice raw.

But he's beyond reason now, driven by a fear for his son and the instinct to protect him at all costs. And it's this knowledge that makes her say: "Are you going to kill me in front of him?"

John tenses. The shovel pauses at the top of its arc. With a shuddering breath, he follows her gaze.

The mask is gone. It means John can see the terror in Calum's dark eyes, the way his trembling lips are pressed together. He can see the way his beloved son is staring at him, shovel raised overhead, about to deliver a killing blow to George's skull.

"Cal," John says hoarsely. "Cal, son. It's all right—just turn around."

Calum rocks back a step, and George sees he's holding the mask tightly against his stomach.

"Cal, just turn around and go home. There's a good lad."

But Calum ignores his father's order as if he hadn't heard it. Instead, his eyes slide to George, sprawled in the grave beneath them. For a moment, he holds her gaze, and she wills every bit of warmth and pleading she can muster into the connection between them.

But she needn't have worried. John told her himself: Calum is smart, smarter than his father. Calum is curious about what makes people tick, observing how they interact with each other, how they move around their tiny world. And Calum understands right from wrong—apparently better than anyone else on this whole goddamn island.

Without looking at his father, he reaches down and offers George his hand. She takes it immediately, and he helps her up and out of the grave. She brushes herself off with her free hand, but keeps Calum's warm hand clutched in hers, unwilling to lose that small connection to the only rational person for miles. Calum has let his fingers go limp, but he doesn't pull them from her grasp.

Across the grave, John stares at Calum as if seeing him for the first time, the shovel still held in a white-knuckled grip.

Their silent stand-off is broken by approaching footsteps. Before she can even think to run or hide, someone new emerges from the shadows.

With his shotgun leveled at her, MacLeod looks at George and Calum standing side by side, then at John. To father and son he says, "Get out of here."

Another sob erupts from John. "She *knows*, Alisdair."

"Go."

But John shakes his head. "If she says that Calum brought her here, I'll be digging his grave next. Or someone will be digging mine, and there'll be nobody to look after him." When MacLeod doesn't react, John's voice climbs in volume. "You know what we have to do, Alisdair. She can't leave here alive or—"

MacLeod's eyes blaze. "Take the boy and go home!"

With a whimper, John drops the shovel and hurries around

the grave toward Calum. Before John can seize his arm, George turns to Calum, a rush of questions and gratitude on her tongue. And then it's too late; his warm hand slides from hers, and Calum lets John tow him away without resistance, looking back only once to flash her a tiny smile before they both disappear into the shadows.

Then it's just George and MacLeod, standing in a secret graveyard in the middle of the night.

The farmer adjusts his grip on the gun, still pointed in her direction. Feeling like she's disconnected from her body, she takes a deep breath and raises her chin. "Put the gun—"

"Shh."

She stares at him. "What?"

He raises the gun slightly and puts a finger to his lips. His eyes slide from hers to the spot in the forest where John and Calum disappeared. The seconds stretch, the only measurement of time George's heartbeats, which are too fast to be reliable.

Finally, MacLeod's shoulders relax slightly; she hadn't realized he'd been holding them so rigid. He looks at her again, taking in her dirt-caked hands and knees, her sweaty face, and sighs. "Come with me."

"Not a chance," she spits. If she can't reach for the knife, the shovel is now within lunging distance. And her body itself is a weapon, if a little dented at the moment.

He takes a step toward her. "If you come with me without kicking up a fuss, you'll get what you want. But you have to come quietly."

She jerks her chin toward the gun. "Or else?"

Before he can answer, a faint rustling above their heads heralds a gust of wind. As it blows through the clearing, sending leaves fluttering across the ground, a familiar sound begins to build. As it grows louder she spins, searching frantically for the source, but it seems to be coming from all around her—until her eyes land on that strange tree in the middle of the clearing.

As the wind dies down, so does the sound.

Her feet move of their own accord, stepping over roots that have ruptured out of the earth. She can see now that the ancient trunk bears a distinct design, deep grooves carved into the wood to shape a beastly face. With trembling fingers, George reaches up to trace the deep eyes, the long snout and gaping mouth. The tree is ancient, alive despite the deep carvings, but it's barely clinging to life—she can tell by the bare branches, by the brittle feel of the bark beneath her skinned fingertips.

It's as she's examining the top row of teeth in the hollowed-out mouth that leaves start swirling around her ankles again, and the beast *howls*.

She jumps away, looking back at MacLeod in shock. But his expression is unreadable as he observes her reactions. As the long, low sound continues, her shock turns to fascination as she realizes that the sound really is coming from *inside* the tree. There must be a hollow somewhere higher up that catches the wind on just the right angle, sending it down the trunk and out of the beast's gaping mouth.

"The sign at the pub ... Calum's mask ... it's all the same face."

"A wulver," MacLeod grunts.

"That's ..." She frowns, trying to recall what Lewis had told her last night. "It's a protector, isn't it?" She eyes the cairns—the *graves*. "Is it protecting them?"

"Protecting the rest of us *from* them."

Her thoughts are racing, trying to piece together what John had told her. "Because they hurt someone?"

"Or were going to."

A twig snaps somewhere off to her left. MacLeod's body tenses; he raises the gun again and directs it into the dark.

"We can't do this here, Inspector," he says in a whisper. "If you're seen, you've got no chance. If you come with me, there's a small one."

She wants to argue, but his apparent concern that they might be joined by other islanders is weakening her resistance. It occurs to her suddenly that the gun might not have been meant for her at all.

However, as if she has spoken aloud, MacLeod then swings the barrel around until it's pointed at her feet. She gets the message.

With a final glance back at the wolf tree, she walks ahead of MacLeod into the dark.

CHAPTER 23

SHE DOESN'T ASK ANY QUESTIONS AS THEY MAKE THEIR WAY THROUGH THE woods, MacLeod's wordless instruction to stay quiet received loud and clear. Besides, even though George has a million questions, she doesn't quite know in which order to ask them.

The first one emerges when, instead of taking the track toward his home, MacLeod prods her along the clifftop path toward the village.

"Where are we going?"

But his commitment to silence lasts all the way to the main street, which she is both disappointed and relieved to find empty. Nobody to call to for help, but also nobody to see her: pale, sweating, and covered in dirt, with a stony-faced MacLeod just a step behind. At least with MacLeod's gun now slung across his back, being ripped to pieces by a spray of pellets is no longer an immediate threat.

She doesn't bother trying to run. The adrenaline that has kept her going all day—which, she realizes with a start, began with her and Richie packing their bags to leave—has finally burned itself out. She feels like a snuffed candle. Her legs are concrete again; it takes a conscious effort to put one foot in front of the other, and her toes keep catching on the uneven ground. After one particularly heavy stumble, MacLeod's strong hand seizes her elbow; she hasn't even got the energy to shake him off.

For some reason, she assumed he was taking her to the

church, but she is not surprised when he pulls her abruptly to the left, down a narrow alley running alongside the post office. The windows are dark, the posters a blur of white paper and indecipherable print. Alan's photo grins at her as she staggers past.

MacLeod leads her to the back of the building and raps once on a green door. About thirty seconds pass before there is movement inside. Light spills under the door, and a voice whispers, "Hello?"

"It's me," MacLeod grunts.

A lock turns; the door opens.

Kathy peers out, wearing blue pajamas, her braided hair piled up on her head. Her eyes are puffy, as if she's been woken from a deep sleep. Those eyes grow round when they flick from MacLeod to George.

"Lord, have mercy," she breathes, taking in George's haggard face, her filthy clothes.

MacLeod shoves George toward the door. "She knows, Kate."

Kathy's lips thin into a worried line, but she steps aside to let them both enter.

Blearily taking in her surroundings, George sees they're in a tiny kitchen—or what is probably meant to be the post office tearoom. There's a small table, a stove, a fridge, and a framed picture of a boat on the wall. Kathy shuffles past and leads them down a short hallway with a weak ceiling light. An open door to the right reveals a small room barely larger than a storage cupboard, into which a single bed has been shoved. A firm hand on her back encourages her to keep moving.

They come out behind the counter of the post office; as MacLeod precedes George around it into the main room, Kathy crosses to a switch and flicks on the lights. They all blink in the sudden glare. George scrubs at her eyes unthinkingly then groans, realizing she's rubbed dirt all over her face.

For a moment, the three of them simply stare at each other.

Then MacLeod clears his throat. "Tea." Without waiting for an answer, he disappears back down the hallway.

George and Kathy remain silent, watching each other carefully as they listen to MacLeod move around the kitchen, setting the kettle to boil, clinking mugs and teaspoons.

"You should sit," Kathy says softly.

George shakes her head curtly.

"You look like you're about to fall down."

"I'm fine," she snaps.

Kathy just bobs her head, her hands twisting over her stomach. MacLeod finally returns, clutching three mugs. He offloads one to Kathy, then approaches George with the other. She shakes her head again, but he just presses it into her hands. Then he moves to a chair beside a stack of newspapers and settles into it with a groan.

Gathering her remaining strength, George straightens. "Talk."

Kathy looks at MacLeod. "Does the other one know?"

He shakes his head. "John MacNeil saw her, but he won't talk—his boy is the one who dragged her into it."

"Is my partner safe?" George interjects.

MacLeod hesitates, then nods. "It's lucky you're leaving tomorrow. Things were getting strained, even after the good you did with Jack today."

"Why? We've finished our investigation. Alan's death was going to be confirmed as a suicide."

MacLeod sips his tea. "People were nervous when they found out you were staying so long. Even more so when you had to stay again tonight." He sighs. "And they were right to be. Look where I found you. Digging up Spud Mackay with your bare hands."

Kathy's hands fly to her mouth, and she looks at George with renewed trepidation.

George glares back at her. "He didn't just die like you said, did he? Someone killed him." Her hand flutters to her bruised cheek. "John said it was because of this."

"We knew he was getting forgetful," MacLeod says. "Young Sarah did a fair job keeping him hidden away. But attacking someone—a mainlander *and* a police officer—in the middle of the street? He was a threat."

"He was an old man and he was sick," George fires back. "He needed specialist care."

MacLeod eyes her speculatively. "Would it change your mind to know that you're not the only one he's ever hit?"

Sarah Mackay's tired, anxious eyes come to mind. George imagines one of them swollen shut by an erratic fist. She presses a thumb to her eyebrow, grimacing. It's been too long since her last pill. "Do you know who killed him?"

MacLeod shakes his head. "It's not for me to know."

Infuriated once again, George nods at Kathy. "And you?"

Kathy's hand drifts down to the cross at her throat. "I can't say."

"You both seem to have forgotten that I am a police officer, and you've just told me that a man has been murdered. If you know who is responsible, you have to tell me."

But Kathy just looks at MacLeod helplessly. George rounds on him. "You promised me answers."

"Inspector, it doesn't matter *who* killed Spud," he says dismissively. "It was one of us. That's all we ever know."

She thinks about the clearing, the number of cairns scattered around it. "How long has this been going on?"

"A long time. A very, very long time. Maybe as long as there've been people on Eadar. It's a duty we inherited."

"A duty?"

Kathy sighs. "You remember Broddy Cameron?"

"The man who burned down the pub."

"Our ancestors had a way of protecting the people here. It was the old way, the wulver way. What Broddy did reminded us what might happen if we turned our noses up at tradition, at duty. Our grandparents knew he was dangerous, but they stayed their hands. After so many of us died that night, we knew we had to resurrect the old customs."

George stares at her in astonishment. "This—what you're describing is vigilantism. You're telling me that you're killing your neighbors and dumping their bodies in the woods because you're scared of what they *might* do? You're saying—" A new chill runs up her spine. "*Why* are you telling me this?"

Kathy and MacLeod exchange a weighted look. MacLeod nods, an almost imperceptible movement, and Kathy sucks in a steadying breath. "Because Alan is out there, and he shouldn't be."

George's eyes narrow. "I saw his headstone up at the church."

"We knew you were coming."

But George shakes her head. "There were cards. People had left flowers." *Blank cards*, a voice whispers. *Fresh flowers.*

Kathy shrugs miserably. "It had to look real."

Her head is still moving from side to side, an unconscious denial, and her eyes catch on the back of the funeral notice in the window. "What . . . what did he do?"

"Nothing," Kathy says tightly.

"No, no, that's not what you just told me," George says, jabbing her finger at the other woman. "The only reason Alan would have been killed and buried out there is because he posed a danger to the community. So what did he *do*?"

"Nothing!" Kathy growls. "He wasn't a danger! He was sweet, he was smart, and he was about to get *out*." Her voice breaks on the final word, and she lifts a trembling hand to her mouth. MacLeod's expression softens as he watches her.

"I thought he hadn't received any acceptance letters."

Kathy whimpers, then crosses to a drawer beneath the counter. George tenses—though she doubts she could react quickly enough to dodge any kind of attack—as Kathy withdraws something from it.

A letter.

Kathy drops the pages onto the counter as if they burn her hands. George approaches and picks up the top sheet to see an ornate letterhead with a red-and-blue logo. Alan's name is printed in black. It's heavy and thick. Not the single sheet of a rejection notice.

"When did it arrive?"

"Two months ago."

The letter suddenly feels ten times heavier in her hand. "Why didn't you give it to him?"

"Things had been strained between Alan and Catriona. I wanted them to make up before Alan could run off to the mainland." Kathy's lower lip trembles. "Catriona and I both knew that once he left, he wouldn't come back."

Anger flares in George's chest. "You're the reason he was still here the night he was killed."

"Don't you think I know that? Don't you think I've had that same thought every single day since he died?" She wipes away fresh tears. "That's why I wanted you to—" Her breath hitches, and she just shakes her head miserably.

George can't stop staring at the letter, at this key to Alan's whole future. "But if you say he wasn't dangerous, why did your vigilante kill him?"

A silence follows her question, and she looks up in time to see Kathy and MacLeod swap another loaded look.

"We don't know who, and we don't know why," Kathy admits haltingly. "And . . . well, I'm supposed to know."

George glances between them, then retrieves a chair from

beside the front door, dragging it all the way back to where she was standing. She lowers herself into it and rests her elbows on her knees.

MacLeod lights a cigarette. Kathy takes a long sip of her tea.

"We all watch each other closely," she begins. "And if we see someone behaving strangely, we're meant to report it."

"To who? You?"

"No, not me. The whole system depends on secrecy."

"Then how do you . . . ?"

Has anyone unburdened themselves to you recently?

I assume you're not about to ask me to break the Seal of Confession.

George inhales sharply. "Father Ross."

MacLeod nods, flicking ash off his cigarette.

"Wait, are you saying *Father Ross* killed Alan?"

Kathy shakes her head. "No, no. The burden isn't placed on just one man; that wouldn't be fair."

"Okay, so who does this killing? Unless the whole bloody island takes turns," she adds sarcastically.

They don't answer.

Whatever remaining blood there is in George's face drains away. She shoots to her feet, and MacLeod rises, too, keeping his hands in sight. "Sit down."

"Stay back," George snarls, putting the chair between them. "You just stay the hell away from me." She darts a glance at the front door—why did she not just run through it when she had the chance?

"Inspector . . ."

"Have you done it? Have you killed someone?"

He watches her carefully. "Are you going to arrest me?"

"*Have you?*"

There's a small cough.

"I have," Kathy says. "I mean, I helped."

George whips around to face her. "*What?*"

She looks Kathy up and down; the image of her as a murderer is made even more ridiculous by the sight of fluffy pink slippers on her feet. "Who?"

"Iain Ferguson."

George's jaw drops. "You killed Catriona's husband?"

"Aye," she says plainly, unaffected by the admission. "And it didn't matter that I'd known him since we were children, that we'd grown up together. As soon as I found out he was putting his hands on Catriona and Alan, I did exactly what we're taught to do—I told our priest. Apparently I wasn't the only one. A few weeks later I found a note in my letterbox that had his name on it." She looks into her cup, swirling the remaining liquid like she's stirring up the memory. "The important thing is the anonymity. It's meant to shield us, I think. So you go to work, you talk to your neighbors, you tuck your children into bed. And then you put on the mask.

"I watched Catriona get Alan ready for bed through the windows. Iain didn't help, didn't even get his fat arse off the chair. By the time Catriona went to bed, there were four of us outside. Not speaking. Just waiting. And when her light went out, we went in. I remember feeling so nervous that I almost laughed and ruined the whole thing." Her face falls. "In the end, I almost did."

Kathy recounts how the four of them had surrounded Iain, who had fallen asleep in an armchair. Someone pointed at a braided rope that secured one side of the curtains, and the others had wordlessly agreed. There was a whisper: "One, two, *three*," and two of them had flung the rope around his neck. As the smallest, Kathy wasn't sure how to help; she only knew that she needed to take part in some way.

"Why?" George interrupts.

Kathy lifts a shoulder. "So the burden is shared."

"So you don't get accused of not doing your bit," MacLeod mutters.

Though Iain was heavily intoxicated, Kathy says they were surprised by his strength. She describes the fear that flashed through her when his thrashing knocked one of them to the ground.

"I realized that even though it was four on one, Iain might win," she says, her voice breaking. "And if he won, he'd never stop hurting my friend and her son. And he would eventually kill her, I was sure of it. If Iain lived, Catriona would die."

Kathy hesitates, then reaches for the collar of her pajamas and tugs it down. Jagged lines of pale scar tissue glow in the firelight. The scar behind George's ear seems to pulse empathetically.

"He got me with a bottle he'd stuffed down the side of the chair," she says, tracing the lines meditatively. "I don't remember much after that—just the sounds of him wheezing."

"You must have been bleeding badly."

"Oh, aye. The last thing I remember is the others dropping me on the doctor's doorstep. I woke up in my own bed the next day with my mother sitting beside me. She didn't ask me what had happened. Nobody did, especially after the news of Iain's death got out." To George's surprise, Kathy's face twists into a fierce smile. "The story was that his drinking had caught up with him finally. When people saw me walking around with my neck wrapped up, they knew it had."

George drags a hand down her face, well past caring about the dirt. "Jesus fucking Christ," she mutters. "So, the priest chose you and the rest of the—the team? What, does he drop the notes off on his morning stroll?"

Kathy's lips turn down. "The priest picks who will do it and writes down their names, but the postmaster delivers them." She nods toward the counter, to that aged timber letterbox

George had seen her handling earlier today: the one with the double spiral carved into the wood.

"And he could pick anyone?"

"Never a child," she says hurriedly, "and none of the elder folks."

"So, anyone between the ages of, say, eighteen and eighty is fair game?" George wonders if there's a cap on the amount of insanity someone can handle in one day. If there is, she's dangerously close to the ceiling. "But if it's all anonymous, can't you just say no? Ignore the note?"

"Have you not been listening, Inspector? Think about it. What if everyone ignored the note on the same night, and Iain was alive the next day? The priest would know that we'd defied him."

MacLeod rumbles, "And everyone is too bloody scared to put a foot out of line in case they're the next name whispered into Father Ross's ear. Even if that means turning on your own kin."

"Some twisted version of self-defense?"

Kathy's lips thin. "It's *protection*." At George's scoff, her hands clench into fists. "You think Iain should have lived? That the others—the men who've beaten their wives, who pulled little girls off the paths, people who have lied and stolen from our precious supplies—should have been allowed to spread their evil infection?"

"I think you're telling me that you knew—you've known this whole time—that Alan was murdered *by your neighbors*. And you said nothing. You *did* nothing. You looked me and my partner in the eye and let us believe you were all mourning Alan, and for five days I have walked all over this fucking island trying to convince myself—against my instincts—that he took his own life."

"I tried to—" Kathy snaps, then reins in her anger. "Do not

make the mistake of thinking the deaths of the people buried out there don't hit us just as strongly as the ones buried by the church. They are still our mothers and fathers and children and friends. We grieve their loss even as we celebrate their absence. We sleep soundly at night knowing that we will live happier lives in a safer community because of how far we're willing to go to protect each other."

That word again: *protect*. They wear it like a shield; use it like a weapon. Symbolized by the wulver carved into the tree that howls so loud the entire island must hear it when the wind blows in the right way; in the beastly masks the islanders wear when they're creeping through the night on their bloody missions.

But George will not allow them to hide behind it.

"You knew that someone exploited your warped justice system to have Alan killed, but you've hidden this secret from me all week. I was *leaving* today, Kathy! I was about to close Alan's file forever!" She sucks in a sharp breath, her lungs feeling too small to power her rage. "You've been wasting time talking in half-truths and riddles when you could have just told me all this at the start!"

"I did! I mean . . ." Kathy throws her hands up in frustration. "I tried."

"Well you didn't try hard enough!"

Kathy just grinds her teeth, but George couldn't care less if she feels misunderstood. "How much does Catriona know?" she asks wearily.

"Just that I didn't send out the notes," she says tersely.

"But someone else did—and you don't know who."

Kathy shakes her head. "Father Ross is just as invested in finding out what happened as I am. If people found out that the system was manipulated . . ." She shakes her head. "Keeping faith is how our community has survived. We can't afford to lose it."

George gestures around the room. "Then why isn't Ross here? So far, you've confessed to enough that I could have you charged as culpable for all the murders. Maybe we should go have a chat with him so he can share the blame."

"Then you may as well just hand him a note with your name on it," MacLeod rumbles. "The priest doesn't give a damn that Alan was killed. He just cares that someone has broken the rules."

"Is that why you're here?" George asks him belligerently.

He shakes his head, but it's Kathy who answers. "He saw me going out to the woods," she says, swiping at her nose.

George frowns. "And that's unusual?"

"Only John really goes in there," she says, "or whoever is carrying the . . . the bodies. It's not a place you go to mourn. When he found me at Alan's grave he, well . . ."

"None of it made sense," MacLeod interjects gruffly. "I knew Alan's da—and I knew people were keeping a close eye on Alan because of what Iain did—but I hadn't seen anything like that with Alan. Hadn't heard anything from my other farmhands . . ." He trails off, shaking his head. "So when I saw her going out there, I followed." He looks at Kathy, his lips twisting into a grim smile. "Only took a wee bit of prodding for her to tell me the lay of things."

Kathy returns his smile weakly, then faces George. "Even though I believe in our ways—and I do, Inspector, so I'm guilty of that, too—there's no point in it if it's being used for"—she swallows—"personal vendettas."

"You want to end it?" she asks doubtfully, then looks at Mac-Leod. "And you?"

"Alan was a good kid," is all he says.

A sudden knock at the front door makes the three of them

jump. The posters covering the windows make it impossible to see out into the street, but George wonders how much someone on the outside can see through the gaps.

"Expecting someone?" she hisses at Kathy.

The other woman shakes her head, her eyes wide with apprehension.

George looks toward the hallway, but there's no guarantee that someone else won't be waiting at the back door to prevent an escape. "If this is a trap . . ."

MacLeod holds up his hand and waves them both back toward the kitchen. For lack of better options, George complies. From the hallway she watches MacLeod approach the door slowly, shotgun in hand. She tenses as he opens the door a crack.

Even with her restricted view, George can read the surprise in MacLeod's body language. And the familiar voice that calls through the door surprises her, too.

"If you wouldn't mind lowering your weapon," Richie says, "I just need to have a quick word with my partner."

CHAPTER 24

ABOVE HIS STEAMING MUG, RICHIE'S EXPRESSION IS STUNNED. "THAT'S A LOT to take in."

"Tell me about it," George says, clutching her own mug, "and I've only known for an hour."

Unable to sleep, and feeling guilty and anxious over leaving George alone in the croft, Richie decided to walk up the hill to check on her when he noticed a light on in the post office as he passed. When he paused to peer in the window, he heard her voice.

"Didn't seem like you three were discussing the weather," he said, taking off his big coat to stand beside the protesting heater.

George has sent Kathy and MacLeod into the kitchen while she fills Richie in on everything she learned this evening. As she speaks, she finds it's a tough tale to lay out in a straight line.

"And you're sure this isn't some ridiculous story? I'm only saying," he says quickly in response to her outraged expression, "when people are starved for entertainment, they come up with strange things."

"I was in a *grave*, Richie. Stephen Mackay is buried out there. Along with Alan and at least one hundred years' worth of the island's undesirables."

Murmured voices float out to them from the kitchen. She peers down the hallway to see Kathy is crying again. MacLeod has his hand on her shoulder, his expression grim.

"If it's true"—Richie blows out a long breath—"this is a wee bit bigger than we anticipated."

"I don't even know how to begin to pull it apart."

Richie raises an eyebrow. "When help arrives, you mean?"

"Rich, we can't afford to wait. Father Ross was arrogant enough to have Stephen killed while we were still on the island. He knows he's untouchable because he's currently got two hundred and four human shields."

"So your plan is to arrest every single person in the village before making a move on him?" He whistles. "I don't know about you, Lennox, but I didn't bring that many pairs of handcuffs."

She jabs a finger toward the door. "The longer we leave this, the more time we give them to start dropping the evidence out at sea."

"I doubt they'll be able to dig up all those graves and load bodies onto boats without us noticing. We may have missed *some* clues, but give us a bit more credit." Seeing her rising frustration, he holds up a calming hand. "We can't handle something like this on our own. We were sent to ask questions about a suicide, for God's sake, and instead you decided to uncover a few centuries of ritual murders." He shakes his head. "If I were you, after I scooped up my Bravery Award from SPF, I'd treat myself to early retirement."

He's right, of course, and she settles back into her chair begrudgingly. If they start reading people their rights without backup, there will be two more cairns by the time the police launch arrives to pick them up. George wonders how the islanders would handle that. They could lie for a while, screen calls from the mainland police, feign bad connections or blame the weather until Richie and George were deep in the ground—though Father Ross is probably smart enough to know that keeping their bodies on the island would be too risky. More likely, they'd be loaded onto a boat and then dropped out at sea. After a few days of calls going unanswered, someone would be sent to check on them, and all they'd find would be Samuel Nicholson's empty croft.

"Fine," she says reluctantly. "But we're coming back. I want to be there when they rip up those woods."

"If we aren't sent for psych evaluations first," he mutters, and she feels a small seed of hope bloom in her chest—with this new revelation, he seems to have forgotten that he was going to report her to Cole. "What should we do about them?" he asks, nodding toward the hallway.

George absently sips her overly sweet tea. "They've risked a lot by telling me this. MacLeod could have shot me on sight and dropped me in with Stephen."

Richie shakes his head. "Their neighbors are their own worst enemies."

"And the worst part is that nobody is *telling* them to do this anymore. The fear and obligation run so deep that they just keep going through the motions day in, day out. They're terrified of each other."

A memory tugs at her. Cold water smacking her chest, lantern light, and Lewis's voice rising above the sound of crashing waves.

If we keep doing things the way our great-grandparents did, then we're already dead.

Suddenly the tea tastes bitter on her tongue.

Lewis knows about this. George's teeth clash together. Lewis . . . and *Cecily*. And every other person who has smiled at her, spoken to her, welcomed her into their home, given her food and tea. They *all* know.

"It's almost midnight," Richie says. "About ten hours until our ride arrives."

George glances back at the huddled pair in the kitchen.

"Why don't we just call Cole now, get her to send reinforcements early?"

"I don't relish the idea of waking our boss in the middle of the night to inform her that Alan's death was not an accident or a suicide, but an act of ritual murder that the people of this island have been committing for a few hundred years, all while dressing up as wolves." He rubs his temples, as if the thought has given him a headache. "Given we're out of here in a few hours," he continues after a moment, "I think that's a conversation I'd prefer to have in person, with our evidence laid out in front of her so she doesn't think we've gone completely insane and fire us on the spot."

Though she chafes at the prospect of waiting so long, she knows that Richie is right. This will require more than a midnight phone call.

"I need to get back to the pub," he says. "The barman saw me head out and I don't want to raise suspicions by not coming back."

"You really think us being separated is a good idea?"

"Not even a little bit. But we don't have many options."

MacLeod and Kathy drift out from the hallway.

"I'm going home," MacLeod grunts. "I'll walk you back up, Inspector Lennox."

George narrows her eyes at Kathy, who answers her unspoken question.

"We'll not say a word. What happened to Alan is against everything our community believes in. Alisdair and I will not stand by and let something like this happen again, and if that means confessing our sins before a judge, or risking our lives to tell you the truth, then so be it." Kathy smiles weakly. "Like it or not, we're on the same side now."

As they wrap themselves up in coats and scarves, Richie pulls George aside.

"I'll stick around for a bit and watch the place," he says in a low voice, buttoning his coat. "I can at least make sure she doesn't go knocking on someone's door."

"And then the two of us will be sitting ducks. You'll be surrounded by them."

"And you'll be all alone up there," he says, looking equally perturbed. "I don't think I need to remind you to lock the door."

They look at each other for a long moment.

"We'll need to talk about everything when we get back," he says.

"I know. Let's just hope we *do* get back." She smiles at him tentatively. "But I'm glad you're here."

He hesitates, then knocks the back of her hand with his. "We're partners, Lennox. Where else would I be?"

The walk through the village is as fraught with tension as the one earlier that night. It doesn't help that the temperature seems to have dropped about ten degrees since they entered the post office; George takes shallow breaths and hears MacLeod doing the same. She has plenty of questions she wants to throw at him, but the recent revelations have left her feeling utterly exhausted. There'll be plenty of time for questions later; she just has to make it through the next ten or so hours without getting herself into a situation that even MacLeod won't be able to rescue her from. Because she's realized that MacLeod did just that.

"Did you see me go into the woods tonight?" she asks through chattering teeth.

There's not enough moonlight to make out his expression, but his voice is the usual grumble when he replies. "Aye. Knew you were headed for trouble."

"So you came to help me?" When he doesn't reply, she persists. "Why would you do that? Because you want me to find out who did this to Alan?"

He grunts an affirmative. "He was one of mine. It's my job to look after them." She thinks he's going to leave it at that, but then he adds, "And also because of the sheep. The one you saved."

She blinks, surprised. "Who told you about that?"

MacLeod makes another noncommittal sound. Those kinds of details might not be important to him, but the sheep clearly are. And George understands that MacLeod had exposed the truth about Eadar in order to seek proper justice for Alan's murder, but his appearance in the woods tonight was about repaying a debt to her.

"Okay," she says to him. Now they're even.

Without any further chat, MacLeod peels off toward his house. She makes it to the croft with relief. She pushes the heavy timber table up against the door, the chairs wedged underneath for good measure. She hangs the blanket back over the kitchen window and checks the latch on the one in the bathroom. But she also realizes the futility of what she's doing. If the islanders come for her, she knows that nothing she can do will stop them. She decides to keep vigil till dawn all the same. If she's to die tonight, she wants to see it coming.

Dragging the armchair closer to the fire, she settles onto it and tucks her knees beneath her chin. And for the next few hours she just watches the flames. Listens for footsteps. And waits for the howling to start.

As the long night slowly turns into pre-dawn, there's one thought that keeps returning to George.

She leaves her post to grab her briefcase from beside the door and, ignoring the alluring rattle of the pill bottles, withdraws the case file, thicker now with the new notes and profiles she and Richie have drawn up during their few days here.

Laying it on the table, she works her way through the pages, each piece of information they've collected already seared inside her eyelids, and slides out Alan's picture. The wispy hair, the gap in his teeth, the movie star smile. All of it—everything he was, loved, and stood for—is about to get swallowed by this village when it becomes front-page news.

The realization drops into her head like an anvil.

When the island becomes front-page news *for the second time.*

She rushes over to the table where, only a few hours earlier, she closed the lighthouse keeper's logbooks for what she thought was the last time. Flipping through the pages now, her eyes catch on the passages she's read over the past few days, the words that made her feel so uneasy. The men's final entries were dated just a year after Broddy burned down the pub—when the island's justice system was already back in full swing.

Did the bad blood brewing between the keepers and the locals—the temperature rising every time they rejected the invitations of the priest, or when Wilson drank too much and started throwing punches—lead to their disappearance? Do three of those cairns in the woods belong to the missing men?

Her thoughts race at the same pace as the growing buzz in her limbs, that old feeling that tells her she's following a tenuous but accurate theory. If their bones are buried beneath the watchful wulver, it means that this century-old mystery could be solved in a matter of months—maybe even weeks, if the keepers have any living descendants to give DNA samples. Is there anyone left in those bloodlines who still wants those answers?

She looks at the papers spread out before her, the photo of the boy who brought her here in the first place. If her theory is correct, and the keepers are buried out there with who knows how many other bodies, will Alan's photo even make the first page? Or will he just become a number, an unbelievable statistic from the incredible case of the Scottish island left alone so long that it learned to be its own god?

Her chest heaves with a shuddering breath, and she has to close the file over the picture of Alan and lock everything back in the case so he can't look at her anymore.

———

Her eyelids are fluttering when the first gull cries. The fire has faded to glowing embers. Her breath clouds in front of her face, and she wonders how long she was dozing as dawn crept into day. Struggling into a sitting position—she slumped onto the couch at some point—she checks her watch. It's seven a.m.

Getting to her feet, she pads silently across to the door, listening intently. There's nothing but gulls for the first few seconds, and the distant crash of waves. In the bathroom she rises up on her toes to peer out the tiny window. The glass is heavily frosted, so she can't see anything outside, but she's survived the night so she guesses that Kathy and MacLeod have kept their word.

Three hours. She and Richie just have to act normally until they climb aboard the police launch and tell them to step on it as soon as they leave the harbor. Hopefully by the time they get a proper team together and make the trip back, the wolves of Eilean Eadar will be just sitting down to dinner.

She spends the next hour and a half writing her statement in her notebook, going over the events of the previous evening in minute detail and jotting down everything she can recall in chronological order. The logbooks, discovering the cairns and the wolf tree, the confessions from Kathy and MacLeod. She knows it's important to be as clear and factual as possible. She can already picture Cole's gobsmacked face and the sideways looks from her colleagues. At least she'll have Richie to back her up. It's a thought that brings her both comfort and guilt.

By eight thirty George has memorized her statement. She decides that she can drag out her walk to the post office enough to make this an acceptable time to leave.

Taking her bag and briefcase, she steps out of the croft for the last time. The air hits her lungs like a knife, and she is astounded by the temperature outside. Then she takes in the changed landscape in front of her.

The keepers described it right—snow falls on Eadar like a blanket.

George's first few steps are on frosty grass, but soon she sinks up to her ankles in fresh, soft snow. She's seen snowfall in the city plenty of times, but Eadar in shades of white and gray is nothing short of breathtaking. What had yesterday been wild green hills and muddy patches has become sweeping mounds of powdery, undisturbed white. MacLeod's paddocks look like the smooth top of a wedding cake, and even the white bricks of the lighthouse look dull from this distance. Gulls circle above, calling out as if to share their own surprise at the sight.

Her trip down the hill is an approximate one, since the track is now inches below the snow. She uses MacLeod's fence as a guide and only stumbles over knots of frozen grass twice before drawing level with his gate. She pauses to survey his house and property. There's a thin trail of smoke emerging from the chimney, but by this time he should be up and working. She wonders if she should knock on his door but decides against it.

It's hard to reconcile what she now knows about the island with the image that greets her when she steps onto the main street. It could be a scene from a postcard, or a fairy tale, with snow dusting the roofs like sugar on gingerbread houses. Even the shopfronts with their flaking paint look charming. Delight colors the faces of the handful of residents who have braved the cold to walk around. The sounds of children's laughter and excited shrieks only serve to make George feel like more of an alien. Keeping her head down as if bracing against a strong wind, she acknowledges greetings and comments on the weather with nothing more than a nod or a wave.

The relief that washes through George when she pushes open the post office door and finds Richie sitting by the counter almost makes her sag to the floor. She hurries over to him with the intention of wrapping him in a hug, but he widens his eyes and shakes his head minutely. A second later she hears voices approaching from the hallway and Kathy emerges, two mugs in her hands—and a few steps behind is Catriona.

George's sudden appearance makes Kathy jump, and tea slops over the sides of the mugs.

"You're early, too," she says, placing the mugs on the counter shakily.

George just smiles at her, then Catriona. "Good morning."

Catriona bobs her head, her face drawn.

The silence stretches uncomfortably long; Kathy breaks it with a strangled laugh. "Can you believe this, Inspector?" She nods toward the window. "What are the chances that we get such a heavy snowfall just days after we talked about how rare it is?" She stares out the window, her teeth worrying her bottom lip. Then she blinks. "You'll want a tea."

Not waiting for George to reply, she scurries back down the hallway. A crease between Catriona's eyebrows is the only indication that she thinks her friend is behaving strangely; with a cautious glance at George, she follows Kathy to the back.

"Everything okay last night?" George asks Richie in a low voice.

"Not a peep. You?"

She shakes her head. "What time did you get here?"

"About forty minutes ago. I woke up early and saw the snow,

so I came here right away to check that the boat was still able to come."

"And?"

"There's no snow on the mainland. I guess it's the island putting on its last show for us. The launch will be here as expected."

George checks her watch again and groans.

"I know," he mutters, then says in a brighter voice, "You make a lovely tea," as Kathy returns with another mug.

"There's an art to it," she chirps as she passes the mug to George. "Double the amount of sugar they ask for. It's naughty, but nobody has ever complained."

Richie chuckles. "I'd start complaining if I had to buy my trousers the next size up."

Kathy's smile doesn't reach her eyes, and it immediately falls as she goes back to chewing her lip.

George seizes the opportunity of Catriona's continued absence to reach into her bag and withdraw the logbooks. "I finished these," she says, placing them on the counter. But when Kathy reaches for them, George tightens her grip. "Last night you said you tried to tell me what was going on here. Is this what you meant?"

Kathy's lips twitch. "Do you really think I wanted you to read them for entertainment? Even I know they're as dry as plain toast. I thought if you read them, if you would figure out what happened to the men . . ." She passes a hand over her face, fingers lingering at her lips. "It was a foolish idea, I'll admit that now. I thought I was being clever—I could help you get to the truth, but still claim ignorance if it came down to it."

Throughout Kathy's explanation, Richie has been looking between the two of them, his brow furrowed. By the end, his jaw has dropped. "You have got to be fucking joking—pardon me. The missing keepers are buried out there, too?"

"I don't know for sure, of course," Kathy says quickly. "That was all long before I was born, and for obvious reasons we don't keep a formal record." She looks at George wryly. "Soon you'll know more about this island's history than I do."

"You mean when we start counting the bones?"

After an uneasy beat, she mutters, "Aye, well. I suppose so." She takes the logbooks out the back and returns wearing a thick orange coat, wrapping a knitted scarf around her neck as she walks. "All right," she says, her voice still subdued, "shall we head over?"

"Our boat won't be here till around ten," Richie reminds her.

"Yes, but the service starts at nine. Mass?" she adds, taking in their confusion. George opens her mouth to protest, but Kathy holds up a hand. "It will help if they see you there," she says quietly. "Capitalize on the goodwill you earned yesterday. You'll need it for when you . . . you'll just need it."

George masks her uneasiness as consideration. "How long will it take?"

Kathy nudges them toward the door; Catriona joins them, shrugging on a smoky gray coat. "You'll be back in time," Kathy says.

They let Kathy shepherd them out onto the street, where they join a crowd of Eadar residents walking up the hill. If evenings at the pub are one of the island's biggest social events, Sunday morning Mass is definitely the other. As they approach the church doors, they're greeted with the warmest reception they've had since their arrival, with most of the smiles and waves directed toward George. Kathy was right: saving Jack Ross has certainly done wonders for her popularity. Catriona drifts behind in a thoughtful silence that's only broken when she's forced to accept someone's hug or soft greeting.

They're carried along with the crowd through the foyer and into the church proper. The lively chatter bounces off the ceiling, making the gathering sound twice its size. The snow seems to be the only topic of conversation. A smiling woman with rosy cheeks invites George to dip her hand in a bowl of water by the door; glancing around, she sees the islanders doing so before making the sign of the cross. Richie follows suit. George ducks her head and moves past hurriedly.

There's an empty pew toward the back; she heads toward it, but Richie gets caught in a cluster moving down the aisle and is driven toward the front. She takes the seat at the back anyway, waiting impatiently as the pews in front of her slowly fill.

After a few minutes, some unspoken signal passes through the room and the congregation settles. George turns in time to see Father Ross enter, resplendent in floor-length robes. The congregation stands, George scrambling to her feet a half-second behind. But there's no way for her to blend in when, as one, they all begin to sing. She simply resolves to draw as little attention to herself as possible.

Father Ross makes his way down the aisle, trailed by two teenage boys with neatly combed hair. It's hard to reconcile that this man, a self-proclaimed shepherd with his mild demeanor, neat robes, and stilted gait, has the power to turn any member of his flock into a killer or a victim with just a slip of paper. The hymn continues as he reaches the front, where he and the boys bow at the altar. After a few moments the priest turns to the congregation. The song ends, and silence falls.

"In the name of the Father, and of the Son, and of the Holy Spirit."

The islanders respond with a murmured, "Amen."

"The Lord be with you."

"And also with you."

Father Ross lets his eyes run over the assembly, as if he means to mark every face in attendance. George slides down in her seat. Then his face breaks into a beaming smile.

"Welcome," he says, his voice resonating throughout the space, "and thank you for braving the elements to join with your neighbors here today. We all awoke to a blessing from our Lord, and though some of us might find the snow a bit of an inconvenience, there's no denying the joy it brings to the faces of our children—of all ages."

A chuckle rolls around the room. George spots Kathy in the front row, Catriona to her left and Richie to the right. Her eye is caught by a flash of red hair to her left. George recognizes Sarah Mackay, her face pale and eyes swollen from crying.

As Father Ross leads them through the Mass, George continues to scan the crowd. She tries to keep one ear on the service, but something is bugging her. There aren't many empty seats in the church, but it strikes George suddenly that several people are not in attendance: MacLeod; Cecily and her children; Lewis. And Ewan.

As Father Ross turns to take some papers from one of the altar boys, she rises from her seat but stays low, whispering apologies as she makes her way to the end of the row. Keeping her eyes on the carpet, she opens one side of the double doors and slides through the tiniest gap, making sure it closes silently behind her. Then she rushes out into the frosty air.

CHAPTER 25

EVEN BEFORE SHE RAISES HER FIST TO KNOCK ON THE CAMPBELLS' FRONT door, George can sense that something is off. It isn't just the smokeless chimney, the stillness of a house usually full of children's voices.

She steps back onto the street and cranes her neck, peering up at the windows. The curtains are still drawn over the main bedroom, which she realizes with a jolt is exactly where she was just five days ago, looking down right at the spot she's standing in now. The memory raises the hairs on her arms and neck.

Approaching the door again, she raises her hand and knocks quietly. The double spiral looms over her.

Almost a minute passes without an answer, and George is just about to turn away when she hears a loud thud from within. She knocks again, louder. "Cecily?" Her eyes slide down to the handle, and she gives it an experimental twist.

Open, of course. She steps in.

She's struck by the temperature at first; the normally cozy house is only a few degrees warmer than outside. A large duffel bag lies at the foot of the stairs, its contents straining against the zip. There are two large backpacks beside it, all seeming to have been tossed from the landing above. George closes the door behind her and climbs the stairs with caution lest another bag come flying. About halfway up, one of the steps creaks beneath her weight.

Cecily's voice floats down to her. "Come help me with this."

Realizing that Cecily must have seen her through the window, she jogs up the rest of the stairs and heads for Cecily's bedroom.

Unlike the last time she was here, the fireplace is nothing more than gray ash, even though there's a stack of logs in the basket next to the hearth. The bed is unmade, the coverlet hanging down on one side, and there are clothes strewn across the floor.

Crouched in front of the wardrobe, Cecily is opening a small suitcase. Her movements are hurried, jerking the zip around the corners roughly. "We've only got room for the essentials, all right?" she says without looking up. "I've done the kids' bags already."

Confused, George replies, "Are you talking to me?"

Cecily gasps and spins around. "George? What are you doing here? I thought you were at Mass."

"I was." She nods toward the case. "Are you going somewhere?"

"Uh . . ." Her eyes flick over George's shoulder. "I'm taking the kids to visit my parents. We're heading off in a few minutes, actually."

Taking in the chaos of the room, George says, "Seems pretty spur of the moment."

Cecily makes a vague sound of assent, rolling up clothes and shoving them into the case. Watching her, remembering the familiar way she called out at the sound of George entering the house, that feeling of *wrongness* returns.

"How did you know I was at Mass?"

"Hm?" Her voice is high.

"You said you thought I was—"

"Oh, I saw you leave the post office," she interrupts, reaching for a pair of trainers and forcing them into a tight side pocket on the case. "You were heading up the hill with Kathy. I just assumed..."

George's body begins to hum. "Right. But if everyone's at Mass, who's going to take you—"

Cecily exhales sharply. "I really can't do this right now."

"Do what? Talk to me?" The hum is spreading through her torso and out to her limbs. It feels hot and prickly, like a rash. "You've never had a problem with that before."

Cecily's chin jerks up. Her eyes are bright; feverish spots of color have appeared in her cheeks. "You know, I didn't invite you in," she snaps, getting to her feet. "Don't you need a warrant before you just barge into people's houses?"

George rocks back a step, surprised by the other woman's sudden shift in tone. "Only if I was here to search the place." *Or to arrest you*, she adds mentally.

She assesses the situation quickly. It would be naive of her to think that Cecily is ignorant of the island's dark secrets. Even though she was born a mainlander, she must know something about the vigilantism, even if only as an observer rather than a participant. And the fact that she's taking off to the mainland after the events of last night...

"What's happened, Cecily? Why are you running?"

The woman's expression hardens, and she stalks forward. "Get out of my home."

George sidesteps so that she's beside the bed, but raises her palms pacifyingly. "Can we just talk for a minute?"

"I don't *have* a minute."

"Why not?"

Cecily ignores the question, so George adds, "Maybe I can help you."

Cecily regards her warily. "Help me how?"

George thinks quickly. She knows they're going to need

more than MacLeod's and Kathy's confessions to sustain a trial. Getting Cecily onside—even just to tell her story as a new bride forced to participate in the grim traditions of her husband's people—would be a valuable addition to their case.

She hesitates for just a moment before saying, "I know, all right?"

"Know *what*?"

"What really happened to Alan," she says, the edge of the bedside table cutting into her calves. "I know about the notes, and the woods, and the wolves."

The color drains from Cecily's face; she reaches out to grip the nearest bedpost. "Oh God," she breathes. "Where—where is he?"

George frowns. *He?*

"Where is he?" Cecily repeats with more force. "Where are my kids?"

"Your kids? Why would I—"

Cecily takes two quick steps toward her. George tries to back up but the bedside table prevents her escape. A few of the framed pictures topple; she glances down, hoping there's something on the table that she can use to defend herself if necessary.

Her eyes flick between the framed pictures on the bedside table: snaps of the kids squeezed cheek to cheek, sepia-toned photographs of stern-faced ancestors, and the Virgin Mary painting. The timber frame of that one looks heavy, and George starts to reach for it . . .

Then pauses.

Another familiar face in a photograph behind the painting has caught her eye. In it, Cecily wears a tea-length white dress, long hair spilling down her back in loose curls. And beside her, in an ill-fitting black suit, clutching her hand with a grin as wide as hers, is a baby-faced Ewan.

Her heart stutters.

She looks up at Cecily, standing close enough that George's stomach tightens. Cecily's face is ashen, her eyes wide and staring.

"Donald never left the island, did he?" she says quietly. "That's who you were expecting when I walked in." The picture from the newspaper cutting flashes across her mind: Alan and Ewan—no, not Ewan, *Donald*—staring at one another. "Did something happen between them?"

"You don't know what you're talking about," Cecily breathes.

"Were they fighting about something?" *Or someone?* George looks back at the wedding photo, her thoughts racing. "Were you sleeping with Alan?"

Cecily's eyes flash. "*I've* never broken my vows."

The emphasis makes George pause, threads of recent conversations weaving together: Catriona saying that Alan and Fiona broke up because he cheated on her; Alan telling Fiona it wasn't going to work out with the other girl because she was with someone else; and Donald's bizarre reaction when George asked if he knew who Alan had cheated with.

"There were rumors about Alan having someone in his room when the crew were on the mainland," she says slowly. "Everyone assumed it was a local girl . . . but it wasn't a mainlander, was it?" She hesitates only for a second before adding, "And it wasn't a girl."

Something breaks within Cecily; her shoulders slump and she clutches the crucifix around her necklace.

"*You* wrote the notes," George breathes, nausea swirling in her stomach. "*You* sent the wolves after Alan . . . because he and *Donald* were having the affair."

Cecily shakes her head, but it's not in denial.

The nausea rises into George's throat, and she swallows thickly. "Does Donald know?"

Cecily shakes her head again, and then, as if she's come to some sort of decision, she straightens. When she starts speaking again, it's almost with relief. "I sent him a note, too. There were others, there had to be, but I wanted Donald to have to live with the knowledge that he killed that boy. That fucking *boy*. It was stupid, in hindsight. He already has trouble keeping a fucking secret, let alone one that's tearing him up."

"Is that why you kept him away from me? Why he gave me a fake name?"

"I told him to leave, to get on his boat and *go*. But he was scared—he thought it would look too suspicious if a boat took off right after you arrived. And then he got paranoid—started talking about all the times I'd complained about missing home." She shakes her head, her expression a mix of frustration and fear. "He thought I'd turn him in and use the opportunity to take the kids and leave for good. He didn't go out on the boats because he wanted to make sure I couldn't make a run for it, and I couldn't have him in the house if you dropped by to ask questions."

George's lip curls in disgust. "And to think you could have saved him the worry if you'd told him you were just as culpable."

"Then he would have killed me," she says simply. "Or if he didn't kill me, if being the mother of his children was enough to warrant mercy, someone else would have done the job eventually. Maybe they'd wait until you and your partner had left. But then again, they didn't for Spud . . . I wonder what excuse they would have fed you," she muses. *"Cecily has a stomach bug, she can't handle visitors. Cecily decided to visit her parents."* She makes a disgusted sound. "It probably wouldn't even be that convincing. They're not used to having to come up with excuses."

Despite Cecily's meandering thoughts, George knows what

312 — LAURA McCLUSKEY

a precarious situation she's found herself in. She's the only one who knows what Cecily has done; the only one standing between Cecily and escape.

Risk risk risk, her heart thumps; a reprimand, a warning. She tries to take a subtle step toward the door, but Cecily mirrors her.

"But why leave now?" George asks, taking another step. "Why the rush? Are Donald and the kids on a boat already? Have you convinced him that you should all flee together?"

Cecily doesn't answer at first; her chest is rising in shallow pants. When she does respond, her voice is flat, stripped of emotion. "That's the fucking irony. I made Donald kill Alan, and it finally poisoned Donald against this island and everyone on it. And I knew it was my only chance to convince him that we—he and I—were on the same team. That we could stay together, with the kids, and live a proper life. A mainland life." A gleam enters her eye; she looks to be on the verge of tears. "I'm finally going *home*, George. For good."

George is in the doorway now. "Running won't fix this. You need to come with me now."

"I *need* to be with my children, my husband," Cecily says, her voice raw. "Everything I've done has been to keep us all together."

"You don't want to put your kids through what will happen if you leave today," George implores. "We will hunt you down, Cecily, and I promise you that it will not be as gentle as what I'm offering you right now."

Cecily's eyes narrow. "Move."

George backs onto the landing. Her thoughts are racing; she knows if she can just keep Cecily talking, she might be able to keep control of this unraveling situation until their launch arrives.

"Cecily, let's just slow down," she says, risking a quick glance around to see how close she is to the top of the stairs—and Cecily chooses this moment to make her move. As George turns her head, she hears swift footsteps, feels two hands against her chest, and then she is shoved violently down the stairs.

———

She's not out for long—no more than a second, one long blink—but when she opens her eyes Cecily's face is looming above her. George's vision swims.

"Fuck. *Fuck.*"

Cecily's fingers circle her neck, almost softly. George groans, trying to twist out from under her. *This is it*, she thinks. *She's going to kill me now.*

But the hands at her throat disappear, and then Cecily's face withdraws. George hears the front door slam.

There's a disconnect somewhere between her brain and her body—she only knows her hand has risen to probe her temple when she sees her reddened fingers in her peripheral vision.

I'm okay, she says to herself, her inner voice sounding small and distant through the bubble of shock around her. *I can think, I can move, I'm all right.*

But she can barely hear it over the other voice, the voice that screams that Cecily is getting away.

Clutching the banister, she drags herself to her feet, but has to brace herself against the wall as she's rocked by a wave of nausea.

I can think, I can move, I'm—

She doubles over, vomit splattering across the floor.

"Fuck," she croaks aloud. Then she wipes her mouth with her sleeve, staggers to the front door, and stumbles through it.

The snow has already started to melt; mud is bleeding

through the pristine white. The main street is a ghost town; everyone must be at Mass still. George can't see Cecily anywhere—she could have made it to the boat already, she thinks, her stomach sinking.

"Inspector!"

George's heart leaps to her throat as she turns toward the voice.

Lewis is beaming as he jogs up the street toward her, coming from the direction of the harbor. But when he gets close enough to take her in properly, the smile slides from his face. "Jesus, you're bleeding!"

She brushes off his concern. "Did you see Cecily?"

"Cecily? Wait, what happened to you?"

"Did you see her?"

"No! No, I—where are you going?"

If Cecily hasn't passed him, then she can't be heading for the boat. Her relief is short-lived as Lewis grabs her arm, turning her to face him. A flare of panic makes her rip her arm away, and she glares at him.

It only takes a few seconds for the realization to hit. Fear and guilt creep into his expression, turning the corners of his lips down. "Inspector, I—"

"Don't bother."

He sucks in a breath, snatching his hat off to rake a hand through his hair. "It's so complicated."

"It really isn't," she says curtly. "I don't give a shit what Broddy Cameron and all those people after him did. This is murder, plain and simple."

He bites his lip and looks back up the street to the houses, the church. When he turns back, there's determination in his miserable eyes. "What can I do?"

George thinks quickly. "Do whatever you can to stop Donald's boat from leaving the harbor." She can see a question forming on his lips but raises her hand to cut him off. "Chain it to the fucking quay if you have to. He's desperate and he's got the kids—I don't want them to get hurt. Do you understand?"

He looks wretched, but he nods.

"Then go."

She watches him jog away, feeling a deep and reverberating sadness penetrate her anger. But both emotions are impractical at a time like this; she needs to focus.

Where is Cecily?

Probing at her head distractedly—the bleeding has already slowed—she surveys the street again. Cecily could have ducked into any one of the houses or shops, trying to figure out her next move.

But she feels a tug in her stomach; a magnet drawing her. She looks back at the harbor, frowning. Cecily *could* have made it to the boat. Just like she *could* have killed George when she was lying prone at the bottom of the stairs. But she let her live, even knowing that it meant the circumstances of Alan's death would come out, that Donald would discover what she'd done, what she'd made him do, and that her children would be taken from them both. Cecily fled the house knowing that she was about to lose *everything* that mattered to her—everything that she killed to keep.

The magnet tugs again—to the right. Toward the clifftop track.

"Oh, shit," George breathes, then launches into a sprint.

She knows exactly where she'll find Cecily.

————

George pushes herself harder than she's ever run before, her lungs burning as she climbs the snowy track. The weather seems to have kept the inhabitants of the woods in their dens and nests—the woods are silent save for the heavy thud of snow sliding off branches. Soon the lighthouse looms ahead of her, and she arrives at the base completely out of breath.

As she guessed, Cecily stands on the edge of the cliff, looking out toward the sea. Her hair flies around her head wildly. The gallery railing rattles over their heads.

"Cecily," George pants, "come away from the edge."

But Cecily doesn't move, and when she speaks it's to the open air. "I used to spend hours here looking at this view while I was waiting for Donald to come. I'd sit up there at the window and think about all the things I gave up to be with him—my family, my friends, the life I'd imagined for myself. But then he'd arrive and I'd push all of that sadness and regret away because I had a husband who loved *me*, who wanted *me*, who'd sailed across the sea to find *me*."

Her arms wrap tightly around her waist, and when she continues her tone is bitter. "Then, a few months ago, I realized that on the nights Donald said he was out at the pub there'd be a candle burning in our front window. Once a week, then twice. Then every night. And so, one evening, I followed him."

She falls silent for a moment, and George remembers the tattered note in the lighthouse—not *code* but instructions, to *look for the candle and you know where to go, you know where to find me*. She sees the letters *D+A* carefully carved into the aged timber of the windowsill. She pictures the melted candle stubs at Alan's fake grave, the blackened wicks now holding only the memory of flickering flames.

"I couldn't think for days," Cecily croaks. "Couldn't eat. I just moved on autopilot. Wake up. Dress the kids. Cook. Take them to school. Clean. Pick them up. Cook. Put them to bed. Clean. The same day over and over and over again. And then, when the fog lifted, I kept imagining Donald looking out at this same view while he waited for Alan to come and find *him*."

George approaches the other woman slowly, and as she

steps from the snow-crusted grass to the salt-poisoned dirt, it feels like the warmth leaches from her bones, her organs. Despite the run here, she feels colder now than she has this whole week.

Hearing George's soft footfalls, Cecily looks over her shoulder. "Stay back."

"Don't do this, Cess. Come on, you said it yourself—your kids need you."

"They don't need a mother they only get to see for an hour a month in some shithole prison."

"Isn't that better than never?"

But Cecily shakes her head, looking back out at the turbulent sea. "When they're old enough to find out what I did, what their dad has done . . . they won't want me in their life anymore, I know it. And when that happens, I'll wish I'd just died today."

George doesn't know what to say to convince her; she doesn't think there is anything she *can* say. All she can do is try to get close enough to stop Cecily before she throws herself over the edge.

"I don't think you're a bad person," she says, chancing another half step. But Cecily mirrors her, her toes kissing the edge. "You were lonely and sad, and your husband broke his vows," George presses, desperate now. "You just wanted to keep your family together."

"And I killed someone to do it." Cecily exhales on a shaky laugh. "To think I was so worried I wouldn't fit in here. Turns out I'm just as damned as the rest of them."

A cry above their heads makes them both look up. A gull struggles against the wind, flapping its wings desperately.

Cecily watches its plight, and when she speaks it's with a deep sadness. "Make sure my parents get custody of my children. Don't let them come back here and end up like us."

"Cecily—"

"*Promise me*, George."

"Don't do this—please!"

"*Cecily!*"

For a second, George is grateful for the new voice; it causes Cecily to freeze. George follows the sound and her gratitude is replaced with cold dread.

Bending to rub his bad knee, Father Ross takes in Cecily's and George's precarious positions, and George's bloody face. He has removed his elegant robes and is now wearing his usual jeans and knitted jumper. "What is going on here?" he demands. "Someone said they saw the inspector running up here like the devil himself was behind her."

George keeps her eyes on Father Ross as she holds out a hand to Cecily. "Come on, Cess. Let's just go back into the village. We can work out the rest on the mainland."

Father Ross zeroes in on Cecily, confusion slowly shifting to a dawning understanding, and George's heart sinks when he then turns those penetrating eyes on her. But there's no reason for her to hide her thoughts anymore; she lets him see it on her face: that she finally knows every twisted thing about the island he presides over as judge and jury.

And he responds in kind; his concerned, avuncular expression slips away. His eyes are cold now as they bore into hers, lips pulled back from his teeth in a snarl. For the first time since she met him, George feels like she's finally *seeing* him; whereas the islanders become wolves by putting a mask on, he's become his true self by taking one off.

"Who told you?" he asks, stepping toward her.

She thinks of Kathy handing her the logbooks; of Calum beckoning her through the window; of MacLeod stepping into the clearing with his shotgun raised. "Nobody."

"You're lying," he says immediately, then scowls at Cecily. "Mainland blood runs thick."

From the corner of her eye, George sees Cecily shudder. Wary of Father Ross closing the distance between them, she beckons to Cecily again. "Come on. Richie is waiting. The launch will be here soon." She doesn't disguise the warning to Father Ross—not only are police already here, but more are coming. "You know," she says to him lightly, "if you are looking for someone to blame, you should blame yourself."

An eyebrow rises. "How so?"

"Stephen Mackay. If you'd just held off one more day before killing him, DI Stewart and I would be gone and Alan's case would be closed."

His scowl deepens. "Even if that's true, I couldn't risk Stephen's presence for even a minute longer. My people depend on me to protect them—from *every* threat."

The chill that rolls down her spine feels more like a claw. If she can just coax Cecily away from the edge before Father Ross can launch . . .

It's Cecily's hesitation that seals their fate. Sensing she has only seconds left, George half turns to pull her away from the edge, and by the time she looks back, Father Ross is moving.

George remembers too late that before he donned the collar, this man was a star rugby player; she just has time to grab Cecily and send her stumbling toward the lighthouse before he's on George, gripping her shoulders and driving toward the cliff edge.

"Stop!" she shrieks, trying to twist out of his hold. The priest's ragged breath is hot against her face, his teeth bared with exertion. She batters frantically at his hands and arms, trying to throw her weight to either side, but his painful grip is inescapable. She can feel his uneven gait, his injured leg almost buckling with every step forward, and she knows that this injury is the only reason she isn't already on her way to the rocks below. But even with the injury, he has size and momentum in his favor; despite her desperate struggles, he continues to march her backward with slow, lurching steps.

She thinks she can hear Cecily screaming, but Father Ross doesn't bother looking her way; he's clearly identified who the primary threat is and will deal with that first. But George has no doubt that once he has tossed her over the side, Cecily will be next.

She kicks a foot backward and her stomach drops when her boot finds nothing but empty space. They've reached the edge. The wind buffets against her back, almost as if it's trying to push her back to safety; she manages to get her foot back on the ground and dig both heels in, but she can feel that she's right on the precipice. A terrified gasp slips out from between her teeth but it's cut off abruptly when one of Father Ross's meaty hands seizes her by the throat.

For a few seconds they struggle like that, Father Ross's grip around her throat both a lifeline and a death sentence. If he lets go now . . .

She's back in Margaret Villo's bedroom, and a skeletal boy with wild eyes is bursting out of the wardrobe, his long fingers scrabbling at her throat. And she's fighting the shock, trying to get her bearings as they stagger straight through the balcony door, glass showering down on them. But the boy's grip on her collar doesn't loosen, even as their hips hit the railing. For a heartbeat, a fraction of a second, she remembers seeing the realization in his eyes as they started to tip over the edge.

The skin on her face is growing hot. Her pulse is pounding in her temples, her ears. "Please," she wheezes.

His fingers tighten and she chokes, her eyes sliding away from his cruel face toward the lighthouse.

He starts to speak, to mock her plea, but realizes too late that her final words weren't for him.

With a wild howl Cecily charges from the side, hooking an

arm around Father Ross's neck and pulling him—and George—backward, away from the cliff. But even when they stumble onto safer ground, Cecily doesn't cease her attack—she scratches and claws at his face until he releases George, twisting to reach for the snarling creature on his back. George's back hits the frozen earth with a thud that knocks the remaining air out of her lungs, and she can only watch helplessly as Father Ross and Cecily stagger over the ground. After the initial surprise, Cecily's primal rage and desperation are no match for Father Ross's strength now. He seizes her around the waist, and drags her to the edge ...

Recalling the events afterward, George will never be sure whether it was luck or a deliberate move. But as Father Ross twists his body to hurl her over the cliff, Cecily manages to raise her leg one final time and kick downward onto his weakened knee. They teeter above the void for one final moment before Cecily drives her heels into the dirt and sends them both down. And down, and down.

There's no scream, and the fall is too far to hear a splash or the crack of bone on rock. Yet even the gulls fall silent for a minute, as if waiting for something deep in the island's core to react to its leader's passing.

It comes a few moments later, after George has torn her gaze from the place where Cecily and Father Ross fell to stare up at the overcast sky. A strong breeze chills the sweat and blood in her hair as it sweeps toward the croft, the woods, the village.

And, as she lies there shivering on the bleached earth, she hears the wolf tree howl.

CHAPTER 26

THE HARBOR IS CRAMMED WITH POLICE AND COASTGUARD CRAFT, AND EAdar's few streets are now filled with dozens of uniformed officers who've landed on the island over the past eight hours.

Cole was among the first of their team to arrive, her head whipping around until she spotted George and Richie on the quay. She listened to their story—starting with the legend of the missing lighthouse keepers and concluding with Cecily's and Father Ross's plunge over the cliff—with an expression that slowly morphed from her normal cool detachment to wide-eyed disbelief.

It took her a moment to collect herself, and, having told the story twice, George couldn't blame Cole when her first two attempts to speak came out as puffs of air. Then George saw the moment she came back to herself, pushing aside her horror and apprehension regarding the incredible task ahead of them to prepare herself to start leading it.

"I need to make about fifteen calls," she said, withdrawing a modern satellite phone from a bag with one hand and flagging down a passing officer with the other. "Take statements from DIs Lennox and Stewart immediately," she ordered. "Actually," she amended, returning her gaze to the detectives, "I need you to point out some of the people from your story first. The farmer and the postmistress, for starters. And which one is the Campbell house?"

The hours have passed quickly since then. A predictably silent MacLeod allowed himself to be led toward the pub, which had become the temporary police headquarters. A teary Kathy was next, her eyes trained on the ground even as Catriona called out to her. And, after the police pounded on his door, an ashen Donald was allowed to kiss his wailing children once each on the doorstep of their home before he, too, was led away.

The sun has long since disappeared over the horizon by the time Cole accompanies George onto a waiting police launch. The main street and harbor are now illuminated with powerful portable lights, and George winces at the harsh white glare.

"I just can't believe it," Cole says again, making it a dozen times since George had shown her the clearing and its beastly sentinel. George can't muster the energy to reply—with the protective bubble of shock and adrenaline long gone, her injuries are clamoring for attention. Cole notices her bloodless face and fetches a blanket from the cabin.

"There'll be an ambulance waiting for you in Stornoway," she says. "No arguments today, Lennox, I'm really not in the mood."

But George just nods dully, pressing her thumb into the storm brewing behind her eyebrow. Cole wraps the blanket around her, her hand lingering on George's shoulder. With some effort, George looks up at her. She's startled by the raw expression on Cole's face.

"I wouldn't have sent you out here if I'd known how badly things would go," she says.

George's jaw tightens. Christ, Cole really wants to have this conversation *now*? "Yeah, I know. Richie already told me that neither of you were sure if I could handle this."

Cole's forehead creases. "That's not what I—"

"It's fine," George says tersely. "Clearly you were both right."

"Lennox," Cole says sharply, then, more softly, "*George*. Being concerned about you isn't the same as doubting you. Even if we'd suspected foul play in Alan's death, I know you could have handled it." Her fingers tighten, a reassuring pressure. "I meant I wouldn't have sent you here if I'd known you'd get hurt again." She sighs, a weary sound. "I know from experience that there are only so many knocks someone can take before they can't get up again. And I really, *really* want you to get back up."

An officer calls out to Cole from a huddled group on the street, and she hesitates only for a second before she jumps down to the quay and jogs over to them.

George's gaze slides past her to the main street above the harbor. The islanders were ordered to remain in their homes while the senior officers figured out what to do next. Despite the urgency in the air when Cole first arrived, George doesn't blame them for taking their time now—none of them has ever investigated an entire community over centuries of ritualistic murders. It's going to take careful planning, and the arrival of several more senior detectives who are due in the morning, to unravel this tangled web. And that's only the beginning of what could be months or even years of inquiries.

Lights are on in almost every shop and house across the island—she guesses that none of the islanders will be sleeping tonight. The custom that forced them to turn on family and friends is collapsing around them. When the sun rises tomorrow, will they understand that they're facing a far harsher reality? Or will they feel a sense of relief now that an invisible blade is no longer pressed to their throats?

A pair of officers enter the main street, coming from the direction of the pub. A third figure walks slightly ahead of them, and he points his finger up the hill toward the church as if giving directions. Although his face is averted, the red hat makes him instantly recognizable. He seems to sense her gaze; after a moment, Lewis glances toward the harbor, scanning the boats until he catches her eye. He raises a gloved hand. She considers ignoring the gesture, but then she remembers that he did what she asked today—with Lewis's help, Donald was prevented from escaping with the kids—and lifts her hand stiffly, before the officers reclaim his attention and he leads them away.

George sucks in a shuddering breath. She kept it together all afternoon, but she can't fight it anymore; an overwhelming despair fills her chest, overflows into her arms and legs. It's a weight full of swirling names: her own, but also Alan, Calum, Fiona, Sarah, the three Campbell children who are already on a boat, Cecily's parents awaiting their arrival. And all the other islanders, including the ones with bloody hands, whose lives will now be forever changed. Kathy and MacLeod. Catriona. John. Lewis. Even Donald, who, despite his fear of being caught, helped pull her and Jack from the water. A murderer who wrapped his arm around her when she was cold.

She thinks about what Cole just said, about some knocks being too hard to recover from, and she wonders if this is what that feels like: this—this heavy, terrifyingly *dark* feeling that is taking root inside her. She thought she'd been through the worst and overcome it, was so determined to show everyone that she couldn't be beaten. But now . . . ?

Before she can spiral too far down into the depths, Richie is climbing aboard with their bags and squashing himself onto the bench beside her. The warmth from his shoulder and thigh slowly leaches into her, and after a few minutes the dark feeling starts to retreat. She shuffles closer to him. A lizard on a rock.

The engine roars to life beneath their feet.

When they're clear of the harbor, the captain opens up the throttle and the boat shoots forward across the waves. It skirts the coastline and, as if on cue, the lighthouse's silhouette appears from the gloom to stand out against the moonlit sky. She rubs her brow again, the pain unrelenting, and Richie silently withdraws the tramadol bottle from her bag. His face remains neutral as he hands it to her. "I'm going in. Call out if you need anything."

As Richie heads to the cabin, George looks back up at the lonely lighthouse of Eilean Eadar, the pill bottle clenched in her fist. Even as she watches, the tower disappears into the night. Soon the whole island will be swallowed by darkness.

She is getting to her feet to join Richie when a sound reaches her ears. She shivers. At this distance, she must be imagining it. Or maybe she's not. Because after everything George witnessed on Eadar, she's certain of only one thing.

The wolves will always be howling.

ACKNOWLEDGMENTS

For the most part, writing a book is a solo endeavor—until it's very much *not*. And I am lucky enough to have many people who are responsible (and now culpable) for getting this book from my brain to yours.

Firstly, my sister Olivia: the first person I go to with a new idea, the one who helps me build my Post-It note plot walls, the one who tells me which lines are cool but ultimately wanky. *The Wolf Tree*, and every amazing thing that's come from it, began with Liv saying, "Tell me the story."

Next up is the Richie to my George—my agent Tom Gilliatt of a4 Literary. I am so grateful for your unwavering confidence in this book and in me, and I look forward to many more phone calls ending with both of us nervously giggling. Thanks also to my international dream team: Felicity Blunt and Rosie Pierce at Curtis Brown; David Forrer at InkWell Management; and Nerrilee Weir and Fiona Henderson at Bold Type Agency, for finding this book the very best homes across the seas.

Speaking of those homes, I couldn't be more enamored by Anna Valdinger and the entire HarperCollins Australia team who continue to wear their hearts on their sleeve for this book; I'm equally as lovey-dovey for Julia Wisdom at Hemlock Press and Daphne Durham at Putnam for believing in this story and its characters. Thanks also to Ali Lavau for your astute edits, to Scott Forbes for casting your sharp eye over everything, and to the proofreaders who picked up the tiniest discrepancies.

Also, thanks to Clare Ainsworth—it's always been a dream of mine to have a map in one of my books, and Clare has created a beautiful piece of art.

I am so fortunate to have three extraordinary best friends who read early drafts of this book and gave me their feedback: Zoe Hawkins, Thalía Dudek, and Gabby Marshall (who pointed out a comma that should have been a full stop and has not stopped talking about it since). I also have to thank my friend Les Zigomanis, who listened to a twenty-one-year-old me say that I didn't consider myself a writer as I hadn't been published, to which he simply replied, "If you write, you're a writer."

To my ever-growing family, who always back me 100 percent (or at least wait for me to leave the room before sharing doubts); to my nephews for taking turns either distracting me from my keyboard or smashing their fists on it—any errors are entirely their fault. To my grandad, Andy, for telling tales of growing up in Glasgow; and to my grandmas Margaret and Kath—you're all name-dropped in this book (as two murderers and a murder victim . . . don't read into that).

A few final shout-outs: to Ashley Flowers for her podcast *So Supernatural*, where I first heard the unsolved mystery of the missing Eilean Mòr lighthouse keepers and felt compelled to come up with an answer; to Hozier, whose rich, haunting music I played almost nonstop whilst writing; and finally to Taylor Swift, for existing.